Alison Roberts has been lucky enough to live in the south of France for several years recently, but is now back in her home country of New Zealand. She is also lucky enough to write for the Mills & Boon Medical line. A primary school teacher in a former life, she later became a qualified paramedic. She loves to travel and dance, drink champagne and spend time with her daughter and her friends. Alison is the author of over one hundred books!

Once making her home in sunny Brazil, **Luana DaRosa** has since lived on three different continents—though her favourite romantic locations remain the tropical places of Latin America. When she's not typing away at her latest romance novel, or reading about love, Luana is either crocheting, buying yarn she doesn't need, or chasing her bunnies around the house. She lives with her partner in a cosy town in the south of England. Find her on X under the handle @LuDaRosaBooks.

Also by Alison Roberts

Their Fake Date Rescue

Royal York Hospital collection

Single Dad's Christmas Wish

Coastside ER miniseries

A Family Made in the ER
Single Dad for the Daredevil Doctor

Also by Luana DaRosa

Falling for Her Miami Rival
Faking It with the Doctor Prince
Falling for the GP Next Door

Valentine Flings collection

Hot Nights with the Arctic Doc

Discover more at millsandboon.co.uk.

DR MADDEN'S MARRIAGE SOLUTION

ALISON ROBERTS

OFF-LIMITS DOC ON DECK

LUANA DaROSA

MILLS & BOON

All rights reserved including the right of reproduction in whole or in part in any form. This edition is published by arrangement with Harlequin Enterprises ULC.

This is a work of fiction. Names, characters, places, locations and incidents are purely fictional and bear no relationship to any real life individuals, living or dead, or to any actual places, business establishments, locations, events or incidents. Any resemblance is entirely coincidental.

Without limiting the exclusive rights of any author, contributor or the publisher of this publication, any unauthorised use of this publication to train generative artificial intelligence (AI) technologies is expressly prohibited. HarperCollins also exercise their rights under Article 4(3) of the Digital Single Market Directive 2019/790 and expressly reserve this publication from the text and data mining exception.

® and TM are trademarks owned and used by the trademark owner and/or its licensee. Trademarks marked with ® are registered with the United Kingdom Patent Office and/or the Office for Harmonisation in the Internal Market and in other countries.

First published in Great Britain 2026
by Mills & Boon, an imprint of HarperCollins*Publishers* Ltd,
1 London Bridge Street, London, SE1 9GF

www.harpercollins.co.uk

HarperCollins*Publishers* Macken House, 39/40 Mayor Street Upper, Dublin 1, D01 C9W8, Ireland

Dr Madden's Marriage Solution © 2026 Alison Roberts

Off-Limits Doc on Deck © 2026 Luana DaRosa

ISBN: 978-0-263-41986-3

03/26

Printed and Bound in the UK using 100% Renewable Electricity at CPI Group (UK) Ltd, Croydon, CR0 4YY

DR MADDEN'S MARRIAGE SOLUTION

ALISON ROBERTS

MILLS & BOON

CHAPTER ONE

'For God's sake, Alice... What's *taking* so long?'

Flight paramedic Alice Barlow's gaze swerved from the central clip on the strap that had been holding a defibrillator safely in place on its shelf during their flight to meet the incredulous stare of her crew partner.

She'd been out of her harness to grab the vital piece of equipment within a heartbeat of the helicopter skids making contact with the grass of this small town's football field. She didn't need to be glared at by a HEMS doctor, who was also the senior medic on this crew, to be reminded of how urgent this response was.

A baby who had stopped breathing for long enough to turn blue? Who had started breathing again when his panicked mother grabbed him from the floor, only to cough so hard he'd made himself sick? The ambulance dispatch technician had been able to hear the sound of the baby's severe respiratory distress on the phone call. This was quite possibly a life-or-death call-out. It was also the worst time a clip could have malfunctioned and be refusing to release.

'It's jammed,' Alice said tersely.

Nate's arm shot past her. He squeezed the sides of the clip and tugged but it still wasn't budging. With a muttered but audible curse, he dropped the arm loop of the kit he was holding and used both his hands to give the plastic clip enough of a wrench to snap whatever part of the mechanism had jammed. Alice reached for the handle of the vital piece of equipment but Nate was faster.

'I've got it. You take the kit.' He shoved the pack towards her with his foot as he used his free hand to reach for an oxygen cylinder.

Their crewman was sliding the side door open. This was a hot landing, where their pilot, Andy, would keep the helicopter idling, ready for a rapid departure. Those minutes saved could be what made the difference in getting a fragile patient to definitive critical care.

Alice was looking at Nate's back as she kept her head down and moved swiftly to get past the danger zone of moving rotors. A glance over her shoulder earned a 'thumbs up' from Andy, the pilot, who'd been watching to make sure he knew exactly where she was and that she was safe. Now she could increase her speed to catch up with Nate, who hadn't even glanced over his shoulder to see where she was.

What was up with him today?

It felt like more than the stress of a kind of call-out that would put any medic on edge. Nate had been noticeably distant ever since he'd arrived for his shift at the Aratika Rescue Base. Grim, even. And, okay, everyone had been cutting him some slack recently because they knew he'd had some personal issues going on but this was on a whole new level.

Alice hadn't seen even a hint of a smile today and now he was snapping at her for something that wasn't her fault? This wasn't like the Nathaniel Madden she had been working with for a long time now. Something was up but now wasn't the time to think about it, let alone try and discover what was going on, so she pushed her concern very firmly out of her head.

A woman with grey hair was waving frantically at them and pointing to a car parked behind her with all its doors wide open. As they got closer, Alice could see a woman sitting on the back seat, a baby clutched in her arms. She was rocking the bundle and she was sobbing.

Alice could feel her heart dropping like a stone.

Were they too late?

'Oh...thank goodness you're here.' The older woman looked close to tears herself.

'What's happening?' Nate asked. 'Has baby stopped breathing again?'

'No...but we keep expecting him to. I'm his grandma.' The woman pressed a hand to her mouth, catching Alice's gaze as Nate stepped past her and crouched in front of the sobbing mother.

'I'm Alice,' she said.

It wasn't like Nate not to introduce himself, either, with his ability to connect and form instant bonds with anybody on scene, from the patient and their family to any local medics or emergency service personnel. Onlookers, even, that he might want to get rid of.

'And that's Nate,' she added, to cover the omission. 'One of our HEMS doctors.' She tried to convey reassurance without saying out loud that this baby was lucky because Nate had to be the best emergency specialist she had ever worked with in her many years as a paramedic.

Another step took her close enough to see past Nate's

broad back. He was doing an initial assessment, talking calmly at the same time.

'This is baby Max, yes? And you're his mum, Louise, is that right?'

'Yes…' The woman started lifting her baby, desperate to give him to someone who could help.

'You keep holding Max for a minute,' Nate told her. 'It will help to keep him warm and he's less likely to get distressed, which will make it easier for me to see what's going on and get some baseline recordings. As soon as we know he's stable enough, we'll get him to hospital.'

'And I'll be able to go with him?'

'We'll talk about that soon. We need to focus on Max for the moment.'

He glanced sideways at Alice, who was right beside him now. She had put down the large red bag with all its internal and external pockets. She was already opening the zip on the airway pocket because she could hear this baby gasping for air at a rate that was well over the upper limit of normal and, even without a stethoscope, it was easy to hear the crackles and wheeze of obstructed airways. He was going to need oxygen. Medication. Possibly intubation if he became too tired or his level of consciousness was dropping.

And, if that was the case, with a critically ill baby on a ventilator, his mother was unlikely to be allowed to travel with them in the helicopter. As hard as it was, they would need the space and focus to do their job. A terrified mother distracting them was a complication it was best to avoid.

'Let's get some oxygen on with nasal prongs,' Nate said. He lifted his stethoscope from where it was hanging around his neck and fitted the earpieces. 'We need an oxygen saturation level, too, please.'

Alice fitted the soft plastic nozzles into the baby's nostrils, using a piece of tape to secure the tubing. The baby looked as if he wanted to cry but the effort was just too much. His skin was very pale but there were mottled red patches on his cheeks.

'So Max has been sick for a couple of days?' Nate tilted his head as he pulled the earpieces of his stethoscope clear.

'Yes...' Louise was still sniffing but she'd stopped crying. She looked almost as pale as her baby. 'There's been a nasty bug going around school and Max's big sister is sick at the moment.'

Alice turned the oxygen cylinder on. She also took a paediatric bag mask out of the kit so she could be ready if Max deteriorated any further and needed help with his breathing. Babies were scary to treat because they could compensate well for a time to cope with challenges like a lack of oxygen or poor circulation but then they could crash with an alarming speed and depth.

'Has he been feeding normally?'

'No... He's been coughing too much today to even suck properly.'

Alice caught the flick of Nate's glance as she wrapped the Velcro strap of a pulse oximeter around Max's tiny foot and she caught the silent communication instantly.

'Don't refasten the leg domes on that onesie.'

'You want access for an intra-osseous line for IV?'

'He's dehydrated. Might be the quickest route.'

The ease with which they could understand each other and work together had been there right from their first mission together. Nate only did one or two twelve-hour shifts per week—the rest of his working time was spent in the emergency department of Wellington's largest hospital as a consultant emergency medicine specialist. Alice had never asked, but had often wondered, if Nate had gone to the manager of the Aratika Rescue Base and put in a request to work with her on his shifts whenever possible after that first time, because it was very rare for her not to be his crew partner.

If he *had* made the request, it wouldn't have bothered Alice in the slightest because she knew it would have been purely for professional reasons. Nate was married. Alice was very happily single. Along with the way they could work together, perhaps that was the foundation for the firm friendship that had grown slowly over the last year. They were both completely safe from the kind of complications that working closely together in an often-fraught environment could so easily generate.

That silent exchange had done more than provide Alice with a flash of the strong bond she had with this colleague. She'd also been reminded of the reason why Nate might seem out of sorts today. He had separated from his wife weeks ago now. The reality of a shattered relationship would be sinking in and Alice knew, only too well, how hard that could be.

But that wasn't a thought that could be allowed to even form properly, like feeling hurt that he'd snapped at her earlier. What it did do was let Alice make allowances for any mood swing Nate might be experiencing and to let go of any concern that might disrupt her focus.

'Oxygen saturation 95 percent,' she relayed. 'No… make that 94.'

Far too low. And it was dropping, despite the level of supplemental oxygen the baby was now receiving. The effort of trying to breathe fast enough to increase blood levels of the vital gas had to be exhausting this tiny person.

She could feel the vibration of the helicopter in the ground beneath her feet. The sooner they could get airborne the better because they could deliver Max into the expert hands of paediatric specialists within half an hour but they couldn't leave until they had a stable airway. It would only take a small shift for this baby to lose the ability to pull in enough oxygen to stay alive, and the familiar prickle on the back of her neck was a warning that it might well turn out to be a difficult task to stabilise and then transfer this patient.

And her intuition proved correct. That shift occurred only minutes later, as Nate was taping a protective shield over the intra-osseous line he had placed.

Max stopped breathing again.

'Okay, Louise,' Nate said calmly. 'I need to take Max now.'

He was slipping his hands under the baby, as he spoke, to take him from his mother's arms and put him down on the clean towel Alice had spread to lay out items they might need. By the time Nate laid the limp form of the baby on the ground and positioned him to make sure his airway was open, she had the small bag mask in her hands. She connected it to the oxygen supply, covered the mouth and nose with a tight seal, and puffed oxygen in gently, watching the chest rise and fall.

For Louise, who was now standing with her mother's arms around her, watching the resuscitation in horror, it must have looked like things were moving too fast to process. Nate's hands were flashing from one checklist point to another, pulling clear plastic kits from where they were fastened inside the pack and ripping open zips. He had the contents of the airway cube set out and was drawing up the drugs to induce sedation and then paralyse the baby so that they could take over his airway and breathing.

Andy was still inside the idling helicopter but the crewman, Nick, who was trained to be able to assist in situations like this, had joined them and knelt beside Alice to take over responsibility for using the bag mask.

Alice stuck the adhesive patches onto the front and back of Max's chest. With their inbuilt electrodes and wires, they could be used for both monitoring heart rate and rhythm and to deliver a shock for defibrillation if necessary. She double-checked the drugs that Nate was drawing up and made sure that all the gear they might need was readily available, like suction and alternative airways and even a surgical pack for the worst-case scenario of *can't intubate, can't oxygenate*.

Seconds later, Nate had a video laryngoscope in his hands and Alice was ready to provide an extra set of hands to position and steady the baby's head, remove the guidewire and help secure the breathing tube when Nate had confirmed its correct placement.

Now they needed to get the baby on board the helicopter. Nate was making sure lines and wires were secure and not tangled, getting ready to pick Max up and carry him while Alice and Nick were stuffing the rest of their gear back into the kit. He was also telling Louise and her mother what was about to happen.

'We'll take Max straight to the paediatric department in Wellington General,' he told them. 'We'll be in contact with the specialists as we're flying so they'll be ready and waiting for us.'

'But...' Louise let go of her mum's hand to touch her baby's head. 'But I can come with him, can't I?'

Alice stuck the clear-sided pack with IV supplies back into the kit by attaching the Velcro patches to each other. Her heart was sinking because she knew that Nate had no choice in what he was about to say.

'I'm very sorry. We're going to have him on a ventilator for his breathing and there will be too much going on for extra passengers to be able to be onboard.'

There was all the warmth and sympathy in Nate's tone that Alice had come to expect, so why did she have the impression that he was still keeping his distance?

That something else was on his mind, at a time when it really, really shouldn't be?

'I'll drive you,' Louise's mother said firmly. 'Come on... We need to let the doctors do what they need to do. We'll get going right now and we won't be that far behind. John can bring everything we need later.' She put her arm around the distraught young mother as she turned her back towards their car.

Nate might be unusually distant, Alice decided, as they got back on board, but it wasn't putting their patient at any risk. They worked fast, hooking Max up to the portable ventilator, making sure all the monitoring equipment was functioning and stowing other gear so they could take off safely.

'Oxygen saturation's 99 percent,' Alice noted aloud, happy with such a big improvement in a vital sign. They had done their job, securing an airway and taking over the work of breathing from an exhausted infant. They were in the air again and on their way to where little Max needed to be. She expected at least a nod of satisfaction from Nate, if not a smile and a look that acknowledged her part in the management of this emergency.

But there was no response from Nate. He was in the seat closest to the stretcher that had the paediatric bassinet attached to it. Baby Max was strapped inside the bassinet, with the tubes and wires of his monitoring equipment carefully secured around him. The ventilator and defibrillator had flashing lights, measurements that were automatically updating and a cardiac graph running constantly across the screen, the spikes close together due to the infant's rapid heart rate.

Nate's gaze was fixed to the screen, as if he was expecting an alarm to start sounding at any moment and indicate a new crisis. It was as if he hadn't even heard Alice, which was impossible because the microphones and headphones built into their helmets made communication crystal-clear. Intimate almost, when you could feel the vibration of someone's voice on the delicate skin of your ear.

And that made his nonresponse to Alice feel like a deliberate snub.

Was she missing something, here? Had she done something to upset Nate?

She tried to retrace the timeline of their day so far. It had been a relatively quiet shift before this with only one call-out, to a medical practice in a small coastal town too far away from a hospital to make road transport acceptable for a man with chest pain and clear signs of an evolving heart attack visible on the ECG. The middle-aged man had needed pain relief and oxygen but it had been a completely straightforward mission with no complications, and their patient had been relaxed enough to have a conversation with Nate about his passion for fishing.

With the information being transmitted directly to the cardiology team at the receiving hospital, they were waiting on the rooftop helipad to whisk the man straight to the catheter laboratory where his blocked arteries could be treated. They were back on base by lunchtime to find that their devoted, volunteer housekeeper, Shirley, had made a stack of cheese and onion toasted sandwiches and everybody had been delighted.

You're a star, Shirley, Andy had said. *Nobody makes a toastie as good as you do.*

Shirley had flapped her hand at him. *Flattery will get you everywhere, young man.*

Alice could remember the laughter around the table. But she also realised she hadn't seen Nate eating one of those delicious sandwiches. He'd excused himself when his phone rang and went to take the call in private. Had Nate noticed the meaningful glances that had been exchanged between his colleagues as he walked away, perhaps? The ones that were conveying hope that this might be the start of sorting out whatever had gone so wrong in his marriage?

But Juliette—one of the base's motorbike paramedics—had shaken her head slowly, when someone observed that he'd been gone a long time and maybe that was a positive sign.

I wouldn't hold your breath, she'd said quietly. *If it*

is a call from Donna, I don't think it'll be good news. I heard this morning that she's heading for Europe. And that she's not travelling alone.

Alice had found herself avoiding eye contact with Nate when he came back. It wasn't that they'd been gossiping, exactly. No one had asked any questions about who Donna's travelling companion might be but the inference that she was leaving with another man had been inescapable, and Alice had been embarrassed that she now knew more than she wanted to know about his marriage.

It seemed easier to join dots now. What if Nate was aware that the fact his wife had left him for someone else could have become common knowledge? What if he'd only just become aware of it himself? That could have been what had tipped the balance prior to his shift today, couldn't it? He'd been subdued for weeks now but there was an uncharacteristic edge of something like anger in his demeanour today.

And Alice, as his crew partner, was on the front line for feeling the brunt of it, and hanging around on base without the distraction of any call-outs this afternoon could well have exacerbated an emotional reaction to something that was happening away from a professional arena.

That didn't make any of it okay, though. There was an unspoken rule that personal issues had to be left at the hangar door on this base. Letting them interfere with team dynamics, or worse, patient care was completely unacceptable and Alice found that her eyes were narrowing as she watched Nate watching the monitors. Maybe she needed to have a word with Nate to let him know that she'd been affected today. That, if he couldn't be sure it wasn't going to happen again, he might need to take some time away from work.

The sudden beeping of an alarm was magnified by coming through the microphone on Nate's helmet.

'Crew harness off.' Nate's voice was as crisp as the click of releasing the clip on his harness. He braced himself against the stretcher and had his stethoscope in his ears as he leaned over the bassinette.

The alarm was still sounding. The oxygen saturation had dropped below the set parameters. It was still dropping as Alice unclipped her own harness.

'Crew harness off,' she said, to alert Andy that she was about to move.

'Roger that.' He knew they wouldn't be taking the risk of being unsecured in any unexpected turbulence unless it was unavoidable. He would be able to hear the alarm going off as clearly as she could.

Max looked as white as the rolled-up towels that cushioned the sides of the bassinette. Nate had the disk of his stethoscope on the tiny chest, intently focussed on what he was hearing,

'Heart rate's dropping,' Alice warned. 'Under a hundred.'

The oxygen saturation was still dropping. Alice's mouth went dry. 'O2 sats under ninety.'

Nate's gaze flicked up to the screen. 'Andy? What's our ETA?'

'Seven minutes.'

Alice looked at Max. His fingertips were dark and his lips, around the device holding the breathing tube in place, were visible enough to see that they were blue.

'Right-sided breath sounds absent,' Nate said, his voice grim. 'He's bradycardic and blood pressure's falling.'

Alice knew what was happening. Possibly due to the underlying respiratory illness and severe coughing or the pressures of the ventilator, damage had occurred to a tiny lung and air was filling the chest cavity to create a situation that would stop both the lungs and heart functioning. They couldn't wait for the seven minutes to get to their destination. They only had a matter of seconds to deal with this crisis before it turned into a full-blown resuscitation for a cardiac arrest.

'I'm going to do a needle decompression.'

Nate's calm statement was for Andy's benefit. As a medivac pilot, he knew how important it would be to keep the aircraft as stable as possible when an invasive procedure was happening. He would be lowering their speed, avoiding any turns or pitch changes and watching out for turbulence that could be avoided.

Alice hadn't missed Nate's choice of words, however. Did he really think he was about to do this entirely by himself?

She braced herself with one hand as she grabbed an IV kit, ripping open the zip.

Nate was pulling on a pair of gloves. 'Find me a twenty-two-gauge cannula, thanks, Alice.'

She put an alcohol wipe down beside his hand. He turned his head.

'Cannula.' It was a clearly enunciated command, not a request. It felt like a reprimand that she hadn't provided what he'd asked for fast enough. She peeled back the top of the sealed package containing the cannula so he could take it out by its base.

Alice watched as Nate gently touched the notch of the baby's neck, went straight down and then sideways to find the exact spot between those miniature ribs to insert the needle and reach the air pocket. She held her breath, sending out a silent plea to the universe not to send a bump of turbulence in their direction for the next few seconds but by the time she'd formed the thought, Nate's hand was out, wanting the syringe she was holding so that he could attach it to the end of the cannula. Nate pulled back the plunger, emptied the syringe and repeated the action.

'Sat's coming up.' It felt like the first breath Alice had taken in some time but she let it out again almost immediately in a sigh of relief. 'Ninety-one...ninety-two...' The heart rate was also increasing. She waited for Nate to catch her gaze. Like he always did in that moment when they knew they'd won.

But he had his stethoscope in place again and the only person he was looking at was baby Max.

'Strap back in.' Andy's voice came through their headphones, moments later. 'We're about to land.'

They were late back to base after delivering their patient to the paediatric intensive care unit before making the changeover from their portable equipment, partly because they waited until a chest drain was inserted to ensure that another pneumothorax couldn't accumulate.

Both Alice and Nate were drained enough, after such a challenging retrieval, for it to excuse the communication that was confined to totally practical requests or instructions.

'Find a three-millimetre ETT tube while you're there, will you?'

'The lifepack needs new patches.'

'And fresh batteries.'

'Swap out that oxygen tank for a new one.'

'Sign off these RSI drugs with me, will you?'

They tidied up, cleaned gear and restocked everything they'd used.

It was well past time they both went home and Alice was about to open the side door in the hangar that led to the car park but she could hear the sound of Nate's boots on the concrete right behind her and, at the last moment, she dropped her hand and turned around to face him.

She couldn't leave things like this. She wouldn't be seeing Nate for another week and she didn't want to be overthinking what had gone down today.

She was blocking Nate's exit. He raised his eyebrows, clearly expecting her to step aside. Instead, she folded her arms.

'What was that all about today, Nate? What is it I'm supposed to have done?'

'What on earth are you talking about?'

'Don't pretend you don't know.' Alice glared at him. 'You snapped at me as if I was hell-bent on making it as difficult as possible for you to do your job. It wasn't *my* fault that the clip broke. You didn't even hear me passing on information, or if you did, you just ignored me which is downright *rude*.' To her horror, Alice could feel the prickle of tears behind her eyes. It had been hurtful but, if he couldn't see that, she wasn't about to tell him. 'And, you know what?' she fired as a parting shot. 'You needed to use an alcohol wipe for skin prep, so it wasn't actually stupid to hand that to you before a cannula.'

Nate was staring back at her. He took a quick glance over his shoulder as if he was checking that nobody was overhearing this rant.

'Are you suggesting I put someone at risk?'

'*No...*' Alice shook her head. 'I would have said something a lot sooner than this if I had. Clinically, you did your job as well as you always do. It was the way you took your bad mood out on me that...that...' she let her breath out in a sigh, the wind leaving her sails completely as she saw the way Nate put his hand to his forehead, rubbing at the lines that had deepened as he scrunched up his face '...wasn't nice,' she finished with a shrug. 'That's all.'

She was turning to the door again.

Letting it go.

But the sincerity in Nate's voice made her pause.

'I'm sorry, Alice.'

'Okay...' She was quite prepared to accept an apology. She didn't want this to be hanging in the air the next time they worked together. She glanced up at him. 'I know you've got stuff going on.'

Nate's eyes were so dark they almost looked as brown as hers even though she knew perfectly well that they were blue.

'You don't know the half of it,' he muttered.

*Oh...*the note in Nate's voice now sounded like very real pain. Maybe they'd only ever been colleagues but there was a solid friendship there as well. They trusted each other implicitly when it came to anything professional. Suddenly, it felt like a barrier needed to be broken. That Nate needed someone in a very personal corner of his life.

The urge to put her arms around him and offer comfort came from nowhere and it was strong enough to be disturbing, so Alice stayed very still.

'What's really going on, Nate?' she asked quietly. 'Is this because Donna's leaving?'

Nate was silent for a heartbeat. And then another. He was still holding her gaze and, when he broke the silence, his voice was raw.

'It's bigger than that,' he said. 'A lot bigger.'

Alice waited. She was here. If he wanted to tell her, he would.

He did.

'I'm going to be a father,' he said. 'And I don't have the faintest idea how I'm going to cope…'

CHAPTER TWO

THE SHOCK OF Nate's words was stunning.

Alice couldn't quite get her head around them.

'Donna's *pregnant*?'

'No.'

'You mean…someone *else* is pregnant?' Alice lowered her voice even though they were still alone in the hangar. 'With *your* baby?'

Stupid question. Of course that was what he meant but this was even more shocking than knowing his wife was leaving him and taking his unborn baby with her. This meant that Nate must have cheated on Donna and maybe given her just cause to walk out on him? Had everyone on-base been offering sympathy and cutting him some slack if he wasn't as nice to be around as usual when he had, in fact, brought this all on himself? The thought came and went in the space of a single heartbeat, followed by another flash that was just as fleeting.

No… Despite the fact that she had been blindsided by her last boyfriend doing exactly that to *her*—it simply didn't fit the man who Alice thought she knew. A loyal, honourable, passionate man who was, outwardly at least, devoted to his work and his family, presumably including the future children that she knew he looked forward to welcoming. For heaven's sake, hadn't she seen Nate poring over a real estate magazine just a couple of months ago, saying that he and Donna were looking to change their apartment lifestyle for a more family-friendly property?

Nate must have seen the shock in her eyes, possibly being washed away by the disbelief. Had that morphed into disappointment, perhaps? Was it actually possible he was just another man who could charm women into trusting them enough to be planning their future around them and then leave them picking up the pieces when they'd realised what a terrible mistake it had been? Like the bad choices Alice had made more than once?

Oddly, a reflection of her own shock was written all over Nate's face.

'It's *not* what you're thinking.' His tone was urgent.

Alice added confusion into how she was feeling. 'What is it, then?'

'It's...' Nate blew out a breath '...complicated.'

Alice's breath came out in a huff that bordered on laughter. 'I'll bet it is.' She wanted to shake her head and say something that might come across as less than sympathetic but then she saw the look in Nate's eyes.

A look that was dark enough to be desperation?

This man was her colleague. Her friend. And he was in trouble.

'Do you want to talk about it?' Her words were tentative but she was holding his gaze, hoping he could see that she was prepared to shelve any judgement. That she had the time to listen and maybe offer at least some kind of support.

Nate looked over his shoulder again. 'Not here.'

Alice looked at her watch. 'It's way past dinner time,' she said. 'Why don't we meet at that pub we always go to for work-related celebrations? You came to the drinks after work for Andy's birthday last month, remember?'

'The Irish pub? In Petone?'

'That's the one. The Emerald Harp. Traffic won't be a problem at this time of night, the food's good and we're almost regulars.'

No eyebrows would be raised that crew members from the base might be grabbing a bite to eat together, as a form of debriefing after a long day or a big job.

Nate looked like he was going to back off fast. Alice fully expected him to thank her but say something like it was no big deal and she probably had much better things to be doing with her time away from work.

'You never know,' she added. 'I might be able to help.' She could feel her lips curve into what was undoubtedly a cheeky smile. 'You know how bossy I can be. Giving people ideas about how they can solve problems is possibly one of my best splinter skills.'

It was nearly fifteen minutes later when Nate followed Alice's vehicle into the entrance of The Emerald Harp's car park.

He cut his engine but didn't open his door immediately because he needed to close his eyes for a moment and pull in a deep breath. He'd been arguing with himself for the whole drive from the base. Did he really want to talk about this? To share details of his private life with someone who was not really anything more than a colleague?

Okay, shoving Alice into a purely professional category wasn't entirely fair. He genuinely enjoyed both working with her and hanging out with her on the base when they weren't working. It wasn't as if they chose to spend time together away from the work they shared, aside from work-related gatherings, of course, like Andy's birthday drinks but that was just the way things were. Donna had left her job as a nurse years ago. The last thing she wanted to do when they had time off together was to hang around with medics who, invariably, started talking shop.

But did that mean that he and Alice weren't really friends?

It was as close to a friendship as any that Nate currently had in his life. He had his work at the hospital, his work at the rescue base and…his marriage. That was his life. Or it had been until a few short weeks ago.

Right now he felt cast adrift, utterly lost, and he knew that the worst was still to come. He also knew that personal information anyone would prefer to keep private was already circulating like wildfire on the kind of grapevine that work establishments like hospitals were notorious for. It was more than likely that Alice had already heard rumours. Maybe the only real control he had over what was turning his life inside out was to make sure at least one person other than himself knew the truth.

And why not Alice Barlow?

He could see her getting out of her car and walking towards him now and she looked like she always did. Dark, wavy hair pulled back into a ponytail, average height, her curvy figure more obvious in civvies than the base uniform. A confident, intelligent, sometimes opinionated and often funny woman who was passionate about her career. She was also a very kind person. Nate had seen evidence of that time and again and it went a long way to explain why she was such a popular member of the Aratika staff.

Perhaps a bit of kindness was exactly what he needed right now. Or company? It had been a bit of a wake-up call to find that this unfamiliar territory he was trying to navigate was a rather overwhelmingly lonely space.

Nate got out of his car to find himself staring at the bright green harp on the pub's signage with a tagline below that he hadn't noticed on his first visit.

Every song tells its own story.

One side of his mouth tilted in a wry smile. Yeah... He had his own story and if he couldn't tell it to someone as trustworthy as Alice it might stay untold forever. Simmering beneath the surface and becoming a toxic brew that could turn him into a person nobody would want to talk to.

He might end up being locked into this lonely space totally alone.

And who would want that?

It was all dark, polished wood and pools of lamplight that made glass sparkle behind the bar. Irish music played in the background but it was midweek and missing the crowds and noise level of the nights they had a live band in the house, like the last time they'd been here.

'Can I get you something to drink?'

They were in a puddle of light and Alice could see that Nate's face had lightened a little since that intense moment in the hangar before she'd asked if he wanted to talk about whatever was going on. His eyes looked blue again. A very dark blue that made him look as if he could be of Irish descent himself with how dark his hair was. Hair that was ruffled enough now to remind her that running his fingers through it was a sure sign that he was stressed.

'Yes, please,' Alice said.

'What would you like?'

'What are you going to have?'

'Has to be Guinness, given where we are. I go for quality over quantity, so I'm thinking Foreign Extra Stout.'

Alice threw a smile at the bartender waiting to take their order. She'd just thought of the perfect way to let Nate know that she was here for him. Ready to listen. And help, if she could.

'I'll have what he's having,' she told the bartender.

She turned back in time to catch Nate's eyebrows lifting.

'What…do you have a problem with women drinking Guinness?'

'Not at all. Are you aware that the Foreign Extra is known as the blackest, boldest Guinness there is?'

Oops. Alice didn't normally drink any beer other than a pale lager on a hot summer's day but she couldn't back out now. She tried a casual shrug.

'You mean you've been working with me all this time and you didn't know that Bold was my middle name?'

Nate gave his head a small shake but he was smiling for the first time today and that made Alice relax a little. She had to admit that being here in Nate's company was feeling more awkward than she'd expected. Maybe it was because they were alone together in a social situation? It was quite possible there were people here that might recognise them. Nate might be separated from his wife but he was still a married man and sometimes people couldn't help jumping to conclusions that might be totally wrong but still had the power to do some damage.

She picked up one of the laminated menus on the bar and scanned it as the inky liquid was being poured from bottles to fill their glasses beneath a layer of brownish foam.

'I'm *so* hungry,' she said aloud.

'Me, too,' Nate said. 'What looks good?'

'Well, I don't know about you, but I can't go past a good slow-cooked beef hotpot.'

'Perfect match for your drinks.' The bartender nodded approvingly. 'That hotpot's got Guinness in it, too.'

It was Nate's turn to smile as he reached to pick up the tulip-shaped glasses. 'I'll have what she's having,' he said.

He led the way to a table in a corner booth and they sat facing each other. They both picked up their glasses. Alice took a cautious sip. Her head jerked up to find that Nate had yet to taste his drink. He was watching her over the rim of his glass.

'Oh...' Alice put her glass down and eyed it with respect.

'You don't like it?'

'I'm not sure,' Alice confessed.

'First time?' Nate's lips twitched. 'I did wonder.'

'I'm being bold,' Alice said. She picked up her glass again and took another, very small sip. 'How do they do it?' she asked. 'Do they go and find random barbecues and scrape all that burnt, black stuff off the bottom of the tray and throw it in with the normal brew?'

Nate actually laughed aloud. The sound went past Alice's ears to flow right through her body and it was impossible not to smile back at him. This felt like a win. The amusement had made his eyes crinkle and his face relax and she could almost forget how desperate he'd looked back in the hangar, but the silence that fell after the laughter faded was full of so many questions it felt almost solid.

Alice didn't need to ask any of them yet, however. Catching her bottom lip between her teeth as she met Nate's gaze was enough of a prompt.

'It's a long story,' he said. 'Are you sure you want to hear it?'

'That's why I'm here,' she responded. She tilted her head towards her glass. 'And I reckon that drink's going to last me for hours given that half a mil at a time is more than enough.'

'No one's waiting for you to get home?'

'No.' Alice didn't offer any more information. This wasn't supposed to be about her.

Maybe Nate hadn't got the memo.

'How old are you, Alice?'

'Thirty-six.'

'Have you ever been married?'

'No.' Alice made a face. 'Don't intend to, either. In fact, I think I'm over men. Been there, done that. Not going to keep the T-shirt.'

Nate opened his mouth as if he was about to ask another question but then closed it with a firmness that suggested he'd thought better of it. Because he knew he could be stepping, uninvited, onto sensitive ground?

'I got married before I even hit the big three-oh,' he told her. 'That's more than ten years ago. My friends were settling down—some of them had started having kids and I'd always seen that as part of my own future.' He was watching a waitress coming towards their table from the kitchens, carrying a tray. 'I was an only child,' he added. 'I'd always thought the one thing that would make life perfect was to have a big family.'

Alice grimaced. 'I was an only child, too,' she told him, 'but I thought the one thing that would make life perfect was not to have a family at all.'

She got a distinctly curious glance this time but they both leaned back as rustic, ceramic ramekins were placed on the table. The thin, overlapping slices of potato on the top were crisp and brown and the escaping steam smelled rich and delicious. The cutlery was wrapped in serviettes and there was a small basket of bread rolls.

'Be careful,' the waitress warned. 'That hotpot's like lava at the moment.'

Alice's stomach rumbled but having broken the potato layer with her fork, she knew it would be unwise to taste it yet. Nate hadn't even unwrapped his cutlery and the look he was giving Alice now was almost a frown, as if he was worried about something. What was it she'd said? Oh, yeah. That she was over men and didn't want a family.

'Don't get me wrong,' she said. 'I don't hate men. I'd even be up for finding a life partner—I just don't want kids. I've found guys who *say* they don't want kids but then it turns out that they're just filling in time until they can find someone who wants to have their babies. Or that's how it feels. I've given up looking.'

'At least you're upfront about not wanting them,' Nate said. 'It's something that everyone should at least talk about before making any kind of commitment.'

'Did you?'

Nate nodded. 'It was something we both wanted, right from the start. We were young. We were both going to work hard for a few years and save a deposit for a big, family house and then start having those babies. At least three. Maybe five.'

Nate paused to take a first, tentative bite of his still steaming dinner. Alice followed his example and found beef that had been cooked long enough to melt in her mouth. She ripped a chunk off a bread roll to dip in the thick gravy.

'This is *so* good... Wish I could cook like this.'

For a while, they both ate in a companionable silence but Nate slowed down and was simply playing with his fork before he'd finished his meal, as if his appetite had suddenly disappeared.

Finally he put his fork down and leaned back in his chair. 'I guess the real start of my story was a couple of years later. Donna's mother rang to tell her that one of her cousin's kids had just been diagnosed with a syndrome. Have you heard of fragile X syndrome?'

Alice shook her head, not trying to pretend that she'd heard of it but forgotten the details. Nate had never judged Alice on any gaps in her medical knowledge. He seemed to enjoy teaching her something new and she always enjoyed listening.

'It's the most common cause of inherited intellectual

disability. It affects boys more than girls, can range from mild to severe and there's no cure. An affected child might need lifelong therapy and support services.'

There was almost a roughness to Nate's voice that made this feel very different to any of those bite-sized tutorials related to a profession they were both passionate about. This information was significant.

'Nobody had even known it was in the family,' Nate continued. 'The doctor involved advised that any close relatives who were planning to have children should be tested—just in case.' He paused to take in a slow breath. 'Turned out Donna is a carrier.'

'Oh, *no*...' Alice felt guilty for entertaining the thought that Nate might have cheated on his wife. Of course there had to have been more to this story. 'That must have been such a shock.'

'The genetic counsellors were great. There were ways around it. It's possible to test prenatally from about ten weeks' gestation but...' Nate pulled in a breath. 'It's a 50 percent chance of it being bad news and neither of us were happy with the idea of having to make a decision about whether to terminate a pregnancy on the grounds of having a potentially severely disabled child.'

Alice nodded. That was understandable.

'There were other options. We could think about adoption. Or go the IVF route where the embryos were tested before implantation and only the unaffected ones used but that's quite a major medical journey and I couldn't blame Donna for needing time to get used to the idea. We got on with our lives in the meantime but... something had changed. The dream wasn't going to be easy any longer and it seemed to have a flow-on effect on the rest of our lives.' Nate shrugged. 'It didn't seem to matter what I said—Donna still felt like it was her fault. We stopped talking about it. We kind of drifted apart. I was focussed on my specialist training and getting a consultancy. Donna did some part-time modelling and then she gave up nursing when she started to get noticed. We were both busy and happy enough, I guess, and another year or two went by.'

They'd both pushed their ramekins aside by now. Their waitress came back to collect them.

'Can I get you guys anything else? Dessert? Coffee?'

'I'd like a coffee, please,' Alice said. 'A flat white would be great.'

'Me, too,' Nate echoed.

He sighed as they were left alone again. 'I knew time was running out with us both nearly in our forties,' he said. 'So I brought it up again about the time I started shifts at Aratika. She said she wasn't sure she wanted to get pregnant anytime soon because it would be too disruptive for her modelling career. She loved the work and she was making more money than I was by that stage.' He shrugged. 'That was when I suggested surrogacy. I was really honest about how much it meant to me to have a family and I think we both knew it was an issue that could break us.'

He looked up and Alice was startled to see something that looked like guilt in his eyes.

'In retrospect, I can see this was partly a Band-Aid baby to try and save our marriage but, at the time, it was definitely what we both wanted. We found an online community and got all the information we needed. We were both excited about it. We made the decision to use a donor egg and my sperm and it turned out to be remarkably easy to find someone who was prepared to help us achieve our dream of having a baby. A gestational surrogate, who has no biological relationship to the baby they're carrying.'

'That's a huge thing for someone to do for a stranger.'

'It is,' Nate agreed. 'And Simone is just the loveliest person. A real "earth-mother" type. She and her partner live on an off-the-grid lifestyle block near the sea right at the bottom of the South Island and she homeschools their five kids. Family is everything to them and she absolutely loves being pregnant but they don't want any more of their own. She wanted to help others discover the joy of becoming a family and she'd been looking for the right couple for quite a while. She said she'd know when she found them and it turned out to be me and Donna. Everything was perfect.' He paused and then let his breath out slowly. 'Until it wasn't.'

'I know almost nothing about the process of surrogacy in New Zealand,' she admitted. 'But I've heard some horror stories about things that have happened overseas.'

'It is complicated,' Nate said. 'It's legal, but only if it's altruistic and the surrogate isn't making money out of it. There are all sorts of hoops to jump through, like meeting ethics committee criteria and getting approval for adoption.' He shook his head. 'That was weird for me, the idea of having to apply for permission to adopt my own child. Our laws state that the woman who gives birth to the child is its legal mother, even if she has no biological relationship to it.'

Alice's jaw dropped. 'Wow…that's a minefield.'

The lines of tension were back in Nate's face. She

could see the muscles in his throat moving, as if it was suddenly hard to swallow.

'That's exactly what it is.' He rubbed the back of his neck. 'And maybe Donna stood on the first mine but I'm the one who's about to detonate an even bigger one.'

The arrival of their coffees broke Nate's story long enough for Alice to get her head around the enormity of what Nate had been through to get this far. But the story was far from over. What had happened for things to have gone so wrong? And what was about to happen next that Nate was so worried about?

She didn't even pick up her coffee cup because the question on the tip of her tongue was all-consuming.

'What happened, Nate? When did it start going wrong?'

He pushed his coffee cup further away. 'Reality happened,' he said quietly. 'I don't think any of us expected the first implantation to be successful but there we were. This wasn't an imaginary baby any longer. We were on the countdown to becoming parents and it was bigger than either of us anticipated. I was thrilled. Donna was... shocked. She might have been happy with the idea of us having children but she'd put her hand up to be a mother to someone *else's* child and it was only after she knew it was really going to happen that she began to realise that perhaps it wasn't actually something she wanted to do.' He cleared his throat. 'That was when she decided to tell me about the affair she'd been having with the photographer she's been working with for the last year or two. Nico. They'd broken it off because he was going back to Italy but...he'd asked her to go with him and she'd decided that *was* what she wanted to do. Things went downhill after that and when I asked what about the baby, she said…she said the baby was only mine so I could have it. By myself.'

'Oh, my God…' Alice breathed. Nico's hand was still lying on the table after he'd pushed his cup away and, without thinking, she reached out to put her hand over his. He didn't pull away from her touch. 'I'm so sorry, Nate.'

He was silent for a long moment. Alice felt his hand clench into a fist beneath her fingers.

'I didn't even see it coming,' he said softly. 'She'd seemed so onboard with the plan. We went house-hunting and had an offer accepted on a real family home—a big old villa with a lovely garden.' He closed his eyes, making a sound like a low growl. 'Donna cleared all her stuff out of our apartment and I moved out of it a few days ago. She's on her way to Italy and I'm living in a sea of boxes and a mostly empty house. But, you know what?'

'What?'

'I was coping. Or I thought I was. And I'm sorry I was unpleasant to work with today but I was confident that I wasn't letting the latest disaster derail me enough to interfere with being able to do my job. I should probably have taken a day off to try and sort out the new issue but Aratika is the most solid rock in my life right now. I know people are talking about me at the hospital. Donna still has friends there. I know it's not possible but I have a horrible feeling that the news might reach Simone any day now.'

'What makes you say that?'

'I got an email from Simone this morning. She wants

photos of the new house so she can daydream about where the baby is going to grow up.' He pulled his hand away from Alice's. 'It hit me like a brick.'

'Why?'

'Because, when she finds out that I'm going to be a single father, she might decide she's going to keep the baby—which, legally, she's perfectly entitled to do.'

'But she knows you. She knows how much you want this baby and if she hasn't worked out what an amazing father you'll be, *I'll* tell her. I've seen you around babies and kids enough to know that and… I can be very persuasive.' Alice attempted a reassuring smile but she knew it was falling flat.

'She only needs to see the house with nothing but boxes in it to know that I'm not exactly coping.'

'So we'll make it look like you are.' Alice's smile was more confident this time. 'That's something I *can* help with. You wait and see. We'll turn it into the perfect family home for those photos.'

CHAPTER THREE

WHAT A DIFFERENCE a day could make!

Alice hadn't expected to see Nate waiting for the first patient she and her crew partner brought into the emergency department the next day by air ambulance but he was clearly the consultant who was leading the trauma team for this case.

It wasn't the time or place to exchange any kind of personal greeting and Nate was completely focused on the patient being wheeled into the resuscitation area, but Alice could feel the difference with no more than a graze of eye contact and she knew Nate was on top of his game today. He wasn't feeling anything like as pressured or miserable as he had been yesterday.

She also knew that the evening they'd spent together at the Irish pub was largely responsible for him feeling better and...for just a beat, until they brought the stretcher to a halt beside the bed, ready to transfer this patient into the trauma team's care, she let herself feel good that dinner last night had been her idea. That she'd done something nice for a friend whose life was currently going more than a little pear-shaped.

Then Alice took a deep breath as a word from Nate drew the attention of everyone in the room. Some people were simply standing to one side, arms folded over the disposable aprons protecting their scrubs, as they waited to play their parts—like the less senior doctors who were poised to begin a primary survey, the radiographer and technicians. An orthopaedic surgeon and neurosurgeon who'd been summoned on the basis of the information already transmitted were arriving. Another consultant who was at the head of the bed, in charge of the airway, looked up from checking his equipment as Nate spoke and several nurses, who had roles with medications, IVs or as a runner, stopped what they were doing and listened.

All eyes were on Alice as the senior flight paramedic on this crew, and the handover she needed to do had once been one of the most intimidating parts of her job with the intensity of the way this group of highly skilled and very experienced trauma experts was about to listen to every word she said. Along with the patient—a very scared teenager—who was lying on the stretcher, with no idea of what was going to happen next. Alice took just a moment to touch her arm and smile at her reassuringly before she began speaking.

'This is Melissa Williams, fifteen years old. She's had a fall from a horse during a jumping lesson approximately forty-five minutes ago. The fall was witnessed. Both horse and rider fell and it appeared that the full weight of the horse was on Melissa briefly as it rolled. Ground surface was grass and she was wearing both a back protector and a helmet.'

Alice took a breath. It felt like all the other people in this room were a supporting cast. It was Nate she was speaking directly to.

'On arrival, Melissa's GCS was fifteen and she had

ten out of ten pelvic and lower lumbar pain which was preventing her moving her legs. She also has tenderness and guarding over her lower abdomen. No obvious signs of limbs fractures and limb baselines normal but slightly reduced in the right leg.'

Alice was speaking rapidly but clearly, trying to get her information across succinctly but not leave anything important out.

'We applied both a pelvic binder due to the mechanism of injury and clinical signs. C-spine immobilisation is due to Melissa's age and the MOI. She has patent IV access and has had fifty micrograms of fentanyl with good effect—pain score now five. Ondansetron given to prevent nausea. Latest vital signs...' Alice glanced down at her glove where she'd scribbled the figures. 'Heart rate one-twenty, blood pressure ninety-eight over sixty, respiration rate twenty-four, SpO2 ninety-nine. No previous medical history of note and no known allergies. Her family have been contacted and her parents are en route.' Finally, Alice let her gaze sweep the whole room. 'Any questions?'

A beat of silence.

'Thanks, Alice.' Nate's tone was crisp but he was smiling at Melissa. 'Don't worry,' he told her. 'We're going to take very good care of you.'

Alice stood back to let the trauma team transfer Melissa to the bed on Nate's count.

'One...two...*three*!'

All the monitoring equipment like electrode connections, blood pressure cuff and the finger clip to measure blood oxygen saturation level were switched on and, moments later, Alice and her crew partner, Jack, were wheeling the stretcher out with all their gear piled on top.

Alice could hear the team swinging into action behind her, a babble of voices and commands, the squeak of trolleys being repositioned and X-ray machinery being readied but she wasn't really aware of the familiar sounds. She was thinking more about what it would have felt like to be Melissa and to have Nate Madden smiling at her like that just before something new and potentially terrifying might be going to happen.

She would have believed him when he said they were going to take very good care of her, she decided.

She would have felt a whole lot safer.

And you couldn't put a price on being able to make a person who was having the worst day of their life feel like that.

Alice didn't get back to The General's emergency department on that shift. She and Jack were dispatched to a car accident but stood down before they got there because first responders hadn't found injuries that were severe enough to warrant the air ambulance resources. They did an inter-hospital transfer of a pregnant woman in early labour with a high-risk pregnancy due to her congenital heart disease but that took them to the city's maternity hospital. There were no call-outs for the last couple of hours of her shift and Alice was more than ready to head home when her phone pinged to advertise an incoming text.

From Nate.

If you're not too tired, come and see the house when you're on your way home. You might want to see what you signed up for last night.

He'd ended the message with a crying laughing emoji that made Alice smile.

She sent him a 'thumbs up' reaction and he sent through his address.

Dusk was falling when she arrived on the doorstep of a lovely old villa in a suburb on top of one of Wellington's hills. The fading daylight only made the view out over the city and the harbour more fabulous as lights came on like fireflies gathering over the hills and amongst the high-rise buildings of the city centre. One of the big ferries that provided a vital link between the north and south islands of New Zealand was heading for its wharf and the lights of a helicopter heading back to the Aratika Rescue Base could be seen not far behind the ferry.

'Oh, my goodness,' Alice exclaimed. She was grinning. 'You can sit here on the terrace and almost feel like you're still at work.'

'It was the view that we fell in love with,' Nate said. 'And I had no idea it would be even better in the dark. There's always something happening out there.'

We...

Alice's smile faltered at the reminder that Nate and his wife had chosen this house together. It was a symbol of the future as the home where they would raise their baby. The enormity of what had already been taken away from him—even without the unthinkable prospect of being denied his child—was sobering. Alice made an effort to think of something positive to say.

'You've got a straight run into the city and all the drama of this amazing view but, when you walk out of the front door, you've got a lovely, leafy suburb and probably a really good school nearby. It really is the perfect family home. Simone's going to be so impressed.'

'Mmm...' Nate's tone was dubious. 'You mean you didn't notice the "warehouse chic" vibe of all those boxes in the kitchen you just walked straight past?'

'Sorry. This view just sucked me in. I'm ready to appreciate all the character now. I absolutely adore old houses. I live in a little heritage cottage in Aro Valley, so this feels like a palace in comparison. Give me the grand tour and then we'll make a plan for how we're going to stage the photo shoot.'

'Follow me.'

Nate had only unpacked the absolute essentials after the movers had done their job last week. A kettle and a toaster sat on the kitchen bench beside a loaf of bread and a jar of coffee. The pantry shelves were empty and boxes labelled 'kitchen' covered the dining table and were stacked high enough to be hiding the chairs.

'I love that they've kept this old coal range,' Alice said. She bent to trace the decorative markings on the cast-iron appliance next to the fridge.

'It still goes,' Nate told her. 'It burns wood as well as coal.'

He was watching her fingers move over the lettering of the manufacturer's name. He'd seen her hands in action countless times, deftly inserting a cannula into a tricky vein, gently examining a break in a bone or slipping a tube into a difficult airway with an ease that only came with practised skill. Alice didn't wear rings and she kept her nails short and unpainted. They were practical, clever, reliable sort of fingers. How come he'd never noticed that they were also so graceful and...expressive? He could almost feel the appreciation that Alice had for this antique cooker.

It was a weird thing to notice. Nate cleared his throat. 'The previous owners used it for heating and cooking. Might be useful in a power cut.'

'It might.' Alice straightened and her gaze went to the bench. 'Are you living on toast and coffee?' she asked.

'Only for breakfast. I get takeaways when I'm home for dinner.'

'Healthy.'

'I've got some wine in the fridge if you'd like a glass.'

'Maybe later.' Alice was heading for the hallway. 'We've got work to do.'

Nate led her through the house and back down the classic central hallway that was a feature of old villas, with their polished wooden floors and a plaster archway halfway down. The rooms on this upper level of the house were big, with high studs, ornate plaster cornices and central roses on the ceilings, and carved wooden fire surrounds. The staircase led down to bedrooms and bathrooms that looked out onto terraced gardens cut into the hillside. The rumpled linen on his bed and all the clothes still waiting to be hung up that were draped over the end of it were a bit embarrassing but Alice didn't seem to notice. She was captured by the part of the garden that could be seen through this window—a space that was entirely filled with a massive, very old pohutukawa tree.

'*Oh...*' Her face lit up with a smile. 'How gorgeous is that going to be when it's in full flower in December?'

The room she really fell in love with, however, was much smaller than the master bedroom. On the other side of the house, with a small lawn outside the window.

'There's a *Wendy* house,' she exclaimed.

'It was left with the property,' Nate said. 'Because they commissioned it to be a miniature villa and painted it to match the house.'

Donna had seemed just as enchanted by the cute playhouse, with its child-sized front door, but she gave no sign of having had the glimpse of a small person enjoying a tea party or making mud-pies on the tiny porch that had squeezed his own heart so hard. For Nate, that had been the moment he'd really fallen in love with this house.

'This has to be the nursery,' Alice said. 'I can see the photo. A cot here, in the corner by the window with a lovely mobile hanging over it, some cute stuffies on the windowsill and the view into the garden with the Wendy house like a peep into the future when they're big enough to go and play in it.'

Alice seemed a bit startled by the way Nate turned his head so suddenly to stare at her.

'What did I say?'

'Nothing…' Nate tried to find a smile but, strangely, it didn't happen. He also found himself holding eye contact with Alice for just a beat too long.

She was the one who broke it, biting her lip as she turned her gaze back to the window. 'You don't like that idea?'

'Oh, I *do*. It sounds perfect.'

He couldn't tell her how much he really liked it, though. Or why. Maybe he didn't want to think about it too much himself, in fact. It wasn't that it was just the kind of picture he needed to send Simone as proof of how much the baby she was carrying was wanted and would be loved. It was more that imagining a happy child playing in the little house had been the first thought Alice had had. It felt like something had reached between them, on a very personal level, and made contact.

It felt like a secret smile.

Nate turned. It was a welcome distraction to move and head back upstairs.

'We should start making a list of things you need to buy.' Alice was following him. 'We can probably order it online but that might be slower. How much time have we got to make the house look like a baby-friendly home?'

'I told Simone I'd try and send some photos in a few days, as soon as we've tidied up a bit from the move. I guess I could spin that out to a week without her starting to think that anything's really wrong.'

They'd got back to the kitchen now. Nate opened the fridge and held up the bottle of white wine he had chilled.

'Just a small one,' Alice said.

'I'll see if I can unearth a couple of chairs,' Nate said, as he handed her a glass.

He shifted boxes and lifted out chairs which he put in front of the big windows and that view.

'Cheers.'

Alice echoed the toast and they clinked their glasses but neither took their eyes off the view for a moment longer than necessary. It was dark outside and the lights of the city and the moving traffic were even brighter. Even the big Interislander ferry was lit up like a Christmas tree as all the vehicles and passengers were unloaded.

'Why would Simone start thinking anything's wrong?' Alice asked. 'How often does she expect to hear from you?' Her eyes widened. 'Is Donna still in touch with her? Will she have told Simone what's going on?'

Nate shook his head. 'I'm the one who's kept up all the contact since the conception and I sign emails or messages from both of us. Simone talked to Donna a lot during all the calls we made in the early stages of getting to know each other but not lately. I've told her she's out of the country at the moment which is why I'm being slow getting the house sorted. She hasn't asked why Donna's away but I'm guessing she's assuming it's for a work thing, like a photoshoot somewhere exotic. She's probably got used to not talking to Donna now.' His face twisted into a grimace. 'She's never actually met her.'

Alice's glass stopped halfway to her mouth. 'Sorry... *what*?' She put the glass down on the windowsill in front of her. 'How can she be carrying your baby without having met the person who's going to be the mother?'

'I know. It's not exactly usual but everything's been a little...different, I guess. This is a very private arrangement. Simone and her partner live an alternative kind of lifestyle. They're relaxed about time frames and not at all bothered by having patchy internet access. I went down to Dunedin, which is the nearest fertility centre for them, for what was supposed to be the joint counselling session for all four of us involved, but Donna got sick the morning we were due to fly out. It was too late to cancel and we couldn't ask Simone to reschedule at such late notice because they were already in Dunedin and a six-hour drive each way with a car full of kids is such a big deal. Donna managed to join us for a voice call and the meeting went so well that we all agreed that we wanted to move forward without any delays. I did everything I needed to do so that the embryo could be created with the donor egg and Simone signed up to get ready for the first implantation.'

'How long ago was that?'

'A bit over six months. Simone's about nineteen weeks now. Almost halfway. She...' Nate had to stop and clear his throat. 'It wasn't obvious on the first ultrasound but she's convinced she's carrying a girl. She's waiting for an appointment to be confirmed for the anatomy scan, probably the week after next. If I can, I'll go down to Dunedin and be there but how I'm going to explain Donna not coming with me might well be a problem.'

He needed a long sip of his wine as those words hung in the air.

'I don't feel good,' he said then. 'Lying to her, even if it's by omission, like not telling her the real reason Donna's out of the country at the moment. Pretending that nothing's changed and everything's okay feels wrong, too, but...'

Could he tell Alice the real truth? Would she think less of him if he did?

He didn't want Alice to think less of him.

'But you're scared to tell her the truth.' Her voice was very quiet. 'Because she might feel that having a mother is a non-negotiable part of being a family?'

Nate didn't need to say anything. He knew that the moment of meeting Alice's gaze was enough. That feeling of contact was there again. That bond that was on such a personal level it was disconcerting. It didn't feel like a smile this time, though. It was more like an imaginary hand hold. She wasn't judging him for not sharing with Simone all the details of the personal problems he was navigating in his life.

She was in his corner and knowing that was enough to give him a bit of a lump in his throat, to be honest. He wanted her to know how much he appreciated her acceptance of how he was handling this. And he wanted her to know just how important this was for him.

'From the moment I knew I was going to be a father,' he confessed softly, 'I've felt so protective of this baby. Losing the chance to be a part of his—or her—life would haunt me for the rest of *my* life.'

He closed his eyes for a heartbeat. The crazy thought that he could beg Donna to come back for just long enough for the adoption to go through got pushed out of his head as fast as it had appeared.

It did leave a realisation in its wake, however. His marriage *was* over. Deep down, he'd known that for a long time. He just hadn't wanted to admit his failure.

He opened his eyes again. 'I have to tell Simone the truth,' he said. 'But…is it a terrible thing to do to wait a little longer? Long enough to buy some time to try and show her how serious I am about being the best father I can possibly be?'

The short silence that fell created a tension in the air that Nate could almost taste.

'I don't think so,' Alice said then. 'So much has happened and sometimes you need some time to clear your head. How confident you feel about being able to cope as a single dad might make all the difference to how Simone reacts to the news. Taking the first step of getting this lovely home ready for a family won't take that long and you might find it makes a big difference for *you*. It's worth a try, isn't it?'

Nate let his breath out slowly, feeling the tension

around him dissipate. There was relief to be found in the prospect of shelving something, albeit temporarily, that could have unpleasant life-changing consequences. It felt like a switch had been flicked and his body was being flooded with a flush of endorphins.

Nate hadn't felt this good in weeks.

Relieved.

Hopeful. Excited, even. With Alice to help, he might be able to get control and start piecing his life back together again.

And yeah…he could add gratitude to the emotions that were making him feel so good.

'Are you hungry?' he asked. 'We could get some food delivered. I might even be able to find a plate or two in one of those boxes.' He waved at the cardboard walls around them. 'Or we could order something that comes in a little box with some wooden chopsticks.'

Alice was laughing. Nate shook his head.

'Okay, okay… I get it. You're *always* hungry.' He was laughing now, too, and it added another boost to the lift in his mood. He liked that Alice made no secret of enjoying her food. He wasn't going to miss watching Donna pick at meals and count every calorie she was consuming. 'What's your favourite to get delivered?'

'Hamburgers,' she said, without hesitation. 'Or pizza. Wait…maybe Mexican?'

Nate pulled out his phone. 'Anything we can eat without cutlery is probably wise.'

But Alice was shaking her head now. 'You order. And then we're going to start unpacking boxes. We might even find your plates and cutlery by the time it's delivered.'

The gourmet hamburgers and hand-cut fries arrived about forty-five minutes later. They had not only found all the plates and cutlery but they were stacked and sorted into cupboards and drawers. They didn't bother using anything that was going to need washing, however. They didn't even sit at the space they'd cleared on the table.

They sat and watched the panorama of lights in the city instead, eating their hamburgers with their hands, the box of chips on the windowsill between their wine glasses.

It felt like a picnic.

'Someone's taking off from Aratika,' Alice observed. 'I used to love being on the night shift crew.' She reached for another chip and dipped it in the little pot of garlic aioli. 'Using night vision goggles is cool and a winch job using the night sun is an incredible adrenaline rush.'

'I've never done a night shift on the base,' Nate said.

'Try one,' Alice suggested. 'As extra crew, maybe.' She smiled. 'Maybe sooner rather than later? You won't be putting your hand up to work at night after your baby arrives. You'll be doing night feeds and watching all the action out of this window instead.'

She made it sound as if there was no doubt that his baby was going to arrive and live here in this house. That he was somehow going to step seamlessly into his new life as a father.

Her confidence was contagious. Nate stuffed the last bite of his burger into his mouth. There were more boxes to unpack. More sorting of his life to get on with and a limited time in which to get it done.

The clock was ticking.

CHAPTER FOUR

THERE WAS ALWAYS a buzz around shift changeovers, and they were favourite times of the day for Alice, with all the promise of unexpected challenges around the next corner in the morning and the satisfaction of doing her job to the best of her ability at the end of a working day.

The Aratika Rescue Base was humming as dawn broke, as usual, with the night shift clearing up any last-minute tasks to get home and others preparing for the day ahead. There were flight crews, pilots and aircraft engineers along with an ambulance road crew and motorbike paramedics that were positioned on base to back up or complement the city's land-based emergency services. The operations manager, clinical team leader, and communications officer were there and, as often as not, there could also be observers, volunteers or trainees there as well.

There was a loud hum of conversation, greetings being called and the occasional burst of laughter. The atmosphere had the feeling of a tight-knit work community and, judging by the smile on the face of the base's most loyal volunteer, this was Shirley's favourite time of day. She was ruling the kitchen, handing out coffees and bacon rolls, unashamedly eavesdropping on reports of night missions and waiting to hear the briefing Don, the operations manager, would be giving the day shift crews that included any potential issues with equipment, staffing, events happening or weather conditions.

'Thanks, Shirley.' Alice happily accepted a bread roll stuffed with crispy bacon and a drizzle of smoky barbecue sauce. She already had a steaming mug of coffee in front of her at the long table in the mess-room. Don was at the head of the table chatting to departing night shift personnel, a sheaf of papers in his hand ready for his briefing.

'Even my mother didn't look after me as well as you do, Shirley.' Nate also scored one of the hot rolls as he slipped into the empty seat opposite Alice. 'This is exactly what I need to get my engine running this morning.'

'You do look a tad tired, love.' Shirley shook her head, her face creased with the unspoken sympathy of knowing that he was still navigating a major life change. 'I'll get you a coffee.'

Nate's gaze caught Alice's as he took an appreciative bite of his roll and gave her a ghost of a wink. She simply held up her own breakfast, like a toast with a glass, and took a bite herself. She knew exactly why he was tired this morning—they hadn't finished organising his kitchen until midnight last night—but there was no reason for anyone else to know about this new out-of-hours arrangement they had. Alice was smiling inwardly as she remembered how satisfying it had been to admire the neat cupboards and pantry and arrange the chairs around a dining table that was now ready to be used for its intended purpose. And how much fun had it been to squash the empty boxes, jumping on them like a couple of over-excited kids? She hadn't laughed that much in a long time.

It was kind of fun to have a secret with Nate, too.

Alice found her gaze straying back to him more than once as Don got on with an update.

'Weather's great to start the day,' he said. 'Light southerly, ten to fifteen kilometres an hour, temperature getting up to nineteen degrees Celsius and just scattered high cloud. Could be a front moving in later this afternoon, though, with deteriorating conditions.'

Alice wasn't thinking about the weather. Andy would be all over it from a pilot's perspective and she would cope with whatever came their way. For some reason, she was more interested in watching Nate take the last bite of his roll.

He did look tired, she thought. He had a bit of a shadow on his jaw and he hadn't had a haircut for long enough to be revealing waves she didn't know he had. It wasn't a bad look, though. If anything, having a slightly dishevelled vibe made him look even better.

Nate Madden was definitely good-looking, there was no doubt about that. Especially when he was dressed in the standard, indoor, Aratika uniform of black technical pants, steel-capped boots and a black T-shirt with their logo below the left shoulder—the outline of a helicopter flying straight towards a mountain range. Alice had taken a second glance herself, when she'd been first introduced to the new HEMS doctor but she'd already seen his CV and knew he was married, so her appreciation of Nate's looks had never been anything more than purely academic.

Until now…?

Oh, my...

Alice had shifted her gaze at precisely the time Nate was licking a dribble of sauce off his thumb, and her awareness of him was so sharp she could feel it in her body. Deep in her belly. Like...

No... Alice might not have felt that particular sensation in a long time but she knew exactly what it was.

Attraction. *Sexual* attraction.

Hastily, she turned her head to focus on Don, but he'd finished what he wanted to say about any current issues being dealt with by other emergency services.

'Have a great day, everyone. And stay safe out there.'

Alice picked up her empty mug. There were plenty of things she needed to get on with before they got their first call-out. She'd already done a check of all the medical packs and the batteries on the defibrillator and portable ventilator, but the drug kit still needed double-checking and she hadn't had time to look at their blood and plasma supplies yet.

She could check all her own gear like her helmet, flight suit and harness. She could even clean her boots if she needed something else to keep her busy. Anything would do, as long as she didn't allow herself to have any more totally inappropriate thoughts or feelings towards her crewmate for the day.

Alice gave herself a mental slap. The man's marriage had only disintegrated five minutes ago, for heaven's sake. And Nate was about to become a father in the near future! Even if he'd been single for a decade, that would be enough of a red flag to make sure Alice was not going to think about Nate as anything other than a friend. With no benefits whatsoever on the horizon.

He certainly wouldn't be having any odd reactions to being around her. She'd met Donna briefly at a Christmas social function at the base not long after Nate had joined the team. The fact that they were both brunettes was the only thing she'd had in common with Nate's wife. Donna was taller, a lot slimmer and far more elegant than Alice could ever dream of being. No wonder she'd given up nursing to become a model.

Okay...maybe neither of them wanted to have children but Alice didn't want to find anything else in common with Donna Madden. Maybe you couldn't judge relationships from the outside but she could be quite confident that Nate had been the one who'd put the most effort into trying to make their marriage work. He was the one who'd dreamed of a happy family future and he was the one who was now rattling around in a big house by himself, determined to do whatever it took to keep at least part of that dream alive.

She was most definitely on Team Nate—more than happy to provide practical help and any support he might accept from a friend. On a deeper level, there was a developing closeness that was making her appreciate Nate in areas she hadn't even considered and she was even more impressed with him as a person. Whose heart wouldn't melt over a man who was prepared to do whatever it took to protect his baby? Or who'd fallen in love with a property because of the adorable Wendy house in the garden?

Alice's heart melted a little bit more when she saw Nate taking his empty mug back to the bench and dropping a kiss on Shirley's cheek to thank her for breakfast. Oh, yeah... Team Nate. She was ready to defend him from any gossip or threat that might undermine his ability to achieve that dream.

The project had just graduated from something nice to do for a friend to something that was more than nice to do for herself.

Something important.

A gift. For Nate.

Nate hadn't had a genuinely close friend who was female since he was at primary school.

By the time he started high school, girls were scary and when they weren't, it felt like there was always a sexual undercurrent to friendships. Or hidden barriers because the girls he would have liked to have been friends with were dating someone and that made it unacceptable to spend time with them alone. Study had been more important than anything else at medical school and it wasn't until Nate had started his final year as a trainee intern position at one of New Zealand's largest hospitals that fate had given him a nudge and he'd met Donna on his first rotation.

The nudge was all the more potent because that first run was on the obstetrics and gynaecology ward and there were babies everywhere—a subconscious shove, in fact, to remind him that there was more to life than his chosen career. They'd become engaged the night he graduated from medical school and were married within a few months. And that, inevitably, put even more solid barriers in the way of having a close friendship with another woman.

Work pressures and a focus on their new life as a couple pretty much made friendship with anyone difficult to maintain. They did things with other couples and the relationships were friendly but not that close. Moving cities more than once to find new opportunities for training and then the consultant position Nate had dreamt of made their social life even more insular. In retrospect, it had created pressure that could have been responsible for the cracks in their marriage to widen beyond a point where they could have been repaired.

Nate wasn't oblivious to the subtle change in the way some women were regarding him as the news of his separation spread, but he didn't have the slightest interest in responding to any invitations. What he *had* needed, without realising it, was a close friend. He might have been wary of that friend being a female but he'd been working with Alice for a long time now and she was already in the friend zone.

Maybe it was strange that they could be real friends when they both wanted completely different things from their personal lives, but perhaps that was also what was making it work. Making this a completely *safe* friend zone because here he was about to become a father and Alice had told him that she never wanted to have children. There was no hidden agenda on her part, that was for sure. There was no need to even set boundaries because it was so blatantly obvious that they could never be anything more than friends, but the change that was happening in their relationship had been a turning point for Nate and he was more than grateful it was happening. It was a lifeline, to be honest. He had someone in his corner and it was giving him a new confidence and hope for his immediate future.

Right now, as they pushed the helicopter stretcher, laden with gear, into a small rural medical centre, he was starting to wonder if it was also changing the way they worked together.

The way they had been in sync professionally had been clear from the first mission they'd ever been on together when they'd had a fight on their hands to save a man whose motorbike had been clipped by a concrete mixer truck. Nate had been so impressed with his new partner that he'd told the operations manager that he was looking forward to working with Alice on future shifts. He'd been crewed with Alice so often since then that they had earned the nickname of Aratika's Dream Team but had he ever felt that he and Alice were *this* solid before?

That there wasn't anyone else he would feel this confident with, walking into a situation that could potentially be a matter of life or death?

The look of relief on the GP's face as they were directed into the consulting room advertised what had been an anxious wait for the air ambulance. Their patient, lying back on the pillows of the bed, looked surprisingly cheerful. He was, in fact, grinning at Alice.

'G'day,' he said. 'I'm feeling better already.'

'G'day,' Alice responded. 'I'm Alice and this is Nate.'

'This is Trevor Henley,' the GP said. 'He's seventy-two years old and he was out doing some fencing on the farm this morning when he got acute pain in his lower back, radiating to his legs, that was bad enough to make him feel a bit faint.'

'It's not so bad now,' Trevor declared.

'He looked very unwell when he arrived here,' the GP continued. 'Pale and sweaty, GCS fifteen, pain score six out of ten, but Trev's inclined to downplay symptoms. He's had some morphine and reckons it's down to four now.'

'Two,' Trevor put in. 'I'm almost cured, Doc.'

Nate smiled at him. 'Is it okay if we have a look at you, mate? I'd like to make sure you're okay to come for a ride with us.'

'Do I really need to? That fencing isn't going to do itself and I don't want my sheep getting out on the road.'

'Better safe than sorry.' Alice was smiling at Trevor. 'And it's a lovely morning for a ride in a chopper.' Her tone was persuasive. 'A bit of time off wouldn't hurt, would it?'

'I guess not.' Trevor leaned his head back on the pillows. The anxious lines on his face that belied his casual cheerfulness softened as he let himself accept that he needed help. 'You do whatever you think's best.'

'And you just relax and let us look after you,' Alice said. 'I'm going to take your blood pressure again, okay?' She took out the blood pressure cuff from the pouch on the side of the defibrillator and wrapped it around Trevor's upper arm.

Nate had been about to ask her to take another set of vitals. Instead, he picked up the twelve lead ECG the GP had recorded.

'Trev's got a past history of hypertension,' she told him. 'Mild to moderate COAD from smoking and he started getting a bit of angina a couple of years ago which is stable and relieved by GTN. Do you want a list of his medications?'

'Yes, please.' Nate looked up from the graph recording the electrical activity of the heart. 'Your ticker looks like it's behaving itself, Trevor. That's good news.'

Nate could feel Alice's glance in his direction. She knew why he was sounding so reassuring. They'd been dispatched due to the GP finding a pulsatile abdominal mass, making a provisional diagnosis of an abdominal aortic aneurysm, then doing an ultrasound to find that blood was leaking from a rupture of the major blood vessel.

The last thing they wanted to happen with someone who had a leaking aneurysm was for them to get really anxious, increase their blood pressure and potentially extend a small rupture into something large enough to be very rapidly catastrophic.

'Blood pressure's one-ten on seventy-five,' Alice said, writing it on her glove. 'Heart rate's one-oh-six and SPO2's ninety-four.' She turned back to their patient and put her hand over his. 'Your hands are a bit cold, Trevor.'

'Cold hands, warm heart,' he said.

'Absolutely,' Alice agreed. 'But how 'bout we get you comfy on our stretcher and wrap you up in some of our lovely warm blankets?'

Nate added the information about Trevor's cool peripheries that Alice had casually given him to the fact that the blood pressure had dropped since arrival at the medical centre and the heart rate was going up—all possibly signs of an increasing internal blood loss.

He liked the way Alice was keeping things so calm. The idea of her tucking someone up in warm blankets was making him feel more relaxed. He saw the squeeze Alice gave Trevor's hand before she let go, as well, and he could almost feel that himself.

Yeah…there was something new in how it felt to be

working with her. They'd always been in tune clinically and able to follow a line of thought or anticipate the next intervention that was needed, and Nate knew this change wasn't due to anything professional, but he didn't give it another moment's thought until they had Trevor safely packaged and on board the helicopter with all the monitoring equipment in place and a new, wide-bore IV line in his arm.

Alice was adjusting the drip rate after hanging a bag of fluid as Nate finished securing the line.

'TKVO?' she asked.

Nate nodded. A minimal amount of fluid to keep the vein open was exactly what they needed. Allowing Trevor's blood pressure to stay high enough to maintain perfusion and consciousness but low enough to avoid increasing any bleeding was the goal.

They had a flight time of about twenty minutes to get to the hospital and they needed to monitor Trevor continuously, taking his blood pressure every few minutes and checking heart and respiration rates, peripheral pulses and skin colour. They'd given him a headset to wear so that they could talk to him about any changes in his symptoms but also so that they could explain what was going on and keep him reassured.

'How's that pain, Trevor?' he asked, noticing a grimace. 'Would you like a top-up of the pain meds?'

'Nah... I'm all good.'

'Don't be a hero, Trevor.' Alice leaned closer. She'd also seen the truth in his face. 'We want you to be as comfortable as possible. I've got it right here, if you'd like a drop more.'

'Go on, then...' Trevor managed a smile. 'Just a drop.'

Alice injected the dose of morphine. She leaned forward once she was strapped into her seat and held Trevor's hand as the noise level increased and they lifted off. Nate could see how fiercely he was gripping it back. Alice's fingers looked squashed but she wasn't moving her hand. Instead, she was trying to distract Trevor's attention to lessen his fear.

'What sort of sheep do you run, Trevor? Romneys?'

'Yep.'

'They're the best choice for both meat and wool, aren't they?'

'Yep. How do you know about sheep?'

'I grew up in the country and Romneys are my favourite—they've got nice faces, haven't they? I bottle-raised one. I called her Barbra. My mother's boyfriend at the time insisted on calling her Sunday.'

Trevor seemed to be forgetting how nervous he was and actually chuckled. 'As in Sunday roast?'

'That's the one.' Alice shook her head. 'Barbra went back to the farm eventually but I was quite happy that she lasted longer than that particular boyfriend did.'

Maybe it was the way Alice turned to catch his gaze to see if he was sharing the amusement. Or perhaps it was because he was suddenly curious enough to want to know more about her childhood. What had happened to her father? And had she ended up with a stepfather she approved of? What he was really conscious of, however, was that he could see what was different about his working relationship with Alice Barlow. She was a lot more than simply a colleague now. More than a casual kind of friend whose help he was grateful for.

He really liked her. He'd always known how much

he liked working with her, but now he knew he liked her without being anywhere near the environment of a shared career they were both so passionate about. He could enjoy eating dinner with her. Pushing furniture around and jumping on cardboard boxes. Talking to her about things that had nothing to do with medicine was surprisingly easy. So natural that Nate felt like he could tell her anything. He'd already told her far more than anyone else knew about what was going on in his life. Being in her company away from work was…

Welcome, that's what it was. Really, really welcome.

Nate hadn't realised how lonely he'd been in the last weeks. Maybe his marriage hadn't been anything like what he'd hoped it would be, especially in recent years, but he'd never been entirely alone, either. A huge part of his life had been ripped away and left a gap that felt painfully raw. Worse, he'd had to pack up everything left after Donna had taken what she wanted from their apartment and then move from one almost empty dwelling to a new one. It had been lonely, beyond sad and totally exhausting. He'd barely smiled for what felt like far too long but he'd laughed out loud at Alice's reaction to that strong Guinness she'd tasted for the first time and he'd laughed even more last night, when Alice had insisted they flatten all those boxes before putting them out for recycling.

Alice had been laughing, too. He could remember the joyful sound of it and the way he could feel it as much as hear it. The way bits of her hair had dislodged themselves from her ponytail. The way her eyes were sparkling from the fun of behaving in such a juvenile fashion.

His thoughts, as he listened to Alice keeping Trevor distracted, had been no more than a flash of feeling more than anything as coherent as words but Nate gave himself a mental shake to get rid of them. He needed to be on high alert right now. If Trevor's aneurysm ruptured, he could crash. He might lose consciousness and need a blood transfusion, intubation or full resuscitation from a cardiac arrest. Nate's focus sharpened as he ran through a checklist of everything they might need in a hurry, like rapid sequence intubation drugs and the airway kit.

Banishing any thoughts remotely personal didn't mean they'd entirely evaporated, mind you. Something was left behind. Something nebulous but pleasant, like a waft of a subtle perfume or the memory of a hug from somebody who mattered. He had Alice by his side and that was making the world a better place to be in.

The drama of flying over the cityscape of New Zealand's capital city and landing on the roof of its biggest hospital never got old for Alice and it was particularly satisfying to have a case with the kind of urgency a triple A generated and get their patient to definitive medical care in time to save his life.

They got Trevor unloaded, into the lift and down to the emergency department without his condition deteriorating any further. A full resus team, including the vascular surgeon on call, was ready for them and after a rapid handover, the switch of monitoring equipment and a repeated assessment, Trevor's bed was wheeled swiftly out of the area, a theatre on standby so that his aneurysm could be repaired.

Alice was coiling electrode wires and slotting them neatly into the side pocket of the defibrillator on top of their stretcher as the doors swung shut behind Trevor's bed. Nate finished the last of the paperwork and handed it to ED staff to file.

'He's a lucky man,' Nate said, taking the front end of the stretcher to help steer it out of the department.

'He sure is,' Alice agreed. 'I was really worried that he was going to crash, especially when I saw how nervous he was about flying.' She kept a hand on the other end of the stretcher as they went down a corridor and then into the busy foyer. The lift that would take them back to the helipad on the hospital's roof was to one side of the main reception desk, just past the gift shop.

Nate steered them to one side, to allow room for a hospital bed to dodge a woman with a pushchair. They were right beside the window of the gift shop and Alice was scanning the usual offerings of hand creams and soaps, fluffy socks, get-well cards and children's toys as they went past. Her tug on the stretcher brought them to a sudden halt and Nate's head swerved.

'What's up?'

'That…' Alice pointed. 'Look…'

She'd never seen anything quite as cute as the honey-coloured, curly-haired rabbit with long, droopy ears but what made it totally irresistible was that it was wearing a doctor's white coat, with a red cross embroidered on the pocket.

Nate looked bemused.

'Wait there. I'll be two ticks.' Alice dived into the shop and came out only moments later, clutching the rabbit. 'This,' she informed Nate, 'is the best possible thing to go on the windowsill of the nursery. It couldn't be more perfect.'

* * *

They needed other items for the nursery, of course, and it was a few days before they found the time to visit one of the biggest baby supply shops in town. The larger purchases, like the cot and change table, shelving units and a rocking chair, would be delivered the next day. The back seat and hatch of Nate's SUV was stuffed with everything else. Linen, clothes, nappies, a baby swing, books and toys, and a mobile that was almost as cute as the gift shop rabbit. Small brightly coloured flowers, leaves and bumble bees made of felt were light enough to move in any breeze, and the mobile could be wound up to rotate slowly to the traditional music of 'Brahms' Lullaby.'

They put the whole nursery together the next weekend when their days off coincided and it *did* look perfect. The cot in the corner had the mobile hanging over it, the rocking chair beside the change table had a soft lemon-yellow blanket draped over it and the cube-style shelving was filled with neat stacks of clothing, soft toys and picture books.

Nate pulled his phone out. 'The rest of the house can wait but I've got to send Simone a photo of this right now.'

'Wait!' Alice ran to where she'd left her shoulder bag. 'We're missing Dr Rabbit. He's got to be on the windowsill for the photos.'

But Nate was already taking photos by the time she got back to prop the rabbit on one side of the window.

'There we go,' she said. 'Now it's perfect.'

But Nate was looking at his phone and Alice couldn't interpret his expression. She went and stood beside him and peered at the screen. The image had everything she'd imagined, with the cot and the view through the window to the Wendy house but he'd taken it as she was putting the rabbit down and the blurry shape of her moving figure filled half the screen.

'Take another one,' she suggested. 'Without me ruining it.'

'You're not ruining it,' Nate said quietly. 'Simone's going to think it's Donna.'

Alice gave a huff. 'Are you kidding? Donna's a *model*.'

'It's the colour of your hair,' Nate said. 'And the way it's blurry. It...' He was taking in a slow breath. 'It looks like a mum who can't wait to welcome her baby.' He cleared his throat. 'Would it be okay if I sent this one?'

Alice blinked but then shrugged. 'Sure...why not? It's not as if anyone could recognise me. Or that we were trying to deceive anyone.'

But for the space of time it took to draw in a new breath, it felt like she was trying to deceive herself. Because, for a split second, she could imagine that she *was* the woman Simone would expect to see. Getting a nursery ready for the baby she was going to love and nurture and...and it felt like a dream. One that would never have occurred to her if it wasn't Nate standing beside her— the man who so passionately wanted a family of his own. It was also one that would be dismissed as soon as she stepped out of this room, of course. It wasn't *her* dream.

It never would be.

Nate tapped on the screen of his phone and then slid the device back into his pocket. 'You're a star,' he told Alice. 'I couldn't have done this without you.'

He was smiling at her. And then, unexpectedly, he was hugging her. Just the kind of swift, squeezy sort of hug that a friend would share when they were grateful for something.

But it didn't quite feel like that.

Alice was too aware of the shape of Nate's body pressed against her own. The way it felt to be inside the circle of his arms. She could feel his warmth and his breath on her hair. She could even feel his heart beating for the beat or two that she was that close to his skin, and it was doing something to her body. Something melty. Something that was making the floor oddly uneven beneath her feet when he let her go.

Maybe Nate could feel it, too?

He was holding her gaze the way she was holding his—as if it was the best anchor to ride out the wobbly floor sensation—but who was going to break it first? Alice could feel it going on that beat too long.

She could see that something else was forming in that space of time. Another nanosecond and she knew that Nate would be kissing her.

Or she'd be kissing him.

However it happened, there would be no coming back from it. And what quicker way could there be to ruin a friendship?

Suddenly, it was easy to break the eye contact. Perhaps because they'd both done it—and stepped back—in the same instant?

Thank goodness it seemed to be just as easy to pretend it had never happened.

And maybe that was because it was what they both desperately wanted to believe?

CHAPTER FIVE

'WHAT DID SHE SAY?'

Alice kept her voice down but the noise level in a very busy emergency department was more than enough to cover having a private word with Nate, who was staring at an X-ray image on a wall screen. They both had their backs to the usual hum of staff and patients moving, trolleys and machines being wheeled from one place to the next, and a cleaner trying to mop up what looked like a bloodstain on the floor.

Alice held up her hand to signal her crew partner who was still moving their stretcher towards the doors. Jack nodded. He knew she would catch up with him by the time he got to the lift.

'Did she love the Wendy house?' she asked. 'And the doctor bunny?'

Nate shrugged. 'She hasn't responded. Could be that the text message didn't get through because it was a picture. I'll email it when I get a minute.' Nate's gaze swept around the busy emergency department. 'But I don't think Simone checks her emails every day, either.'

'She'll love it, don't worry.'

But, even though Alice only saw Nate from a distance the next day, it was obvious that he still hadn't had any contact. She could see it in his body language. When he looked up and saw that she was in the department, just a heartbeat of eye contact made her realise she could actually feel that he wasn't happy—as if his mood was something invisible but tangible in the air—as obvious as the smell of the disinfectant often was around here.

And that was when Alice started to wonder if something was amiss. She called Nate that evening.

'She gave the picture a "thumbs up" reaction but didn't say anything. Not a word.'

'At least she likes it.'

'It just feels like she doesn't want to talk to me for some reason. I'm wondering if Donna's been in touch with her and she knows what's going on and she's trying to decide what to do about it.'

'She might just be busy. Didn't you say she's got *five* kids? That would make anybody's life hectic.'

'That's true. And she'll have some organising to do so that she can get up to Dunedin for the day and have the anatomy scan. She's never been great with communication, either. They only need a bit of bad weather to lose their internet connection. Or get a power cut. Maybe her phone's dead.'

'Has she got an appointment for the scan?'

'Yes. End of this week. Friday.'

'Are you going down?'

'I'm wait-listed for a seat—there's a big rugby game on that weekend and everything's booked out at the moment. If I can't make it, Simone's going to get a video of the scan and then she'll ring me as soon as she can.'

'There you go, then. Not long to wait.'

The silence told her that it felt like a long time to Nate.

'Why don't you send her another picture? Of the garden or the rest of the house?'

'I did think of that. I wandered around looking for something that looked…' His voice trailed off as if he hadn't actually been too sure of what he was looking for.

'Something homely?' Alice suggested. 'Like a happy parent-to-be is living there?'

'Yeah…and the only room that looks like that is the nursery. Everything else is a bit…empty? As if nobody's *really* living here. Maybe I need to hang up some pictures.'

'That would be a good start. And you could fill the bookshelves. Books always make rooms look like home. Put some photos around, too. A fruit bowl on the dining table? And knick-knacks.'

'Knick-knacks?' Nate sounded bemused.

'You know…things like souvenirs or small sculptures or bowls. Vases. Antique bottles or jars. Candlesticks. Pretty things or personal stuff.'

'I think Donna took most of that kind of stuff. And the only books I've kept are textbooks. That built-in bookshelf in the living room is completely empty.'

'That's an easy fix,' Alice assured him. 'We could hit the second-hand shops. Are you working tomorrow?'

'I've swapped to cover someone for the last half of a swing shift—5 p.m. till midnight. He got invited last minute to a stag do and has promised to cover a full shift for me sometime in return for the favour.'

'Excellent. I've got a day off. Let's go and do some power shopping. There are some great antique shops in the central city and I just happen to know the best second-hand bookshop in town.'

* * *

Nate had expected their mission to add to the tension of not knowing what was going on in Simone's head but, in fact, it did the opposite.

Not just by being enough of a distraction.

Or even that it was far more fun than he expected it to be.

It almost felt like he was travelling back in time. Reminding himself of long-forgotten parts of his life and, even better, sharing them with someone who was genuinely interested.

They started in a huge, second-hand bookshop where he recognised the covers and titles of books from the days before he began to study so hard. When he could banish any loneliness that came from being an only child by escaping into other worlds and the company of fictional friends and enthralling adventures.

He picked up a set of Tolkien books.

'My dad read me *The Hobbit* as a bedtime story when I was about seven years old,' he told Alice. 'I had nightmares about giant spiders and dragons but that didn't stop me going back to read it for myself a couple of years later.'

'Scary stuff is kind of delicious when you know it's safe.' Alice was smiling. 'If it gets really bad you know you can just shut the book.'

'Oh, I knew it was safe. It was my dad reading it to me and he was my absolute hero. I would have felt safe if it had been *real* dragons in my bedroom as long as he was there with me.' Nate was smiling. The sadness had become muted over the years but it would always be there in the background.

The look Alice gave him made him wonder if she could hear more than what he was saying in his voice.

'What did your dad do?' she asked.

'He was a firefighter. A real-life hero.'

Yeah... Alice knew that this was breaking off a little bit of his heart. How astonishingly perceptive was this woman? And how sensitive. She wasn't about to pry into something he might not want to share. Except he did. There was something about Alice that made him feel, in some ways, almost as safe as he had with his dad.

'He died on the job,' Nate added quietly. 'A warehouse fire where the roof collapsed without warning.'

'How old were you?'

'Fourteen. Old enough to know I needed to step up and look after my mum. Young enough to be totally lost without my dad. It wasn't just that he made me feel so safe. The best feeling in the world was when he was proud of me. It...' He eyed Alice. 'This is going to sound daft but it made me feel like I could do anything as long as he was there to watch. Fly, even...'

Alice's smile was softer than he'd ever seen before. 'It's not daft,' she said. 'How lucky were you to have a dad like that?'

Nate nodded. It was time to change the subject before that lump in his throat got any bigger. He found a smile.

'It's why I've always wanted to be a dad myself,' he told her. 'To be able to make my own kids feel like that. I reckon that would have made my dad the proudest he'd ever been.'

'You need this book,' she said, taking the slightly tattered old version of the beloved story from his hands.

'It might be a while before you're going to be reading it aloud but it'll be good to have it handy.'

She added it to the box on the floor that was already full of the science fiction and mystery books that had also been favourites.

'I'm going to get another box,' she said. 'You need some chick lit on the shelves as well. Oh...and recipe books for the kitchen.'

They went to a coffee shop for morning tea after loading the boxes of books into Nate's car and then to a massive antique shop, with room after room of everything from total junk to priceless collectibles.

Alice found an old crystal vase. He found a huge yellow ceramic bowl that was hand-painted with the leaves, flowers and fruit of a strawberry patch.

'My grandma had one just like this,' he said in amazement.

'Good find.' Alice nodded. 'Everybody has a couple of precious things they've inherited in their houses.'

'And look at these...' Nate peered into a glass cabinet that was stuffed with Matchbox cars a few minutes later. 'I had some when I was a kid. Might still have a couple buried in a box in my parents' garage.'

'Buy some more,' Alice said. 'You can add yours later. They'd look perfect on the top of a bookshelf or the mantelpiece in the living room.' She was smiling at him. 'I can just see you playing with cars when you were a wee boy. Making roads in the dirt or the sandpit. You would have been so cute.'

Nate smiled back. He liked that Alice thought he might have been a cute kid. He liked that she was interested in his childhood. He was, he realised suddenly, very interested in hers.

'What did *you* play with?' he asked. 'Dolls?'

Alice made a face as she shook her head. 'I had a doll,' she said. 'A very realistic baby one. I gave it to the girl who lived down the street.'

'Wow...' Nate blinked as he remembered something that Alice had said that night at the Irish pub.

I thought the one thing that would make life perfect was not to have a family at all...

'You started early, didn't you?' he asked quietly. 'Not wanting kids?'

Alice nodded. She had turned away to look at a display of antique cast-iron pots and pans.

'My mother got pregnant when she was nineteen,' she said, glancing over her shoulder at Nate. 'And her boyfriend refused to be involved. So there she was, in her twenties, stuck at home with a baby, when all her old friends were out having fun, going to uni, starting jobs and finding relationships. By the time I was four or five, I knew that it was my fault that she was never going to find a husband. Never going to be happy. That was about the time I decided I never wanted to be a mother and I gave the doll away.' She shrugged. 'Don't you think these pots and pans would be fabulous hanging over the old coal range?'

She was changing the subject but that didn't stop Nate continuing to think about Alice as a small girl.

That she'd been made to feel unwanted was heartbreaking.

He picked up a pair of rather tarnished silver candlesticks that still had half-burned candles in them but turned his head towards Alice again.

'Did she find what she wanted? Did things get better for your mum?'

'She kept trying,' Alice said. 'But nothing lasted, even when I was old enough to not be in the way so much. She died when I was thirteen. She stepped off a footpath and got hit by a bus and...that was that. She was gone. I got sent off to live with my grandmother in a small town up north. Neither of us was that thrilled about it.'

Nate was staring at her. Had her mother's death been an accident? Had her grandmother also made her feel like she was in the way? He didn't feel like he could ask such personal questions, especially not in public, but he couldn't blame Alice for still believing that having a family wasn't the road to happiness. What else had she told him that night? That she'd found men who said they didn't want to have kids but they were just filling in time until they found the women who *did* want to have their babies?

It was probably just as well that Alice was looking at the candlesticks and didn't see the sympathy that had to be written all over his face.

'Good choice,' she said. 'Put it on the dining table and it'll look as though you and Donna make a habit of romantic dinners. Simone will notice that in the photos.'

Nate said very little as they walked back to the car with their purchases. It wasn't just that he'd found the glimpse into Alice's childhood sobering. Her comment about the candlesticks had made him realise he couldn't remember the last time he'd felt the magic of real romance.

Maybe he'd never find it again but he could live with that. At least he'd know he was safe.

That was when he felt a solid beat of something much

stronger than sympathy for Alice. He understood why she'd built walls around the very idea of having a family of her own. She was simply trying to keep herself safe. To protect her heart.

He got that.

The recent setbacks he'd encountered were far less than Alice had dealt with in her life, but it still felt like a real bond between them. That Alice chose that moment to create a physical bond by putting her hand on his arm to stop him walking felt like more than a coincidence.

They were in front of a modern homewares store.

'Look at that.' Alice was pointing at a framed picture of a row of old silver spoons overflowing with vibrant spices like saffron and paprika and pink peppercorns.

'You need that,' she declared. 'In the kitchen. It would look fabulous in that gap between the fridge and the door into the living room.'

Nate was staring at the picture but all he could think about was the feeling of Alice's hand on his arm.

'You could put a wine rack underneath it. I'll bet they sell wine racks in here, too. Come on…' Her hand slid down his arm and grabbed his hand to pull him towards the doors of the shop.

She let go as soon as she was happy that he was following her, and Nate tried to brush off the memory of the touch. The way he'd brushed off that odd moment in the nursery the other day—after he'd hugged her as an impetuous way of thanking her for helping him bring the fantasy of his child's bedroom to life.

The moment when he'd thought about kissing her? A tiny flick of time when kissing her was the one thing he really *wanted* to do?

The last thing Nate wanted was for this lifeline of a friendship to get ruined by the kind of sexual undercurrents that always made things turn awkward when only one person was having those thoughts. The eye contact had been broken so decisively that he'd known it had only been wishful thinking that he'd seen what looked like a reflection of his own, errant desire in *her* eyes.

He didn't need to try and read anything into being touched on the arm, either. Not when Alice was clearly intent on something else. She'd asked a shop assistant if they had wine racks available and, on the way, had picked up a big bunch of brightly coloured artificial flowers.

'For that crystal vase,' she said with satisfaction. 'We'd better stop after this so you've got time to put things where they belong before you have to get to work. Send me some photos later?'

A photo pinged into Alice's phone when she was sitting in her small apartment that evening looking at the mess she'd made after she got home, inspired to sort out some of the clutter stuffed into the cupboard under the stairs.

The first photo was simply the silver candlesticks on Nate's dining table on either side of the antique bowl which was unexpectedly filled with an array of fresh fruit. Bananas, red apples, oranges and kiwifruit. Beyond the colourful display, Alice could see the blurry twinkle of city lights through the window and it reminded her of sitting there with Nate eating burgers. After she'd agreed that it wouldn't be a bad thing to cover up what was going on in his personal life long enough to give the impression that, even though he was going to be a single father, he was going to have his life completely under control.

With the speed of light, that memory morphed into standing in the newly furnished nursery and the feeling of Nate's arms around her as he gave her a hug and seeing that look in his eyes, yet again, with a clarity that didn't show any signs of diminishing. If anything, it was sharper. She could feel the points of it digging into some deep places in her body and it felt very much like…

Lust. If she was honest with herself, the more she thought about that moment, the more enticing the thought of kissing Nathaniel Madden was becoming.

She actually shook her head to dislodge the thought, her thumbs busy responding to the message.

Looks great. Did you get the pots hung up?

No. I need to go to the hardware shop for some hooks.

That felt like the end of the conversation. Nate was probably busy with a constant flow of patients in the emergency department, so Alice opened the box she'd dragged out of the cupboard. It was full of half-finished craft projects like a jumper she'd started knitting last year, cross-stitch patterns and some very dried-up oil paints and brushes from even longer ago when a paint-by-numbers project seemed like a nice hobby for winding down after work. She was taking the paints and small canvas to the rubbish when her phone pinged again.

Alice enlarged the picture so she could see what Nate had done with all the sections of the built-in shelves in the living room beside the fireplace, smiling at the instant effect that books could have to make a room look lived in and friendly. The vase full of pretty artificial flowers was on one corner of the top shelf and, beside it, the collection of tiny cars and trucks were lined up. Her smile widened. She could imagine Nate arranging them.

She could almost see him as a small boy, playing with his own small cars. In a room by himself because he didn't have the siblings he'd wanted so much for company, and it squeezed her heart. Hard.

Good job, she messaged back. Love the cars and the flowers. I think you need some pot plants in the house, too. I can go and choose a couple, if you like.

Please. I wouldn't have a clue about pot plants.

I'm off on Friday. I'll go to the garden centre and drop them off on your doorstep.

Might be here myself, waiting for a call from Simone. Haven't got a ticket yet and they're not putting on any more flights.

What time is the scan?

First thing in the morning. But she didn't say what time she'd ring and I don't want to pester her.

Alice went back to the box and started sorting all the balls of wool that were getting tangled up. She was still thinking about Nate. She knew that the anatomy scan was a big deal. It was a milestone in any pregnancy and it was a long and possibly tense appointment if someone was worried about potential complications like a low-lying placenta for the mother or issues like congenital heart defects for the baby. Would being so far away make it harder for Nate to wait for the results? Maybe he'd be bursting to tell her all about it when she arrived with those pot plants, because she was the only one he could tell, wasn't she? The only one who knew his secret.

Alice was smiling again. She was about to throw the ball of wool she'd rewound back into the box but, instead, she stared at it thoughtfully. It was lovely and soft in a pale shade of yellow. Somewhere in this box, she was sure she had a book of patterns for baby clothes, like little hats and bootees. She kept the wool out and began searching for a pair of needles. Baby stuff was so quick to make and what better way to spend an evening by herself than by finding a good movie and knitting?

Really?

Good grief... Had her personal life shrunk enough that having the kind of evening an elderly woman might enjoy was appealing?

Alice found herself picking up her phone. Reading Nate's texts again.

If he couldn't get on a flight he'd be home on Friday morning when she dropped off those plants. Would he want some company if he was stressing about the phone call he'd be waiting for?

Would he want *her* company?

Would she *want* him to want her company?

Judging by the way her heart rate had picked up noticeably as she'd been scanning those messages and that any desire to start knitting had completely evaporated, the answer to that question was more than obvious.

Yes...

CHAPTER SIX

DESPITE BEING AT the airport ready to take advantage of any no-shows for the early flights to Dunedin that Friday morning, Nate was more than disappointed to find himself out of luck. Passing a hardware store on his way home from the airport gave him the distraction that he knew he was going to need. Getting stuck into the final touches his new home was begging for was as good a way as any to fill in a long morning, waiting for a call he was probably not going to get before lunchtime.

He put up hooks to hang the antique pots and pans in the alcove above the old coal range and put the copper kettle on a hotplate beneath them. Then he hung the picture of the spice spoons in exactly the spot Alice had thought it would work. Having positioned the elegant wrought iron wine rack beneath it, he stood back to admire the effect and found he was nodding in admiration. He'd have to tell her that she had a real gift for interior design the next time he saw her.

As if he'd somehow made it happen, the doorbell rang and he found Alice standing outside, with pot plants in her arms and a larger one at her feet. She must have been unloading her car while he had been standing there admiring the new additions to his kitchen. This was an even better distraction than the handyman tasks he'd been keeping busy with and he knew he had a stupidly wide smile on his face. He hadn't intended sharing what was going through his head but it came out anyway.

'I was just thinking about you,' he said. 'And here you are.'

'Were you?' Alice was smiling, too. 'And yes, here I am. Bearing plants. I thought you'd be in Dunedin by now, though.'

'No such luck. I missed out on getting a seat.' Nate dropped his gaze from where it seemed to have caught on her smile. 'That plant's more like a tree!'

'It is. It's a fig tree. I thought it would look great in that empty corner of the living room beside the bay window. Can you carry it? My hands are kind of full.'

'Of course.'

Alice put the plants down on the kitchen bench. 'The little pots of herbs are for the windowsill here and this fern can hang in a bathroom, perhaps.' She took off her coat and draped it over the back of a chair, along with her shoulder bag. 'There was a café in the garden centre so I got some sandwiches because I was really hungry.'

Nate was on his way into the living room with the largest pot. 'Is there any time when you're *not* really hungry?' he called over his shoulder.

Alice didn't respond. When Nate put the tree in its place and went back, he found her taking in the artwork and wine rack and the accessories for the coal range.

'This looks *amazing*,' she said. But her smile faded a little as she held his gaze. 'Has Simone called yet?'

'No.'

'She will. Probably by the time we've had some

lunch.' She produced paper bags with freshly made sandwiches in them. 'Ham and cheese or egg salad?'

'They both sound good. I forgot to eat breakfast. Coffee?'

'Yes, please.' Alice wandered to the door of the living room. 'That tree is just right there, isn't it?'

'It is. Hope I remember to water it.'

'I'll remind you.' She turned away so quickly it felt like she was avoiding eye contact. 'Or just make a habit of doing it when you do some weekly chore, like putting your bins out.'

Nate had his phone nearby as they sat and ate the sandwiches a short time later, but it remained silent and he barely tasted even the mustard in the ham and cheese. He got Alice to help him choose places to hang some other artwork he had but another hour ticked past with no contact. Alice had, of course, noticed how often he was looking at his phone.

'Text her,' she said, with a smile. 'If she's in Dunedin she won't have any problems with reception and hey... this is about *your* baby. She must know that you'll be hanging out to hear the results.'

Nate picked up his phone. He sent a message.

An hour later, he still hadn't had a response and the tension was getting unbearable.

'Don't feel you need to hang around,' he said apologetically. 'You've probably got a lot you want to get done on your day off and I'm not exactly great company.'

'I'm not going anywhere,' Alice said quietly. Again, it felt like she was avoiding direct eye contact, looking around the room as if hunting for a distraction. Her gaze landed on her shoulder bag. 'Hey... I've got something for you. I totally forgot.'

'You shouldn't be buying anything for me,' Nate told her. 'And I need to know what you spent on all those plants this morning so I can pay you back.'

'Didn't buy these.' Alice had fished something yellow out of her bag. 'I made them the other night when I was watching a movie.' She bit her lip as she opened her hand. 'Don't laugh at my knitting. It's just a pair of bootees.'

Nate blinked. For some reason, the fact that Alice had created a pair of baby shoes for *his* baby brought a huge lump to his throat. He opened his mouth to say something but a sound interrupted him. They both turned to look down the hallway at the front door. Then they looked at each other.

'It couldn't be,' Alice whispered. '*Could* it?'

Nate didn't say anything. If, for some reason, someone wanted to deliver news in person, it could only be bad.

He went to open the door, his heart sinking. It landed with a thump when he saw who it was.

'Hi, Nate.' His visitor knew she had given him more than merely a surprise. 'Can I come in?'

'*Simone*...' His voice cracked. 'Oh, my God...is something wrong?'

Alice had heard Nate's horrified greeting and she was frozen to the spot, the bootees still in her hand as Simone came into the kitchen, her long, auburn hair flowing loose over her shoulders and a huge smile on her face.

'Donna,' she exclaimed. 'I'm so happy to finally meet you properly.'

Alice opened her mouth to correct her but she could see Nate over Simone's shoulder and there was no mistaking the panic in his eyes as he pushed his fingers through his hair.

This was stunning. For some inexplicable reason, Simone thought she was Donna. What would happen if the truth came out now? When Nate was alone in his house with a woman who wasn't his wife? Just a 'friend'? What assumptions might Simone actually make about why his wife had left? And about how fit he was to be a father, single or otherwise? What if it turned out she hadn't helped Nate at all? That she had, in fact, been responsible for making his worst fears come true?

'It's—ah—good to meet you, Simone,' she managed before she was folded into a hug. She saw Nate mouth something that looked like 'thank you' before he was hidden from view.

She was still frozen. What on earth had she just done? She could feel the roundness of Simone's belly through the soft corduroy dungarees she was wearing.

'I'm so sorry not to have given you any warning,' Simone said. 'But this was such a spur-of-the-moment thing. I was about to ring you, Nate, but Olly had made a video of the whole scan because I felt bad that I had shared it with him instead of you but we knew it would be too big a file to try and send. And Olly had this *brilliant* idea as we started driving south—' Her words were tumbling out with excitement. 'We passed the turn-off to the airport and he said why didn't I just jump on a flight and come and surprise you and when we found there was a seat available and we could make it work, it felt like fate... I can't stay long—only an hour or so.

The only flight I could get back was later this afternoon and Olly's waiting at the airport in Dunedin to drive me home.' Simone paused to snatch a breath.

Alice was watching Nate. It looked like he was holding his breath.

'Nothing's wrong,' Simone said happily. 'She's perfect. Guys...' She looked from Nate to Alice and back again. 'Your little girl is absolutely perfect.'

Alice felt tears welling up in her eyes as she saw first a wash of relief and then the glow of joy on Nate's face.

'Aww...' Simone gave her another hug. When she straightened, she looked down at Alice's hands. 'Did *you* knit those adorable bootees?'

Alice nodded. She swiped at a tear before it could escape.

'I used to love knitting,' Simone said. 'Just listening to the click of my needles and dreaming about meeting my baby. I don't get much time for it these days, though.' She took a deep breath, stepping further back. 'I don't imagine you get much time, either, what with having to travel so much for your photo shoots.'

Alice swallowed. Hard. She turned her head to find that Nate was walking towards them. What should she do? How could anyone believe she could be making a career out of looking beautiful enough to model clothes? Nate was holding her gaze. She could almost feel the message he was trying to send.

Please...don't say anything. Can we pretend? It's only for an hour...

He stopped right beside her. Close enough for his arm to be pressing against hers. When he took the bootees from her hand, Alice could feel the touch of his skin against hers—an electrical current that was enough to shock her back into life.

She could do this. She had to—for Nate's sake.

'I'm sorry you've found us in such a mess,' she said. 'We've been busy sorting out the last of the house.' She pushed a stray strand of wavy hair back from her face.

'Don't apologise.' Simone flapped a hand. 'It's lovely to see you in real life. Not that I haven't loved the photographs and those glamourous magazine shots. And that wedding picture you sent me a while back. Oh... how romantic was that?'

'You didn't tell me you sent Simone a wedding photo.' Nate looked as if he might be gritting his teeth for a moment. 'That's almost ancient history.'

'I loved it,' Simone said. 'So romantic, that silhouette of you guys holding hands and watching the sun set.'

A back view photo? The glamour that could be created by makeup and hair artists for magazine shoots? Being in the house with the husband that Simone had already met? It could explain why the assumption that she was, indeed, Donna, had been made, especially when Simone had something more important on her mind.

'Come and see the scan.' Simone pulled a tablet out of her woven straw tote bag. 'Let's not waste any more of the precious minutes we've got. You sit here, Donna—' she pulled out a chair at the dining table '—and you sit here, Nate.' She dragged another chair so that they were side by side. She propped the tablet up on one of the silver candlesticks and tapped the play button.

Alice watched the paler blobs moving on the black background of the screen as the technician angled the transducer to sweep the uterus and find how the baby was lying. Suddenly, and very unexpectedly, a tiny hand was in the centre of the screen for a second. Alice heard the way Nate caught his breath and she could feel the magic of this from his point of view. They both had their hands resting on the table and it took only the smallest shift to let the side of her hand and her little finger to touch his—to let him know that she knew how important this was to him and that it was a privilege to be sharing it with him.

She hadn't expected Nate's hand to slide over hers and his fingers to curl so that they could hold her hand. His eyes were still fixed on the screen.

'That's the skull,' the technician said. 'There's the spine…and…here's the heart.'

They could see the flutter of movement inside the tiny heart and then they could hear the beat—a rapid swish of sound. Nate's fingers tightened on Alice's hand and she squeezed back when she saw the tears in his eyes as he turned his head just far enough to catch her gaze.

Oh-h…

It was a feeling like nothing Alice had ever experienced. A connection with another human that was deeper than she'd ever felt. And it felt like the most natural thing in the world to keep holding Nate's hand while the detailed examination of the baby began and views and measurements were taken of the brain and spine, the heart chambers and blood flow and each internal organ and limb were checked.

They sat in stunned silence for a moment as the scan ended.

'Aww…' Simone wiped away a tear. She leaned to put her own hand on top of where Nate's hand was still gripping Alice's. 'I knew it would be like this for you guys. I'm so glad I came...'

Nate cleared his throat but his voice still sounded hoarse. 'Thank you. I can't tell you how much it means.'

'I can feel it.' Simone pressed her hand to her chest as she got to her feet. 'My taxi's coming back in ten minutes,' she said. 'I can't miss that flight but I really want to see that gorgeous nursery before I go. *Oh*...' She pulled in a gasp of a breath.

'What?' Nate was on his feet now, the physical link between him and Alice finally broken. 'What's wrong?'

'Nothing.' Simone reached out to take his hand. 'Your daughter's woken up, that's all. Here...fecl...' She put his hand on her belly and then turned to Alice. 'You, too?' she invited. 'Come and feel her kicking.'

If Alice had thought the connection between herself and Nate had been something extraordinary as they watched his baby on the screen, it paled in comparison to his hand over hers and the baby actually moving beneath her palm and fingers.

The busyness of giving Simone a whirlwind tour of the house, and the nursery in particular, and then going with her to see her into the car meant that there was no time to process what had just happened, and Alice's head was spinning as they stood at the gate to wave her off. Simone was turning to wave at them out of the back window.

'She's still watching us,' Nate said as the car began to move. 'Do you think she really believed that you're Donna?'

'I think so,' Alice said. But then she looked up to catch his gaze. 'But we could make sure.'

She could see the flash of comprehension in his eyes. There was no time to second-guess anything, because they would be out of Simone's view in a matter of moments. Alice found herself stretching up onto her tiptoes. Nate was bending his head to meet her.

The last Simone would see of them was the kiss between an apparently happy couple—the parents-to-be of the baby she was carrying.

It had only needed to last a heartbeat or two but Alice could feel them both falling into this kiss, and it went on for long enough to feel like more than simply a performance for the benefit of someone else.

Unbelievably, for Alice, *this* was going to be the most memorable part of an extraordinary day.

CHAPTER SEVEN

'Aratika One... Aratika One...you're tasked to a single vehicle crash on Highway 60, south of Tākaka. Male driver, mid-thirties, trapped and unconscious. Police, fire and ambulance on scene...'

Alice and Nate had already begun moving away from the morning briefing as their pagers sounded, before the announcement came over the speaker system as backup communication. Their pilot, Andy, and the crew person Nick were ahead of them.

Alice pulled on her helmet as she crossed the helipad. Nate followed her into the cabin of the helicopter, closed and secured the side door, sat down and put his harness on.

'Crew ready?' Andy's voice was loud in their headphones.

'Crew ready,' Alice confirmed. She had her tablet on her lap. Further information would be arriving to update them as they headed to the scene and she was hoping the patient would have been extricated from the vehicle by the time they arrived. Right now she had the map on her screen that would follow their route across the channel that divided the north and south islands of New Zealand. The accident site was at the tip of the South Island and that made them the closest crew available.

Nate was also adjusting what information he was getting on his tablet but, weirdly, it felt like they both looked up at each other in exactly the same moment. A glance that was held long enough to be significant.

And how could it *not* be significant after what had happened only yesterday?

Oh, they'd made light of that kiss that had been only for show the moment it had ended. Alice had been the first to find some words, probably because she'd been embarrassed. What if Nate thought she was moving in—that she might be interested in taking the idea of pretending that she was his wife even further?

'Wow...who knew you were such a good actor? That almost felt real...'

'I could say the same about you. I completely believed you when we were in the nursery and you told Simone how overwhelming this all was because you'd never thought you'd have the joy of becoming a mother.'

'That was probably the most honest thing I said.'

'Of course it was.' Nate's smile had been apologetic. *'I'm sorry I forced you to be part of my deception. It was overwhelming, which was probably why I couldn't see a way out of it fast enough.'*

'It was me who agreed that it wasn't a problem to wait before you let Simone know you were planning on being a solo parent. It's okay, Nate. I wasn't going to drop you in it and...hey...' Alice had found her brightest smile. *'I'm not complaining. You're a good kisser. But...it's time I went home. See you at work tomorrow?'*

And that was that. They'd both dismissed the kiss, along with the unspoken connection of watching that scan together and feeling the baby move, as no more than doing what needed to be done to buy Nate a little more time to protect his future.

Something that would never have been real. And something that was never going to happen again.

But...oh, my...it was still there in that brush of eye contact, wasn't it? Alice could still feel an echo of that sensation of falling into something...huge... The attraction that had always been there but had never been allowed to see the light of day had well and truly had its cover ripped off. It was real. Not that it could come to anything. Alice had no desire to be a mother to any child. Or to be in a relationship where the emotional well-being of a child was any of her responsibility. Why would she, when she could still hear her grandmother's disappointed tone?

This apple didn't fall far from the tree, did it? You're just like your mother...

How could she have contradicted that? She hadn't even wanted to take responsibility for a doll when it was what every other little girl wanted to do.

And Nate? Well, he had far bigger things in his life to deal with than the fact that he was single. He probably didn't even feel the need for a sex life right now and, judging by the way he was focussed on the screen of his tablet again, he hadn't allowed any hidden depths in that shared glance to distract him in the slightest from the work ahead of them.

She needed to follow his example.

Could Alice tell?

That he'd been thinking about that kiss every time he looked at her? That he'd been thinking about it even more, last night, when she wasn't even there?

He had been trying to figure out what had made it so…intense and he'd finally decided that it was because Alice had demonstrated—yet again—that she was in his corner by insisting on staying with him when she knew he was getting anxious about the results of that scan. Knowing that she cared that much about how he was feeling had opened up a space in his heart that he'd thought he'd slammed shut recently—a space that was only available to the people he could really trust.

She'd stepped up even more by letting Simone believe that she was Donna. That his marriage was still intact and his baby was going to have an entire family.

But maybe most significantly, Alice had been there when he'd seen his unborn baby for the first time. They'd been linked by skin-to-skin contact as the enormity of seeing his daughter's face and those tiny fingers and hearing her heart beat had brought tears to his eyes and again when her hand had been beneath his to feel the miracle of the baby moving in Simone's belly.

No wonder the emotional connection had been off the charts well before they'd staged that kiss. Adding an intimate touch of lips on lips into the mix had been like lighting a fuse. A long and very unexpected fuse that was leading to a bomb that represented…

Sex, that's what that bomb was.

The closest physical—and emotional—connection any two humans could have.

He shouldn't even be thinking about it but it was impossible not to. Because that kiss had given him the distinct impression that Alice was also aware of that fuse. Letting it reach the bomb would be a disaster. A dead-end road to ruining what was shaping up to be the best

'They've only just stabilised the vehicle with chocks and a winch. Be lucky if they've got him out before we get there.'

'At least we've got a place to land.' Andy joined the conversation. 'There's a passing lane that widens the road after that corner and a picnic area that leads down to that creek.'

There was no chance of Nate being distracted by anything that wasn't purely professional by the time they landed a few hundred metres from the accident scene and made their way along the road that was now closed to general traffic in both directions and clogged with emergency service vehicles, including an ambulance and first response unit, fire trucks and several police cars. Personnel who weren't down the bank were standing at the top, watching what was going on.

For the next thirty minutes, that was all Nate and Alice could do as well because there was no room for any extra medics in or around the vehicle. The roof had been cut and folded back and the driver, in a rigid extrication jacket and hard collar, was being strapped to a backboard, with further neck immobilisation from soft blocks, secured by bandaging, on either side of his head. It took six people, mostly fire officers who were the experts in extrication, to lift the backboard and carefully inch the victim clear of the car's interior and the sharp edges of the twisted metal. Still on the backboard, he was lowered into a Stokes rescue basket and secured, padded and covered with blankets for warmth. Lines were attached to winch the basket up the steep bank and, finally, Nate and Alice were able to meet their patient and do their own assessments as they took over his care for transport.

It was Alice who crouched beside the rescue basket.

'Hi… I'm Alice. I'm a paramedic. And that's Nate there, who's a doctor. You're Ben, aren't you?'

'Yeah.'

'How are you feeling?'

'C-cold…'

'Anything hurting?'

'Just my neck. I… I can't feel anything else…' There was a note of terror in Ben's voice. 'I'm never going to be able to walk again, am I?'

Alice took hold of Ben's hand. Could he feel that? Nate knew what it felt like. How reassuring it could be.

'I know how scary this is,' she said. 'You've got an injury to your neck but we can't know how serious it is yet. What we're going to do is take the very best care of you and keep you safe until we get to the specialists.'

Nate moved so that he was right beside Alice. Crouched down close enough to touch Ben's shoulder. Alice was still holding his hand. 'You're breathing on your own,' he said. 'Your heart rate's good and we're happy with your blood pressure. You've had a nasty crash but you're doing really well. Try and focus on that and let us take care of you.'

He glanced sideways to find Alice's gaze on him. There was a softness to her mouth and eyes that suggested she approved of the reassurance he was offering.

Ben tried to nod his head but Nate put his hand on his forehead. 'Try and keep your head completely still,' he said. 'How's that pain in your neck?'

'Bad.'

'On a scale of zero to ten, with zero being no pain and ten being the worst you can imagine, what score would you give it?'

'Nine.'

'Okay. We're going to give you something for that and then we're going to shift you onto our stretcher for the helicopter. We've got a special mattress on it that we can take the air out of and it moulds around your body to keep you still and protect your neck.'

Alice had moved as he was speaking and, when Nate looked up again, she was unzipping the IV pack, ready to hand him everything he needed to establish a line and give Ben some pain relief and fluids.

'Thanks, Alice.' His smile was as subtle as hers had been only seconds ago but he was grateful for more than her anticipating what was needed next. This was exactly how it needed to be during working hours in a valued partnership where skills and knowledge were shared to the benefit of all.

No undercurrents.

No fizzing fuses.

Professional.

By the time they'd got back to base after delivering Ben to the nearest major trauma centre that could take care of an acute spinal injury and provide the intensive care and possibly surgery that Ben would require, it was halfway through their morning.

'It's Saturday,' Andy said happily as he began the helicopter's shutdown. 'Do you think Shirley's made cheese scones?'

'What's her story?' Nate asked as he walked into the hangar with Alice. 'How did she get so involved with the rescue base? I've never asked her.'

'She's a legend,' Alice told him. 'As much a part of

the place as any crew members. You should ask her one day. She loves telling the story of her son who went tramping about twenty years ago and fell down a cliff. He would have died if he hadn't been winched out in the nick of time. She brought a cake in to thank the crew and it just grew from there. Cakes, scones, cookies. Getting involved with any fundraising that was going on.'

'She seems to practically live here,' Nate said. 'Not that I'm complaining. Closest thing I've had to a mum around for a very long time.'

'It's the people connection that she needed, too, I think. Her son moved away. To the States. But it was after her husband died that Shirley started coming in a lot more. We're her family. She must be well into her seventies now but, man, she can cope with anything—even a Sunday roast dinner for about fifteen people.' She grinned at Nate. 'I want to be Shirley when I grow up.'

The sound of Nate's laughter as he reached to pull the door open made Alice's heart thump as it made up for a missed beat. Or was it that she'd caught his gaze and the eye contact felt like a physical touch. She had to look away. Otherwise she was going to start thinking about that kiss. Again.

What made them both look away was the sound of their pagers going off. Nate was holding the door open with his shoulder as they read the message but then he stepped away and let it close again. They shared another glance that was an acknowledgement they weren't going to get a coffee and one of Shirley's cheese scones anytime soon, and they both turned to walk back to the helicopter.

'No rest for the wicked today,' Alice said brightly. 'We

love Saturdays when everyone's out doing their sports and recreation.'

They barely got time for a late lunch. It was one job after another. A bad fall on the cross-country course at an equestrian event left a teenage girl with a head injury and rib fractures. A man suffered a heart attack climbing a steep hill track and was more than an hour's drive away from a hospital so needed urgent transport. A woman with a low-lying placenta had gone into early labour and was bleeding heavily and, just when their shift was due to finish, they were tasked to a car crash but stood down when an ambulance crew arrived on scene and found there were no serious injuries.

It was even later by the time they'd cleaned up and restocked but people were still busy getting sick and injured. As Alice was peeling off her overalls and boots in the locker room and putting her street shoes on, she heard the clatter of the night shift crew heading out of the hangar. The whine of a helicopter's engine warming up outside distracted her slightly as she pulled the locker room door open and maybe that explained why she walked straight into Nate, who was coming on his way in.

'Oh...' The warmth of him hit her like a solid wave, followed instantly by a memory of how it felt to be even closer to this man. 'Sorry,' she added, hastily. 'I wasn't thinking.'

Alice had taken a step back. Nate was still in the doorway. They'd both stopped moving. Alice could hear the rotors gathering speed now and feel the steady thump of displaced air reverberating through the huge hangar. It felt like a heartbeat.

Or perhaps she was feeling her own heartbeat. Because she'd lifted her gaze to Nate's. After a long moment, his gaze dropped to her lips. And then it lifted again and Alice knew.

He was thinking about the kiss.

The noise outside was loud enough to drown the gasp of Alice's indrawn breath. Maybe she imagined the low growl that came from Nate as he stepped closer and pushed the locker door closed behind him without breaking that eye contact. Alice lifted her face, her lips parting and Nate bent his head and still their gazes were locked. Until they were too close to be able to see each other but it didn't matter because that wasn't what either of them wanted.

They wanted to *feel* the touch of each other's lips. To go back to the taste of something extraordinary that they'd been left with yesterday. To find out if there really was something that could justify a magnetic pull that was this powerful.

There was nothing staged about this kiss. Alice was letting herself fall, further and further into this pool of sensation. The softness of Nate's lips, the glide of his tongue. She could feel his hands holding her face and then moving over her body but it still felt utterly safe— as if he was catching her as she fell.

The helicopter was long gone when they both pulled back to try and catch a breath.

Alice definitely heard a groan from Nate this time. His voice was low. Roughened by what sounded like desire.

'Is it my turn to apologise?'

'No...'

Dear Lord...how had they managed to pretend there was nothing significant about that kiss yesterday? The tension in the air between them at the moment was so thick it was hard to breathe.

'Good,' Nate growled. 'Because I want to kiss you again.'

Alice couldn't say anything. She couldn't find the words that would encompass how much she wanted him to.

'But I don't want to ruin our friendship,' Nate said. 'You've been amazing, Alice, and...an absolute rock and I can't tell you how much I appreciate everything you've—'

'Nate?' Alice interrupted.

He blinked. 'What?'

Alice reached up and put her hands around his neck. 'Just shut up,' she told him. 'And kiss me again.'

There was pretty much zero danger of being disturbed. Administration staff and the other day crew members had left some time ago. The night crew of a paramedic, crewman and pilot were who knew where, flying towards an emergency that had the extra challenge of being a scene cloaked in darkness.

The operations manager on shift was nowhere near the hangar or locker rooms and they would be focussed on monitoring updates from the current mission, tracking where the helicopter was and fielding any other incoming calls.

Not that Nate was actually thinking that straight.

He wasn't thinking of anything other than *this*...

This astonishing response from this woman in his arms. The scent and taste of her. The taut muscles of her back as she pressed into him. The incredible softness of her breasts against his body. The tiny sounds she was making.

The *heat*...

Okay...a tiny alarm bell was sounding. They did need more privacy. Preferably their own scene that was cloaked in darkness. Somehow it didn't surprise him at all that Alice picked up on the thought the moment it occurred to him. Or had he picked up on hers? They broke the kiss to stare at each other. It was a moment that either of them could have used to slow things down. Back off completely, even.

But that eye contact only seemed to be ramping up the heat. Nate could almost imagine a flicker of flames like an aura around their bodies.

'An on-call room?' Alice suggested in a whisper. 'Upstairs?'

'Through the staff room?' Nate shook his head, albeit reluctantly.

The night-shift operations manager would be upstairs somewhere. They might both be off-duty and single, consenting adults but Nate didn't want this to become an item of gossip. Alice had made the assumption that he'd been having an affair when he'd told her that he was a father to a baby that wasn't Donna's. If anyone saw them together they might make even wilder assumptions— like that Alice had been a part of why his marriage had failed? Keeping this private was a way he could protect Alice and, no matter how powerful this physical attraction might be, he had every intention of protecting Alice.

Alice was shaking *her* head now, but it wasn't for a negative reason.

'The fire escape.' Her gaze went to the spiral staircase

in the corner of the hangar, which provided access to the platform built into the wall that was used for winch training purposes. Nate had never done any winch training, so he'd never had any reason to notice the door at the top that must lead into a corridor that led to the staffroom and offices. A space that divided the bedrooms on either side that were provided for any base crews on call overnight.

An almost secret passage.

As exciting as the thought of taking this connection with Alice to the next level. Did she want that as much as he did? But was it still risking too much to give in to this overpowering pull right now?

'Come home with me,' he said softly.

'You want to wait *that* long?'

Nate could feel his smile beginning to curl as any doubts evaporated. Yeah…she *did* want this just as much as he did. He didn't have to say anything aloud. She took one look at that smile and grabbed his hand. Seconds later they were at the top of the staircase, opening the first door they came to and slipping inside without bothering to even try and find a light switch.

How perfect was this?

Sex, spiced with a level of physical attraction like none Alice had ever experienced. A totally gorgeous man who clearly knew what he was doing. The way he could kiss— as if he was savouring the most delicious treat imaginable and he wanted to make it last as long as possible.

The way he was touching her! Sliding his hands inside her clothing, removing that clothing with far more skill than she was demonstrating as she fumbled with the stud on his jeans and then…oh, *my*…his fingers on her bare skin—gently tracing the shape of her body as if he needed to be sure that his touch was welcome and then, when Alice had been ready to beg for more, holding her with a strength that made it impossible not to surrender completely and simply melt into his arms.

It was a rollercoaster of sensation like nothing she'd ever known. Nate had a talent for finding a way of eliciting a stifled groan of delight and then teasing her, making her wait a beat and then, somehow, taking it to a whole new level. The release, when it came, was another revelation of just how good sex could be.

It wasn't until she was trying to catch her breath, some time later, that Alice realised what might be adding so much to this pleasure.

There was no hidden agenda. Neither of them was taking tentative steps towards a possible relationship. They liked each other. They fancied each other and… they trusted each other enough to make this safe.

Safe and so astonishingly *good*…

Alice could feel the rapid pulse of Nate's heartbeat finally beginning to slow as she lay pressed against his body in this narrow, single bed. Had he found it as good as she had? Would he want to do it again? As much as she did?

When she looked up, he had that smile on his face again. That drop-dead sexy smirk that he'd had in that moment before they'd made a dash for the fire-escape staircase.

'My place next time?' he murmured. 'I've got a much nicer bed.'

CHAPTER EIGHT

IT *WAS* HIS place the next time.

Hers, the time after that.

It should have been enough to have taken the edge off any curiosity about each other and blunted what they had both acknowledged was a friendship with a surprisingly strong streak of lust involved but, in fact, it seemed to be having the opposite effect. The more they discovered, the better they got to know each other, the more irresistible the sex became.

One week slipped into another with no signs of the attraction being sated. It felt more like a growing addiction.

It could never last, of course. They both knew that. There was a ticking clock in the background. Nate was going to become a single father and his life would never be this relaxed out of work hours. He'd probably be too tired for any desire for sex to be registered, let alone acted upon and perhaps that became an unspoken excuse to be together—to make the most of it before it evaporated. This bubble of time had an expiry date.

It wasn't only the pleasure of the sex that was filling the bubble. What came alongside the physical intimacy—the deepening of their friendship and the trust between them—was something that felt like it could last a lifetime.

Something precious.

As that level of trust grew, the words they could share were sometimes an echo of the closeness they had discovered with physical touch. Part of the safety net of knowing they weren't in a 'real' relationship meant that Nate could talk to her about the crushing disintegration of his marriage and she loved that she could, completely sincerely, offer reassurance that he couldn't blame himself.

Like tonight, when they were sitting in the dark, watching the lights of the city from the windows in Nate's house, sharing a bottle of wine and having an animated conversation about the interesting cases they'd been involved with that day.

Nate stopped with a shake of his head. 'No wonder Donna got so sick of my talking shop. I'm married to my job as much as I was ever married to her.'

'You're a passionate person—that's why you're so good at what you do. I'd be willing to bet that was what attracted her to you in the first place. You're determined to be the best you can be and you're already good enough to be better than anyone else I've ever worked with and that's not just because you're so smart. It's because you're…' Alice smiled at him. 'You're a nice guy, Nate. You're compassionate. You have a lot of love to give and—' her smile widened '—you're going to be an amazing dad.'

Nate made a face. 'I had every intention of being an amazing husband, too. Where did I go wrong? Was it because I wasn't prepared to let go of the dream of having a family?'

Alice stared out at the lights for a long moment. She could see an emergency vehicle, probably a police car, racing along the main road leading away from the city.

'If you're with someone who doesn't want the same things from life as you do, it's inevitable that you'll drift apart. It's nobody's fault. And if they're really big things like whether or not you want kids, it's never going to work. Nobody can live their best life if they're unhappy.'

'But why did she agree to the surrogacy? I really thought that was going to give us a second chance.'

'I'm sure she did, too. Maybe she felt guilty about the affair and that it was *her* fault your marriage was in trouble and this was her way of trying to fix it. She cared enough about you to try but, as you said, when it became a reality, that was when she had to admit the truth—that it wasn't what she wanted.'

'It was a bit late by then, though, wasn't it?'

Alice took in a deep breath. 'You're both getting a second chance to be the people you want to be,' she pointed out quietly. 'She's chasing the career she wants so much. And you're going to be a dad.'

'I am, aren't I?'

Nate's smile began slowly but Alice could see he was now looking forwards, not backwards. She got the impression that he was feeling a lot happier than he had moments ago.

She brushed off a feeling of pride that she'd had something to do with making him feel good. It was just what friends did, wasn't it?

Nate shared the regular updates Simone sent him, like a text message with a laughing face emoji that said his daughter was kicking her so hard now she was beginning to wonder if she was destined to join the New Zealand Black Ferns who were the country's international women's rugby team.

It was definitely a step too far for Alice to send messages to Simone herself, pretending that they were coming from Donna but she helped write messages that they knew would be taken as coming from both parents-to-be.

Like the one that was about the child-sized table and chairs they'd found in a junk shop and taken home to paint in bright, primary colours. The table was blue and the little wooden chairs were red and yellow and green. Alice had taken a picture of Nate with smears of paint on his hands and a proud smile on his face. Alice had found an equally bright, plastic tea set online and they'd set them out on the little blue table when the paint was dry. A small teapot, milk jug, and cups and saucers, along with a few cupcakes that were pink and white and as sparkly as any princess could desire.

Just practising, Nate had captioned the photos. Next time we might even bake the cupcakes ourselves.

Simone sent a picture of her bump the following week and, when she was transitioning into her third trimester not long after that, she emailed all the blood test and other results from her midwifery check.

It's all going so well, she wrote. And I know you'll both be as happy as we are. Carrying your baby feels like the best decision I ever made.

Alice was happier than she'd ever been but it wasn't only because of how smoothly the surrogate pregnancy was going. Or that she was enjoying the best sex life she'd ever discovered and building a lifelong friendship.

Life in general just seemed to be particularly enjoyable at the moment. Work was more satisfying than ever, especially on the days she was crewed with Nate. They'd always had the connection that allowed them to work seamlessly together, not only making the most of each other's skills and knowledge but allowing them to improve as well.

Like the time he coached her through a particularly difficult intubation on a patient with major facial trauma when she thought a surgical airway might be the only option.

Measure the distance between incisors. Three fingers is enough room for the laryngoscope.

I'll keep the field as clear as I can with suction for you. Use the bougie even if you can only see the epiglottis. Feel for the clicks of the tracheal rings.

The satisfaction of securing that airway had been something that Alice would use as encouragement to tackle a difficult challenge for the rest of her career.

The pride from Nate's nod and the quiet praise of 'good job' had taken a small moment in her life and transformed it into something she would remember for the rest of her life.

She might only have an evening with Nate once or twice a week but it was enough. Keeping their alliance discreet added an extra level to the pleasure of working together and the infrequency of their private time together increased the level of anticipation for it to be a noticeable factor in how alive she was feeling these days.

Life had never been quite this good before.

Nate looked happier than he had in a long time, too, and Alice wasn't the only person to notice, but then Shirley had a sharp eye when it came to what was going on with the people she loved to care about on the Aratika Rescue Base.

'It's good to see you with a bit more spring in your step, lad,' she told him, putting a plate with one of everyone's favourite breakfast bacon rolls on it. She leaned down and spoke more quietly but Alice was sitting close enough to overhear what she said. 'You've had a tough time of it, lately, haven't you?' She patted his arm. 'You deserve better and that's all I have to say about it.'

Alice and Nate shared a glance. It was highly unlikely that Shirley wouldn't have more to say about it in the not-too-distant future but nobody minded her treading on personal ground. She was a real mother-figure on the base and well-loved.

They didn't get to finish their breakfast that morning, however. The strident sound of pagers going off had the crew moving fast towards the operations room where Don held up his hand to signal that he wasn't finished with the phone call he was taking. He was watching information being added to the computer screen in front of him at the same time. Alice and Nate were scrolling their tablets, getting the same updates. Andy was already checking weather reports on his device.

'Where's Nick?' Alice asked.

'He's called in sick. Sounds like food poisoning and there's no replacement available as yet.'

'Right…' Don's tone was crisp. 'As you can see, we've got a twenty-four-year-old woman who's thirty-six weeks pregnant. Has a low-lying posterior placenta and was down for an elective C-section at thirty-eight weeks.

She's bleeding.' Don paused for a beat. 'She's on the Cape Palliser Coast. In Ngawi.'

Alice's head jerked up. 'Wow...that's about as isolated as you can get around here.'

Ngawi was a tiny fishing village on the south-eastern base of the North Island, sandwiched between rugged hills and the sea. It had a small population of permanent residents rather than holidaymakers and it was famous for the tractors lined up on the shingle beach to haul fishing boats ashore.

Don nodded. 'Nearest GP or first responders are more than an hour away. You'll get to them in half the time they would need to take off in a car to meet an ambulance en route.'

'She's getting intermittent contractions,' Nate noted. 'But there's no indication of any trauma?'

'She's got UTI symptoms.' Alice was scrolling her tablet again. 'That can precipitate labour.'

Don was looking at Andy now. 'Cloud ceiling's currently just over eight hundred feet at Ngawi, with wind gusts up to thirty-five knots. Marginal VFR given the hilly terrain.'

Both Alice and Nate looked up this time. They knew that if they couldn't fly with the visual flight rules they needed for a safe distance from the ground, Andy could refuse to accept the mission.

'I wouldn't want the ceiling to get any lower,' he said. 'But we'll give it a go. From what I can see here, there looks like a good landing area beside the community hall or in the camping grounds over the road. Is there a local cop who can make sure it's currently clear and keep bystanders away?'

'No local police. They're as far away as the nearest medical help in Martinborough. I'll get Comms onto it. They can contact the manager of the camping grounds or maybe the person who's in charge of the rural fire station.'

The briefing had taken less than two minutes and the process of getting from the operations room to the helipad wasn't going to take much longer than that, even when they were collecting their gear and the extra supplies they might need. Like blood products.

Especially blood products.

'If she is in labour she's also at high risk of a post-partum haemorrhage.' The glance Nate gave Alice had an edge she'd never seen before but she recognised it instantly.

This felt personal to him. Running into trouble in late pregnancy, somewhere where advanced medical care was a long way away, could be catastrophic.

Simone lived in an isolated area.

'Crew ready?' Andy had the helicopter ready for lift-off by the time Nate and Alice were clipping into their harnesses.

'Ready.'

'We recommend that you keep those safety belts fastened at all times while seated, in case of unexpected turbulence.'

Alice's huff of laughter was audible. She knew that Andy loved a bit of rough weather and those wind gusts over hills and around coastal cliffs were more than likely to deliver some buffeting and downdrafts. Was that why Nate wasn't sharing the amusement of Andy's tongue-in-cheek instruction? Or was he worried that they were heading to a potentially serious case minus a crew member—to a case that might be very close to his own heart?

Andy wasn't joking now. He was on a different channel. 'Aratika One to Wellington Tower. We're ready for departure to Ngawi. Requesting clearance.'

'Cleared for take-off, Aratika One. Track east of harbour, not above fifteen hundred feet.'

Alice caught Nate's glance and offered a reassuring smile.

I've got your back, she tried to convey. *We've got this*.

It was one of the bumpiest rides Nate had experienced in his time working as a HEMS doctor but that kind of suited his mood.

This could be a high-stakes scenario for both a mother and a baby and, okay, he was possibly more invested on a personal level than he should be but that was inevitable, wasn't it? Just like it would be for any medic going to a situation that had important links to their private lives, especially when it involved the most vulnerable patients. He might have to live with this for the rest of his life, dealing with babies coming into the emergency department and then toddlers and children. Teenagers, even. He suspected this was part and parcel of becoming a parent, and now was as good a time as any to start learning how to deal with it and push any emotional reaction into a space that would have no effect on his professional decisions or skills.

It turned out that it wasn't an issue at all as soon as he walked into the room where Nicole, the young mother, was sitting on the floor of her living area—a large bloodstain visible on the dress she was wearing. Her eyes were closed and her skin very pale.

Nate crouched beside her and took hold of her wrist to take her pulse. 'Hi, Nicole. My name's Nate,' he told her. 'I'm a doctor. I've got Alice with me and we're both here to take care of you and get you to hospital, okay?'

Nicole made a strangled sound, gave up trying to speak and nodded instead. Her face was scrunched into lines of pain.

'Are you having a contraction at the moment?'

Another nod.

Alice was reaching for Nicole's other hand. 'Squeeze my hand,' she said. 'Try and breathe through it.'

Nicole's husband, Gareth, had met them at the door moments ago and relayed the information that the contractions seemed to be getting stronger and more frequent. Nate glanced at his watch so they would know how close together the contractions were. A vaginal examination was contraindicated with any antepartum bleeding because touching the cervix could break blood vessels and turn a small bleed into something far more dangerous.

'Can we get a BP and O2 sats, please, Alice? And some nasal prongs for oxygen. Throw me the IV roll, too, would you?'

'No worries.'

Nicole was opening her eyes as the contraction faded and Alice was already turning to open pouches on the defibrillator case. She pulled out the blood pressure cuff to wrap around Nicole's arm. As the cuff inflated, she unfurled the tubing of nasal prongs and fitted them into nostrils and around ears.

'You're doing really well,' she said, with a smile.

Nate was keeping his voice deliberately calm but his mind was racing. He needed to establish a wide-bore intravenous access. Preferably two. He wanted fluids running and some tranexamic acid administered.

'I'm going to pop a needle into your arm, Nicole,' he told their patient. 'We're going to need to give you some fluids and medication. Is that okay?'

'Y-yes...'

'Have you been feeling unwell in the last few days?'

'Just since I got up. It hurt to pee.'

Nate had swabbed the skin over a large vein in her arm. 'Sharp scratch,' he warned. He slid the tip of needle in and then gently pushed the cannula into place. 'All done.'

Alice was setting up the bag of IV fluids. They had carried in the polystyrene container that kept blood products cool along with all the other gear. Just in case.

'She kept having to go back to the loo every few minutes.' Gareth was hovering near his wife, looking very anxious. 'And that was when she found she was bleeding.'

'BP one-ten over sixty,' Alice relayed. 'Oxygen saturation 97 percent.'

So far so good, Nate thought. He caught Alice's glance. 'Let's get Nicole into a left lateral position until we're ready to load and go.' The less time they spent on scene here, the happier he would be. He reached for the drug kit to extract the medication that could reduce the bleeding. 'An estimate for the blood loss would be helpful.'

He was drawing up the TXA as Alice helped Nicole to lie down and put a cushion beneath her head.

'I'm going to find a fresh pad for you,' she said. 'This one's getting pretty soaked.'

That told Nate that the blood loss could be significant already. Another glance at his watch told him that it had been over two minutes since the last contraction and he blew out a tiny breath that could have been relief. It would be better for everyone if this baby stayed where it was until they were a lot closer to all the equipment and expertise a major obstetrics department could provide.

His relief had been premature.

The slightly surprised sound that came from Alice made his skin prickle. She'd seen something unexpected and was deliberately trying to sound calm, as he had been earlier.

'Um... Nate?'

'Yep?'

He pushed the last drops of the medication out of the syringe into the cannula port and then shifted far enough to see what Alice was looking at.

A dark shape, with whorls of wet hair, that was unmistakably a baby's head crowning.

They weren't going anywhere just yet.

'Nicole?'

'What is it? Is something wrong?'

'Not wrong, but your baby is very close to being born—maybe with the next contraction.'

'*No!*' Nicole sounded horrified. 'That can't happen. I'm supposed to have a Caesarean.' She burst into tears.

Gareth was staring at them, shocked.

'Come and help Nicole,' Alice told him. 'Sit behind her and she can lean against you and hold your hand.'

Nicole was gasping between her sobs. And then the sound became a cry of pain.

'I have to *push*,' she cried, seconds later.

Nate knelt beside Alice. He cupped his hand over the baby's head, providing a gentle pressure to stop it emerging too rapidly. He felt the cord around the neck but it was loose enough to slip over the head.

'One more push, Nicole,' he said. He guided the head down and then up, to deliver the shoulders and the baby came out with a rush of blood that made Nate's heart sink. Alice had a clean towel in her hands and she met his gaze for a heartbeat as he put the baby onto it. This was the worst-case scenario. A postpartum haemorrhage to deal with so far away from hospital and...a very flat-looking baby.

Alice put the baby boy onto Nicole's chest but she was using the towel to rub the skin on his back and chest briskly, trying to stimulate the newborn.

'Why isn't he crying?' Nicole lifted her head and then dropped it back against her husband. 'Oh... *God*...something's wrong, isn't it?'

'Why is he so *blue*?' Gareth sounded just as horrified.

'It can take a minute or two.' It was only because Nate knew Alice so well that he could hear the note of fear in her voice. He saw her flick the baby's feet and then start rubbing again. 'It's a big transition, coming into the world, especially if it happens a bit fast. His heart rate is good, his breathing just needs to catch up.'

He wasn't only blue. From the corner of his eye, Nate could see Alice shifting the position of the head to make sure the airway was open and he could tell that the baby was completely limp, his eyes shut. He had to leave the initial resuscitative attempt to Alice, however. Nicole's welfare was his priority and he needed to deal with the heavy, ongoing bleeding. There were drugs, including oxytocin and more TXA that needed to be administered, IV fluids and blood products to be infused. Nate wanted an update of all vital signs and the uterus would need to be massaged—compressed, even, if the bleeding continued to be severe and Nicole's condition was deteriorating. It might well be a tense trip back to the city. As soon as he had a few free seconds he would radio Andy and get him to have the chopper ready for take-off and to heat the cabin as much as possible. It couldn't have been a worse call-out to be short of an extra pair of hands to deal with this.

They were not out of the woods yet, that was for sure.

Alice had never been this afraid.

Her efforts to stimulate this baby seemed to be failing.

It was the bluest, floppiest baby she had ever held in her hands and...it was terrifying.

How devastating would it be to lose this infant? She could see the shock and fear in the faces of both these young parents, and she hoped she wasn't showing how concerned she was herself. And what about Nate? He was already invested in this case on a personal level. She *had* to succeed. She was trying to think ahead to what she needed to do as the next priorities. She needed to know the heart rate, and the oxygen level. Provide ventilation. Clamp and cut the cord? Start CPR?

She rubbed harder with the towel.

'Come on, sweetheart,' she said aloud. 'Take a nice, big breath for me...'

A sideways glance showed her that Nate was flat out drawing up drugs, adjusting the IV. As much as she desperately wanted him to come and help her, she knew she was on her own for the moment. The mother's life took priority. As if he'd felt her glance, Nate looked up. The eye contact was so brief it barely happened but it was enough.

Alice wasn't really on her own, was she?

They were doing this together. And they were a team that had proved their strength time and time again.

And, just as she had that comforting thought, she felt the baby move beneath her hands. Saw the tiny mouth open and heard the first air being dragged into the baby's lungs.

'That's the way.' Her whisper was fervent. 'Come on, baby.'

The first warbling sound from the infant made Nate's gaze swerve up from where he was injecting medication into the IV line. It shifted from the baby's still-blue face to Nicole, who had buried her face against Gareth's shoulder as they shared their relief at hearing their baby begin to cry and then, finally, it caught Alice's gaze and the message she received was so clear, it might as well have been said aloud.

Good job... I knew you could do it...

Another breath and a stronger cry and the dreadful shade of the baby's skin began to change. Pink was fighting the blue and, best of all, the eyes were open. The baby was looking right at Alice. She wanted to put the infant skin-to-skin with his mother as soon as possible, to help keep him warm and to reassure Nicole because her distress could only make her own condition worse but, instead, she held the baby close to her own chest.

She had to make sure it was safe to put the baby down and she needed to know that the heart rate was at least a hundred beats per minute.

She cuddled the baby, still wrapped in the towel, her fingers around a tiny arm to feel for the brachial pulse. The baby stopped crying and hiccupped instead, his gaze fixed on Alice's, his face a much healthier colour now.

'You're fine, aren't you, sweetheart?' she said. 'You were just a bit slow to get used to the world.'

The relief was almost overwhelming. She could tuck the baby against his mother's chest, clamp and cut the cord and cover them both to keep warm. Then she would be able to help Nate with whatever he was doing to control any ongoing bleeding. But, for a moment, Alice couldn't move. She couldn't let go of this baby just yet. She was so aware of his warmth and weight in her arms and the rapid beat of his heart against her fingertips. But, more than that, she was totally captured by the way he was looking at her with eyes that were too dark to be able to discern what their colour would be. He could *see* her and Alice was suddenly aware of a connection that was doing strange things to her. Creating a sensation that she'd never felt before.

A yearning that was so deep, it was profound. It felt like *this* was what life was all about.

For the first time in her life, Alice was feeling the desire to have her own baby and it was so unexpected and so strong, it caught her unawares and that made it terrifying.

She had to move and she did so with the confidence that she knew she had. That wash of emotion had been so fleeting nobody could have noticed she was doing anything more than assessing this baby.

'Heart rate's over a hundred,' she reported. 'Sat's are 82 percent and I'd put the five-minute Apgar at eight.'

'Fantastic.' Nate was smiling at Nicole as she gathered her baby into her arms but Alice could see the shadow in his eyes that reminded her of the personal undercurrents here.

She could also still feel the echo of that astonishing wave of her own emotion when she'd been holding this baby.

It felt like something was changing.

Something that Alice didn't *want* to change, because it felt as if the whole foundation of her life was in danger of crumbling.

CHAPTER NINE

It stayed with Nate for the rest of what felt like a very long day.

A clear image in his head that came with a wave of something emotional enough for him to know he'd never forget it.

The surprising thing was that it had come from a totally unexpected direction.

It hadn't been the satisfaction, or maybe relief, that he and Alice had managed an out-of-hospital obstetric emergency well enough to have possibly saved two lives today. Nate had rung the hospital for an update just before they left the base to learn that both Nicole and baby Edward were now tucked up in a maternity ward, basking in the afterglow of creating a brand new family.

They'd been on scene longer than anticipated to get Nicole stable enough to transport and then they'd hung around until they got another call so that they could get an update on their patients. Nicole had needed to go to Theatre for the removal of the placenta and definitive control of her bleeding, and the baby boy, Edward, had been taken to NICU for a brief period of observation.

The generous platefuls of Shirley's much-loved Sunday roast that she had kept warm in the oven so that

Nate and Alice could have a late lunch when they finally got back to base had been very much appreciated. The delicious roast beef with all the trimmings, including Yorkshire puddings and made-from-scratch gravy, was definitely memorable but that wasn't what he was still thinking about.

No…

The image that had been slotted into a memory bank that was kept for really significant things was that of Alice holding baby Edward. That moment after the baby's first cry, when the horrible fear that they might not win the battle to resuscitate the shocked newborn began to fade rapidly, and Alice was holding the baby in her arms to check his pulse and calculate that first Apgar score.

The way she was cradling the baby in her arms. The way she was looking at that tiny, crumpled face. As if it was her own baby.

As if it was the one thing she'd been waiting for to make her life complete.

She might not know it herself, Nate had thought in that instant, but if she really thought a family was the last thing she wanted, she couldn't be more wrong.

Maybe that was why, when he took her home that evening, the first thing he did after pushing the front door closed behind them, was to take Alice in his arms and simply hold her close. It was Alice who broke what had become an overly long silence.

'I don't think I've ever been quite that scared on a job,' she confessed. 'There was a moment when I thought we might lose them both.'

'You and me both,' Nate murmured. 'But we didn't. How good is that?'

Alice pulled back far enough to see his face. 'I know it was hard on you,' she said quietly. 'I wasn't going to say anything in front of anyone but...you must have been thinking about Simone living so far from a hospital. And you'd know how terrified Nicole and Gareth must have been, knowing that their baby was in danger.'

'It did feel different,' Nate admitted. 'But I knew it was something I had to learn to deal with. I think it's there for every parent—that fear that something might happen that they can't protect their children from.'

Alice's gaze slid away from his. She was nodding but he could sense that she wasn't comfortable talking, or perhaps even thinking, about it. Because she'd been denied the ability to trust that she'd been wrapped in that kind of protection when she'd been a child? His breath caught in his chest again. To be allowed to think that it was her fault her mother was less than happy was worse than her not being loved as much as she'd deserved.

What he wanted more than anything for Alice was that she could find someone to offer that kind of protection to her now. He wished he could offer it himself but they didn't have that kind of relationship, did they? That kind of commitment to protection and safety were the bonds of family and Nate had not forgotten what Alice had said to him in the first truly personal conversation they'd ever had—that she'd grown up thinking that life would be so much better if you didn't have a family.

It was heartbreaking that she'd never been offered the kind of unconditional love that family could provide. How could she know that the risks that came from both giving and receiving that kind of love were so absolutely worth it?

He needed to steer the conversation back to the question Alice had asked.

'Any background thoughts of Simone or the baby were gone the moment we arrived,' he added. 'There's nothing like a medical emergency to push any personal considerations away, is there?'

He saw the tiniest flicker of something in Alice's eyes which suggested that she was remembering the very personal moment for herself but it was gone almost before he saw it properly. In its wake, he thought he could see a beat of confusion. Or sadness, even?

Whatever it was, it made him want to wrap Alice in something that was going to make her feel good again. He might not be able to tell her that she had as much of his protection—and his trust—that he could give her as a friend, but maybe his kiss could convey a hint of it. It was a soft kiss. Tender.

'It was a privilege to work with you today, Alice Barlow.' He pushed a stray wave of hair back from her face. 'You really are something special.'

He didn't give her time to respond, because he knew she would deny it. Instead, he kissed her again. With just as much feeling but a little more heat.

'You hungry?' he asked when he broke the contact.

'After one of Shirley's Sunday dinners?' Alice was smiling. 'Not likely. You?'

'Oh... I'm *so* hungry,' Nate said softly.

That was her line, they both knew that but he'd been unable to resist borrowing it. Alice's smile was fading. Judging by the way the pupils in her eyes dilated and her lips parted, she had a very good idea what he was about to add to that line.

'But not for food...'

Oh, my...

Alice had lost count of how many times she and Nate had been to bed together over the last weeks. She'd given up trying to define what it was that made it so good, and simply put it down to their chemistry being particularly well-matched and the level of attraction being off the charts—along with that extra dollop of knowing that it was something special that wasn't going to last, which seemed to have the effect of making her so much more aware of every aspect of it.

Oh, yeah...and knowing that it was safe because Nate wasn't pretending that there was any more to this than a 'friends with benefits' thing. He wasn't going to break her heart by dumping her in favour of someone who wanted to make babies with him. You couldn't dump someone that you weren't officially in any kind of relationship with anyway. And Nate already had the baby thing sorted. He was happy to be tackling the parent thing as a single dad. Even this afternoon, he'd been talking about the kind of woman he hoped to find as a live-in nanny.

A slightly younger version of Shirley would be perfect, don't you think?

If Alice had wanted to define what it was like to share intimacy with Nate, however, she would never have thought of using words that might describe what it was like *this* time. Because it had never been like this before.

So slow.

So tender, Alice could actually feel a lump forming in her throat as she tipped her head back to let Nate trail kisses down her neck, all the way to her breast. She had her fingers in his hair, cupping his head, but the only thing she was really aware of was the feeling of being... cherished.

Loved...

Weirdly, the level of heat from a powerful physical attraction was still there but it was being tempered with something that felt both incredibly soft but solid at the same time. Something real and dependable and still safe.

This was the difference between having sex and making love, wasn't it?

A tiny alarm bell rang somewhere in the back of her mind, but was it really something to worry about?

Alice couldn't begin to think about that right now. Not when Nate's hand was gliding over the curve of her hip and heading towards the part of her that was desperate for his touch.

Thinking could wait.

The only thing that mattered in this moment was a sea of sensation that she would be happy to swim in for however long it was going to last.

And she was just as content to lie in Nate's arms when they were both limp with the relaxation that could only come in the wake of unbelievably good sex. Alice could feel her eyes drifting shut but she couldn't go to sleep like this. Having sex with Nate was one thing. Waking up with him was crossing a boundary that would make this more than what it was.

It wouldn't hurt to stay here for a few more minutes,

though, would it? Just to have one of those lovely pillow-talk kind of chats? It didn't matter what they talked about, she just wanted to hear—and feel—the rumble of Nate's voice.

'I should have let Gareth cut the cord,' she said. 'Do you think he was disappointed?'

'We had rather a lot going on right then,' Nate responded. 'And I don't think he even noticed. He was too busy watching the miracle of their baby getting pinker with every breath he took. And so proud that they were giving him his father's name.'

'Have you thought of names for *your* baby?'

'Not really.' Nate sounded suddenly shy. 'It kind of felt too early. Like it might be tempting fate or something.'

Alice could hear what lay beneath his words. That desperate desire to be a father. To have a family of his own. She had the strongest urge to reassure him.

'It's not too soon,' she said. 'Simone's into the third trimester. Even if the baby did arrive early, she's going to have every chance of being absolutely fine.'

'I know. I just…worry a bit.'

'I know.' Alice turned her head just enough to let her lips touch his skin. An almost kiss that she hoped would tell Nate that she understood. That the fact that he cared enough about his baby to be worried was part of what was going to make him such a great dad. 'So…what's your mother's name?'

'Ruth. Bit old-fashioned now, isn't it?'

'It might be a lovely middle name. Any other family names you like?'

'I had an Aunt Winona. And my gran on my father's side was Daisy.'

'Oh...' Alice was smiling. 'I *love* Daisy.'

'You know what?'

'What?'

'I think I do, too.'

'Are you going to be at her birth?'

'I hope so,' Nate said. 'It will depend on how fast the labour is, of course. Who knows? Simone's had so much practice, she might end up having her at home before she gets anywhere near a hospital.'

Alice could feel his breath being released in a long sigh. 'I can't wait to hold her,' he said, very softly. 'I want to know that she's safely in the world and to let her know how much she's loved. That she's always going to be the most important person in the world to me.'

'You're going to be such a wonderful father,' Alice reminded him. 'Daisy is going to be a very lucky little girl.'

His arms tightened around her a little. 'Do you know anything about *your* father?' he asked.

'Not really. He went to the same school as my mum. They hooked up at some end-of-term party. When she told him she was pregnant, he said it wasn't a problem, it was easy enough to get abortions these days.' She swallowed hard. '*He* definitely didn't want me. I don't know why my mother didn't take his advice. Maybe she just left it too late...'

Nate was still holding her close. 'It's no wonder you grew up to spend your life caring for others,' he said. 'You knew too well what it was like to not be cared about, didn't you?'

'I guess.'

Her voice wobbled. Tucked into Nate's arm like this,

with the warmth of his skin under her cheek and not having to make direct eye contact made it easy for words to fall out that she might never have otherwise spoken. She couldn't tell him about how she'd felt when she'd been holding baby Edward today—that, for a moment, she'd actually felt such a deep desire to be holding a baby of her own. She didn't want to remember how powerful that feeling had been. What she needed to do was to remind herself of the reason why she had decided so irrevocably that it couldn't be allowed to happen.

'I'd never forgive myself if I made someone feel like that,' she whispered. 'As if they had so little importance that the world would be a better place if they weren't in it.'

'Oh... *Alice*...' There was a catch in Nate's voice now. 'I hate that you ever felt like that.' He pulled in a slow breath. 'I want you to know that *my* world is an infinitely better place because you're in it.'

'Aww...that's probably the nicest thing anybody's ever said to me.'

'I mean it.' Nate pressed a kiss to her hair. 'If it wasn't for you, I'd still be living out of boxes and feeling like my life was a complete train wreck. Now I'm looking forward to a whole new future. With my daughter... with Daisy...'

Alice wasn't really listening to his soft words. She was still hearing him tell her that she was rocking his world. She could still hear that note in his voice when he'd said her name. *Alice*... As if his heart was breaking for her.

It would be so easy to fall in love with this man. She could feel it hovering around her like a mist. Or perhaps it was more like a magnetic force because she could feel herself being pulled into it.

The alarm bell was louder this time and the fact that it had sounded twice in such a short period of time meant that it couldn't be ignored.

This wasn't supposed to be happening.

She had to make sure it *didn't* happen.

Alice eased herself away from Nate's side. 'I'd better get going,' she said. 'Early start again tomorrow.'

'You could stay,' Nate said quietly. 'I've got a spare toothbrush somewhere.'

'Maybe another time.' Alice rolled away and got her feet onto the floor, reaching for the first item of her scattered clothing. Crossing that boundary was the complete opposite of what she needed to do right now.

She had to get out of this room. Out of Nate's house. She could have a peek in that adorable nursery as she went past to get to the stairs. She could remind herself that she'd always been adamant that she did not want to have a family. What had happened earlier today had been nothing more than hormones. Her body trying to make her take notice of the ticking of her biological clock.

She could also remind herself of what Nate had said only minutes ago—that he couldn't wait to hold his daughter in his arms. To let her know that she would always be the most important person in his life.

Was Alice destined to never know what that might feel like, to be that important to someone? She'd missed out on it as a child. Was that what she'd been trying—and failing—to find in every relationship she'd had as an adult? To be enough. Just on her own. To know that she could make someone's world a better place, just by being in it. So much better that they didn't need anyone else in that innermost circle of their lives. They could simply be a couple, not a family.

Too much had happened today. It had pushed her even closer to Nate and she knew he was feeling it as well. The evidence had been there in every moment of their love-making. In Nate's invitation to cross that unspoken boundary.

They were turning into a couple.

What was waiting around the next corner? Would Nate start to hope that she might change her mind about motherhood? That she could step into the gap that he—and the baby—would have in their lives?

The thought sent a chill down her spine. She couldn't do that. Her grandmother had helped to ensure she would never change her mind. There was no getting away from the fact that she was her mother's daughter and there was only one way to be absolutely sure that history was not going to repeat itself.

For the sake of everyone involved, including a baby that wasn't even born yet, she needed to rein it in. Before someone got hurt.

There was no choice to be made here. It was going to happen anyway so it might as well be now.

It was time to back off.

CHAPTER TEN

NATE STARED AT the phone in his hand.

He wanted to ring Alice. Not just text her. He wanted to hear her voice but he was hesitating. Because they'd only ever messaged each other and an actual phone call and conversation, especially late at night, felt like a boundary line.

Like staying a whole night with each other?

He'd made a mistake suggesting that the other night, hadn't he? It had been obvious that Alice wasn't feeling comfortable by the way she'd got dressed again so hurriedly—as if she was escaping.

But he was missing her. Missing her voice. Missing her touch even more. So much, it was almost a physical ache.

It would be well within the boundaries of friendship to ring and ask how her day had been today. To check in that she hadn't had to deal with any more cases as dramatic as that birth had been. But that wasn't why Nate wanted to talk to her.

He started tapping his screen.

Heard from Donna today, he texted. She and Nico are heading to the States to live. She wants a divorce.

A sad face emoji landed moments later along with a short message.

Are you ok?

Surprisingly, Nate *was* okay. It had been a very emotional exchange but amongst the swirls of regret and grief for a lost relationship, there was relief to be found. His marriage was definitively over after limping along for far too long. He and Donna could tidy up the mess they'd made of the recent years and get on with their lives. As Alice had said to him herself, not that long ago, nobody could live their best life if they were unhappy and he hadn't realised how miserable Donna had been for a long time. Nobody went looking for someone else to fall in love with if they were happy in their marriage, did they?

I knew it was coming, he responded. I'm thinking it might be time to tell Simone what's going on. She asked today if Donna was having phone problems because she hasn't had her messages picked up.

The silence seemed to stretch as he waited for the ping of a response.

That will give you a starting point to say something's changed. At least she knows how important this baby is to you now. Good luck! Keep me posted.

Nate blinked. He'd been hoping for a different response. A reason to put it off even longer? Advice on what to say?

Support...?

Yeah...he'd been counting on support from the only

other person who knew what was going on in his life, and that message was leaving him feeling oddly...abandoned?

Good grief...where had *that* come from?

Will do, he messaged back. See you at work.

Not this week. Auckland friend's husband broke his big toe and she's persuaded me to take his place on a 3-day horse trek. Driving up to Napier tomorrow.

Nate was staring at his phone again. That unpleasant sensation of being rejected was growing in intensity and—added to that need to talk to her and the desire to be even closer than that—it could only mean one thing.

He was relying too much on Alice. Their friendship was becoming too important. He was, he realised, in danger of falling in love with her and that could only end badly. The warning signs had been there when she couldn't get away fast enough after that invitation to stay the night—as if they were a real couple.

How had he not been aware that they were drifting too close? That boundaries were beginning to feel as if they could be pushed? It was a good thing that Alice was going to be away for a few days. They needed a reset, here. Finding a way to tell Simone he was going to be a single parent was more than enough to cope with right now.

How stupid would it be to even be thinking about sailing into another relationship disaster? That was another pearl of wisdom Alice had shared once, wasn't it? That a relationship was never going to work if they weren't on the same page for the big things, like whether or not they wanted kids. He might be convinced that Alice was wrong about not wanting them but it might be something she would never be ready to admit.

Will do, he sent back. Have fun and don't fall off.

'I didn't fall off.'

Alice was beaming at Nate when he found her in the storeroom, restocking one of their kits before his next shift at Aratika started. She'd caught some sun on her days away, which had given her some new freckles on her nose. She looked proud of herself and very happy and...

And how had he never taken that much notice of how gorgeous she was? He'd been physically attracted to her, of course, but there was so much more to Alice Barlow. She had her life sorted, didn't she? Any partner she chose would have to be just as free. Just as adventurous. Just...totally different to how his life was going to be for the foreseeable future. A pang of regret came from nowhere, that Nate couldn't be that man.

'Was it fun?'

'*So* much fun. We covered farmland and stayed in shearers' quarters but there were the most beautiful forests to go through. And beaches! Have you ever galloped a horse through the waves on a totally deserted beach?'

'Can't say I have.'

'Try it sometime. Soon.'

Nate managed a chuckle. 'Like that night shift you said I needed to do before my life is totally taken over by a tiny human?'

'Absolutely. Three days on horseback would be even further out of reach.'

'I did a night shift. While you were away.'

'Really?' Alice reached up for a box of dressings but then she groaned loudly. 'I can't believe how stiff I am. I hadn't ridden for years and now every muscle in my body is hurting.'

'Sounds like you need some paracetamol. And a massage.'

Oh…imagine that. Some oil on his hands and Alice's skin beneath them…

Alice threw him a smile but didn't quite meet his eyes. 'Paracetamol's a good idea.' She took a couple of tablets from a bottle. 'I think I'm done here. Let's go and grab a coffee so I can wash these down.'

Nate picked up the backpack. Alice held the door to the room open. 'So how did it go?' she asked.

'The night shift? It was good. Only one call-out, to a car versus tree about an hour north. The night vision goggles were fun.'

'That wasn't what I meant.' Alice lowered her voice as they reached the main staircase that led up to the staff room. 'How did it go talking to Simone? About… you know…'

It was Nate's turn to avoid direct eye contact. He pretended a need to adjust his grip on the backpack straps. 'I haven't talked to her yet,' he admitted.

'Oh…'

Such a small word. It was a wonder it could pack such a punch that Nate could feel it in his gut hard enough to make him wince.

Was she disappointed in his lack of action?

He couldn't blame her. He was disappointed in himself, to be honest, and he also had the horrible feeling that he was losing the control he thought he'd had regained over his life. Could he admit that he'd been missing Alice?

A lot?

That he'd been waiting for her return because he really wanted to talk to her? After several dead-end attempts at a written confession, explanation and sincere apology, he was worried that it might make things worse to handle something like this via the impersonal route of a text message or email. A phone connection was quite likely to be patchy, however, and quite possibly get cut off and that could leave things unsaid and hanging awkwardly. It felt like he was between a rock and a hard place and the only person he could talk to about it was Alice but now wasn't the time to try. Andy was coming into the hangar, heading their way.

'Good to see we've got the Dream Team on board today,' he said cheerfully. 'Hasn't been the same without you two.'

Alice had to wonder, as the day wore on, whether Andy was still so pleased with his medical crew for the shift.

She was finding the atmosphere reminiscent of what it had been like to work with Nate when she knew about his marriage falling apart but had no idea of the real turmoil going on in his life, and she was uncomfortably aware that this might be due to her decision to try and create a safer distance between them. Maybe she was trying too hard and there was a danger that she was going to lose what she most wanted to keep—that level of friendship and that trust, both personal and professional—but what else could she do?

This *was* hard.

The flip side of the coin that the ease of falling in love with Nate would have been.

It was, in fact, a lot harder than Alice had expected it to be, but that only made her more determined to succeed. For both their sakes.

And maybe this new tension was due more to the fact that he still hadn't told Simone about Donna? It was perfectly understandable that it was proving a difficult thing for him to do. He'd been worried all along that Simone might be shocked that the baby she was carrying was going to be raised by a single parent but, having made that spur-of-the-moment decision to use the accidental deception that was available when Simone had arrived on the doorstep so unexpectedly, he'd inadvertently given her another reason she might not consider him an ideal parent, hadn't he?

He'd lied to her. He'd let her think that Alice was Donna.

She'd played her part in that deception. She could still remember that look in Nate's eyes and an unspoken plea that was coming straight from his heart that she couldn't possibly refuse.

Please...don't say anything. Can we pretend? It's only for an hour...

She could remember the touch of his hand, too. That sizzle of electricity that should have been all the warning she needed that she was in danger of falling in love with Nathaniel Madden.

Did she heed that warning?

Ha! She'd practically run past any red flags that might have been waving. She'd kissed him, for heaven's sake.

She'd convinced herself that she'd be helping Nate even more by letting Simone see them kissing, like happily married parents-to-be.

Alice sighed. Even thinking about that kiss was like giving her body, and her heart, permission to relive exactly what it had been like to kiss Nate that first time and open a door to so much more. To mix in the pang of longing to experience it again. Longing that was strong enough to feel like a *need*.

Yeah…if things became difficult, she would have to shoulder her fair share of the blame.

She knew how devastating it would be for Nate if things became really difficult, so it was hardly surprising that this palpable tension was there.

Thank goodness it turned out to be one of those days where it was a bonus to find time to have a bathroom break. Alice hoped it was as easy for Nate as it was for her to forget about anything personal as they treated and transported patients. Half the morning was taken up with their first call to a remote farm, where a young man had managed to roll his ATV down a bank and had fractured his pelvis, judging by the level of pain he was in and the instability of what was normally a rigid, bony structure.

It was an injury that carried the possibility of life-threatening internal bleeding and required the air ambulance team's full focus. They got IV access and provided strong pain relief but needed extra help from the local volunteer fire brigade to get their patient out from under the heavy, four-wheeled bike without making his injury worse. It was only then that they could apply the pelvic binder that would help tamponade any bleeding and continue the intensive monitoring for signs of shock as they got him to the emergency department of The General.

There was a quick turnaround after the handover as they were dispatched to back up another helicopter at a major scene where a car had collected more than one rider in a motorbike club's road trip. Lunch was sandwiches from a cafeteria in the hospital foyer and time on-base was only long enough to restock the kits and refuel the aircraft.

The next job was more sedate—simply a transfer from a rural hospital for a patient who had suffered a heart attack that was severe enough for her to need to be in a catheter laboratory for angioplasty within a window of time that could prevent ongoing cardiac damage. It was as they arrived back on base that Nate got a text message on his phone. His expression, as he read it, made Alice's heart sink.

'It's Simone,' he said. 'Her midwife says her blood pressure is too high. She's going to take her into Invercargill Hospital as soon as Olly gets home from the farm he's working on, so he can look after the kids.'

'Did she say what her blood pressure was?'

'I'll ask.' Nate texted swiftly and didn't look up as he waited for a response. 'One-fifty over ninety-five.' His tone was grim. 'That's pre-eclampsia territory.'

Alice bit her lip. Pre-eclampsia could morph into full-blown eclampsia the moment a seizure occurred and that was an obstetric emergency for both the mother and baby. It could cause lack of oxygen during seizures or a placental abruption. There was a risk of stroke or organ failure and, in a worst-case scenario, it could be fatal.

Nate was still focussed on his phone. 'She says she hasn't got any visual disturbances but she does have a headache and her ankles are swollen. She'll let me know more when she's been seen at the hospital.'

It was just as well there were no further call-outs that afternoon. Even with the best of professional intentions it would have been a challenge to shut this down. If further tests confirmed that Simone did have pre-eclampsia, she would have to be admitted to hospital for continuous monitoring and medications to try and lower her blood pressure, prevent seizures and prolong the pregnancy. Delivery was the only cure, however, and it would have to happen with any signs of danger to either mother or baby, regardless of dates.

Simone was barely into her third trimester. Nate's precious baby would be very premature and that could add a whole new layer to the complications in his life. Alice's heart was aching for him as she watched him pacing the base, his phone in his hand, glancing at the screen frequently. Sometimes he was staring at it as if he was willing it to ring or sound an alert for a message.

In the end it did ring. Alice could see Nate walking outside, near the helicopter, making sure the call was private. She went down to meet him when he came back into the hangar. It was time they should be heading off shift, anyway.

'She's had blood tests and an ultrasound,' Nate told her. 'The baby's fine. They've got her on continuous CTG monitoring and she's on bed rest. They're going to keep her in for observation for the next twenty-four hours.'

Alice nodded. 'That's good. They haven't confirmed pre-eclampsia, then?'

'Not yet.'

The shadows in Nate's eyes were haunting. It was all Alice could do not to offer him a hug.

'You want to get down there, don't you?'

A single nod from Nate. 'I've been checking flights. I've got a day off tomorrow and I could get there by mid-morning. They should know how serious this is by then.'

Alice mirrored his nod. She wanted to reassure him but how? She would go home with him tonight just to be there for him but that didn't feel like enough.

She cared about this man. Too much, maybe, but that was beside the point right now. She had to *do* something.

'If we let Don know what's going on, I know he'd get someone in to cover for me,' she said quietly. 'Would you like me to come with you? To see Simone?'

Alice could see the softening in his eyes that was a kind of melting. She could *feel* it happening in her own heart.

'Yes,' he whispered. *'Please…'*

CHAPTER ELEVEN

'OH, MY GOODNESS...' Simone was astonished to see Nate and Alice come into her room the next morning. 'You've come all this way! *Both* of you...'

'We were worried about you,' Nate said. 'I'm sorry we couldn't get here any sooner. I rang a couple of times overnight but all they would tell me was that you were sleeping comfortably.'

'I feel fine,' Simone said. 'Just a bit of a headache, that's all. I'm sure they're going to let me go back home today. They're just waiting to see what the results of the latest blood tests are, I think. I'm sorry to have given you such a fright. Are you okay, Donna?'

Alice swallowed hard. She'd known this would be the hardest part of supporting Nate through this, but she had no choice but to continue the pretence of being his wife. They'd both agreed that today was not the time for honesty. Upsetting someone whose blood pressure was already too high would be an irresponsible thing to do. Unacceptable from both a professional and personal standpoint.

'We'll both be fine, too,' she said. 'Once we know that *you're* okay. And please, just say if there's anything we can do to help. We've got flights booked back for this afternoon but they can be changed if we need to.'

Simone shook her head. 'Olly's got everything sorted with the kids. I think he loves an opportunity to show off what a great dad he is. He's going to bring them all in for the ride this afternoon, either to visit me or take me home.' She smiled. 'You'd be welcome to come for dinner, if you want to rent a car and stay the night. I'd love you to meet the kids and see where we live.'

Alice didn't know how to respond to the invitation. She turned to Nate but he seemed to be focussed on the screen of the cardiotocography machine although it looked reassuringly normal. The line for the transducer measuring contractions was completely flat and the fetal heart rate was a healthy, rapid blip of about a hundred and forty beats a minute.

They were both saved from having to say anything by the arrival of the medical team doing their ward round. They stepped back out of the way as the small group of doctors, a nurse and a midwife surrounded Simone's bed.

The consultant opened Simone's notes. 'Latest blood results are looking good,' she said. 'Your kidney and liver function is fine and your platelets are normal. How's that headache?'

'Not too bad.'

'On the pain scale of one to ten?'

'Still only about two. It's just a nuisance, that's all.'

'Let's have a look at that swelling in your ankles.'

A nurse lifted the covers of Simone's bed to reveal that the swelling had decreased overnight.

'Amazing what staying off your feet for a while can do,' Simone said. 'My blood pressure's down a bit, too, isn't it?'

A junior doctor picked up the chart on the end of the bed. 'Last reading was one-forty over ninety,' he said.

'Still a bit high,' the consultant told Simone. 'But it's stable and not enough to warrant starting medication at the moment. Try and stay off your feet more, if you can. We're going to give you an easy-to-use automatic cuff so you can take your blood pressure daily at home and we'll be asking your midwife to check on you more often. We're happy that this is gestational hypertension and not pre-eclampsia but we also want you to come back here immediately if you notice any new symptoms, like visual disturbances, abdominal pain or a reduction in baby's movements.'

She nodded at Nate and Alice as she turned back to the door. Had she assumed they were family members or simply visitors?

'These are the baby's parents,' Simone told her. 'Nate's a doctor, too. From Wellington.'

Nate put his hand out. 'Nate Madden,' he said as she accepted the handshake. 'Nice to meet you.'

'I'm Maria. I've delivered three of Simone's babies in the last few years and we're happy to support her in this surrogacy.'

She turned to Alice with a friendly smile. 'You've come a long way. I'm Maria,' she repeated as they shook hands. 'Good to meet you.'

'And you.' Alice smiled back. 'I'm Alice.'

Oh, *no*... The minute her name left her lips and Alice realised what her automatic reaction had revealed, she cringed inwardly and her smile vanished. She could feel the atmosphere in the room changing around her.

Maria hadn't noticed. She was still smiling. 'You'll

both be happy to know that the results of the ultrasound we did yesterday are all on track. Normal growth, no problems with the amniotic fluid volume or the blood flow through the umbilical artery. Baby's doing well.'

'That's great news.' But Nate's voice sounded tight.

'I'll be back soon,' the midwife told Simone as she turned to leave. 'I'll bring the blood pressure cuff and teach you how to use it.'

Simone nodded but said nothing.

Within seconds, the medical staff had moved on to their next patient and it was just the three of them in the room again. Alice could feel Simone's stare but she was transfixed by the expression on Nate's face.

He looked as though she'd just betrayed him. She felt like she'd betrayed him and she wished the floor would just open up and swallow her. She'd hurt Nate but she could feel the pain and it was…unbearable.

A single word, from Simone, fell into the silence in a tone of both confusion and accusation.

'Alice…?'

'I can explain.'

Now that the initial shock was wearing off, Nate felt a wash of something like relief. 'I've been wanting to tell you for a long time but—'

'Tell me *what*?' Simone demanded. 'That your wife has changed her name? Wait…' Her gaze swerved to Alice. 'You're *not* Donna, are you?'

'No.' Alice had to stop herself from looking at Nate. 'I'm sorry,' she added. 'It just kind of happened. When you turned up that day and assumed I was Donna.'

Simone was shaking her head. 'Of course I did.

You were in Nate's house. You were so obviously a...a *couple*—'

'No...' It was Nate who interrupted this time. 'We were just friends.' His sigh was resigned. He couldn't keep lying. He should never have let this happen in the first place. 'Then...'

Simone was rubbing her forehead and Nate's heart fell even further. Was her headache getting worse? Had he been justified in wanting to keep up the pretence to avoid exacerbating what could still be a complication in this pregnancy?

'How stupid could I have been?' Simone muttered. 'If I hadn't been so excited about sharing the video of that scan with you, I would have paid more attention. I knew that your wife looked different from her photos. I just thought it was because she wasn't expecting visitors and didn't have any makeup on or something.' Her head jerked up. 'Where *is* Donna?'

'She's gone. She's been in Italy and is now moving to the United States.'

'I'm not surprised.' Simone sounded disgusted. 'How long has this been going on?' Simone looked from Nate to Alice and back again. 'This...*affair*?'

'Please...' Nate moved closer. 'Let me explain.'

'Um...' Alice sounded uncertain. 'Would it be better if I left?'

Nate hated that he'd created this situation. He'd made Alice complicit in a deception that might have happened unintentionally but he'd chosen to prolong it. He couldn't blame her for having used her own name when she introduced herself to Maria. This might be a very difficult situation but it wasn't Alice's fault. He had to take the blame and try and put this right.

'If might be better,' he agreed. 'This is between me and Simone and I need to tell her everything.'

The whole story. About Donna walking away from the prospect of bringing up a child when she wasn't the biological mother. Of walking away from being his wife. About the affair she was having that he hadn't known about. Of how Alice had been helping him to try and show her how committed he was to being the best father to his baby. *His* baby...

'I'll meet you at the airport, then,' Alice said quietly.

It was an hour later that Nate arrived back at the airport. He spotted Alice almost instantly, sitting on the far side of the waiting area. Even from this distance he could see that she'd been anxiously watching for him.

'I'm *so* sorry,' she said as soon as he got close enough. 'I can't believe I did that. I just...wasn't thinking.'

'It's not your fault.' Nate tried to smile but his lips wouldn't cooperate. 'I was the one who let it happen in the first place. I could have just said you were a friend and none of this would have happened.'

He wanted to sound reassuring but it was too difficult. He'd known all along that precisely this would have happened. His entire future had been hanging on that conversation with Simone that he had put off for far too long.

Nate was totally drained.

And afraid.

'Is Simone okay?' Alice asked.

'Physically? Yes. She's upset but it hasn't made any difference to her blood pressure.'

Alice was biting her lip. 'What did she say?'

'That she needs to talk to Olly about it. That she needs time to think about it.' Nate turned away. 'Have you checked in?'

'Yes.'

He nodded. That meant Alice already had a seat so it was unlikely they would be seated together and that was probably a good thing.

There really wasn't anything more to say at the moment, was there?

He had given his evidence to the best of his ability and now the jury was out.

There was nothing either of them could do other than wait for the verdict to arrive.

CHAPTER TWELVE

THE WAITING WAS the worst.

Alice texted Nate two days later but he hadn't had any communication from Simone at that point. He said he'd let her know when he heard something.

So she kept waiting and resisted the urge to find another reason to make contact.

It wasn't what she wanted to do. What she wanted was to turn up on Nate's doorstep. To walk into his house and...

And what?

Hope that he would pull her into his arms and tell her that everything was going to be okay? That he'd fallen in love with her and couldn't live without her? That she was just as important to him as the baby?

No...all she really wanted to do was to hold him in *her* arms. To comfort him. To tell him again how sorry she was. To let him know how much she cared about him, even if she couldn't say it aloud because it might well be the last thing he wanted to hear when his life had got even more complicated.

But neither of those scenarios were going to happen, were they?

Nate had made it very clear, when he'd opened up to

her in the first place, that his unborn baby was the most important thing in his life, and his ability to be a father to that baby was in jeopardy. While Alice knew that it really wasn't her fault that this had happened, that didn't stop her feeling responsible. She'd been well-trained, after all, to know that her presence in someone's life was enough to be a problem. That just her existence could diminish someone else's happiness.

Perhaps the best thing to do was to stay well clear of Nate.

She also thought he might be deliberately avoiding her, giving that he wasn't even texting, so she wasn't really expecting to see him turn up for his next rostered shift at Aratika but there he was, already in the staff room when she arrived, with Shirley fussing over him, trying to tempt him to accept one of her delicious bacon rolls.

'Or at least an egg on toast? You look like you're losing weight.' Shirley tutted. 'You're not looking after yourself well enough, are you?' With a sigh, she gave up. 'What's that book you've got? It looks very old.'

'It's *The Hobbit*.' Nate showed her the battered green cover of the book that he'd found in that second-hand bookshop. 'I started reading it last night and I couldn't put it down. Thought it would make a change from medical journals if we get time on base today.'

He did look tired, Alice thought. The lines around his eyes were deeper and his smile looked like it was taking considerable effort. How much sleep was he getting? Had he been up half the night reading to try and distract himself? Had he *still* not heard back from Simone?

As if he'd caught her thought, Nate glanced up and

gave a clear message with a subtle shake of his head. There was no news.

Andy and Nick broke off the conversation they were having as Don came out of the operations room.

'Your pagers are about to go off,' he told the crew. 'Car versus cyclist on the Paekākāriki Hill road. Sounds like someone came down the off-ramp like there was no tomorrow. According to the first responder it looks like a partial amputation with a fracture/dislocation of an ankle. They've only got methoxyflurane as an analgesic and it's not doing much to help the poor guy.'

Pagers sounding drowned out his voice but the crew were already moving. Weather was not an issue with a cloudless sky and little wind, Andy and Nick had already done the pre-flight checks on the helicopter and any further information could be relayed during the time it took them to get airborne and over the hills to the west coast.

Alice was grateful for the call. It had to be better for both herself and Nate to be busy and working. Sitting around the base, sneaking glances at him and worrying about his state of mind would make for a very long and miserable day.

They were back to square one and Alice was beginning to wonder if this was going to affect Nate's ability to do his job effectively. It felt like a lower dip in the rollercoaster of their professional and personal relationship, however, because she'd learned what it was like to be close to him. To share his secrets and know what hopes and fears he had for his future. She knew what it was like to be really close, in fact, and that made this so much more personal. What was bothering Nate mattered to her as well.

It mattered a lot.

They could see traffic banking up below them in both directions as they neared the scene. Emergency vehicles with their beacons flashing made it easy to spot their target. An ambulance, fire trucks and police cars had responded and a tow-truck was trying to weave through the snarled traffic. Police officers had blocked off part of the adjoining state highway to give the helicopter a safe landing area not far from the group of people clustered around the accident victim.

The local first responders looked very relieved to see expert help arriving and it was easy to see why as Alice and Nate crouched beside a young man who was screaming with pain. His whole ankle joint was visible, the foot hanging on an angle below, looking very pale and completely lifeless.

'Do you know his name?' Nate asked the first responder.

'Peter.'

Nate crouched. 'Peter? Can you hear me? My name's Nate and I'm a doctor. We're going to get on top of that pain for you, okay?'

Their patient gave him an agonised glance but just groaned in response.

Alice was right beside him, unzipping the pack. Nick was setting down an oxygen cylinder near Peter's head.

'Want O2 on?'

'Yes, thanks. Let's get some leads on and a BP, too. Peter?' He leaned closer. 'I'm going to put an IV line in your arm so we can give you some stronger pain relief. Is that okay?'

Peter was sucking on the mouthpiece of the Penthrox inhaler but managed to nod this time, which rang an alarm bell for Alice. Peter might have been wearing a helmet but, with a mechanism of injury like this, the head and neck could well be involved and the distraction of the pain he was in from his ankle, any signs or symptoms could be buried.

'Try and keep your head as still as you can for the moment,' she told him.

'Blood pressure's one-fifty over ninety,' Nick reported as Alice handed Nate the Luer plug to attach to the end of the cannula. 'Heart rate one-twenty. Resps twenty-four.'

Alice leaned down so Peter could hear her over the reverse beeping signal of a tow-truck backing in to hook up the car that had been involved in this incident. 'Are you allergic to anything that you know of, Peter?'

'No...'

His groan became a crescendo into another scream. Alice gripped his shoulder. 'Hang in there, Peter. The doctor's drawing up some drugs right now that are going to take that pain away.'

She assumed he would be using ketamine because it was the most potent analgesic and sedative they had available and something powerful was going to be needed to align this fracture. The wound was heavily contaminated so it would also need irrigation with saline before sterile wound dressings and immobilisation in a splint.

Alice saw Nate looking around them before he injected the drug and she knew he was worried about how busy the scene was. Ketamine was the ideal drug to use in this situation but it did have the potential to cause hallucinations and severe agitation in some patients, and there was a lot of stimulation around them that could trigger a reaction. Flashing lights were very close, horns were blaring from irate drivers who were fed up with being caught in a traffic jam because there was a helicopter sitting in the middle of the road, people were shouting and a siren from another emergency vehicle arriving could be heard.

Nate caught Alice's gaze and gave his head a slight shake. There wasn't much they could do to try and make things calmer and quieter but Alice put her face close to Peter's and kept talking to him. Reassurance and distraction could be helpful as well.

'You're doing really well, Peter,' she told him. 'We're going to give you some medication now so we can get your leg sorted and then we'll put you in the helicopter and get you to hospital. Have you ever been in a helicopter before?'

Peter's eyes were open and he was staring up at her. When Alice saw the involuntary movements as his eyes flicked from side to side, she knew that Nate had administered the ketamine and it was taking effect.

Nate moved Peter's leg gently to check the level of sedation.

'All good?' he asked.

Peter's eyes were still open but he wasn't showing any sign of being aware of what was going on or experiencing any pain.

'All good,' Alice responded.

'Can I get you to support the leg above the ankle, please? I'm going to put some longitudinal traction on the foot to get the joint back in. Nick, keep an eye on his breathing and sedation level.'

They didn't need their crewman to warn that there was a problem as the sedative effects of the ketamine began to wear off. Peter suddenly began struggling to sit up. He was ripping the oxygen mask from his face and shouting.

'Get them away...we're going to get trampled...'

Nick put his hands on Peter's shoulders to reassure him and push him gently back to a lying position.

'Watch his neck,' Nate snapped. 'C-spine isn't cleared yet.'

'It's all right, Peter. Nothing's going to trample us.' Alice tried to catch hold of his hands but he swung his arm towards her and she fell backwards as the blow connected to her cheek.

She heard Nate swear under his breath. She rolled on her side and pushed herself upright again, ignoring the stinging of the side of her face and the metallic taste of blood in her mouth. Nate was injecting more medication into the IV line as Nick held Peter's body in a tight hug.

'Midazolam?' she queried.

'Luckily I had some drawn up, just in case.' His gaze flicked sideways. 'Are you hurt?'

Alice touched the back of her hand to her lip to wipe away any blood that might be obvious. 'I'm fine.'

'He's settling,' Nick said, lowering Peter to the ground again.

'Let's get this dressed and securely splinted, then.' But Nate's gaze was searching Alice's face as she reached for some large, sterile dressings.

'I'm fine,' she repeated, more firmly. 'Forget about me.'

Nate had to do that, at least for now, but he could see that Alice had a cut on her lip and a red mark on her cheek and his mind was demanding to replay the moment she'd been struck and turn that spear of empathetic pain in his own gut into something solid and heavy. It was harder than it had ever been before to bury a personal reaction and do what had to be done.

Which was a rapid but thorough secondary survey now that the overwhelming distraction of the ankle injury had been dealt with. The steps of the head-to-toe sweep might be so well-practised for Nate that the process was automatic but this still required a level of focus that would ensure nothing got missed.

Like CSF fluid leaking from an ear that could indicate a skull fracture, perhaps. Reduced breath sounds, which could be a symptom of a serious chest injury or abdominal signs of internal bleeding. Another set of vital signs needed to be recorded, medication topped up and then they would be ready to secure Peter to the stretcher and get him into the helicopter for transport. The whole crew was kept busy and it wasn't until they had completed their handover in the trauma resuscitation room of the emergency department that Nate let himself take a more searching look at Alice's face.

Her cheek still looked red and her lip was swelling now.

'You need to get your lip checked out. And your cheek.'

Alice shook her head. 'It's nothing,' she muttered, not looking up from the paperwork she was completing.

Nate went to get some ice from the staffroom freezer and wrapped it in a gauze dressing pad.

'Here...' He handed her the cold pack. 'Keep this on your face for a while. I'll look after the stretcher.'

What he really wanted to do was hold her face between his hands and examine it properly. To touch her lip and make sure there wasn't a hidden cut deep enough to need stitches.

But Alice had made it obvious she wouldn't welcome that kind of attention. They'd barely spoken, in fact, since that awful moment in Simone's room when she'd suggested it would be better if she wasn't there. They hadn't been seated together on the plane and Alice had been as determined to escape the airport when they got back to Wellington as she had been to leave his bedroom the last time they'd slept together.

And maybe that would turn out to *actually* be the last time they were ever that close.

The distance had been growing ever since that night but Nate was doing his best to convince himself that this had been inevitable. That Alice had only ever been interested in something temporary and without any kind of strings.

With the horrible tension since Simone had learned the truth about their deception, he had even wondered whether it might help her decision-making if he could tell her that what she saw as an 'affair' with Alice was over. That he was not going to let anything other than his child have a claim on his attention for the foreseeable future.

Even that he was prepared to sacrifice a friendship that he knew *was* significant? Alice might have told him to forget about her but he knew, beyond any shadow of doubt, that was never going to happen.

The cold pack helped a lot.

Alice checked her lip in the bathroom mirror when they got back to base and she knew that the cut was small enough to heal easily on its own.

As she'd had to tell Nate more than once, she *was* fine. Physically, anyway.

The fact that Nate had cared enough to make the ice pack for her wasn't helping her emotional state, though.

She hated this distance between them. She was missing him so much it hurt, dammit, and it didn't feel like it was going to wear off anytime soon.

Alice turned away from the mirror. Surely there was some way they could at least salvage the friendship they'd discovered before they'd allowed the attraction between them to make things complicated? She knew Nate was on tenterhooks waiting to hear from Simone and she knew how incredibly important this was to him.

He needed a friend right now more than he had when she'd first stepped up and pushed herself into his personal life. Alice gave the door a rather determined push and headed towards the staff room. She was just as determined to let Nate know that she was still in his corner and that a real friendship—like theirs—could survive anything if they both wanted it to.

She didn't get to say anything, however.

She found Nate standing by the floor-to-ceiling windows that made up the wall in this central, third-floor office area of the Aratika Rescue Base. The view was spectacular. Wellington Harbour straight ahead, the distinctive central city skyline a background on one side and rugged, forest-covered hills on the other. Directly below was the helipad but Nate wasn't watching Andy as he walked around his beloved yellow helicopter, possibly looking for a smudge of dust he could brush off.

Nate was, instead, looking at the screen of his phone.

He looked up as Alice got close that the look in his eyes made her breath catch.

She didn't need to ask if it was a message from Simone. Nate handed her his phone and she could see that the communication was an email.

Dear Nate,
Thank you for your patience. Olly and I had a lot to talk and think about after this unexpected development in our surrogacy journey and we also decided that we should seek some legal advice.

As I'm sure you know, under NZ law, the woman who gives birth to a baby is the legal mother, regardless of any lack of genetic relationship. You will also be aware that the intended parents must apply for an adoption order and that this requires the surrogate (and her partner) to consent to the adoption. Without this consent, the adoption cannot proceed.

Alice couldn't breathe. She knew what was coming.

I'm very sorry, Nate, but Olly and I feel very strongly that, as a loving and complete family, we can offer this baby a better future than you will be able to.

The screen went blank but Alice didn't want to tap it back into life. She'd seen enough. She handed Nate his phone. She could feel tears gathering in her eyes as she met his gaze, but it still felt like she couldn't breathe and that meant she couldn't say anything, either.

Even if she'd been able to find the words…

The only thing she could do was to open her arms. To offer the comfort of a hug.

For one long horrible moment, Alice thought that Nate was going to refuse. That he would shake his head and turn away. It was quite understandable that he might want to be alone to deal with what had to be an unthinkable pain but...

But it would break Alice's heart.

Because this was how much she loved Nate. She could feel his pain as if it was her own and the need to offer comfort and support was so big it was filling her, body and soul.

And, in a moment that Alice would remember for the rest of her life, Nate didn't refuse. He not only stepped into her arms, he wrapped his around her and held her so tightly she could almost believe that he needed this physical contact as much as she did.

That he needed *her*?

But, what Nate did refuse, moments later, was her offer to go home with him so that he wasn't alone.

'No.' The word had a finality that seemed to echo around Alice. 'Thanks, but I'm going to go and see my solicitor. He's a friend so he won't mind talking to me away from work.'

'Call me when you can,' she said. 'Let me know if there's anything I can do to help.'

That wry smile nearly undid her.

'Thank you,' he said quietly, 'but you've already done more than enough. I shouldn't have involved you in this at all. I'm sorry, Alice. This is my problem. And it's up to me to find a way to fix it.'

CHAPTER THIRTEEN

SHE HAD DONE 'more than enough.'

There was no way Alice couldn't pick up her fair share of the blame for this new challenge that Nate was facing.

He rang her that evening.

'It's not good news,' he said, without preamble. 'My solicitor, Rob, was straight with me and he said that it would be an uphill battle to persuade a family court to override the birth mother's rights.'

'But you're the father.' Alice was shocked. This was so unfair. 'You're the person who chose to create this baby—the only person here that's got a genetic connection.'

'Rob said I'd have to prove that there were serious concerns about the child's welfare so that I could go for a guardianship or custody.' He sounded even more tired than he'd looked this morning. 'I know that Simone and Olly are amazing parents, so that would be dishonest. I couldn't do that. It was a lack of honesty that's brought this to where it is and…it's not me.'

'I know,' Alice whispered. 'I knew that all along. I also knew that you had the best intentions in the world.'

There was a huff of sound that could have been an equal mix of laughter and a sob.

'Isn't that what the road to hell is paved with?'

Alice closed her eyes. What could she say?

'Rob said the best way to resolve this is to negotiate with Simone and Olly,' Nate said, into the silence. 'I just need to decide what the best way to go about that is. Wish me luck.'

'Of course I do. You know that.'

'I do.' Alice could hear Nate drawing in a deep breath, as if he wanted to say something else but, judging by the final tone of his next words, it seemed that he had changed his mind. 'Catch you later, Alice.'

There was no point trying to sleep yet, Alice decided later that evening. And she might end up missing Nate even more acutely if she was lying there in her bed, wide awake.

She wasn't hungry and she didn't want the noise of either a movie or music that might have distracted her. She decided to do some housework, instead, but the first thing she picked up to put back into the cupboard under the stairs was that box of wool that had been sitting beside the end of her couch ever since she'd made that pair of booties for Nate's baby.

She found herself sinking onto the couch, with that soft ball of pale yellow wool in her hands and, suddenly, knitting something seemed like the perfect distraction from the thoughts and emotions that were as tangled as some of the wool at the bottom of this box. The book of baby patterns was still on top of the box, along with the needles, and it didn't seem like a stupid idea to use them. She could use the rest of this yellow wool to knit a tiny hat. Maybe she could post it to Simone with a note of apology for her part in complicating what had been supposed to be a wonderful gift of creating a family for others.

It was soothing to focus on how many stitches to cast on and then follow the instructions to the lacy pattern for a sweet baby bonnet. For a while, even, Alice forgot that she was making an item of clothing for a newborn baby but, as the shape began to emerge, she found herself remembering the birth of Nicole's baby.

Or rather, the way she'd felt when she'd been holding that baby boy in her own arms.

And, this time, that surge of yearning was so strong, her needles stilled and she rested her hands in her lap.

Was this how Nate felt when he thought about the baby he wanted so much? When all he wanted to do was to hold his daughter and let her know how loved she was?

No…it had to be far worse for him. This was just the concept of a baby that was making Alice feel like this.

Nate's baby was *real*. She already existed. She was growing and she would be born and taking her first breaths in the very near future.

Alice barely noticed the tears trickling slowly down her face. She wanted Nate to be holding his baby as she took those first breaths.

She wanted to hold her *own* baby one day. To love her the way a baby should be loved. The way Nate would love his baby if he was allowed to.

The way every baby should be loved?

This flood of emotion couldn't be attributed simply to hormones or a biological clock. Alice could see that it had been there forever. Deeply locked away in order to dodge the painful memories that were inextricably linked to her own mother. But this was different. This flood was washing away the walls that had kept it locked up. She could see it for what it was. A childhood fear.

She wasn't a child now.

She knew how much love she was capable of giving. To a baby. To the father of that baby. And it mattered.

She mattered.

I want you to know that my world is an infinitely better place because you're in it...

Dear Lord...that emotional flood was washing away the final lumps of rubble that she'd believed had been keeping her safe all her life.

What was being left behind was the love she had for Nate. And for the little girl who should be called Daisy and be brought up with the father who loved her to the moon and back.

What was happening to Nate wasn't fair. It wasn't right.

She *had* to try and find some way to help fix this.

It was a day off for Nate but he was making a quick visit to the Aratika Rescue Base because he'd left something behind when he'd left yesterday.

He'd been so shocked by that email from Simone that he hadn't even thought to go back to the staff room and collect his book. He'd only remembered where it was, in fact, in the early hours of this morning, when he'd needed something to distract himself from the dark space his thoughts were trying to lure him into, and what better way to find a rock to cling to than to remind himself of his own father. It had been a real surprise to find he could almost hear his dad's voice in his head when he was reading *The Hobbit* but there was comfort to be found in that.

And Nate had never been in quite this need of comfort. He'd felt lost when his life seemed to be falling apart and he had no idea how he was going to cope with a new home to settle into and fatherhood just around the corner. But now…he felt broken. The dream he'd had of his own future had been well and truly shattered with not even a glimpse of a possible solution to be found yet.

The helicopters were on the ground when he arrived. He could see Andy standing in the sunshine, having a yarn with one of the other pilots. The back doors of the ambulance were open and it looked like the paramedic crew were doing a check of all the gear that was kept on board, in the overhead lockers and other storage areas.

There would be other staff members inside the building but Nate wasn't sure he wanted to be sociable enough to return greetings and field any jokes about how he couldn't stay away from the place. Alice would be on duty today and he didn't want to see the concern that would be in her eyes, because that would make it harder to try and stay in control. And what if Shirley was in the staff room today? One look at his face and she'd probably be wrapping her arms around him and offering him some of her home baking and that could well be his undoing.

Maybe he should go and have a quiet word with Andy and ask him to pop upstairs and collect the book? As he walked into the hangar, however, Nate's glance caught the spiral staircase and he remembered the door at the top and the corridor that led to the central hub of the base with the staff room and offices. Nobody would be using the on-call bedrooms during the day and, if he went up that way, he could open the door far enough to see how crowded the area was and whether he could face it. If he couldn't, he'd go and talk to Andy.

He hadn't factored in how he would feel going up these steel stairs and quietly opening the door that led into the corridor, mind you. Oh, man…the memories of the way that physical attraction between himself and Alice had ignited with such force that neither of them could resist giving in to it right then and there…

He'd never experienced a physical connection to anybody like that, including the woman he'd married, and he doubted that he would ever find it again. The way it had felt as if they'd always known each other. As if their bodies were made for each other. Sex had never felt wilder or more exciting but oddly, it had never felt that safe, either.

Nate was halfway along the corridor, sinking into emotions rather than coherent thoughts, when he heard a voice that stopped him in his tracks.

Alice?

What on earth was she doing here?

In one of the on-call rooms. The one just ahead of him, its door ajar.

'I'm in a completely private area,' he heard Alice say. 'So no one will be able to hear and I'm on my lunch break, so I won't be called out unless it's a real emergency.'

Nate was turning. He needed to retrace his steps. Alice was trying to make a very private call and he didn't want her to know he was here.

Alice cleared her throat as he was about to move. 'Thank you so much for this. I hope you didn't go into town just so we could get a good enough reception for a video call.'

'It's okay. I had to come in for a midwife appointment, anyway.'

Nate froze. He knew that voice. Alice was talking to *Simone*. There was no way he could move now. He might not be a part of this conversation but it could only be *about* him. He had to know what the hell was going on. Simone didn't sound that happy. Was Alice about to do something that might make it even less likely that he could somehow negotiate a change of heart from his surrogate?

'Olly said it was only fair,' Simone added. 'I listened to what Nate had to say, so I should listen to you. So, shoot…what is it that you're so desperate to tell me?'

'Oh…' It sounded like Alice didn't know where to start. 'I just think there are some things you probably don't know about and maybe what you do know isn't the whole story.'

'Like what?'

'Like how committed Nate is to being a father. To having a family. I've been working with him for over a year but I've only got to know him because of this baby. Because of how important it is to him to have his own family. He lost his father when he was too young and he's still Nate's hero. His dad made him feel like he could be a hero, too, and you know what? That's exactly what he is. He doesn't just save lives in an emergency department—he gets on a helicopter and flies into places that make his job so much more difficult and he does it with an absolute passion for helping the people who need him the most. Any kid would think that a dad who did that was something special, wouldn't they?'

'He is special,' Simone agreed. 'That's why I chose to be a surrogate for him.' Her sigh was audible. 'And his wife.'

"Did you know how protective he's been of the baby you're carrying—ever since he knew you were pregnant? He was a real mess when his marriage fell apart because he was scared—really *scared*—that you might think he couldn't be the best parent if he was a single dad. He told me that if he lost the chance to be part of his child's life, it would haunt him forever.'

'That's something we've talked about.' Simone sounded more sure of herself now. 'Nate's the biological father of this child. We know he needs to be involved to some degree. We'll figure something out.'

Nate was leaning against the wall of the corridor right outside the door. He closed his eyes when he heard Simone say this. It was a small step towards acknowledging his rights as a father, but it wasn't enough. Not nearly enough.

'Did he tell you that it was Donna that ended the marriage? That she left him for a man that she's been having an affair with for maybe a couple of years? That she told him that the baby was only his so he could have it—by himself?'

Outside the door, Nate winced at the private revelation but could hear Simone's shocked gasp.

'No…he never told me any of that. But…she seemed to be just as keen to have a baby as he was. Was she lying to everybody?'

'Maybe she wasn't sure what she really wanted,' Alice suggested quietly. 'But when the reality hit that they had a child on the way, she realised what she really *didn't* want. And I think Nate realised just how much he *did* want exactly this.'

Simone was silent. The sniff Nate could hear from Alice revealed that she was struggling with tears and he had to press himself against the wall to resist the urge to go into the room and put his arms around her.

'I grew up without a father,' Alice said then. 'A few contenders for a stepfather but nothing ever worked out because none of them wanted someone else's kid. I never had anyone that wanted me that much. Not even my mother or my grandmother. I can't imagine what it would feel like to have someone want me as much as Nate wants his baby. Or who would love me the way he could. He's the most wonderful man, Simone. He's clever and kind and gentle and so…loyal. He bought that house you came to see us in because of the Wendy house in the garden. He painted the table and chairs in the brightest colours he could find. And now…' Alice's breath escaped in an almost sob. 'Now he won't see Daisy playing in it.'

'Daisy?'

'It's a family name. Nate's grandmother. I think that's what he would like his daughter to be called.'

There was a longer silence from Simone this time and then she spoke slowly. 'But that's the problem, don't you see? It's family that we want for this baby. Not for her to be raised by a single, working father and maybe an endless stream of nannies.'

'He didn't set out to be a single father,' Alice said.

'And he might well get married again one day, after his divorce comes through. What if...?' Her next words were whispered. 'What if *I* was there instead of a nanny?'

'You'd want to look after someone else's baby?'

'This isn't "someone else's" baby. This is *Nate's* baby. And yes... I'd love to help take care of her.'

She would, Alice realised. She could love that little baby if she was allowed to. As much as if it was her own. She'd never let Daisy feel unloved, not for a heartbeat.

'But you work full time, don't you?'

'I'm not the only person who would want to help. Aratika Rescue Base is full of people that think the world of Nate. We'd all help. I could cut back on my hours and juggle my rosters so I can fill in gaps when Nate can't be at home.'

'Why would you want to do that?'

'Because...' Alice cleared her throat. 'I love him. I'm never going to love anyone else the way I love Nate.'

'Does he know that?'

He does now, Nate thought. And it was giving him a warm glow that came from somewhere very deep and was now spreading right through his body, all the way to the tips of his fingers and toes. It was making him feel...*happy*. Safe. As though he could stop wishing for things he didn't have and simply be grateful for...*this*— something that most people dream of having.

He'd known he'd been in danger of falling in love with Alice but of course he hadn't known how she felt about him. Quite the opposite. That night when he'd invited her to stay, had she been running away from him because she thought she needed to hide how she felt? *Why?*

Was Alice shaking her head? Was that what was making her next words wobble?

'I haven't told him. It was too soon after his marriage had broken up. I knew that the only important thing in his life right now was his baby. He even said that to me and I knew that the last thing he needed was the complication of getting into another relationship. I thought it was the last thing *I* needed, to be honest. I was only trying to help him show you that he would be the best father ever, whether he has a partner or not. I… I didn't mean to fall in love with him but… I'll always be there for him, if he wants me…'

'Of course he wants you.' Simone sounded as if she was crying now. 'It's obvious how much in love you two are.' She made a frustrated sound. 'Sorry, but I have to go,' she said. 'I'm going to be late for my appointment.'

'Okay. I hope everything's fine. Take care, Simone. And…thank you for listening.'

'Tell Nate…no…don't say anything. Could you just ask him to call me later? This evening, when I've had a chance to talk to Olly.'

Alice ended the call.

Her lunch break was over but she didn't make a move to leave this on-call room yet. She needed a moment to try and breathe through the emotional aftermath of that intense conversation.

It wasn't easy. Because this was the room where she and Nate had given in to the overwhelming level of attraction between them and broken through the conventional boundaries of friendship. She could remember every touch. Every kiss. Every murmured word. Had she really thought that she had pulled the plug before she fell in love with Nathaniel Madden by sticking to a new boundary of not staying a whole night with him? She'd lost any control over that long before then, hadn't she?

Maybe it had been when he'd told her how much he'd wanted to protect his baby from the moment he knew she'd been conceived.

Or had it been when she'd seen that plea for help in his eyes and she'd known that, if it was humanly possible, she would give him anything he asked for?

The real crunch had been the baby, though, hadn't it? Nicole's baby. When she'd been hit with the realisation that she wanted her own baby.

She just hadn't dared to acknowledge that it wasn't simply a baby she wanted.

It was the whole package. A family.

And there was only one person she would ever choose to create that family with.

Nate…

It had only taken the space of time it took to draw in a single deep breath for her brain to process the flash of her thoughts and feelings. It was her body's turn to react a heartbeat later, as it jerked in alarm at the sound from just outside the door of this room.

A door that she hadn't realised she'd left open that far.

A door that was opening even further as she watched it.

Her jaw dropped as she saw who was stepping into the room.

'*Nate?* Oh, my God…how long have you been out there?'

'Long enough.'

Alice could feel the colour draining from her face. 'I wasn't trying to interfere,' she said. 'I'm sorry… I might have even made things worse but… I couldn't *not* try to help. Because…because…'

Nate was closing the gap between them. 'Because you love me?'

He looked as though he was trying to smile but it wasn't quite working. The intensity in his eyes was overpowering anything else his face wanted to do. He was close enough to touch Alice now but he was simply standing there, in front of her.

'I love you, too,' he said. 'I've never felt like this about anyone. Ever. You're the best friend I've ever had. The best colleague. The absolutely best lover.' His lips curled a little but the embryonic smile faded just as fast. 'I knew I was pushing things further than you were comfortable with when I asked you to stay the night with me but, if I'm honest, that's what I want—every night for the rest of my life. I want to wake up and find you beside me every morning for the rest of my life.'

'But I'm not what's important right now,' Alice said, with a gulp. 'What matters most is Daisy.'

Incredibly, Nate's head made a side-to-side movement to contradict her.

'What matters most right now,' he said softly, 'is you, Alice Barlow. It was you who gave me the confidence to step up to being a single dad and get my life sorted. Who let me see that future I'd dreamed of by reminding me of what that Wendy house represented. It was you who gave me the strength and focus to do my job when there was a case where we could have lost a mother and baby and that could have derailed me.' He was really smiling now. 'It was you who reminded me of how much I loved my dad and how much I want to be like him for my own child. How much I want a family.'

Nate closed his eyes for a long blink as he took a new breath. And then he opened them again.

'You make me the best person I could be,' he added. 'And I need you in my life. In my family.' He was pulling Alice into his arms, now. 'You *are* my family.' His voice was raw. 'But I couldn't tell you that, not just because it's taken this long for me to see what's been in front of me all along but because of what you said that night you discovered that you hated Guinness.'

A huff of laughter escaped Alice.

'Do you remember what it was?'

She bit her lip. 'You mean about life being perfect with having no family at all? Or was it the bit about not wanting kids?'

Nate held her tighter by way of response. Was he holding his breath?

She looked up so that he could see her face properly. Her heart was hammering against her ribs.

This was it.

The moment where she could reach for a totally new future, if she was brave enough.

'You're not the only one who can go a long time with not seeing what's in front of you,' she told him. 'I've spent my whole life, ever since I gave that doll away to the girl down the street, believing that children are the last thing I would ever want. But you know when I saw the truth?'

'Yeah…' Nate's lips were on her hair. 'It was when you were holding Nicole's baby, wasn't it?'

Alice nodded.

'I knew the truth then, too, but I wasn't sure if you would believe it.'

The love Alice knew she had for this man was already filling her heart to bursting but this made it overflow.

She hadn't been ready to believe it then. He knew her *that* well. He understood just how huge that had been. He was always going to be there for her, just the way she would be for him. Helping her to be a better person than she could ever be without him.

There was so much she wanted to say but there were only three words that escaped her lips.

The ones that mattered the most.

'I love you…'

EPILOGUE

Three years later...

'Happy anniversary, darling.'

Alice Madden turned her head sharply, to where her husband was sitting beside her on a rustic wooden bench in the garden, her eyes wide with surprise. 'Oh, no… have I forgotten something important?'

Nate smiled at her. 'Think about it.'

Oh…the *love* in that smile…

Whatever it was, it had to be something to do with what Nathaniel loved most in the world—his family. Alice turned her gaze to where Daisy was playing on the veranda of the Wendy house, sitting on the top step with her tea set arranged around her chubby little legs.

It was only water in the teapot but Daisy was pouring it into the little plastic cup as if everything depended on not spilling a drop. It was too much of a challenge to get to her feet, holding the bright red cup without slopping water over the edge but Daisy didn't seem to mind. She was on her way from the Wendy house steps towards the wooden bench that Nate had built under the pohutukawa tree, a triumphant smile on her face.

'It's not Daisy's birthday,' Alice said. 'That's two

months away. Oh…did I tell you that Simone's coming up for the party? She said there was no way she was going to miss Daisy's third birthday—especially when it's a princess party. She's borrowed a crown from the kids' dress-up box and Olly's going to look after the kids for the night.'

'That man's a hero,' Nate said.

'He is,' Alice agreed. 'I will love him forever for standing back and letting you cut Daisy's umbilical cord.'

You're her father, he'd told Nate. *You need to do this.*

They'd arrived only minutes before Daisy made her appearance, after a mad dash to the airport and the assistance of people who knew them both from their work at Aratika. Someone in the control tower actually paused a plane from beginning to taxi out for take-off so that the air bridge could be opened again and allow two extra passengers on board. Nobody on the flight minded being held up. The pilot had apparently told them they were waiting for a dad who desperately wanted to be at his daughter's birth and they all clapped as Nate and Alice came aboard.

Olly was also a hero for whispering in Simone's ear not long after that, when Nate was holding his daughter for the first time and the medical staff were happy to leave the room, and he made the suggestion that saw him help his wife into a wheelchair and push her out of the room to leave Nate, Alice and baby Daisy alone for those first precious minutes of bonding as a brand new family.

Nearly three years ago. And here she was coming towards her parents, a very happy and healthy little girl.

Nate was watching her progress across the lawn. His daughter was watching him. Her smile widened and she was walking faster. She didn't seem to notice that more water had gone over the edge of the red cup.

'Cuppa tea,' she announced proudly as she got closer.

'Oh, thank you...' Alice reached out her hand but Daisy shook her head. 'For Dadda,' she said firmly.

Alice wasn't the least bit offended. She laughed aloud. 'You're such a daddy's girl,' she told Daisy. She threw Nate a sideways glance. 'Like me...' she murmured.

Nate winked at Alice but then gave his daughter his full attention as he gravely accepted the cup. There couldn't have been more than a teaspoon of water in the bottom by now but he made an impressive slurping noise as he pretended to drink it.

'That's the best cup of tea I think I've ever had,' he said.

Daisy beamed.

'Do you think Mumma might like one as well?'

Daisy nodded. She took the cup from Nate and turned around to toddle back to where her teapot was.

Alice was still smiling but she shook her head.

'It's not our wedding anniversary,' she said. 'We haven't even got to six months yet and I don't think either of us are going to forget our first anniversary.'

Nate let his breath out in a contented sigh. 'I'll never forget that day,' he vowed. He reached to pick up Alice's hand. 'That moment when I was standing right here, under this tree, and you came around the corner of the house and down the path in your wedding dress I knew that I was marrying the most beautiful woman in the world and that made me the happiest man on the planet.'

'And I was the happiest woman.' Alice echoed his sigh. 'And wasn't Daisy the cutest flower girl ever? The way she stopped every few steps and stared into her little basket and then picked out one rose petal at a time and had to crouch down to put it so carefully on the ground.'

She'd been wearing a pink dress that had flowers and butterflies embroidered on it. It had little pink wings attached to the back of it and there'd been a halo of flowers in Daisy's soft, dark curls.

She'd sat at their feet, taking out the rest of the rose petals, one at a time, from the basket, as Nate and Alice had exchanged their heartfelt vows and the rings.

'She was adorable,' Nate agreed.

Everybody would have agreed with that. Especially the celebrant. She'd just pronounced them husband and wife when Daisy discarded her basket, got to her feet and held out her arms.

'Up,' she commanded.

In Nate's arms a moment later, the celebrant had joined in the laughter of all the guests and pronounced them a family as well.

But, however wonderful those memories were, it wasn't what Nate was referring to.

'I'm good with dates,' Alice protested. 'What am I missing that's special enough for you to remember?'

'To be honest,' Nate admitted, 'I wouldn't have remembered this particular date if I hadn't upgraded my phone yesterday.'

Alice blinked. 'What's that got to do with it?'

'I was deleting some old photographs and messages.' Nate took his phone out of his pocket and swiped the screen. 'And I found this.' He handed the phone to Alice.

It was a text conversation that had happened, three years ago today, between Nate and Simone. Alice hadn't ever seen this even though she'd been sitting with Nate as it happened. She'd been too focused on watching his face and then too overwhelmed with the joy of its conclusion to ever ask to see exactly what had been said. Nate had sent the first message.

The signal's terrible. The call won't go through. Are you okay to text?

Yes. All good.

I have to confess—it was unintentional but I overheard Alice talking to you.

She loves you.

I know. I love her just as much.

I knew that. Have you told her?

Yes.

Does she want this baby as much as you do?

Yes. Absolutely.

I've talked to Olly. We think you're going to make a perfect family. We'll both be happy to sign the consent when it comes time for Daisy's adoption.

I can't tell you how happy I am.

I know. I also know that the love you have for each other is strong enough to last a lifetime. Never forget that, will you?

I won't. I promise.

    Alice didn't need to read the sign-off and arrangement to talk again soon. The words had blurred, anyway, and she was blinking as she handed the phone back to Nate.

'It's a date we should both remember from now on,' she said, leaning her head against Nate's shoulder. 'That was really the day we became a family, wasn't it?'

'It was.' Nate's arm went around her back to hold her against him.

They were both watching Daisy, who had finished pouring the second cup of 'tea' and was getting unsteadily to her feet. Most of the water was spilling.

'Just as well,' Nate muttered. 'That tea tasted a bit funny.'

Alice laughed but then stopped suddenly, with a tiny gasp.

'What?' Nate's head swerved. 'Is something wrong?'

'No…' Alice reached for his other hand and placed it, palm down, on her belly. 'I think I just felt the first real kick.'

She was only just beginning to show in this pregnancy and this was a real milestone.

'Did you feel that?'

Nate didn't need to say anything. He looked up and

caught Alice's gaze and she could see tears shining in his eyes.

Tears of joy.

'Mumma...' Daisy called. 'Here I come...'

But Alice was still holding Nate's gaze. 'Simone was right,' she said. 'I'm so glad I've got a lifetime to love you.'

Nate was leaning in to kiss her, his hand still on her belly. 'Me, too,' he whispered.

* * * * *

*Look out for the next story in
the Aratika Air Rescue Trilogy
Coming soon!
And if you enjoyed this story, check out these other
great reads from Alison Roberts*

Single Dad for the Daredevil Doctor
A Family Made in the ER
Single Dad's Christmas Wish

All available now!

OFF-LIMITS DOC ON DECK

LUANA DaROSA

MILLS & BOON

CHAPTER ONE

Day One, Naples

'You are by far the worst best friend I've ever had.' In Catalina's mind, it was a fair assessment to lob at Amelie Morgan, her—soon-to-be-former—best friend since medical school. She narrowed her eyes in a glare to make sure the message came across.

From the screen of her phone, Amelie looked up at her with huge eyes and a frown so devastating it looked more cartoon than human.

'Cat, I'm sorry! You know I wanted to be there with you, but I can't get on a cruise ship like this.' She lifted her leg into view of the camera, showing off the cast on her leg.

'Again, why did you think riding a horse for the first time was a good idea right before shipping out on a cruise?' She pushed down on the twinge of guilt in her chest threatening to replace her anger.

Catalina hadn't been there when the accident happened a few days ago. They'd finished their internships a few weeks ago at Alexander Attano Memorial, and while Catalina had gone back to visit her family in the Dominican Republic, Amelie had apparently decided she'd always wanted to be a show jumper.

Though bearing in mind how aggravating—as usual—

her visit home had been, she wasn't sure she wouldn't trade places with her best friend despite the injury. She'd take anything to avoid her family.

'You know my parents didn't let me do anything adventurous when I was younger. Growing up, it was always "study this, grades that". And it's not like we had any time to do fun stuff during med school or in our internship year.' Amelie let out a dramatic sigh, sinking back into the mountain of pillows Catalina could see she was propped up against.

'You get a piercing or an ill-advised tattoo if you have these urges. What you don't do is pretend to be an experienced rider and fall off a horse.' She understood wanting to have fun. Hell, the reason she was weaving through a crowded port in Naples was that they'd decided joining a cruise as working crew would be fun.

Now Catalina was going solo. No, not true. She *wished* she were on her own. But instead—

'*Your brother?* Of all people, your replacement is Theodore?' She knew complaining to Amelie was a mistake. The two siblings were day and night but somehow still thick as thieves. How they got along as well as they did was a mystery for the ages. Like when you tried to plug in a USB thing it was somehow always the wrong way around twice.

It made no sense to think about it because her brain would simply fold in on itself.

Where her best friend was bright and bubbly and over the top, her brother was a surly, broody hunk. That a man this strait-laced was also one of the most beautiful people she'd ever met was no doubt some cosmic joke. The powers that be had looked at Catalina specifically and thought, *On top of middle child syndrome and hyper-competitive-*

ness, let's also give her a hot best friend with an even hotter older brother. But said older brother looks at her like she's gum on his shoe. Oh, and let's make her a virgin. What a lark!

Amelie covered her face with her free hand, and Catalina thought she caught the flash of a grin. It only deepened her scowl. 'I didn't know what to do, Cat. They told me I needed to find someone else or pay a fine since they are required to have a certain level of staffing. Nautical law or something like that.'

Catalina raised an eyebrow. 'Maritime law?'

'Pretty sure it's nautical law. But whatever, it doesn't matter. I'm really sorry I can't go, but Theo also needed to get busy again, so it's not the worst timing. He's been living the hermit life for too long.' Amelie pulled a face. 'He's grown a beard!'

A flash of heat pulsed through Catalina, bright and quick and gone before she could dwell on the picture of a bearded Theo.

Some of Catalina's annoyance fell away, giving way to a tiny spark of sympathy. Not too much, considering who they were talking about. She'd heard of Theo's burnout and his subsequent quitting as the head of emergency medicine at Morgan Greywater Institute—his family's hospital. *His* hospital.

Everyone had heard of it. Or at least everyone who had even a tiny interest in the goings-on of the medical world. Morgan Greywater was the hospital group at the forefront of medical science and innovation. Whenever any new technique was pioneered or any breakthrough got announced, chances were high it came from Morgan Greywater.

And Theo had been raised to carry the family legacy

forward, according to Amelie. Even though she'd gone into medicine, just as their parents had expected their children to, Amelie had soon discovered she wasn't about the legacy life. Instead of doing her internship at the family hospital, she'd chosen to go to the same hospital as Catalina, and so they'd spent the last year living together in Chicago.

'Maybe you can convince him to shave it. It's not a good look on him.' Amelie shook her head. 'But just like…ignore him. You're not the only two people on the medical crew.'

'Avoid each other? Amelie, we booked *one* cabin. I'm stuck in a cabin with your *brother*.' The thought was so outlandish, renewed waves of heat flooded through her. Clearly her body was rebelling against the idea.

'Oh, right…' Wait, Amelie hadn't considered that when she'd asked Theo to sub in for her? 'But it was two beds, right?'

'I sure hope so. Otherwise, your brother is going to sleep on the floor.' The surrounding noise grew louder as more people arrived at the port. Catalina followed the path signposting check-in for any staff. The queue grew longer as she stood there, glaring down at her phone.

'There you go. I knew you'd have a plan. Put up a privacy curtain, and you won't even know he's there. I promise you. As kids, I would randomly poke him for a sign of life because he was so quiet.' A small smile spread over Amelie's lips at the fond memory, and Catalina reminded herself to remain annoyed at her best friend even as her heart softened.

She didn't have memories like that about her seven siblings. Or maybe she did, but they were buried beneath far too complex dynamics for her to recall. Whenever she recalled them now, all she could think about was how she and her older siblings had been wrapped up in an unhealthy rivalry around who could get the most attention from their parents. And how she'd *become* the parent to her younger siblings when no one else stepped up for them.

Catalina pushed the thoughts away.

'Look, why don't you get on board and see how it goes? You might even have fun.'

'Doubtful.' Catalina blew out a breath. 'But at least I have access to the ship's pharmaceutical stash. If I can't stand him, I'll just give myself a sedative for the next three weeks.'

'That's the spirit.' Amelie's laugh sounded more genuine than before, and despite her resolve to stay mad, Catalina felt a glimmer of excitement. She had been looking forward to the cruise for so long and couldn't quite quash the anticipation bubbling beneath her reluctant acceptance.

Thanks to a last-minute dropout from the regular staff roster—and Amelie's countless connections in the medical world—they'd been able to get a contract for the duration of this one cruise. Without a plan on what to do next in her professional life, spending some time exploring the most beautiful parts of Europe while still keeping her skills somewhat honed seemed like the perfect opportunity.

In a life mainly lived to impress others—her parents, tutors, siblings—this was the first thing she was doing just for herself. Not even her best friend's grumpy older brother, who she'd inexplicably had a small crush on since the day they'd met, even though he'd shown literally no interest in her.

'Fine. Getting on the ship now—I'll talk to you later.'

'Love ya, Cat. It'll be great!'

She hung up and shoved her phone into her backpack, as if the act could physically silence the echo of Amelie's optimism. The line in front of her crawled forward, punctuated by the chatter of fellow crew. And even though Amelie wasn't here—and her stupid, sexy brother Theo *was*—Catalina reminded herself that this was *her* time. Her opportunity to let go and find herself outside of work so that the idea of finding her next steps in her career didn't feel so daunting. Find out who she was outside of her role as the middle child of a huge family, always vying for attention by performing even though she knew she wasn't ever going to get the praise she coveted.

Finally see the world with her own eyes instead of living vicariously through the hundreds of travel influencers she followed on Instagram.

Because doing things because they were the *right* things to do hadn't got her any closer to getting acknowledged. Not even after she'd spent years—and hundreds of thousands of dollars—going to med school, thinking that surely with those two letters at the end of her name, she'd get some acknowledgement from her parents. She still remembered the day when she'd shown them her medical licence. *Catalina Reyes, MD*. She also remembered the silence that had followed. And the rather affected 'Good job, *mija*,' before her mother went on to tell Catalina about her sister Sonya and how she was pregnant again.

Twenty-six years she'd tried to impress her parents, get them to tell her how proud they were of her. How well she'd done to carve her own way without help from the family. And what did she have to show for it? She was a whole-ass adult—a *doctor*, for crying out loud—and she was still a virgin. She also had no idea what she wanted to do with her life professionally, but that was a problem she would tackle after the cruise.

This cruise was supposed to be her chance to change her personal life. To stop performing and start living. To let go, maybe hook up with someone hot and emotionally unavailable, and finally close the chapter on her overachiever virgin era. But without Amelie there to play distraction and hype woman, and with Theodore 'fun sponge' Morgan as her new roommate, the odds weren't exactly in her favour.

The thought of Theo sent a nervous jitter through her, and Catalina ignored it, opting to stare at the sleek white hull of the ship as it appeared before her like a promise.

Who cared if Amelie wasn't here? She could do this, right? Could have some no-strings-attached fun? Learn how to live like the rest of the population, who weren't constantly wondering if they were doing their parents proud. Craving the attention and never getting it no matter what.

Shaking those thoughts off, Catalina gripped the handle of her suitcase more tightly as she approached the check-in area. So what if Amelie wasn't here? She could do this on her own. Not a big deal. Like, at all. Right?

'Welcome to *The Aurelian*!' a bright-eyed receptionist greeted Catalina when she stepped into the little foyer somewhere in the lower half of the ship. The name tag read *Sam, they/them* and their smile set Catalina at ease. Well, kind of at ease. There was still the Theo-shaped shadow looming over her, and even though she told herself not to care, her eyes darted around, scanning the face of each crew member as they stepped into the foyer.

He was nowhere to be seen. Bummer. No, wait. Good. Or was it? This entire thing with Theo had her so turned around, Catalina didn't know how to feel. So she pushed it away, focusing on Sam instead.

'Thank you, I'm excited to be here,' she said as she handed her ID over to Sam for them to find her details in the system, wishing for the words to ring true in her mind.

She *was* excited, even without Amelie. 'I'm part of the medical crew led by Dr Chen. She sent an email that orientation would be later in the afternoon.' Catalina knew she still had several hours to get settled in, yet she still flicked her wrist to look at her watch as if to confirm time hadn't suddenly skipped ahead.

Sam smiled, their eyes scanning over the screen in front of them. 'Ah, I have you here. Here is your starter package.' They pulled a sleek navy box from behind the desk, the ship's crest stamped in gold foil on the lid.

'Your crew kit. Everyone gets a badge to identify them as crew, a map to the ship for those first few days when it seems labyrinthian, and some coupons for services like the movie theatre and the spa.'

Catalina's eyes went wide, her fingers skating over the crest embossed in the cardboard. Amelie had talked about all the amenities of the ship and what they could do on their days off, but now that she was riding solo she didn't know what to do with any of their plans. Would it be weird to show up on her own for everything? Would she even try?

Between the two, Amelie was the more adventurous one, dragging Catalina along with her regardless of her willingness to participate. But what was the alternative? Sitting in her cabin for three weeks, scrolling through her phone until she knew every corner of the internet? She'd spent so much time on the virgin side of TikTok, figuring out her game plan to finally take that step. Amelie had promised to make herself scarce, but now with Theo…

Heat rushed to Catalina's cheeks at the thought of her involuntary roommate. No chance she would bring anyone to her cabin when *he* would be there. Talk about awkward.

Maybe Amelie had been right. Maybe she could just ignore him. Pretend he was a ghost. A sexy, judging ghost.

'Your room assignment is in there, too. Let me find the key for you,' Sam continued, opening a drawer filled with white keycards sorted alphabetically. When they got to the letter R, they flipped open the pouch and pulled out a few cards, reading the Post-it notes on them before dropping them back in the drawer. 'Strange... I can't find your keycard in here.' Their frown deepened when they looked back up at their screen. 'Oh, right. You are sharing accommodation with someone. Let me check if the cards are under your roommate's name.'

Theo wasn't even here yet and it was already becoming hard to ignore him. She'd been happy to let Amelie handle everything cruise-related, but now that Theo was in the picture she needed to make it clear they were two separate entities.

'We definitely need two keys and receive things in duplicate,' Catalina explained while watching Sam rifle through the drawer. 'I was supposed to room with someone else, my bestie. But now I'm stuck with her brother, who has this gigantic stick up his—'

A shadow fell over Catalina. One that smelled like expensive sandalwood. A scent that shouldn't feel familiar, and yet... A shiver ran down her spine, and she knew what—who—her senses were warning her of, just as she turned around.

Theodore Morgan was somehow even taller than she remembered, and she had to crane her neck to look up at him. His expression was an unimpressed scowl directed towards her. At this point, she would have thought she'd be immune to his glares since they'd accompanied her through his final year at med school.

But no. Her heart still sped up, almost leaping into her mouth, which was suddenly as dry as a desert. Sweat slicked her palms as Catalina gripped her starter box to her chest.

She should say something, right? Only what? Because the thing she wanted to say—*I hate your sister for sticking me with you*—didn't seem like a good way to start their forced roommate-ship.

Luckily, she didn't have to come up with anything, for Theo said, 'You were saying?'

Catalina blinked several times, the low tone of his voice sending a *zing* through her. Stupid voice. 'I didn't say anything to you.'

'But you were about to say something to Sam.' He tilted his head to the side, eyes flicking up and down her body—appraising. No, *judging*. The way he always looked at her when they saw each other. 'Something about a stick I have somewhere?'

Heat crept up her neck, flushing into her cheeks. 'Oh, you... How long have you been standing there?' Of course he'd heard her talk trash about him. Why wouldn't he? After all, what would be more hilarious than the man she was forced to share a cabin with standing right behind her when she called him uptight?

The corner of his mouth twitched, and she could practically see the disdain ooze from that little gesture. What had Catalina ever done to him that he held her in such low regard? Yeah, sure, she and Amelie were annoying at times, and could have been considered *obnoxious* in their younger years. But really, wasn't their amusement at him his fault for being so strait-laced?

'Long enough. Came back here because it looked like there were two keys in my envelope.' His hand disappeared into his pocket, and when it came back up he held a white keycard with the ship's branding between his fingers. 'Didn't want my *roommate* to get stuck waiting for me. Despite what she has to say about me.'

Catalina's eyes flared. From the corner of her vision, she could see Sam shuffling on the spot. No doubt that was a first for them, too. Or did colleagues and crewmates often have tense discussions within an hour of boarding?

Before Theo could drag this out any more, Catalina snatched the keycard from his fingers and slapped it on top of her starter box while giving him the best version of a withering glare she could muster. Not that it affected Theo. His mouth remained pressed into a thin line, every twitch in his expression signalling how utterly unimpressed he was with her. Well, he could get in line. Catalina had more than enough experience vying for people's attention and running herself into the ground while doing so.

But that era of her life was over. She was here to choose herself for once. Let go of the incessant need to prove herself to get the attention she'd craved all her life, only for it to be yanked away from her. For the goalposts to move and put her further away from simple acknowledgement.

'Thanks for bringing me my keycard, Theodore. If you don't mind, I will settle in before orientation.' Catalina turned away, taking a steadying breath through her nose, and then shot Theo a look over her shoulder. 'Amelie was right: you look ridiculous with a beard.'

Then she stalked away, as fast as she dared to without giving away how saying that had made her voice wobble. And from behind her, she could have sworn she heard an incredulous laugh.

CHAPTER TWO

Day One, at sea

'And that should all be sufficient for you to do your jobs. The first shift starts as of right now, and there will be a continuous presence in the med bay until we arrive back here in three weeks' time. You can access your individual shift plan through the app.' Dr Sarah Chen looked around the conference room filled with doctors, nurses and various support staff, then nodded their dismissal.

Theo had already looked around the facilities earlier in the day, having had a quick chat with Dr Chen to introduce himself. During the conversation it had become clear she was aware he was one of *the* Morgans, and so was his sister. Apparently, Amelie hadn't played up that particular fact.

She never did. Unlike himself, his sister had managed to divorce herself from the family name—from the weight attached to it. Even all these years later, he couldn't figure out how she'd done it. How she'd swatted away the expectations of their parents as if they were mere suggestions. As if she hadn't been raised to support a dynasty of medical excellence where failure couldn't be accepted.

Like, for example, facing burnout and quitting the job he'd been raised to do since he was old enough to make memories. Yeah, that hadn't gone over well with his parents, who not only owned the hospital but had also installed him as the head of emergency medicine at Morgan Greywater.

The sound of chairs scraping over the hardwood floor filled the room as people got to their feet. Then soft murmuring followed as people introduced themselves to their new co-workers for the next three weeks. Theo caught the names of the different cities people wanted to visit as they checked the schedule, trying to match their time off to specific stops the ship would take.

He didn't care much about any of this. His presence here was a favour to his sister. One he was coming to regret more the longer he spent on this ship. Which wasn't a good sign, since it had only been a few hours since they'd set sail—could he even say sail when there were none on this ship?—and had left Naples behind.

'Theodore.' A shadow fell over him as he heard his name, and even though he knew the voice—somehow even knew the cadence of the steps—he wasn't prepared to be back in her orbit.

There were a few reasons not to be thrilled. He was trapped on a floating piece of steel where the preferred way of consuming food was buffet-style—hello, salmonella. His work wasn't exactly what he would call challenging, though that might be a good thing considering he was still recovering from burnout.

But the biggest reason Theo couldn't shake his dark mood had appeared in the form of Dr Catalina Reyes. Ever since they'd met in the lobby, she'd been hovering at the edges of his perception.

'Dr Reyes,' he replied, and got a derisive snort from her in response.

'Really, that's how we're going to do this? Titles?' Her

honeyed voice rolled over him, drowning out the noise of the room. One minute into the conversation, and he was already losing his grip on his thoughts. Just as he had when he'd spotted her in the foyer, talking to the receptionist about all the reasons why she hated being near him.

And despite knowing that, he couldn't keep his eyes off Catalina.

'Given we are colleagues now, I thought you'd appreciate some decorum. Or maybe that's not something you're used to from your time at Attano Memorial?' Theo couldn't resist the jibe. Even though his feelings for Morgan Greywater weren't the best ones, the pride in his family's legacy—of his name—was hard to shake.

Spending the last year of med school in close proximity to Catalina, thanks to his sister, he'd learned of her fierce competitiveness, and recognised the signs here as well. She'd spent the entire orientation perched at the front of the room, notes jotted so furiously into her phone it was a wonder the device didn't catch fire.

Given they were on a cruise ship, where most of their patients would have either minor injuries, alcohol-related ailments or the aforementioned food poisoning, he wasn't sure how she planned on channelling her hyper-competitive spirit.

He'd tried not to stare at her throughout Dr Chen's presentation, but it was as if his eyes had developed a will of their own, constantly going back to her in quiet observation.

She'd gathered her coily hair into a puff at the top of her head. It was a practical style but drew his attention to the graceful curve of her neck, the smooth, dark brown skin catching the light. She was wearing a simple white T-shirt, loose but somehow accentuating the lines of her body, and he'd had to force his gaze away before she'd caught him in his silent assessment.

She looked him up and down, frowning. 'You know, when I imagined this cruise, I thought it would be with Amelie. Champagne. Bad decisions. Possibly one good one.' Her eyes dragged over him pointedly. 'Instead, I get Broody McJudgy and a buffet full of norovirus.'

He stared at her, trying not to look amused at the impromptu nickname. Catalina had always had this disarming quality about her, and Theo wasn't about to fall for it now when it hadn't worked on him during their time at med school either.

'You think I'm super excited to be here instead of literally anywhere else?' he asked with more bite than necessary, but it was what came out of his mouth.

When it came to Catalina, he couldn't help himself. The moment he was in her vicinity—since they'd first met in med school—a subtle undercurrent needled at him, demanding all of his attention be on her.

Theo couldn't explain it. He didn't *desire* her. The thought was ridiculous. She was an uninhibited ball of chaos, chasing down opportunities and victories where they didn't exist. A small part of him admired the utter lack of inhibition because it stood in such stark contrast to his own life and how he'd been raised. Always proper, representing the Morgan family, and never allowed to stray for even a moment.

Maybe that was why Amelie had asked him to stay away from her best friend. When she'd asked him to sub in for her here, the warning had struck him. Why had she thought it was necessary to point it out? Now that she was towering over him, pillowy lips downturned and brown eyes pinning him with a combative stare, he felt himself drawn into the challenge he saw in her eyes—even if he didn't understand it.

'No, and I think everyone else can tell you are here against your will. Like, can you try to look a bit less like a hostage and more like a person who had a choice in being here?' Catalina crossed her arms, mouth pressed into a thin line. 'Or is this some burnout thing you still got going on? Amelie warned me about the beard, but I didn't think your personality could get even more sour.'

The prickle of heat Theo had sensed in the back of his neck disappeared as one word rang in his ears. *Burnout*. He shouldn't be surprised Amelie had shared his history with her best friend, yet a part of him had hoped he wouldn't have to explain anything. Come to think of it, why should he explain himself to her? He hadn't asked to be here or to be anywhere near her.

Catalina's eyes widened, her mouth dropping open in an O-shape. 'Sorry, that didn't come out right. I meant—'

Rising to his feet, Theo stuffed his hands into his pockets and shot her his best withering glare over the hammering of his heart. She didn't know. Didn't know how bad it had been at the end, or what it had cost him. She couldn't know because he hadn't told Amelie the whole story either of how he'd crashed out during a shift and had simply never returned to Morgan Greywater.

'Sorry to disappoint,' he said, each word clipped, and then he turned away from her and walked out of the conference room.

Only apparently Catalina had decided they weren't done yet. The clicking of heels followed him only briefly as the wooden floor gave way to carpet, and he heard her call his name behind him. Then her hand wrapped around his bicep, forcing him to stop if he didn't want to drag her around the ship like a rag doll.

He turned around, looking her up and down, and when he noticed the electric-purple suitcase she was dragging behind her, he paused. Looking back at Catalina, a sheepish smile split her lips.

'What's in your luggage that you felt the need to drag it around all day?' He'd given her the key to his cabin—*their* cabin—right after they'd embarked a few hours ago. Wanting to give her some space to unpack, he'd found a quiet corner of the ship to go over his missed messages and emails. Most of them were from his parents, demanding answers he didn't have. Those remained unread.

'Well, funny you should ask. You see...' Catalina looked down to where her hand was clutching the white keycard. 'After I said goodbye to you—'

'After you stormed away while insulting my beard, yes.'

Colour rose to her cheeks, giving them an even softer glow. 'After I said goodbye and went to look for the cabin, I realised I didn't know which one was mine.'

Theo couldn't keep the smirk off his face. A few seconds ago he'd wanted nothing more than to get away from her before she could say anything else about his burnout and what her thoughts were on his utter failure as the head of emergency medicine at the hospital his parents had built from scratch. The one they'd expected to leave in his hands before he'd torched his life.

Something about Catalina—watching her stare at her hands in clear discomfort at having to ask *him* for a favour—cleared his head more than a meditative walk along the shoreline ever could. For a second, he forgot about the life events that had brought him here and could focus on the ease that was the antagonistic pattern he and Catalina had developed over the years.

'I see, so you've been wandering around the boat since earlier with your luggage, unsure where to put it. Why didn't you just call me?' Theo was pretty sure she didn't have his number, but details like that had never mattered to them when they sniped at each other.

His eyes dipped down to her lips when he noticed a muscle move in her jaw, enjoying the sight far more than he should. But focusing on that was better than trying to reconcile the changes in his life and where things would go after the cruise. Maybe that was why his sister had warned him to stay clear of her best friend. Catalina was already turning out to be an excellent distraction, and they'd spent no more than five minutes together.

'This is a ship, not a boat,' she said, and Theo couldn't help but laugh at the pure defiance in her voice. Not that it helped their situation as her glare turned angry.

'You've been part of the crew for a few hours and already an expert on all things boats—pardon, *ships*?'

Catalina let out a huff. 'A boat is smaller and can be controlled by an individual or a small team of people. A ship carries cargo or passengers and needs an entire crew to operate. Did you see how big the medical staff alone is here? Therefore, we are clearly on a ship.' Her sparkling brown eyes narrowed on him, and the sight affected him far more than it should. 'Did you do any research before coming here?'

Of course he had. From the moment he'd been born, he'd been trained by his parents to be the most type-A personality to ever walk the earth. But it was more fun to pretend otherwise.

'Not really. Amelie sent me some of the crap she'd researched, but it seemed frivolous.'

'Frivolous?' Catalina's voice pitch became higher, filling him with an inappropriate amount of glee.

He shrugged, playing at nonchalant. 'You know, things like "Top Ten Things to Do in Dubrovnik" or "Don't miss these three spots in Santorini". Not really helpful to life on a ship.'

'There was a lot more information in there outside of things to do in Santorini if you'd read it all carefully enough. Like a list of the most likely ailments we would encounter here, or what to do in case of an emergency.' Her speech sped up as she rattled off the information, and part of him wanted to let her know he'd read it all. And that he knew Catalina had been the one to put it all together. He knew his sister, and she had got all the spontaneity in the family.

'Is it buffets infested with norovirus?' he asked, recalling her previous comment.

'That's a big risk, believe it or not. But that's not why I followed you.' Her grip on her luggage tightened, tension flickering across her knuckles. 'Can you just show me the room?'

Right, the room they were supposed to share. There was no way that was going to happen, though Theo hadn't devoted much time to figuring out how to solve that particular problem. After dropping his stuff off, he'd needed a moment to regroup and make a plan of how the hell he was going to survive the next three weeks on this *ship*. One thing had become clear: there was no way they could share a room. Especially not *that* room.

He thought about telling her the glaring issue he'd encountered the moment he'd opened the door. But then he decided it would be funnier if she saw it with her own eyes.

'Fine, let's go,' he said, turning around and waving her along.

They weaved through different parts of the ship, taking the lift up with a group of people who had already hit the bar far harder than Theo would recommend this early in the afternoon. He looked at her over his shoulder when the lift stopped on the crew deck and felt her presence behind him as a prickle at the back of his neck.

The corridor buzzed with the thousand tiny operations that kept a ship like this from veering into chaos, despite feeling like chaos itself. Cabin doors clicked open and shut, voices scooted from room to room and the faint briny tang of the ocean soaked even the recycled air. Theo led them down two bends in the hall, then another, leading them into the bowels of the ship where the crew accommodation was.

He stopped in front of a nondescript door. The vinyl letters beside it read CREW DECK 8, CABIN 1264, and a tiny plastic placard below that read MORGAN/REYES, MD.

Theo let himself take a moment to appreciate the symmetry of their names, side by side like that. Only to quickly realise what he'd just done and push the thought away. They didn't live in a world where such a thought could move from fantasy to reality, and it was time he got a grip on it. Not in the *before,* where he'd played too big a role in his family's legacy to let anyone get tangled up in the mess and misery that involved. And now, in the *after,* his life was a burning wreckage. In neither version had his attraction to his little sister's best friend ever made any sense.

It was unfortunate that now he faced three weeks of close proximity to her.

Theo tapped his keycard. 'After you.'

She entered and stopped dead. A laugh—almost a bark—escaped her. 'You have got to be kidding me.'

There it stood, just the way Theo remembered from when he'd arrived here a few hours ago: the single queen-sized bed jammed up against the far wall.

Catalina whirled around, eyes narrowed on him just as he entered. 'Did you do this?' she asked, and he couldn't swallow the incredulous snort.

'Yes, of course I planned this. When Amelie begged me to sub in for her so she wouldn't have to pay the contract termination fine, I thought to myself: You know what would make this whole thing even more *fun*? Sleeping in the same bed as my sister's best friend.'

She cut him a glare which, granted, he deserved for being a smartass. Something he needed to check himself over the next three weeks. Regressing to petty insults and jabs wasn't becoming of a doctor of his status. Even if doing so let him step away from the mess inside his head. As much as he wanted to, using Catalina to escape his own head was probably why Amelie had even felt the need to warn him about not doing anything 'inappropriate' with her best friend.

Stepping into the room, Catalina dropped her luggage on the rack with a *thunk* and then spun around once, inspecting the room. He watched her face as she twirled again, her eyes darting into every corner of the room. She frowned as she came to the same conclusion he'd reached when he had first come into the cabin.

'What about—'

'There's only a shower. No bathtub. Already checked. Not that I'd recommend either of us sleep in a bathtub for three weeks.' Theo had already made the decision to leave the room to Catalina and see if the ship had any open rooms. Even if he had to pay for his own room on the passenger side, he'd be happier than sleeping next to Catalina for the next three weeks. Not when he was already enjoying himself way too much in her presence.

Strange how a bit of needling could get him out of his head when nothing else had post-burnout.

'So...are we going to fight over it?' Catalina asked, her voice loud in the small space. 'Or is this one of those free-for-alls where we both pretend not to care and then one of us cracks and sleeps on the floor?'

'There isn't really much floor to go around,' he replied, gesturing at their feet. Another thing he'd contemplated earlier and decided it wasn't a feasible option to solve this problem. But he was having too much fun watching her squirm to let her off the hook just yet. 'We could top and tail, strictly back-to-back. Minimal contact guaranteed.'

She rolled her eyes. 'Thank you for the helpful suggestion, Theodore. Clearly, you've never shared a double bed with three siblings before.' She crossed her arms and leaned against the desk, and Theo kept his eyes trained on her face even as he felt them draw downwards.

He forced a shrug, not admitting to either of them the effect her proximity had on him. 'No, I was busy being installed as the future of Western medicine. You know, the thing that sent me into...what did you call it? The *burnout thing*?'

Theo wasn't sure why he went there. What had led to his abrupt departure at Morgan Greywater was something he kept under lock and key. Amelie had tried multiple times to talk to him about it but he'd found he couldn't even mention what had happened. How he felt.

Now he stood here making jokes about the pressure

under which he'd cracked, as if his decisions hadn't upended his life. This was not good.

Though his sister would argue that escape was something he desperately needed, it wasn't what he was looking for. But the relief of the pressure when he was near Catalina was already so seductive, he needed to stay away if he actually wanted to *work* through his issues during the cruise rather than drown himself in the next distraction.

Catalina didn't answer right away. For a moment, she just watched him, the teasing in her eyes dimmed to something quieter. Then, as if snapping herself out of it, she gave a shrug and turned to unzip her suitcase.

'Well, if you're planning on being insufferable, I call the right side.'

Theo snorted. 'I'll alert the media,' he said again because he couldn't help himself with her. He'd better leave now before she could drag him into something neither of them really wanted. 'I'll be back later. Need to talk some stuff through with Dr Chen.'

Theo didn't wait for her to look up from her packing, retracing his steps until he was back at the lifts. With each step, the knot in his chest that had eased during their entire conversation tightened again, reminding him of the work still in front of him. The cruise wasn't a chance to escape his life. No, he was doing it as a favour to his sister. Instead of getting distracted, he needed to spend his free time examining his life and figuring out where he was headed.

He had no job, no career, and his abrupt departure had left his reputation in tatters. After years of grinding, never-ending work, his professional contributions had been reduced to nothing. And he had no idea what he was supposed to do about that. If he had ever belonged in such a high-ranking position in the first place.

And yet, as he stepped into the lift and pressed the button to return to the reception area, his thoughts weren't on how to rebuild. They weren't on where he wanted to go with his life, either.

All he could think about was the smell of coconut butter on supple skin as he'd stood far too close to Catalina.

CHAPTER THREE

Day Four, at sea

THERE WERE FAR fewer opportunities to let her hair down than Catalina had anticipated. Yesterday they'd stopped in Kefalonia, but she had a shift at the clinic on that day and hadn't been able to leave the ship at all. Since then, they'd been at sea, crossing over the Ionian Sea on their way towards Corfu. Her heart had kicked up a beat standing on deck and watching the white stone walls appear. All her life, she hadn't even thought about going to Greece once. With a family as big as hers, their holidays had consisted of local adventures to different places in the Dominican Republic. Catalina hadn't set foot on a plane until her interview for med school in the United States.

Now she finally got to see the world. Sure, she got to see it in between treating mild cases of alcohol poisoning, the common cold and—surprisingly—an STI on her first day, but the point was, she was doing it. Seeing the world.

She was, however, not doing *it*. And with the situation she found herself in, she wasn't sure if project 'Cat loses her virginity' was still on. When she'd told Amelie she wanted to find someone to pop her cherry during the cruise, her best friend had squealed in excitement and promised she would vacate the room if she ever needed to bring her designated lover there.

Catalina wasn't sure Theo would extend the same courtesy. She certainly wasn't about to ask. Mainly because the only time she'd seen him had been in the clinic. Had he found somewhere else to sleep? He certainly hadn't come to the cabin at any point in the last four days; she would have noticed that. Still, what if he did come back the moment she asked someone to join her in bed?

The wind picked up as the ship approached the port. It tore at her clothes—a floral summer dress cinched tight at the waist and flaring out in a voluminous skirt—and a laugh slipped through her lips as Corfu's sun-washed villas and terracotta roofs gleamed against the hills thick with cypress and olive trees.

'Never seen anyone this excited to arrive at Corfu.' Theo's familiar drawl made her turn around and she watched him approach.

She hated how her breath hitched in her throat as her eyes roamed over him. Okay, yeah, he was a beautiful man. She avoided the word *handsome* because somehow it didn't seem enough. He wasn't just intruding in the space of beautiful people, but he might actually have founded the club. Not that it mattered too much because his beauty didn't come with a kind personality. Quite the opposite.

'How many people have you seen arrive in Corfu in general?' she asked, crossing her arms in front of her to protect herself from his aura as well as to stop her hands from doing anything foolish like reaching out.

'That's fair enough. Let me rephrase: I don't think I've ever seen *you* this excited about anything.' He stepped next to her at the railing, leaning his hip against the metal bar, and looked out at the sea.

'Well, you haven't seen much of me since leaving med school.' She wasn't sure if the reminder was for him or for herself. Occasionally, Catalina had travelled back with Amelie to New York City, where the Morgan clan had built their empire, to celebrate Christmas and Thanksgiving. Amelie's family was plenty dysfunctional, but still miles ahead of the mess awaiting her back home in San Cristóbal. At least the Morgan parents had cared about their children's careers and pushed them towards excellence.

Whereas Catalina might as well not have bothered going to med school and becoming a doctor, her parents cared so little. Whenever she'd called them to tell them anything about her life—about her achievements—they had the same thing to say: *'That's nice, dear'*. Followed by whatever impressive thing Esteban, her oldest brother, had done. Like she gave a single crap that Esteban had added another van to the growing fleet of vehicles he rented out when she had helped to literally save someone's life on the same day.

Another problem Catalina had planned to deal with during her time on the cruise: her professional future. When starting her internship, she'd thought she would go into a specialty straight away. But the closer she'd got to the end, the less appealing the thought had become. But she *had* to continue her education, right? Pick a career path and excel at it, the way she always had.

What else could she do, if not the one thing she knew she was good at?

'The walls are so bright, it looks almost fake. More like a painting than real life,' he said, repeating her own thoughts from earlier almost verbatim, and ripping her out of her spiralling career crisis thoughts.

She shot him a sidelong glance, trying hard not to appreciate what she was seeing. Because he wasn't wearing what she would call typically Theo clothes. Even during the family holidays she'd spent at the Morgan estate, he'd worn what could only be described as business casual: a button-up shirt and chinos that were starched to oblivion and back. To the point where she'd been astounded about his ability to sit down. It was how he presented in front of patients in the clinic, too.

They'd worked together over the last few days, and the word *together* was doing a lot of heavy lifting. Occasionally they'd see each other as they popped their heads into the waiting room and asked people to come through. Unlike a structured GP clinic, their patients were all walk-ins, and they saw quite a few patients an hour. Which meant lots of bumping into each other.

Though today Theodore Morgan was wearing a loose white linen shirt and a pair of dark brown trousers of the same fabric and style. And Catalina couldn't swallow the surprised gasp when her eyes got all the way down to his feet.

'Are you wearing sandals?' The words shot out of her mouth before she could consider whether she even wanted to engage in more conversation with him. The answer was most likely no.

'Oh...yeah.' Theo looked down as well, as if he couldn't remember putting them on. 'Amelie gifted them to me.'

'I didn't take you as someone who'd wear sandals.'

'I don't. When my sister gave them to me, she said, "I've never seen you wear sandals so you must want some".' He chuckled, the sound low and strangely addictive. Catalina wouldn't mind hearing it again.

'That sounds just like her. You should see our apartment in Chicago. It's filled to the brim with things she thought we could-slash-would use one day. Including a bread maker that's still in its original box.'

Something about their conversation was off, though Catalina couldn't figure out what it was. Maybe how easy-going it was? After sniping at each other the entire time on their first day, she'd thought the trend would continue whenever they saw each other. Except the only times they *had* seen each other had been at work. Which was odd, given...

'How come you haven't been back to our cabin?' she asked. She'd had the thought before but had put it off because a part of her didn't want to look beneath that rock if she didn't need to. Especially if this particular rock meant he might have found some other person he *didn't* mind sharing a bed with.

Catalina swatted the thought away so fast it had no time to sink its teeth into her.

'Oh? Miss me that much?' He smirked, running a hand through his short hair, the movement slow and deliberate.

She let out a sigh. 'Is this how it's going to be? Each time we see each other we either behave like children sniping at each other or like strangers?'

Theo turned to look at her, surprise rippling over his face. Had it never occurred to him they could be more than that? Not that Catalina had ever *really* considered it. Her little crush on him was mere physical attraction paired with annual forced proximity due to family visits. Her *interest*, if she could even call it that, had been one-sided from the start and was never meant to be acted on.

The thought alone was absurd.

A tremor ran through her when their eyes collided, a connection she'd been ignoring for years flaring back alive. He was the first to break eye contact as he dropped his head to stare down at the moving water beneath them. The silence stretched on, interrupted only by the passengers milling around them and the droning of the ship, which had already become so familiar she barely heard it.

Catalina was about to excuse herself and pretend she needed to get ready for the day in Corfu when Theo said, 'It's been nice handling the day-to-day in the clinic here. Less stressful. Almost feels like a vacation.'

He didn't raise his head as he spoke, and Catalina had to step closer to hear every word. There was an edge to his voice that drew her in. Could it be…vulnerability? Theo? No, that couldn't be right. In all the years she'd known him, he'd been stone-faced as a gargoyle in every single one of their interactions. To the point where Catalina had seriously questioned herself since she had developed a huge crush on this man that had hardly dulled in the years since he'd left med school.

'You prefer handling food poisoning over life-or-death situations in the ER?' she asked, though she knew the answer already. Had read studies about burnout in all disciplines of medicine, and those working with daily trauma were so much more likely to not just burnout but do irreversible damage to themselves.

A small smile curled his lips, though it didn't quite reach his eyes. 'Don't tell my parents. If they heard their son is enjoying the equivalent of family medicine, they'd probably send a team of doctors out to the cruise ship with sedatives and a straitjacket.'

Theo was passing it off as a joke, but she suspected there was more behind his words. She and Amelie shared everything with each other. Everything except things about Theo. Catalina had never questioned it because the less she knew about him—the less she was *around* him—the sooner this pesky infatuation would go away. The crush itself was too clichéd for her to stand it. The young impressionable med student from a poor upbringing falls for the protege of a prestigious medical dynasty? *Gag.* She'd seen that plot unravel in several medical TV dramas.

Whether Amelie was protective of her brother or she was looking out for Catalina and her dumb crush, she didn't know. She wasn't even sure if Amelie had ever suspected what fuelled the antagonism between Catalina and Theo. No matter if she did or didn't, her best friend never talked about her brother or what was happening in his life.

But Catalina wasn't blind. She knew when a person was struggling. And that wasn't something she could walk away from.

Swallowing the sigh—and the roiling in her stomach warning her that spending any extra time with Theo would be a bad idea—Catalina straightened up and asked, 'Seeing how you're dressed, you're going to see Corfu today?'

The question made him look up, and the intensity in his eyes was as sudden as it was brief. Then his usual gargoyle expression fell back into place. 'Thought I might have a walk around since I didn't get to leave the boat in Kefalonia.'

'Yeah, me neither.' She paused, unsure how to approach this. Maybe she was misreading this entire situation and he wasn't lonely. He didn't need her help with anything. 'Do you want to see the island together? Fair warning, the detailed itinerary Amelie shared with you was mine and I intend on hitting every single spot at the intended time.'

His brows shot up, and she wished the stony expression back. Because the look rippling across his face right now did something annoying to her stomach. Made it swoop like she'd boarded a roller coaster. 'I should have figured my sister didn't write this.'

'Oh, yeah? How come?'

Wrong question because it made his lips kick up in a smile—a genuine one this time that reached his eyes in a sparkle.

'Because Amelie hasn't organised anything in her entire life. I'm surprised she even made it through med school.'

Catalina laughed, the knot in her chest loosening a fraction. 'I think we pulled each other through it. Me by sharing all of my notes with her, while she reminded us to take breaks, hydrate and eat normal food and not just instant noodles.'

Though even to this day nothing hit quite as right as some instant noodles blasted in the microwave.

'I don't think anyone has ever survived med school without copious amounts of microwavable noodles,' he said, earning himself another laugh.

'Literally what I was thinking right now!'

The wind picked up, tearing at their clothes, and around them some passengers gave excited squeals as the port manifested in front of them.

Crew hurried around, yelling things into their walkie-talkies, and Catalina thought the entire thing might have been overwhelming. Except there was one person she was focused on, with the bustling of the ship no more than irritating background noise.

Was he really going to make her ask again?

'So...?' This was as far as she would go. The ball was in his court. If she had to repeat herself, she would shift from casual to needy, and that was not something she would do with Theodore.

He straightened, towering over her enough that she had to stare up at him. The wind tousled his hair, sending the strands in a myriad of directions. It was longer than it had been when she'd last seen him for his father's seventieth birthday party. He'd kept it cropped ever since he'd started in the ER at Morgan Greywater, not letting it get any longer than a centimetre. The last time she'd seen it this long had been during their shared year at med school, and back then she'd already wondered far too often what it would be like to feel the silky strands between her fingers.

Oops. Nope, not where her thoughts should be going. Damn it.

'Sure, let's go,' he said, yanking her out of her thoughts.

'Wait, really?' Even though she'd asked the question, Catalina hadn't expected a positive reply. Since when did Theodore Morgan hang out with anyone?

But this wasn't the man she knew. This was the *after* version of whatever had happened to him in that ER. He was almost the same. *Almost.* Except she'd seen the cracks during this conversation without anyone needing to mention them or point towards them. Hell, that he was even here instead of continuing his legacy at Morgan Greywater was a testament to how much trouble he really was in.

Theo shrugged, either because she'd read too much into it or because he wanted to play this moment of vulnerability down. Did it matter? 'You seem to have a plan, and I've not thought through anything other than stretching my legs. So why not?'

When she'd issued the invitation, Catalina hadn't expected him to accept. Leaving her now to puzzle over the appropriate response here.

'Okay, then…but keep up with me. If we want to see anything, there is no margin for lingering and *enjoying the scenery.*'

The flash of teeth accompanying his grin shot right down her spine, and before she could react outwardly, she took a step back and clutched her phone with the itinerary mapped out.

This was fine. Theo was clearly going through some stuff and she was being a good person. A good best friend, looking after Amelie's broken brother.

Totally fine.

CHAPTER FOUR

Day Four, Corfu

THIS DIDN'T COUNT as getting closer, right? The thought ate at Theo as they walked up one of the winding streets of Corfu.

They'd started their day weaving through the cobbled alleyways of Corfu Town, the smell of strong coffee and orange blossom clinging to the warm morning air. Bright shutters lined the pastel buildings, most cracked open to let in the breeze. They'd passed a sleepy *kafeneio* where two old men were deep in a game of *tavli*, dice clicking against the wooden board, arguing in murmurs that sounded affectionate even in disagreement.

Later, they'd wandered up to the Old Fortress, its weathered stone walls casting long shadows as the sun climbed higher. Catalina had insisted on taking the narrow steps up to the top, where the view had stunned even Theo into silence—an endless blue horizon broken by the curve of the coastline, the rooftops below tiled in sun-warmed terracotta.

Now, hours later, their route had grown quieter. The cruise tourists had thinned, replaced by sun-struck cats and the distant echo of a church bell. Wrought-iron balconies overflowed with bougainvillea and drying laundry, and the scent of grilled sardines drifted from a tiny taverna with checked tablecloths and no English menu.

No, this definitely didn't count. If anything, Amelie would be thrilled he'd left the ship behind for the day. Wasn't that why she'd sent him Catalina's itinerary in the first place? So he could find some inspiration and get out there? Except what he couldn't figure out was why she hadn't altered it. Wouldn't she have figured out that if he followed the same itinerary as Catalina, they would bump into each other? It flew in the face of his sister's request to stay away from her best friend.

So did the room situation. To his utter bafflement, there had been no open rooms on the ship according to the reception desk, leaving him with no alternative than to sleep on one of the stretchers in the clinic. Thankfully, Dr Chen seemed to assume he was just resting rather than squatting, and he had yet to explain himself to anyone.

And until a few hours ago, Catalina hadn't even seemed to notice his absence. When she'd asked, he'd wanted to tell her the truth. He'd decided to find somewhere else to stay for her comfort. He was only one step above a stranger, and there was no scenario in which he was comfortable forcing his presence on someone like that.

'Have you ever been to Greece before?' Catalina asked in between breaths. The island was deceptively hilly, each new destination forcing them up and down several hills to the point of exhaustion.

He shook his head. 'I haven't spent any time travelling that wasn't for work. And most of that was fairly local. Medical conferences and such. Close enough to get back to New York City if required.'

It sounded just as pathetic out loud as in his head. He'd built his entire life around this one job—the legacy he'd never asked for—and had given up so much of his life, only to lose it all in the span of a week.

Less than that. When he'd reached his limit, he'd simply got up from his desk and walked out, not thinking about the consequences. Those had come later and were still plaguing him now.

'Me neither. It's my first time in Europe,' she said, keeping the conversation on the light side of things—just as she had since they'd disembarked. 'Whatever free time I had during med school I spent studying, like the try-hard I am. The only place I'd ever travel to was back home.'

They had this much in common: giving far too much of themselves to the pursuit of greatness. Though he looked for the signs he'd ignored in himself in Catalina, and he couldn't see any of them. Maybe it was the reason she was here, seeing what had happened to him. How he'd only stepped back when it had been already too late.

'Home is the Dominican Republic for you, yes?' Theo framed it as a question even though he knew the answer. There wasn't a single thing he'd learned about Catalina Reyes he had forgotten over the years of knowing her.

She nodded, her smile more subdued than it had been a moment ago. 'It's what we're told to call it. *Home*. Regardless of how accurate it feels.'

They reached another taverna with its seats spilling out onto the cobbles. The menu sat on a stand right outside the door and when Catalina approached it, she clapped her hands in excitement. 'Never thought I'd be this happy to see the Latin alphabet.' Before Theo could ask what she meant with that comment about home, she whirled around with a smile bright enough to blind him. 'Let's have a bite to eat.'

'Does that even fit in today's agenda? I would have thought you'd make us eat sandwiches while walking.' He actually didn't mind that idea, but Theo wasn't about to tell her that her tour of Corfu had been so much better than he could have imagined. He might go as far as to say he was enjoying himself.

Not something he'd done in the recent past.

'Please, you think I'd plan a visit to a Greek isle and not plan a stop for real Greek food? How foolish do you think I am?' She shook her head, and when he nodded his agreement she plopped herself down on a chair with him taking the one opposite.

When the waiter approached them, Catalina leaned forward with a smile that could charm stone. 'Hi! Can we get—' She paused and tilted her head. 'What's your most traditional dish that doesn't involve lamb? I'm trying not to eat mammals today. I had a moment with a goat statue earlier and now I'm emotionally compromised.'

The waiter, perhaps used to odd tourist declarations, only smiled. 'Moussaka without meat? Or perhaps spanakopita, dolmades, grilled halloumi?'

'That,' she said, pointing to the halloumi, wide-eyed and licking her lips. 'And the dolmades. And tzatziki. And—Theo, what are you having?'

'I'm being guided by a woman who fell in love with a goat statue, so clearly I'll trust your judgement,' he said, then turned to the waiter. 'Same for me. And maybe a Greek salad for the table?'

Catalina gave a little approving nod, as if he'd passed a test. Why did that send a thrill down his spine?

'Good choice. You're learning.'

Their water came first, ice cubes clinking in mismatched glasses. For a few minutes they drank in silence that was more companionable than strained, the quiet broken only by the hum of traffic a few streets down and the clatter of plates from inside the taverna. Theo let himself lean back into the metal chair and—just briefly—breathe.

This was almost peaceful, each lungful of air filling him with the tranquillity of the island. Muscles which had been bunched up from the moment he'd left med school relaxed, knots loosening, and for a moment he let himself believe that life might be this simple after all. That the consequences that awaited him back home didn't matter. That he didn't torch his family's entire legacy by leaving the hospital one evening and never returning.

The legacy that had been slowly killing him day by day.

'See? I told you.' Catalina's voice drifted across the table, warm and teasing. 'I know where the good stuff is.'

'Not the worst place you've brought me,' he admitted, unable to keep the smile from his face.

Her eyes brightened, flicking over him. 'Considering I've never brought you anywhere, I don't think this is the compliment you pretend it is. Unless this is you inviting yourself along to any other stops when we both have the day off.'

Theo realised he didn't hate the idea. His original plan had entailed nothing more than doing his sister a favour. He'd not thought about what else there would be to do outside of his shifts. But a calm he hadn't felt in far too long infused him, and so the next words came out without much resistance.

'If you'll have me.'

Catalina's lips parted, still wet from the water she'd drunk. For a second, she looked as if she was going to say something, but the waiter reappeared with their food, a riot of colour and comfort across the tabletop. The halloumi was crispy and golden, tasting like light and salt and grease. They stabbed into each other's plates with mismatched forks, trading and tasting and pushing the salad back and forth between them.

'Here.' Catalina's eyes were intent, watching for his reaction as she held out a vine leaf wrapped tight around fragrant rice. Her fingers brushed his, and he took it from her hand, his own hand clumsy and too slow. When he bit in, she cocked her head, appraising his expression. 'Well?'

'Not bad,' he said, wiping oil from his mouth. 'But I still prefer sandwiches on the go.'

She clicked her tongue. 'I knew Amelie was uncultured, but I didn't realise this applied to you, too. Didn't you attend all sorts of fancy galas and fundraisers as the heir apparent of the Morgan family?'

Theo's entire body stiffened at her words, the warmth that had just begun to settle in fleeing on the breeze brushing over them. Even though it was nothing more than polite conversation and something anyone could ask, it was a reminder of everything waiting back home. Everything he didn't know how to deal with yet.

She must have caught the shift in his expression because she went wide-eyed and said, 'Sorry, what I meant to say was—'

'It's fine,' he said too quickly, trying to look casual as he stabbed his fork into the salad. 'You're right. I did a lot of those things. Not that I had much of a choice. I had to be there.'

Was it too much to admit that to Catalina? Compared to everything else he was keeping locked away, it was the smallest of truths. But it still left him feeling exposed, like an unhealed scrape.

Catalina fell silent, the kind of heavy silence that seemed to unspool between breaths until she eventually said, 'I grew up thinking that families like yours must be perfect.

That it must be so easy to have parents who care about your life and want you to succeed. But even though Amelie dances to her own tune, she told me how hard it had been to defy her parents' expectations of her. And how they all fall on you now. It's so unlike my family, who…'

She didn't finish, but he knew what came next. That the grass wasn't greener, and that his story wasn't much different from hers. Always reaching. Never good enough.

'Living someone else's dream is never easy, is it?'

Understanding bloomed on her face and it hit him in a way he hadn't expected. It showed him that even though this woman had spent a fair amount of time at his family's home, he didn't know all that much about her. Didn't know her circumstances, her upbringing or what lay beneath the beautiful façade.

Catalina opened her mouth, brows drawing together as if she was choosing her words with care.

A sharp crash broke through the haze of their conversation. At the far end of the taverna's patio, a chair scraped against stone. A man had slumped sideways, limbs limp, a knocked-over glass of wine seeping into the tablecloth. His dining partner—a woman with cropped grey hair—was already shouting, voice rising in panic.

'James? James!'

Theo was out of his chair before she'd even finished saying his name.

The other diners froze, forks halfway to mouths. Catalina's chair screeched against the stone as she stood, moving to follow. Her expression had dropped all trace of humour, hands steady even as adrenaline surged behind her eyes.

Theo crouched beside the man, pressing fingers to his carotid. 'Pulse is faint,' he said aloud for Catalina's benefit, and maybe his own.

The man's skin was clammy, his face rapidly draining of colour. His breathing was shallow, lips tinged a bluish-grey.

'Sir? Can you hear me?' Theo asked, shaking his shoulder gently. No response.

'Could be a syncopal episode,' Catalina murmured, already pulling her phone from her bag. 'Or hypoglycaemia?'

Theo shook his head once. 'Call emergency services. If we can stabilise him, we'll let the local team handle transport.'

She nodded and stepped away, already dialling. Theo caught the clipped edge of English as she spoke into the phone, slow and clear, pausing when the operator asked something she clearly didn't understand. 'Corfu Town, yes. A tourist collapsed at a restaurant. We need medical help.' She looked around, locking eyes with Theo first and then the waiter, who hurried over to her as she put emergency services on speakerphone.

Knowing Catalina had it covered, he turned back to the patient on the floor. 'Breathing's becoming more shallow,' he muttered, then raised his voice. 'Ma'am? Does he have any medical conditions? Medications?'

The woman was frozen, her hands fluttering at her chest. 'I think it's his blood sugar,' she said, breath hitching. 'He's type two diabetic—but he's on insulin. I know most people aren't, but he's had it for years, and it just got worse. The tablets weren't enough any more, and the consultant said his pancreas was basically giving up. But James, h-he watches what he eats and everything…but this morning… this morning he skipped breakfast because we were late, and I told him it was a bad idea, but he said he felt fine—'

She stopped when Catalina put a hand on her shoulder, giving it a squeeze. Her tone was soft when she said, 'He may have taken insulin without food to buffer it. Thank you for telling us. We'll help him, okay?' The woman's panicked eyes searched Catalina's face and then, trusting, let her hands drop.

'Theo,' she said when she crouched down next to him. 'Ambulance is en route, but they didn't give an ETA. Could be a while.'

He nodded, gaze sweeping over the patient again. 'We need glucose. Do you know whether he has anything with him?'

The woman blinked, as if trying to shake herself out of a fog. 'His bag—he has a little pouch, but I don't know what he keeps in there. He doesn't like it when I get involved in his medical stuff.'

'Check it,' Theo said, then turned to the waiter who was hovering nearby, eyes wide. 'Do you have juice? Coke? Anything with sugar?'

The waiter nodded and bolted back into the taverna.

Catalina reappeared at Theo's side a beat later, already crouching with the pouch in hand. 'Insulin pens, glucometer, but no snacks.' She flicked it open, reading the monitor's last log. 'Last reading was five point nine mmol/L but that was yesterday.'

Theo swore under his breath. 'We'll have to assume he's hypoglycaemic. If we can get sugar into him orally and he's conscious enough to swallow, we'll do that. Otherwise, we're going to have to find another way.'

The waiter returned with a glass of orange juice sloshing wildly in his hand. 'Is this okay?'

'It'll work,' Theo said. He turned to the patient prone on the floor again. 'James? Can you hear me?' Still no response.

Catalina leaned closer, voice low and even. 'His eyes are fluttering. I think he's semi-conscious.' She tapped his cheek gently. 'James, you with us?'

There was a faint groan.

'That's something,' Theo muttered. 'Let's try.'

With Catalina supporting the patient's head, Theo tipped a bit of the juice into his mouth. The man coughed and choked, but then swallowed. Theo glanced at Catalina, who nodded once.

'Keep going. Small sips.'

A small crowd had begun to gather now, tourists peering over from their tables, some filming, others whispering. The air had grown tight with tension, the late afternoon heat suddenly oppressive.

'We need space,' Catalina called out, her voice calm but firm. 'Please give us some room.'

The woman—James's partner—looked up. 'Is he going to be okay? He was fine this morning. I don't understand.'

Catalina put on a soft smile again, and Theo fought not to get distracted by it. There were too many things jumping at him right now and vying for his attention. Like the way her hands cradled their patient's head with such care. How she kept James's frantic loved one updated even as she helped Theo handle this situation.

It made him realise how little he really knew about her. He didn't know what kind of doctor she was, how she dealt with the pressure of the job, or even how she preferred to practise medicine. What was she going to do once the cruise was over? Travel medicine? Or a less adventurous specialism? Whatever it would be, he knew her ambition was boundless.

He pushed those thoughts away when the patient on the floor stirred. Minutes passed in tense silence, broken only by the clink of the glass as Theo coaxed another sip past James's lips. Then—slowly—colour returned to the man's face. He blinked, eyes glassy but open. 'Lynne...?'

and each time he'd fallen short he'd not only let his family down but everyone he was in charge of, too.

The sirens grew louder, and the ambient chatter of the taverna fell as the ambulance jerked to a halt nearby. A pair of paramedics rushed over and they transferred James to a stretcher. He was already more alert.

Lynne hovered beside him, her expression a mixture of gratitude and lingering panic. 'Thank you,' she said, and took Catalina's hand. 'You saved his life.'

'You did,' Catalina replied, squeezing back. 'You told us everything we needed to know.'

Theo watched the exchange, a small smile tugging at the corner of his mouth. Watching Catalina work was... surprising. Impressive.

Goddamn irresistible.

With the patient en route to the hospital and the crowd dispersing, they found themselves alone amid the debris of their meal.

The adrenaline should've worn off by now, but Theo felt charged, as if every nerve-ending was awake and alive. He glanced at Catalina even though he knew he shouldn't. It would only give the *thing* inside him room to breathe.

Hadn't he promised his sister he'd stay away from Catalina? Theo had made the promise without thinking, because of course he wouldn't start anything with Catalina. The thought had never crossed his mind.

Now that he was in her orbit, he remembered what she was like. The magnetism humming between them whenever they clashed. How much fun it was to have verbal sparring matches with her.

How Catalina marched to the beat of her own drum, always making him wish he could do that, too. And wasn't he doing it now?

The woman gasped, crouching beside them. 'I'm here, love. I'm right here.'

James's hand moved, seeking hers, and Theo let out a breath. 'He's coming back.'

Catalina pulled back at the same time, her shoulder brushing Theo's. 'We stabilised him.'

He nodded, still scanning James for any sign of relapse, but the worst seemed to have passed.

Sirens echoed faintly in the distance.

Catalina looked at him. 'You did well.'

'So did you,' he said. And for a moment—surrounded by the mess of knocked-over chairs, sweat on his brow and adrenaline in his blood—he felt something more than just relief. He'd expected a familiar pressure to push on his chest, the crushing sensation of an incoming anxiety attack unfurling in the pit of his stomach. It was how he'd felt every time he'd set foot in the ER of Morgan Greywater the last few months before he'd quit.

But the emergency had triggered none of that. His adrenaline had spiked, of course it had, but then he'd jumped into action and...

Theo looked up at Catalina, who sent him a tentative smile. As far as emergencies went, this wasn't even comparable to what he used to handle, but something about the situation—them working together—struck him.

Support. Throughout this entire emergency, Catalina had done everything he needed for support without even asking. Why was that a novel experience? Had it been something lacking at Morgan Greywater? He remembered his colleagues with fondness, the team trying their hardest in any situation. The pressure hadn't come from a lack of support, but rather the expectations piling on top of him,

'Most exciting meal I've had in a while,' he said, and she let out a shaky laugh.

'I thought you were going to say fastest. Did we even get to that salad?'

'I think we inhaled most of it,' he replied, letting the familiar back-and-forth ground him. The aforementioned salad had, of course, gone mostly untouched between all the other delicacies they'd ordered. But they'd reached a silent understanding: they would both pretend to have thoroughly enjoyed it. They were doctors, after all.

'Thanks for your quick reaction,' he said when silence settled between them, and Catalina waved her hand.

'It's kind of why we got hired in the first place, right?' The corner of her mouth kicked up, and he felt himself return the smile before he could think otherwise.

'I guess. Though this might count as overtime. We should ask Dr Chen about that.' Around them, tourists were flooding the streets, most of them heading back in the direction of the port.

'Wait, doctors get overtime?' Catalina widened her eyes in what he knew to be mock shock. 'How could Morgan Greywater even afford to spend all of that extra money?'

The mention of his family's hospital was like a bucket of ice water decanted directly into his veins. His muscles seized, his body reverting to the same fight-or-flight reaction that had pushed him through endless days and nights in the emergency room, trying to hold all of it together through sheer will. So much time and effort given of himself, so many opportunities to lead a normal life passed over, only for him to lose it all. To give it away.

Cracked under the pressure of his last name.

The shock on Catalina's face turned genuine as she no doubt read his body language. Not for the first time, he wondered how much Amelie had told her about him. It couldn't be all that much considering he'd kept most of the things haunting him internal. His sister had broken through the toxic cycle of the obligations that came with their family name, and he didn't plan on dragging her back into it by telling her what had happened to him.

'I think we need to get back to the boat. Dr Chen won't be happy if they leave without us,' he said, both to move on from the topic and to have an excuse to turn away from her as they threaded into the flow of people around them heading in the same direction.

CHAPTER FIVE

Day Five, at sea

OKAY, SO THEODORE MORGAN wasn't *only* a foul-tempered man with a hot face and an even hotter body. Underneath the stony façade lurked a surprisingly funny guy. Or maybe she was just telling herself that. Maybe she was chickening out on starting her new life by hanging out with him rather than focusing on the pleasure that—theoretically—awaited her on the social side of the boat. Even on her days off, she'd not set foot in any of the seven bars or three nightclubs *The Aurelian* offered its guests. At least not until today, when she'd sat down with a drink at an empty table and had begun staring at the crowd, as if she could find a suitable mate like that.

It was the most effort Catalina could muster right now. She'd told herself it was because of the unresolved Theo situation. How was she supposed to bring someone over if Theo could pop into their room at any second? She was already nervous enough about finding a hot stranger and getting rid of her virginity. Maybe thinking of it as 'getting rid of it' was part of the problem. But with almost a week of the cruise and no sign of him ever sleeping in their shared accommodation, she kind of knew he'd found some other place to stay.

There were no traces of him after all. No luggage with his clothes. No toothbrush in their shared bathroom. And she had yet to wake up in the middle of the night with him sleeping on the floor like some homeless raccoon.

Wait, weren't raccoons homeless by default? The thought made her laugh out loud, and a few heads turned towards her. Fair enough. She'd also be glancing at the lonely lady laughing by herself in the corner of the room with an untouched drink sitting right in front of her.

The truth was simple: Catalina had no idea how to pick up anyone. It was the reason she was still a virgin at the delicate age of twenty-six. Between vying for her parents' attention by outperforming at literally everything she had tackled—and never getting the praise she craved—and then throwing herself into the most competitive and high-performing medical program in the country, she'd had no time or energy to figure out dating. She'd made exactly one friend—Amelie—and had nailed it on the first try.

To Catalina's dismay, she'd also only ever developed one crush—Theodore—and a part of her blamed his sheer proximity more than anything else. Was his lush dark hair the envy of every man crossing his path? Probably. Did his gaze send tingles running up and down her spine? Unfortunately. Was he going to be the one to take her virginity? Not a chance in hell. He wouldn't give her the time of day even if her life depended on it.

Except he had taken her up on the offer to explore Corfu Town together, and hadn't it been sort of nice? Not date-nice, and definitely not 'let me make sweet love to you' nice. But...like...friendly? Comfortable? When their conversation had veered into more personal space, she'd thought she had glimpsed something beneath the stony exterior. Another soul fighting a battle for parental appreciation, even if it came in a completely different shape.

Ugh, feeling a sympathetic spark for Theodore Morgan was the opposite of what Catalina needed right now. Sure, they had fun on Corfu, and maybe he wasn't as stern and gargoyle-y as she'd always thought. But still, what was one nice day compared to all the times she'd met him and he hadn't even found her worthy of his attention?

'You look like you could use some company.'

Catalina yanked her head up from where she'd been inspecting the table in all of its magnificence and stared into the unfamiliar face of…some guy? Maybe a patient?

She tried to place him since he was looking at her rather expectantly. Had they spoken on her last shift?

And then it clicked. Her lips parted as she let out an 'oh' sound. Her spine stiffened the moment she realised he wasn't here to see her in her professional capacity. He was here because he'd seen a woman sitting by herself at a table at a bar, and he was trying his luck.

This was the moment she'd been waiting for. Someone was hitting on her. Only whenever she'd gone through the scenario in her head there had been no doubt about it, unlike right now. And her first reaction to the person hitting on her hadn't been mild confusion followed by instant discomfort.

'I'm not *not* looking for company,' Catalina said, cringing right away. She should have really taken some flirting lessons ahead of this trip. Was that even a thing? It sounded bizarre, but surely capitalism would find a way.

'May I?' The guy stared at the empty chair next to her, and she forced herself to nod. Truth be told she didn't want to spend any time with this stranger, but the idea flew in the face of the whole 'losing your virginity in a fun night of debauchery' idea so she really had to accept when the universe threw opportunities her way.

A picture of Theo flashed through her mind, and she pushed it away before any dumb ideas could take root. His being here and sharing a cabin with her, at least in theory, was *not* the universe's way of getting her to take a hint.

Nope.

'I'm Dave,' the guy said, holding out his hand towards her.

Okay, Dave. Unorthodox move, starting with a handshake, but Catalina needed to keep an open mind. Maybe handshakes were popular again. Or an essential part of the dating experience. With her having done exactly zero dating, she needed to take the lead from other people.

A shiver ran down her spine when his fingers wrapped around her hand with far too little pressure, leaving a clammy imprint behind. She fought with all the strength inside her to keep her expression neutral. This flirting business wasn't off to a good start.

'I'm Cat,' she replied, dropping her hand down into her lap and hoping he didn't notice her gently wiping it on her thigh.

Definitely not a good start.

'Oh, Cat. I like it.' His face split into a far too eager grin as he made a cat noise and bent his fingers so they looked like claws. 'Why is a cute kitten like you sitting all by yourself at the edge of the party? I almost didn't see you.'

He made a sweeping motion behind him. The bass of the electronic music was strong enough to rattle the furniture the closer it was to the source. Catalina had spent two minutes in there before finding this table and making it her home for the evening. How could she even approach anyone when it required screaming through a conversation?

And had this guy really just called her a cute kitten? Instant boner killer. Or whatever one said for the female version. Dry peach?

'It's a bit too loud in there. I was giving my ears a break,' she said, attempting a smile that said, *I'm not all that interested in talking to you.* It clearly didn't work, since Dave kept staring at her with that smile on his face.

'Right, right. Not so easy to chat someone up. I thought so too.' The way he nodded had her believing he hadn't thought about it for even a second.

Dave leaned in, his arm brushing against hers on the table, and gave her a once-over that wasn't even pretending to be discreet. 'So, are you one of the dancers or something? You've got that look.'

Catalina blinked. 'The…look?'

'Yeah. You've got this sexy, mysterious vibe. Bet you're trouble.'

He winked, and it took everything in her not to recoil. She reached for her drink just to have something to do, fingers curling tightly around the glass.

'Not really. I'm a doctor working at the clinic here. So I'm part of the crew and not a regular guest.' This interaction was turning into a mistake. Nothing about Dave was giving her the reaction she knew would be essential to take him back to her room—or, rather, ask him to take her to his. Inexperienced as she was, she knew the amount of cringe running through her body as he looked at her wasn't the way to go.

Nothing about this felt like a spark. No flutter in her stomach, no tilt in the world, no inexplicable rush of heat that made her catch her breath. None of the things that—annoyingly—had started to happen around Theo.

Like when he'd brushed past her in that tiny exam room,

close enough that her pulse had jumped without permission. Or when he'd made some grumpy offhand comment, and she'd found herself smiling at the crinkle in his brow instead of the words.

God, was her body *actually* so broken that it only responded to sarcasm and disapproval in a six-foot-something grump?

'A sexy doctor. That's even better,' Dave drawled, hinting at his inebriated state, and Catalina took that as her sign to extract herself from this table, call it a night and try again the next day. Practice made perfect and all that. She offered a tight-lipped smile and angled her body away ever so slightly. He either didn't notice or didn't care.

'I've always had a thing for women who take charge. You're the kind of girl who likes to be in control, huh?' He grinned, as if it was a compliment.

All right, time to go, she told herself as she set her glass down. Bracing her hands on the table, she said, 'Sorry, but I should—'

'Hey, don't go yet. I'm not done talking to you.' His hand landed on her arm. Light. Casual. But enough to snap a warning into her system.

Forced to lean closer, she could smell the alcohol on his breath and it sent another shiver through her. Her eyes narrowed, and she flexed her hand, ready to give this guy what he was asking for by laying a hand on her.

'You've clearly had too much to drink to have a pleasant conversation with anyone. I suggest you go sleep it off,' she said, but when she pulled her hand free of his grip she saw it darting straight back at her.

She flinched instinctively, but instead of touching her again, his hand stilled in mid-air. Stopped there, to be precise, by another hand wrapping around his wrist with a grip hard enough that Dave yelped.

So did Catalina when she followed the muscular arm up and found the rest of Theo staring at the guy accosting her. His eyes had a dangerous spark in them as he stared the drunk guy down. Nothing in his stony expression let her glimpse what he might be thinking.

Not until he spoke, voice low and rumbling. 'I believe she said she's not interested,' he said, every word somehow also a threat.

'She did not. I'd never bother someone who said no.' Dave wiggled his hand, but Theo's grip didn't falter, turning tight enough that she could see his knuckles whitening.

'A hint for next time: when someone gets up to make an exit, it means they don't want to be there. So don't go grabbing them to restrain them,' Theo said, and why were his words sparking something low in her stomach?

Dave blinked, first at her and then up at Theo. 'Oh, mate, I didn't realise she was with you. Totally my bad. I didn't mean anything by it.'

Theo simply stared at him, a muscle in his jaw jumping for a few quiet seconds before he let go of the guy's hand. 'I'd better not see you anywhere near her again. *Mate.*'

The guy vanished as fast as he had appeared, leaving Catalina alone with Theo's brooding presence and the unfortunate conundrum where she found herself indebted to him. The least she could do was thank him, even if the thought sent nervous flutters through her.

'You don't have to thank me,' he said, seemingly reading her mind. Was her anguish that obvious, or was it possible that Theo actually knew her?

'Of course I have to. You helped me out of a potentially sticky situation. I would be a bit of an ass not to acknowledge that at the very least,' she replied, and debated for a second if that was enough of a thank you, before sadly coming to the conclusion that it was not.

Plopping down on the chair she'd just got up from, she let out a sigh and gestured at the other chair for Theo to sit. He did after a moment of hesitation. The low drumming of the bass filled the space between them, and Catalina reached out to run her fingers up and down her empty glass, just to give her hands something to do.

Intellectually, she knew what was about to happen. Dave's unwanted attention had triggered a spike in adrenaline, making her ready to fight. Now that the issue was resolved, the adrenaline was coming back down, and with it came the familiar symptoms of the crash: shaky limbs, shallow breathing and a ridiculous awareness of how tight her dress suddenly felt against her chest. Textbook catecholamine dump.

Fight-or-flight, now firmly in the post-game analysis phase.

She'd read about it. She'd lectured patients about it. But somehow, knowing what her autonomic nervous system was doing in clinical terms didn't stop her from feeling the lingering heat on her skin or the way her pulse kept fluttering as if it hadn't quite decided whether it was still in danger.

Which was absurd. The threat was gone. Theo was here. And that was *not* a soothing thought.

If anything, he'd made it worse by showing up like some dark knight with a grudge against unsolicited touching. And now he was sitting across from her, looking at her as if he wasn't sure whether to ask if she was okay or interrogate her about her poor decision-making.

She hated how steady he looked. How composed.

As if *he* hadn't just gone from zero to dangerous in five seconds flat.

'Did Amelie tell you why she was dragging me to this cruise?' she asked to take her mind off the riot of sensations pouring through her body. Catalina was almost certain she would regret opening up, but right now she needed to say anything to keep her mind off the dampness of her sweat clinging to her.

Theo leaned back in his chair, his eyes fixed on the window to their side and watching the dark sky pass them by. 'Just assume my sister has told me absolutely nothing about anything. Ever. And even then you'd assume too much,' he said, and it was enough to make her look up.

'What? I know you guys are close. She texts you all the time.'

Truly, it was hard to tell her best friend *not* to share things.

Theo let out a low chuckle, which somehow crossed the space between them and slithered down her spine in a pleasant spark of warmth. 'She sends me anywhere between seven and twenty-four Instagram reels a day, and that's about it. Her style of communication when it comes to me is very much "interpretive memes".'

Catalina let out a laugh, because she couldn't have described Amelie any better. 'You should see the artwork she's put up in our apartment.'

'Oh, I'm well aware of Shrek adorning the wall above the fireplace. Unclear if the artist painted this erotic rendition of Shrek under duress.' His lips twitched in what Catalina knew to be his version of a smile. Theo leaned forward, bracing his arms on the table, and his gaze swept over her. 'You okay?'

'Yeah, of course I am.' She said it reflexively and cringed

when the hollowness of her voice reached her ears. It wasn't lost on Theo, either. His lips pulled into a frown and his gaze swept over her, scrutinising. The hair along her arms stood on end at the intensity in his eyes.

'Catalina.' It was all he said. Yet hearing her name in his dark voice cracked something inside her. Maybe it was the disappointment this week had been so far regarding her mission of finally getting with someone. Or that she was all alone on this ship when she was supposed to have her best friend by her side. Or maybe it was this thing between her and Theo, the elusive push and pull that had existed since they'd met all those years ago—now exacerbated by their forced proximity to one another.

Though how forced was it at this point? Catalina would never admit it even under oath, but the day out in Corfu had been far better than she'd expected. Sure, wandering around with Theo had put a considerable dampener on any conversation she might have had with any eligible bachelor. Or bachelorette. Or non-binary babe.

With her lack of experience, Catalina wasn't fussy. The point of this cruise had been to explore her sexuality at warp speed as she approached her thirties, since everyone else in her peer group seemed to already have it all figured out.

'Ugh, okay, fine. I guess I can talk to you about my crap. But then you will officially become my Amelie surrogate. So no judgement, no scowls and don't give me any advice on how to fix things unless I specifically ask for it.'

Catalina had no idea if this was the right way to go about things, but these were desperate times. She had lost control of basically every aspect of this trip, but at least she could use the opening Theo had provided her with to reclaim some of that control—regardless of whether he knew what he was signing up for.

'I'm here to…find someone,' she said, the words failing her at the very last second.

Theo picked up on the hesitation, his eyebrow rising in a silent question. Her heart stuttered in her chest when he looked at her like that—or when he looked at her in general, to be honest—and she bit her lip.

Just get it out, she told herself. *You'll feel better with a confidant.* And who knew what could happen from here? Theo had intervened with this creep right now; maybe he could also help her find an acceptable match. It wasn't as if Catalina was looking for her happily-ever-after here. She wouldn't have time for that idea in her life until long after her medical training was done.

What was this woman struggling with? Theo swallowed several barbed responses and fought his inner demons to keep his expression neutral. There was something she was working up to tell him, and even though he couldn't imagine anything to be this nervous about, her hesitation was apparent.

Catalina was here to find someone? A long-lost sibling? A person she'd met while playing an online video game? A missed connection?

The last thought sent a jolt through him, and he pushed it away. It was none of his business who she was here to meet. And he was therefore not entitled to any kind of reaction.

'Okay, this sounds so dumb because I'm twenty-six years old and a whole-ass doctor. Like, I don't even know why I'm telling you this,' Catalina rambled, her nerves obviously getting the better of her.

Theo silenced the part of him that wanted to say something. To assure her she could tell him whatever she wanted and it wouldn't matter. He would still—no. Not a path he could go down, even mentally. His feelings for Catalina—whatever they were—needed to remain unacknowledged, the way they had been over the years of knowing her. So instead he stayed silent, letting her work through whatever mental block she needed to get through.

And if by the end of that she chose to share her thoughts, he would be thrilled. But if she didn't, he needed to be fine with that. Needed to deal with the dread humming at the lower part of his spine.

'When Amelie suggested we do something fun between our internship ending and us choosing our respective fellowship programmes, she came up with the idea of this cruise to force me out of my shell.' She paused, her hand gripping the empty glass in front of her. 'The idea behind it was that since I'll be forced to be on the ship and around people, I might find it easier to…connect with people. It's something I struggled with during med school and also during my internship year. Like, watching *Grey's Anatomy* seriously messed with my head about how much social time junior doctors get.'

'I'm familiar with the workload,' he said, unable to keep the brittleness out of his voice. The stress placed on doctors in training was bad enough. If you combined it with a medical dynasty then it became a time bomb just waiting to explode. Like it had in his life.

'What I'm trying to say here is that, outside of Amelie—and I guess you, to some extent—I didn't hang out with people or get to know anyone or have…*been* with anyone. You know?' She dropped her gaze at the last part, staring at where her fingers connected with the glass as if it was the most interesting thing in here. And, to be fair, it might actually be true, seeing that creep seemed to be the calibre of people coming here.

She hadn't been with… His thoughts ground to a halt, heat blossoming in the pit of his stomach before he could control any of this reaction. Wait, was Catalina really telling him that she'd never been in a relationship? Never been…?

A tendril of awareness—hot and persistent—unfurled in the pit of his stomach, and though he batted it away it remained there, suggesting *something* he had no business entertaining.

'I see.' Theo knew it was the wrong thing to say even as he said it. The sound came out too clinical but somehow also too…curious? A strange divide to straddle, but somehow he had managed it with the efficiency of a contortionist. And here his former girlfriends had all said he wasn't flexible enough. What did they know?

'And this is my chance to catch up. Or at least I thought it was, but you see how that turned out.' Catalina dropped her head, waving in the direction where the guy had run off to.

He still wasn't sure why she was telling him all of this, and a small part of him wished she hadn't. What was he supposed to do with this information? There was nothing *he* could do about it, and yet the thoughts unravelled in his brain as if she'd tugged on a loose strand. Fantasies coalesced in front of him unbidden, and he swallowed several times to get rid of the thickness coating his throat.

'Because of my predicament, I apparently don't even know how to pick them. Like, could I have known Dave was a creep not worthy of even five minutes of conversation?' When she looked back up, Theo had to ball his hand into a fist not to reach out and touch her.

'I promise you he wasn't. Anyone worth your attention

doesn't have to beg for it,' he said without thinking, and something in her eyes lit up. The dejection he'd seen there a few moments ago was transforming into a different expression right in front of him.

'Did you know he was a sleaze when you saw us talking?' she asked, eyes wide enough to reflect the strobe lights behind him.

He paused, unsure where this line of questioning was going and whether he really should be the one to follow it to the end. 'I had a pretty good guess,' he admitted.

Her expression turned radiant. Even in the dim light, he could see the energy coming back into her body. Only he couldn't see her like that. It would make staying away from her even harder. Something he'd struggled with during his time in med school until he'd been glad to leave because the constant distraction of Catalina Reyes was finally out of his life. Or at the very least contained to major holidays.

Theo didn't have time for distractions like that, and because he didn't he could not let himself think about how much he might have liked to be distracted. How much fun it might have been. Or if his life might have been different if he'd chosen different priorities.

The cruise was starting to look like a glimpse through a window into a past he had denied himself.

Was that why Amelie had told him to stay away from Catalina?

'How?' Catalina asked, eyes still wide in wonderment.
'How...what?'
'How did you know he was a sleaze?'
Theo blinked several times as his thoughts crashed back into reality. 'What do you mean?'

'Because...look, I think I knew as well. But I wasn't sure. There was a sinking feeling in my stomach. A sense of impending doom. But I brushed it off because I thought maybe that's my inexperience. What if I'm just uncomfortable with flirting?'

'You're not.' The words were out before he could stop them and as they floated between them, Theo cursed silently. He knew exactly what she was going to ask next, and he had no idea—

'How do you know that?' Yup. There it was.

'Because I've been around you, believe it or not. We might not talk much, but you're far from quiet. You…grab people's attention. And you know how to talk to people. Flirting is just that: talking.' Subtext weighed down his words to the point where anyone else would have called him out on it. But this was Catalina sitting across from him. She'd not once acknowledged what lay beneath the snipes between them, had never even hinted at being interested in more—on the other side of the coin that was their contentious relationship.

Though with what he knew now—and the questions she was asking—he wondered if maybe she genuinely didn't know. That she hadn't picked up what he'd put down all those years ago—not because she hadn't been interested but because…she couldn't tell?

The way she stared at him, mouth as wide as her eyes, it had to be the latter. Which put him in a far more dangerous situation than he'd previously thought. Years ago, he'd believed himself rejected. But what if it wasn't true? Had he mistaken a lack of experience as a hard no? With an ego far bigger than his achievements warranted, Theo had retreated back into the safety of his peer group, where people knew him and appreciated him for who he was—regardless of what he'd *actually* achieved so far.

The way she spoke of their shared past now, he realised

Catalina had no idea of his intentions back then. Which, in turn, meant there was a chance.

And Theo couldn't have that. Considering how thoroughly his life was in shambles right now. With his reputation in tatters, any connection to him would only hold her back in her future career. He wouldn't have it on his conscience.

'I do?' Catalina paused, and he wasn't sure if she was speaking to him or to herself. Then he flinched when she clapped her hands, her expression transforming from puzzlement to something steely. Resolved. 'Here's the deal, Theodore. I know how you'll make up for all of this: you'll be my wingman.'

That was not at all what he'd expected to come out of her mouth. It was, in fact, so absurd that he snorted in the most undignified, non-Morgan appropriate fashion. 'Your wingman? You didn't even know the guy was a sleaze. How do you know what a wingman is?' As he asked, he realised the answer and held his hands up. 'My sister, of course.'

'She was supposed to be my wingwoman and land me with someone who can, you know...take care of *it*.'

Another burst of heat rippled through his body, hotter than the previous one, shooting through him and into every extremity. He clenched his jaw to regain control, tamping down on the *thing* inside him that had stirred when he'd first seen her again in the lobby five days ago and which was now projecting ungodly pictures in his mind. Except he didn't see himself in there, but rather the creep—or a loose approximation of him—with Catalina, and the heat turned into something discomfiting. A feeling he couldn't remember ever feeling this intense: jealousy.

What terrible things had he done in a past life that he would be tormented like this? Having Catalina, of all the women on this planet, ask *him* to help her get laid. For the first time. That was knowledge he couldn't un-know now. Nor could he forget how she intended that man to be anyone but him—or how he shouldn't *want* to be him.

It didn't make being around her any easier. Not that he idolised virginity or anything like that. No, simply thinking of her in this way was provoking thoughts he could—*should*—do without.

'I don't think I will.'

In fact, there was no chance in hell Theo was going to do that. He'd already had to employ a breathing technique when he'd seen the guy touch her without her consent. How was he supposed to help her find someone else when he—?

Nope. There was no way he would let himself go there. His silly infatuation—because that was what it was—would stay in the past. Maybe he should help her with her harebrained idea. Just to prove to himself that these lingering thoughts were nothing but a result of their forced proximity. That there was a reason he preferred to stay away from her, and it was because he needed to keep a lid on things.

'You owe me, Theo.' Catalina couldn't hide the wince as she said that, just as he couldn't help the smirk from appearing on his lips.

'How exactly do you figure I owe you?' he asked, now leaning close enough that her scent drifted up his nose. The same hint of lavender he'd caught that first day when he'd stood behind her. A smell he knew was all over the cabin they were supposed to share. The one he hadn't set foot in since showing her the way, because there was no way he could withstand the proximity to Catalina. He would lose his sleep along with what little of his sanity remained.

'Well...it's technically not your fault Amelie fell off a

horse and broke her ankle. But, as both an older and a younger sibling, I know there are certain responsibilities that come with being the eldest, and so I'm okay holding you accountable for it.'

Theo couldn't stop the laughter bubbling in his throat. 'You went through an awful lot of mental gymnastics to get to this point.'

Catalina shrugged, but he could see she was trying to fight off a smile. Or maybe he just wanted to see her smile because he enjoyed it too much. Probably a combination of both.

Now was the time to stop the jokes and walk away. They had their fun teasing each other, but avoiding Catalina was still one of his top priorities. Especially since she had a way of eroding his defences—and of late he didn't have very many left. The circumstances of his life had left him scrambling to hold on to *anything*. Who knew what might happen if he let himself slip too far out in these unknown waters?

Not that he *wanted* to. Nope, he definitely didn't.

'Fine, say I agree. What's your plan of attack? What do you need in a wingman?' he asked instead of shutting the entire idea down.

Catalina's lips split into a huge grin that stole all the air from his lungs. 'Yes! I knew I could count on you. There's lots to do. First is, of course, checking out people's vibes. Like, you're already good at observing and judging people. Put that power to good use and weed out anyone I should avoid.' She clapped her hands once, clearly delighted. 'Excellent. Tomorrow night's karaoke at the Sunset Bar. Prime vibe-checking territory. Wear something non-threatening.'

He blinked. 'Non-threatening?'

'You know, less brooding serial killer, more supportive bestie. I can help if you need it.'

Theo scrubbed a hand down his face. What had he just agreed to?

Catalina stood, grabbing her drink and shooting him a look over her shoulder. 'Come on, wingman. Let's go back before the good ones are all taken.'

She didn't wait for him to follow, just strolled off into the blur of lights and music as if she hadn't just handed him a live grenade and walked away smiling.

Theo exhaled slowly and dragged himself to his feet. One night. A bit of recon. He could manage that.

Probably.

Maybe.

God help him.

CHAPTER SIX

Day Eight, at sea

AFTER TWO SUCCESSIVE nights of hunting, Catalina had to admit that her plan to make Theo her wingman in her mission to lose her virginity wasn't working out the way she'd imagined it. In her desperation, and also caught up in the moment of her valiant rescue from sleazy Dave, she hadn't realised the fatal flaw in the plan: Theodore Morgan was far too handsome to be her wingman.

The people in the clubs and bars took one look at him before backing off, not wanting to mess with what they thought was his girlfriend. It didn't help that Theo couldn't get rid of his resting bitch face long enough to talk her up to someone.

So instead of making progress in her virginity-losing quest, she'd mostly hung out with her best friend's brother, talking about the most random things.

Which led her to the second problem in this whole scenario—she was kind of enjoying herself. And by *kind of* Catalina meant she didn't feel as if she was missing out on anything when spending her time with Theo.

Which was bad, right? The innocent crush she'd nursed over the years of knowing him was one thing. Completely harmless by virtue of his being utterly uninterested in her and also because they hung out—what, maybe two hours *a year*? It was easy to forget about this man's magnetism when she rarely saw him.

But now that they were spending more time together—both on and off the clock—things had veered into the uncomfortable range.

'So, no pool for me today?' Sam, the receptionist from her first day, asked, their voice raspy.

'Afraid so, Sam.' Catalina gave them a sympathetic smile. 'You caught a virus from someone. Seems it's going around since you aren't the first here with those symptoms. I'd suggest you lie down for the rest of the day and see how you feel in the morning. Lots of fluids and rest.'

'Why did it have to be on my day off? I—' The rest of their sentence was swallowed by a hacking cough sounding painful enough to make Catalina wince.

She got up from her chair, and Sam followed suit, swaying on their feet as they got off the exam bed. Catalina frowned and stepped closer. 'Will you be okay to get to your cabin?'

Sam gave a slow nod. 'I'll be fine. Thanks, Dr Reyes.' Catalina opened the door and waved at Sam as they trotted out and down the corridor before disappearing from the clinic.

The sound of coughing hit her before she even stepped out of her office. Catalina frowned, caught off-guard by the muffled chorus echoing from the waiting area. She'd expected maybe one or two more cases before the end of her shift, but as she rounded the corner her jaw dropped.

Every seat in the waiting room was taken. A family of four huddled around a single crossword puzzle, each of them coughing in counterpoint. The two elderly women—chess rivals Catalina had seen battling it out yesterday on the entertainment deck—now sat slumped beside each other with identical boxes of tissues clutched in their laps. Even the normally unflappable bartender from the ship's mid-deck lounge was doubled over, face buried in his hands as if seeing everyone else swaying set him off. Hadn't he been serving her and Theo drinks last night?

She scanned the room, counting. Fifteen. At least half the patients she'd usually see in a day, now assembled all at once and multiplying by the minute. Whatever this respiratory disease was, it spread a lot faster than Catalina liked. Had Theo seen a similar trend? After spending the evening together yesterday, they'd realised this morning they were scheduled together in the clinic as well. Not that they had any time to see each other with the amount of work waiting in the patient room. Also, why would she *want* to see him?

It wasn't as if he could help her pick someone up right now.

No, she wanted to see him because the number of patients still trickling in worried her, and she needed to know if it was appropriate. Theo had worked in one of the largest metropolitan emergency rooms only a few weeks ago. He would know what was going on.

As if her thoughts had summoned him, a door behind her opened and Theo stepped out, along with Dr Chen, heads bowed in discussion. If those two were meeting behind closed doors, there was definitely something wrong.

Catalina stepped forward as soon as she caught Theo's eye, intercepting him before he could disappear back into the staff corridor. Dr Chen had already turned around and vanished behind her office door.

'What's going on?' she asked in a low voice, glancing over her shoulder at the full waiting area. 'I thought this was just a trickle, but it's turning into a flood. This many cases in one day feels…wrong.'

Theo nodded once, his mouth set in a grim line. 'It's a cluster. We've logged twenty-eight symptomatic cases since this morning, and they're all showing the same progression: low-grade fever, dry cough, sore throat, malaise, some with mild dyspnoea. One or two borderline hypoxic, but nothing needing intubation so far.'

Catalina blinked. 'But what *is* it? Influenza?'

'Possibly,' Theo said. 'Could also be adenovirus or para-influenza, maybe even a seasonal coronavirus strain. We won't know for sure until we get swabs to the mainland. But whatever it is, it's highly contagious. We're looking at a confined-space outbreak—classic cruise ship scenario.'

Her brow furrowed. 'You've seen this before?'

He gave a short nod, rubbing the back of his neck. 'Yeah. We had something almost identical at Morgan Greywater last winter. Two nursing homes got hit at the same time, and we were overflowing within hours. Same presentation, same acceleration. It's the incubation window that screws you—people are contagious *before* they realise they're ill.'

Catalina frowned. 'This is going to be a nightmare.'

He nodded again, glancing over her shoulder towards the waiting room. 'Be extra careful. Don't take off the mask or those glasses. I can't have you getting sick.'

It was a throwaway line, and Theo couldn't possibly have meant anything by it. Yet her heart still stumbled as the words settled into a squishy place inside her chest. Of course he was worried about her getting sick. She was his colleague in this mess. Plus, he was a doctor and didn't want *anyone* to get sick. This wasn't about her. Except maybe it was, because as it turned out, Theo maybe didn't think she was a piece of gum stuck to his shoe, the way she had always believed. He just had a terminal case of grumpy face.

'W-what are we supposed to do though? Tell them to isolate?' She bit down on her cheek when her hesitation turned into a stutter. Four years of medical school and an additional year as an intern had taught her a lot about being a doctor and how hospitals worked, but this wasn't exactly a regular hospital environment. 'Should we alert the CDC?'

Theo shook his head. 'Dr Chen has already alerted the Maltese health authorities since the ship is registered in Malta. But as the senior medical officer on the ship, she has the authority over how we proceed with this. She's on the phone with the Captain to confirm the plan of action.'

As if his words had summoned her, Dr Chen's office door swung open and she stuck her head out, making eye contact. With a quick wave of her hand, she beckoned them both to enter and when Catalina closed the door behind her, Dr Chen was already sitting back behind her desk.

'Here's what we decided: mild cases will be ordered to self-isolate in their cabin until we reach Dubrovnik tomorrow, at which point we will reevaluate the situation. The Captain decided against turning around and going back to Split port. With how the waiting room is looking right now, I'm expecting more serious cases to come in.' She paused, looking between them. 'I know your shift is supposed to be over soon but, unfortunately, I will require you to stay until the situation is contained. I asked more of the staff to start early as well.'

Next to her, Theo nodded, unsurprised about the decision Dr Chen had made. Was it because he would have made the same decision? Meanwhile, Catalina hadn't even known where to begin triaging, let alone deciding the fate of so many people at the drop of a hat.

'The Captain asked his staff to prepare a room on Deck Four as an overflow in case we need to move critical patients there,' Dr Chen continued when they both stayed quiet.

'Do we have any ICU-grade equipment?' Catalina asked as she played through the scenario in her head. More critical cases would require specialised care—intubation, ventilation, potentially an isolation room.

'We have a few ventilators on board. The crew is currently hauling them out of storage. But it's not—'

'*Help!*' A screech interrupted Dr Chen's words.

Theo was already moving, his long stride swallowing the office in two steps, Catalina tight behind. The waiting room had become a centrifuge of chaos. The bartender, grey-faced, slumped sideways in his chair as his neighbour—a twitchy college kid in a faded Pink Floyd shirt—tried to prop him up while yelling for help.

Theo dropped to his knees beside the bartender, fingers already at the man's wrist. 'Pulse is thready. He's febrile and tachycardic. Catalina—'

'I've got it,' she said, crouching opposite him and pulling on gloves. 'Sir, can you hear me?' She tapped the man's cheek, but he didn't stir. His skin was flushed, sweat clinging to his brow.

'We need to move him.' Theo looked around and spotted a wheelchair. 'Clear the hallway,' he called out, and the crowd shifted without hesitation.

Catalina rolled the chair into place while Theo and the college kid lifted the man in. He slumped to one side, head lolling.

'Hold him steady,' Theo told her, grabbing the handles. 'We'll take him to Exam One. If his breathing worsens, we'll need to start oxygen—maybe prep for escalation.'

Catalina's eyes went wide. 'Do we even have oxygen?' The thought of starting someone on oxygen was so far out from what they'd been told things would be like in the clinic and she couldn't remember whether the orientation day had touched on the subject. Maybe, but she'd been too busy feeling self-conscious about being in the same room as Theo. Great.

'Storage cabinet by the crash trolley,' Theo said without missing a beat. 'Green cylinder. Regulator should already be attached.'

Right. Catalina spun on her heel and dashed to the cabinet, heart thudding as she yanked the door open. Her fingers hesitated for a split second before closing around the oxygen kit. By the time she turned, Theo had already wheeled the patient into Exam One and lowered the backrest.

'Here.' She passed him the tubing. 'Mask or nasal cannula?'

'Start with a mask. His sats must be dropping fast.'

Catalina connected the tubing, slipped the elastic behind the man's head and adjusted the flow. 'How's he doing?'

'Breathing's shallow, but steady. Chest rising symmetrically, no obvious distress.' Theo placed the pulse oximeter on the man's finger and waited a beat. 'Ninety-one. Not great. Hopefully, it climbs.'

She moved to the IV cart. 'Fluids?'

'Wide open,' he confirmed. 'One litre Ringer's. Let's cool him down too—he's roasting.'

She nodded, grabbing a cool pack from the fridge and wrapping it in a towel before placing it under the man's neck. 'Temp must be sky-high.'

Theo glanced at the thermometer. 'Forty-point-two. Damn. Fever wasn't one of the symptoms I saw on any patient today. You?'

She shook her head while tearing open the IV kit. 'Nope. Low-grade, maybe, but nothing like this. This could be secondary. Dehydration, maybe?'

'Or an opportunistic infection due to the compromised immune system,' Theo muttered, moving to the cabinet and pulling down a box of antipyretics. 'I'll draw up paracetamol. IV, right?'

'Yeah,' she said, already finding the vein. Her gloved fingers moved steadily now, confidence kicking in. 'Good flashback. Threading.'

Theo turned with the syringe just as she taped the line in place and flushed it. 'Nice stick.'

She smirked. 'Didn't even need a second try. Try not to be too impressed. Us doctors at non-top institutions do just as well.'

'That's not— You think that's how I see you? Like the name of your hospital matters more than how you handle yourself?' Theo let out a laugh and shook his head. Before Catalina could muster a reply, he handed over the paracetamol for her to push through the port. 'Keep an eye on pulse and oxygen. Let's recheck sats, BP and temperature in two minutes.'

As she administered the medication, the heart monitor gave a steady rhythm. No alarms. No panicked spikes.

Catalina exhaled and peeled off her gloves. 'He's stabilising. Colour's better already.'

Theo nodded, eyes still scanning the monitor. 'Breathing's improving too. That oxygen's helping.'

The bartender gave a weak cough and stirred, blinking sluggishly. Theo crouched down beside him, his energy gentle. 'Sir? You're okay. You fainted, but you're stable now.'

The man gave a faint groan in response, eyes fluttering closed again.

Catalina glanced at Theo. 'I guess we'll need to keep a close eye on him?'

'Definitely. I'll radio the crew to see if the room on Deck Four is ready.' He paused, looking at the bartender with a frown. 'Let's keep him in the chair. It's not the most comfortable, but I don't know what the transport situation looks like.'

'Got it. I'll stay and check him over again while we wait for word on what to do next,' she replied with a nod, ignoring the burst of butterflies in her stomach as the adrenaline faded out of her system with the emergency winding down. This persistent feeling should go away, too. Yet it stuck around to annoy her. And made her blurt out the next thing without thinking. 'Look at us. Teamwork.'

She braced herself for his smirk of derision, but when their eyes met, his smile was a lot softer. Or had it always been like that and she hadn't seen it for what it was until now?

His eyes sparkled with amusement. 'Not bad for a girl who forgot where the oxygen was.'

He had not just said that. Catalina huffed out an incredulous laugh and said, 'Not bad for a guy with chronic resting bitch face.'

His smile turned brighter, showing her a flash of the one crooked canine that always caught her attention. 'That's just my neutral.'

'Your neutral scares small children.'

'And yet *you* keep showing up.'

'I don't...' Her voice trailed off when the butterflies in her stomach turned into tiny fireballs, bouncing around her body in an erratic pattern and setting everything they found inside her on fire. Heat prickled at her skin, making it impossible to focus on any single thought she might have. The reply to his words she now couldn't find.

He had noticed her hanging around him despite her own insistence that she shouldn't. But not just that, the implications of his words wormed into her. Had he liked it? Theo certainly hadn't made a concerted effort to avoid her. Except for seemingly finding another place to stay, given he hadn't set foot in their shared cabin after the first day.

A question she still had to ask. Later.

Outside, another cough echoed down the corridor. The next wave was coming, but for a moment they stood in the eye of it—just the two of them, connected by the hum of machines and the steady pulse on the monitor.

Theo hesitated, eyes flicking to her for a beat too long. 'You did well.'

The praise slid under her skin, warm and steady. She shouldn't enjoy his words as much since they didn't mean anything. Who was Theo to her that she would crave his compliment? It was ridiculous how much he fuelled the fire raging within her.

'You're not too bad yourself, Morgan,' she said in an effort to deflect. 'Go radio the team. Patients are piling up, and we need to clear the waiting room.'

Theo gave a quick nod and stepped out, the door swinging shut behind him. Catalina blew out a breath, forcing herself to move. There was no time to stand still and analyse what had just happened. Patients were waiting. Her job wasn't to decode mixed signals—it was to keep people breathing.

Fatigue sat deep in Theo's bones. The only times he'd ever felt anything that was comparable to this level of tiredness had been after long days in the Morgan Greywater boardroom, talking to his parents and the rest of the board about the state of the emergency room. Those were usually followed by nights actually in the ER, making sure his staff members knew he was around. Because he knew what the optics looked like: rich parents appointing their freshly qualified son to a position far beyond his capabilities. He knew the nepotism narrative was impossible to avoid, and he needed to show his mettle to convince the staff he was more than just his family name. Unfortunately for him, that meant stretching himself beyond his means.

With the outbreak of whatever virus had taken hold on the ship, Theo had worked just as hard. But his level of exhaustion was nowhere near similar. Yes, he was tired, but his mind wasn't circling all the problems he hadn't solved or the people he couldn't save.

No, it was quiet in his head as he lay on the lounger on the empty pool deck, staring up at the night sky and scanning the stars as they drifted by.

The pool deck was empty, save for the occasional crew member walking up and down the sides of the ship. Theo had befriended them on his first day here to make sure he could access this part. They had an understanding: the crew would let him spend time alone, and he would be the responsible doctor he claimed to be and not abuse the privilege his crewmates—and new friends—were giving him.

Between these loungers and empty beds in the overflow room next to the clinic, Theo had avoided the shared cabin with Catalina. Though now that the rooms were actually occupied by patients in isolation, he wasn't sure where he would spend his nights.

'You're like weeds, you know that?'

Theo's eyes flew open at the sound of the familiar voice. He hadn't even realised he'd drifted off to sleep. Blinking several times, the blurry figure slowly took on the form of Catalina.

'I'm relentless, even though people try to get rid of me?' he asked, and her chuckle slid down his spine and settled at the base there in a warm buzz.

'Kinda? I more meant I've seen you all day and now that I'm looking for some time alone, there you are.' Catalina hovered over him and even in the dim light of the night sky he could see the exhaustion etched into her features.

They'd worked together until two hours ago, when Dr Chen had finally dismissed them to get some rest. The medical officer's prevailing sentiment was that they had contained most of the virus, but some passengers would be staying in Dubrovnik when they arrived tomorrow, both because they needed the attention only a hospital could give them and to mitigate further risk of spreading.

The crew roster had several built-in redundancies, but even those could run thin if they didn't manage it properly and let some virus eat itself through the ship's population.

'I'm not sure weeds is the right metaphor here. More like a shadow? I follow you wherever you go?' He paused, then sat up enough so there was space at the foot of the lounger for her to sit down. To his surprise, Catalina didn't hesitate before plonking down, her head tipped back in equal, silent wonder at the constellations above them. The hush of the sea and the throb of distant engines were white noise, a perfect buffer against the spooling anxieties neither wanted to examine right now.

She pulled her knees up, arms looped around them. 'Never thought I'd end up pulling an all-nighter as a doctor on a cruise ship,' she said after a minute. 'I mean, I've done night float shifts before, but at least there's a cafeteria and places to hide when you want to scream into the void.'

Theo snorted. 'You could scream now. The only thing that would answer is seagulls.'

She grinned, a slow, tired sunrise of a smile. 'Not my most dramatic breakdown, then.'

Her gaze drifted to him, softer than he'd seen it before, and something in his chest hitched at that. And then it squeezed even tighter when she asked, 'How are you holding up?'

The question caught him off-guard. Not because no one had asked it—Amelie had, countless times, cajoling him to talk instead of turning into an emotional dam—but because he didn't want to lie to Catalina. He realised, in this odd half-life on *The Aurelian*, that he had started to value her opinion more than he wanted to admit. That in a weird turn of fate, he'd found parts of himself he'd thought forever lost, by stepping *away* from his life.

How was it possible when he hadn't even wanted to be here? Something inside him told him the answer lay in the woman sitting next to him. Even with so little contact, Catalina had a way of getting under his skin—flipping some internal switch that left him thinking of nothing but her.

Which was strange, considering the reverse wasn't true for her. She was here actively looking for *someone else*, with his express help. And seemingly unaware of the fact that the thought was killing him inside. Or maybe what was really bothering him was how he was powerless to do anything but help her, now that she was in his orbit.

How he wanted to give her whatever she desired, as long as it wasn't himself.

At least not fully. Small pieces would have to do.

'I'm okay,' he replied, letting the truth settle in between them. That she cared enough to ask meant something. He wasn't sure what, but it was there, a flicker of warmth in a cold place.

'Don't make that face,' Catalina murmured, nudging his knee with her own. 'I can't categorise it, and it freaks me out.'

The air tasted briny, a salty sharpness that was both clean and abrasive, clearing out whatever clouds had settled around him. She looked genuinely concerned, a strange contrast to their default mode of mutual antagonism. He found himself grinning, a small, unguarded twitch that surprised even him.

'I didn't realise I had so many faces,' he said.

'You don't,' she replied, wrapping her arms tighter around her knees. 'Mostly you have "neutral", "I'm judging you" and "Why am I surrounded by idiots?". This one's new.' Her voice softened then, quieter. 'I like it.'

His chest squeezed tight at her words—at how the slight hesitation in them told him all he needed to know about her frame of mind. They'd never sat this close to each other, hadn't ever been this open about, well, anything. It wasn't how their dynamic had worked with Amelie between them acting as a buffer.

Theo had forced himself to keep his feelings hidden beneath an expression of neutrality. Though how Catalina had picked it up had been so much different as he'd learned over the last few days of interacting with her. She'd seen it as disdain.

It couldn't be further from the truth, and that was what made this entire thing so dangerous. He could not let his true feelings out—this was as true now as it always had been and always would be. His sister had been right to warn him away from Catalina.

Yet under the starlight, surrounded by the quiet of the

ocean and with the long shift in the clinic wearing down his defences, Theo couldn't muster the usual air of distance. Not when she sat this close, her scent wrapping around him like a soft cocoon. Lulling him into safety.

He leaned in, a thrill running through his body when Catalina didn't flinch.

'I thought the hectic nature of the outbreak would trigger something in me. That it would remind me of how running the ER had ground me down. But it didn't,' he said, the words finding their way out with no resistance. He wanted her to know this, though he couldn't explain why.

Catalina rested her head on top of her folded arms, tilting to the side so their eyes met. 'There was a lot less trauma in that room today. Like, yeah, it was stressful. But I imagine it doesn't compare to the number of high-degree injuries coming into an emergency room like Morgan Greywater. It can't...'

He shook his head as she spoke, her words trailing off before she could finish her sentence. 'It doesn't matter *what* it is. If you feel like you're going to fail, or you're not good enough, that's what gets to you. It's the only thing.'

Catalina stayed quiet for a few seconds before answering him. When it came, her voice was so soft he barely heard it above the lapping of the waves. 'Yeah. I know exactly what you mean.' Her lips pressed tight, teeth pulling at the inside of her cheek as if she was deciding whether to keep going or shut it all in again. But she kept her eyes on the sky as she went on. 'I used to think that if I was perfect—if I got the grades, did the work, made it into the right schools—my parents would finally notice me. Or at least care about my achievements, you know?' The laugh that followed was brittle. 'Turns out, it didn't matter if I made it to med school or got my name on a plaque. There was always something more impressive my siblings had done. Or some new kid on the way. I couldn't ever be enough.' She shrugged, trying to play it off.

Theo resisted the urge to put his arm around her. Instead, he leaned closer still until their shoulders brushed against each other.

'Going on this cruise and experiencing all these things—it's supposed to be me taking charge of things. Finally living for myself rather than for the expectations of others, you know? Even when it comes to the continuation of my medical training, whenever I look at a path forward, I can't shut up the voice that asks: is this the right way to gain their attention?'

Theo was silent, but it wasn't the uncomfortable hush that sometimes happened when people shared too much. He took a deep breath, exhaling slowly. How had they ended up sharing these things with each other unprompted? 'Sounds like something I need to do as well.'

He wasn't sure how he would even begin to 'live for himself', as she put it. When she'd asked him to help her, something in his chest had stirred. An unease he'd pushed away in denial. If she wanted to meet people it was none of his business. But now that he understood why—understood more of Catalina—the unease came rushing back.

Was that really how she wanted to reclaim her life from whatever ghosts she'd spent chasing all these years? By finding some random guy at a bar? Wouldn't the experience be so much better if he—

The thought was so loud, so intrusive, Theo forgot how to breathe. How could he sit here and continue to support her with her plan when his entire being recoiled from the thought? When in every stray fantasy there was no random guy, but just her with *him*. His mouth exploring her body. His fingers teaching her what pleasure looked like—sounded like.

Dear God, how was he supposed to go through with any of this?

Theo looked at her, the sharp shadow of her profile painted by the distant light of the ship's navigation beacons. She was still, and her expression raw and unguarded in a way he'd never seen before. Maybe she'd never meant to say any of this. Maybe it was the exhaustion, or the hour, or the way the stars went on forever above their heads and nothing felt as heavy as it did during daylight.

But it would be a lie to say he didn't want to be the one to help her rewrite her story. Not as a surrogate or a bystander or a facilitator, but as himself. Theo Morgan, whose entire life had been about denying himself the things he really wanted, because wanting was always dangerous, always selfish, always a threat to the order of things.

He'd spent years telling himself that what he wanted—how he felt about her—didn't matter and would only ever get in the way of the important things in his life. Now, the space between them felt charged as their eyes met, an intense spark jumping between them.

'If anyone would have told me a few weeks ago I'd be sitting with Dr Theodore Morgan on a cruise to stargaze, I don't think I would have believed them,' she said, her voice taking on a quality that sent a trickle of warmth shooting down his spine. She leaned into him now, enough that he could feel her weight against him. So close, he could count her eyelashes, watching their mesmerising dance with each blink.

He huffed a low laugh, wanting to look away but not being able to. If he kept staring at her for much longer, he would forget himself and do something dumb. Act on the attraction that he had felt for her since they'd first met. Because whatever was floating between them now was mutual.

'Yeah, I'm not used to seeing you outside of the rigid programming of our Thanksgiving dinners.'

A smile ghosted across Catalina's lips—soft, a little sideways, part incredulity, part dare. 'We're a lot less horrible with each other than I thought we'd be,' she said. 'Isn't that weird?' The question was half rhetorical; the rest hung between them, open.

'We could fix that,' Theo offered, his voice low. 'We could start bickering again. Re-establish the natural order.'

The silence that followed was long and risky. Theo reached up, brushing a stray curl from the edge of her brow, letting his hand drift just long enough that she could feel the shape of his fingers, the weight of whatever he wasn't saying. It was a deliberate slow-motion act—one that left no room for doubt about intent.

His eyes darted down to Catalina's throat when she swallowed. But she didn't move away from his touch, didn't shift or give him any other indication that he was too close. That he was overstepping. Theo thought he was, knew this wasn't a good idea under these circumstances, or any other. But he couldn't stop himself as his thumb brushed over her cheekbone and a sigh dropped from her lips.

His heart lurched into his throat when she met his gaze again, eyes ablaze with the same forbidden temptation raising its head in his chest.

'Are you going to kiss me, Theodore, or will you just keep staring at me?'

Something deep in his gut tightened. 'Amelie told me not to.'

She snorted, her nose wrinkled from the effort not to laugh. 'Are you going to listen to her?'

He was both relieved and bereft, because the room for denial had officially closed itself off. Whatever happened next, it was wilful. Chosen. Maybe that was why he hesitated: the old, calcified routine of denying himself in favour of expectations, and the certainty that to want was to set himself up for disaster.

What if he treated his life as suspended here on the ship? Maybe for the duration of his time here, he could be someone else. Try on the skin of a Theo who wasn't so wrapped up in his family's legacy he couldn't escape it. Catalina was looking for someone to give her back control of her life—maybe she could do the same for him?

When he finally leaned forward, it was with a carefulness that was less like hesitation and more reverence for the moment itself. He stopped just shy of her lips.

'You're sure?'

She didn't answer in words. Her hand skimmed the rough line of his jaw, palm cupping the side of his face. There was no tremor—she was as steady as he'd ever seen her.

'Yes,' she said, and that little word made him feel precariously on the edge.

He closed the distance, hesitation burning away in the heat between their mouths. Her lips were soft and tasted like all the fantasies he'd quietly indulged in the time he'd known her. Her body angled towards him on nothing but instinct, pressing into him with a needy, tentative certainty.

He felt himself smiling against her mouth, all the tension of the day evaporating as she kissed him back, equal parts desperate and giddy. The electric charge between them broke as their bodies met, following the rhythm of their bodies. Time seemed to slow when they touched, and the more of *her* Theo got to feel under his hands, the more intoxicated he became.

Theo threaded his hands through her hair, a zing of electricity shooting through him when her low moan reached his ears. Catalina clawed at him, fingers finding purchase in his shirt, and as she pushed towards him, he lay down, pulling her with him until he was flat on the lounger with her straddling him.

The weight and motion of her hips sent a searing jolt from his chest straight to his groin, and for a suspended second Theo was no longer the master of anything—not his body, not his brain, not the wild animal thrum of desire that made his world tilt. He could feel her through the thin summery fabric of her skirt, and all at once his self-control, the one thing he'd always believed in, snapped like a brittle leash, and the friction made him dizzy.

His hands found their way to her hips, relishing the feel of her bare skin against his fingertips when he found the exposed strip of flesh where her shirt was riding up. Was this really about to happen? For years, Theo had imagined what it would be like—fantasising about his complete surrender to this woman who he could never have.

His want had never been an active thing or something he pursued in his life, but rather a slow boil, constantly there in the back of his mind, and he'd lived with the idea that it was all he would ever get. Their lives had diverged before they had even met, and with his future entirely wrapped up in the world his parents had created for him, he knew he couldn't have her. Someone as ambitious as Catalina would have choked in his world.

Only this world wasn't his any more. So maybe he could have her, even if it was just for the duration of this cruise.

The thoughts dispersed when Catalina let out another

throaty moan, her hips jerking against him and building the hardness there. The pressure was so unexpected—*delicious*—his head lolled back, making impact with the cheap plastic of the lounger.

Her thighs tensing on either side of his body sent another ripple of pleasure through him, and he surged up, wanting to drag her back onto his mouth and continue down the inevitable path they'd chosen. Only Catalina's eyes were no longer hooded with desire but wide enough for the starlight to bounce off them in a sparkle. Her body was no longer pliant under his touch but rigid.

'Cat…are you…?' He let the words hang in the air because he didn't know how to complete the sentence. His heart, still racing from their kiss, took on a completely different beat, one reflecting the mounting panic he could see in her eyes.

Catalina scrambled off him as if she'd been burned, knees wobbling slightly as she stepped back. Her hands flew to her hair, pushing it back from her face in quick, agitated motions.

Theo sat up, heart still hammering, the sudden chill of her absence making every inch of his body feel exposed.

'Cat?' he said quietly, careful not to spook her further. 'Hey. It's okay.'

She shook her head fast and jerky, as if she was trying to shake something loose. 'I… I shouldn't have—this was a bad idea.' Her voice cracked around the words, the earlier warmth and teasing entirely gone. In its place was a brittleness that made something cold bloom in his chest.

She pressed her palm to her lips, as if to keep anything else from escaping. 'We shouldn't,' she said, voice thin. 'I don't know what I'm doing, I don't—' She cut off, brows knitting as she stared at the deck between her feet. 'Everything is so… We're both… This isn't smart.' She let out a shaky exhale caught between a laugh and a sob.

Theo nodded before she could finish, already feeling the undertow of regret. 'Okay,' he said, giving her the route out. 'You're right.' He forced a steadiness into his voice, the same tone he'd used to call time of death or break bad news to a patient's family. Clinical, because that was how their relationship should be. 'We don't have to—none of this has to mean anything. Just something that happened after a day of high stress, which messed with our judgement.'

Catalina remained quiet, teeth biting into her bottom lip so hard he was sure she'd leave a mark. Then, without another word, she turned and fled across the deck, the sound of her sandals slapping solitary against the composite planks.

Theo couldn't move, too thrown by the events leading up to all of this. He waited until he'd lost track of time. The sea wind picked up as the hour deepened, bringing with it a chill that cut through the humidity. When he finally let himself collapse back onto the lounger, arms splayed and chest rising and falling in uneven increments, the world felt hollowed out.

CHAPTER SEVEN

Day Nine, Dubrovnik

'I MADE OUT with your brother.' The words were both a whisper and a scream, the syllables all fusing together until her sentence became a garbled mess of words.

Amelie peered up at her from Catalina's phone screen, eyes wide as saucers. Her lips parted, then moved wordlessly. Catalina's insides wound tighter with every second of silence ticking by, and she forced herself not to fidget in her chair.

Amelie's entire face lit up in real time. The shriek that followed was so loud Catalina had to jerk one earbud out or risk permanent cochlear damage. She recovered just in time to see Amelie's excitement collapse into a fit of delighted giggles as she pounded a triumphant fist into her mountain of pillows.

'You did *what*?' Amelie's voice rose an octave, and the joy was so unfiltered, so completely uncontained, Catalina didn't know how to process it. Amelie was happy about it? Of all the reactions she had mentally prepared herself for, this one hadn't even occurred to her.

'But you said…' Her voice trailed off as she thought back to several conversations she'd had with her best friend leading up to the cruise, and none of them had involved

Theo. Other than the conversation they'd had about Amelie's poorly timed horse-riding debut, all the advice her best friend had given her before her voyage had very much centred around Catalina's need to break out of her own lane and try something new.

Theo hadn't been more than a footnote to that. But then why—?

'You didn't tell me to stay away from him,' she said, levelling an accusing glare at Amelie. Her best friend tilted her head to the side, giving an excellent impression of an owl as she blinked her big eyes.

'No, why would I do that?' she asked, the picture of innocence.

'But you told *him* to stay away from me.' It was what he'd said last night. In the moment, Catalina hadn't even questioned it. Having several siblings, she was more than aware of the dynamics and the specific rules she had to obey as a sister. Even though her relationship with her siblings was more akin to that between rivals, she knew some things were taboo even with the Reyes clan.

Only she would have expected to receive the same warning, given Amelie knew everything about their proximity and how much time they'd be forced to spend together—more willingly as the cruise went on.

Amelie looked somewhere off to the side, a sly smile accompanying the rosy blush crawling up her cheeks. 'Okay, listen…'

'Why did you tell him to stay away from me?'

'Because…' Amelie let out a sigh. 'I know my brother, and after everything that's happened to him, he needs to let loose a little. A part of me actually believes that breaking my ankle is some divine intervention on my brother's behalf. So he would be forced to leave his house, go on a cruise and actually be around some people. Work a job that is *not* destroying him.'

Catalina frowned. 'Okay, but then why tell him to stay away from me? I could have helped him "let loose", as you put it.' In fact, she was. But now she was wondering how Amelie's command to stay clear of her played into it.

'It's hard to explain. I just know my brother. If I hadn't told him something like that, it wouldn't have even occurred to him he *could* hang out with you. He would have just done his shifts, returned to his bed, rinse and repeat. Even just mentioning you put a dent in that plan.' Amelie shrugged. 'And I was right, wasn't I? Though I thought maybe you'd take him sightseeing, not suck face.'

Amelie burst out laughing when Catalina made a face at her words, and the sound was so infectious she joined in despite herself.

'So what I'm hearing is you basically pimped me out to your brother to get him out of his funk. Are you also planning on letting him take care of my little problem?'

Her best friend screwed her eyes shut. 'Ew, no. Or like, if you really need to, fine. But then we just found the first thing you and I can't talk about openly, because there is no way I will survive hearing about you and my brother doing it.'

Heat burst alive inside Catalina when her thoughts wandered down the path Amelie didn't want to discuss. Last night had not gone the way she'd expected. When she'd headed up to the pool deck, she had been looking for fresh air and a moment alone with her thoughts that wasn't inside her dim cabin.

But seeing Theo under the starlight, alone and so obviously untethered, she'd ended up sitting beside him. And then—God, she'd lost herself in the hush and the heat and the undeniable pull between them. It had been perfect. And then, less than a second after it started to feel real, she'd vaporised the moment. Sunk deep into her own panic and bolted.

She could still feel the press of his hands on her hips, the rough drag of his beard along the corner of her jaw, the way he'd asked if she was sure. It was only after she'd fled—like a cartoon character leaving a dust cloud and debris in her wake—that the shame had set in. She had chickened out, and not for the first time during this trip. Theo had been right there, his desire for her undeniable, and something within her had balked at it.

The confirmation of the knowledge that her one-sided crush hadn't been, well, one-sided had thrown her for a loop. When had that happened? She thought back to the moments they'd shared throughout the years, none of them standing out to her. He'd always been this brooding, unapproachable presence to her.

This development had to be more recent, right? Maybe as recent as the cruise. With what had happened to him back in the States, that would explain it. Weren't people more prone to rash decisions after a major life event?

This could be an opportunity she hadn't even realised she'd been waiting for.

Amelie's shocked gasp sounded metallic through the phone's speakers. 'Oh my God, you *like* him. I don't know if I should say *aw* or *ew*.'

Catalina bristled, her defences kicking in without her input. 'Girl, you've always known I had a crush on him.'

'Yeah, but I thought it was like my crush on Adam Sandler. Not like a *real* thing. How can you like Theo? He's literally the worst.'

Catalina rolled her eyes, but her pulse thudded in her

neck. 'He's not always the worst,' she muttered, and instantly regretted how plaintive it sounded.

'Gag. That's even worse! Now you see him doing, like, normal human things and you're in love?' Amelie clapped a pillow to her face, but not before Catalina caught the smile crimping at the corners of her mouth.

'That's…not… I mean—' She fumbled, mortified by the flash of heat rising through her cheeks. 'We didn't actually do anything, okay?'

'But you wanted to.' It wasn't a question.

Catalina closed her eyes, letting her breath escape in a hiss. 'No! *Maybe*. I panicked, and now I don't know how to be around him.'

Now, to be fair, she hadn't exactly been confronted with him today. Come to think of it, she *still* didn't know where he had been spending his nights. She'd meant to ask him on the pool deck last night but they had got…distracted. He'd said things she couldn't stop thinking about. Had opened up about what the pressure of his family name had done to him. And she'd shared things with him only Amelie knew. The closeness had wrapped around her like a fog, making her forget who was actually sitting in front of her—and how far-fetched the thought of them together really was.

Above her, the ship's PA system whirred to life, announcing their imminent arrival in Dubrovnik. With a sigh, Catalina sat up. 'Listen, I know you had fun with this. But it was a mistake. A moment of weakness after a long shift that had left both of us feeling vulnerable. Nothing serious has or will happen between me and your brother.'

Going by Amelie's unimpressed expression, she didn't believe a word she'd said. 'Right.'

'And to prove it to you, I will go to Dubrovnik today

and mingle—for real, this time. No Theo to ruin me for potential single men with his brooding presence.'

'Now that's the spirit.' Amelie perched higher on her pillow tower, tucking a leg beneath her as if settling in to a grand saga. 'Go forth and sow your wild oats, Cat. I want a ten-photo minimum. Extra points if you get at least one hot local to buy you a drink.'

Catalina snorted, waved goodbye and then ended the call.

By the time she made it off the gangway and onto Croatian soil, the sun was already bruising the sky over Dubrovnik's terracotta rooftops. Catalina stood at the edge of the old port and tried to summon an emotion other than exhaustion or a vague sense of cosmic embarrassment. The city shimmered, beautiful in a way that felt almost staged—white limestone walls, bougainvillea, alleys paved with centuries of intent. She wanted to feel something: thrill, wanderlust, even loneliness would do. Instead, all she could feel was the imprint of Theo's hands on her hips, the press of his mouth, the impossible ease of their conversation as they'd stargazed on the pool deck.

She'd spent all morning bracing herself for a run-in. Maybe he'd be on the shuttle bus into the city, or at the breakfast buffet, or in the queue for Customs. But he'd vanished. She'd spent the entire ride craning her neck to spot him, convinced that at any moment he'd materialise, looming and silent. Instead, she'd ended up sandwiched between a bachelorette party from Leeds and a pair of elderly German tourists who'd spent the entire trip arguing over which *Game of Thrones* episodes had been filmed on location.

Catalina tried to enjoy the city despite herself. She

wound her way through the old town, checking off the list she'd put together to distract herself—*Walk the walls. Find a dragon egg. Buy a fridge magnet*—and even managed to grab a coffee at a tiny bar tucked into an alley, where the server spoke five languages and insisted she try the local fig liqueur 'for luck'.

She was at Pile Gate, eyes closed and letting the late-afternoon sun coat her skin, when a voice behind her said, 'Melanin is not a force field, you know? You have to wear SP. I can see you're beginning to burn.'

It was so perfectly him that Catalina's heart skipped hard enough to leave her dizzy. She turned, and there he was: Theo in simple jeans and a navy shirt, the sleeves rolled up to show the muscles in his forearms, his hair messily windswept and his face clean-shaven for the first time since they'd boarded.

'You shaved.' She blurted the words out, the vision such a stark contrast from last night. The rough hair had abraded her skin, mixing pleasure with pain as they'd deepened the kiss. The memory was enough to summon the unwanted desire she'd been fighting all day—and all night before that.

His hand came up to his face, rubbing his cheeks. The corner of his mouth kicked up in a boyish smile. 'It was time for the beard to go.'

'How come?' She missed it. That was weird, right? She'd yelled at him about how hideous it was, yet eight days had somehow been enough to change her picture of him. Or maybe it had more to do with the fact that she now knew what it felt like against her skin.

Theo dropped his gaze down to his shoes, nudging a tiny rock before looking back up. When he did, a slice of vulnerability flashed in his eyes—the same thing she'd seen last night. It lasted no more than a second before it disappeared, leaving the usual mask of indifference in place.

'It was time to let go.'

'Oh...'

Her throat squeezed at the admission, and for a heartbeat she thought he might actually say more. That he'd lay it all bare, the thing that had been simmering just beneath the surface since...since always? Maybe she should say something? Tell him that last night had been a mistake. Fun up until the point where she'd bolted, but still a mistake.

'How are you enjoying Dubrovnik?' she asked instead, feeling like a right chicken as they fell into a slow walk.

'Not bad,' he said, and the words drifted lazily between them. 'I didn't expect much, but the city's beautiful. Even the air smells different here.' He seemed distracted, or maybe just uncertain—his hands kept finding and leaving his pockets.

Catalina tried to orient herself, to find the familiar tension, the old comfort of their mutual antagonism. It stubbornly refused to surface.

'What does it smell like?' she asked.

Theo considered the question, then shrugged, glancing over at her. 'Stone. Sea. And a little like burnt sugar. I passed at least three gelato places.'

'Don't tempt me,' she muttered, then caught herself. 'I'm trying to pace myself after the local speciality coffee that was more sugar than coffee. And a fig liqueur the bartender swore would change my life.'

'Did it?'

Catalina shrugged, trying her best to ignore the tension following their words. They had to address it, right? That was the reason her stomach wound itself into a tight knot with every step they took, immune to the Croatian beauty surrounding them?

'Jury's still out. It spiked my blood sugar and it's giving me some cravings. Not the worst problem to have in Dubrovnik.'

'Did you eat already?' He didn't look at her as he spoke, walking forward with the confidence of someone who knew where they were going. Catalina, meanwhile, was so frazzled by his appearance, she wasn't able to do more than follow—not even contemplating where he might lead her.

'Just some snacks here and there. I didn't feel like sitting down and having a whole meal. Too...' Her voice trailed off when she realised what she'd been about to say.

Was there a chance Theo would let her get away with this? Her stomach did another loop when his head tipped to give her a sidelong glance. 'Too what?'

I'm too freaked out about us making out, and if I stop for even one second, that's all I can think about. The words were right there in her amygdala, along with all the other stuff Theo brought forth in her. But she wouldn't say them. No, that would be weird.

So yeah, she might have figured out that her crush was a bit more reciprocated than she'd thought it would be. Not a big deal. Except in all those years, Catalina hadn't even once entertained the idea of acting on said crush. A part of her was busy convincing herself the reason for it was because Theo was her best friend's brother. Forbidden fruit.

But now that they had stepped over the line she'd never thought they'd cross, she had to admit her reluctance had come from a different place: his obvious dislike of her.

Only that idea lay in tatters at her feet, his desire for her so clear it had freaked her out and beaten her into a retreat that was still causing her no small amount of embarrassment.

'I feel a bit...frazzled,' she ended up saying, lacking the proper vocabulary to say—or rather *avoid* saying—what she really wanted to say.

Theo, of course, didn't let the matter drop. 'Frazzled?' he repeated, head tilting to the side in such a familiar way she now couldn't see the gesture without seeing him, too.

'That's the most accurate word I can come up with, Theo. Take it or leave it.'

They continued to walk in silence, the low mumbling of the surrounding people wrapping around them. Her steps were aimless, her brain wiped clean of her intended itinerary and simply following the street one step at a time. Or maybe she was following Theo, even though she had no idea why. They'd said what they were willing to say—which evidently wasn't a lot—so they should go their own ways again. Slip back into what their relationship used to be before the kiss. Before this entire cruise.

'Are you okay?' They'd reached a quiet viewing platform overlooking the port, and they stood there, watching throngs of people boarding the ship again.

Theo's words took a few seconds to register as Catalina disentangled herself from her thoughts. She blinked a couple of times and then looked up at him. Nope. That was a mistake. With the beard gone, his handsomeness had evolved to a new level. Not that she didn't like the beard. The feel of it still lingered on her skin, invading her thoughts whenever she let them drift too far from the safe zone.

'Yeah, I am...' Catalina gave the words a moment to sink in and become the truth through sheer willpower. They did not. Before Theo could say anything else, she hung her head and let out a deep sigh. 'No, I'm not. I'm not—'

Catalina's whole body tensed so hard she could feel the muscles twitch in her legs. She hugged her arms to her ribcage and blurted, 'I'm sorry about last night.'

Theo's lips parted; she watched the words hit him, watched his eyes flicker with too many emotions to interpret. She pushed on before he could respond. 'I know I was telling you all these things about what I'm hoping to get out of this cruise and how you should help me. But I didn't mean... I wasn't talking about *you* doing all of...ugh.'

Theo stilled beside her, his focus so sharp she felt its pressure on her skin. She expected a quip, a smug arch of brow, proof he'd won some private game she'd never agreed to play. Instead, when he spoke, his voice had a distant quality to it.

'Don't apologise. This is on me. I promised to be your wingman and I should have stuck to that. I shouldn't have let myself get carried away. It was a long day, and I shouldn't have put all of my problems on you. Or kissed you.'

Yes, of course. That made sense. Catalina had struggled with the same thoughts of vulnerability all day, leading her around the city without actually taking it in. His words should be the relief she'd been chasing. The confirmation that even though something had happened, it wasn't a big deal. Nothing had been broken between them, and they could go back to their normal ways where they repelled each other like oil and water. Where the most he had to tell her was a snide comment here and there. Where she didn't have to contemplate if he maybe liked her too.

So why did his words press down on her, making it harder to breathe? What was that sludge-like substance her blood had turned into? Catalina knew what it couldn't be: regret.

'Okay, cool…yeah. Sounds like we are on the same page.' She struggled through those words, finding them somewhere in the back of her brain, and because of that they didn't sound sincere or even real.

Theo picked up on it, too. A line appeared between his brows, and when his gaze swept up and down her entire form, a shiver crawled down her spine. The concern in his eyes was clear, but it came with a flavour of something else that contradicted what he'd just said. A hunger that had been clawing at her for longer than she was willing to admit.

'Where are you sleeping?' Catalina blurted the words out, the question the first thing that came into her head as she looked for a distraction from the searing heat his eyes raised in her.

Something inside her squirmed when she saw the surprise ripple over his expression. Not often could she surprise him, but the question kept nagging at her whenever she settled down in the cabin, waiting for the door to open. All the nights leading up to yesterday, the thought had filled her with quiet unease. Last night, however…

Theo looked down at his shoes again, a gesture more familiar by the day. She'd always thought of him as stalwart—unshakable. But even without knowing what she knew from Amelie, she could see beyond the abrasive façade now. See the man behind the figure he'd created to keep himself safe. Sane.

'You noticed my absence?' he asked, and was there a flirty tone to his voice, or was Catalina's desperate brain conjuring things? Hadn't they just agreed that the kiss—and any potential additions—had been a mistake?

'Given you are quite...um, noticeable...yes. I did *notice* that a seven-foot tall man did not show up in my cabin every night.'

A thrill went through her as he looked back up and the corner of his mouth kicked up in a half-smile. 'I'm six foot five.'

She pursed her lips. 'I rounded up.'

'I hope you don't round this liberally with your prescriptions.' Now his lips split in a smirk, sending her heart rushing through her body.

'I—well, of course not. I'm a fully qualified doctor even if I haven't decided on a specialty yet.' Catalina's voice came out more breathless than sharp, betraying her lack of composure. This was the other thorn in her side—her complete lack of motivation to find a residency and continue her training.

Which was so unlike her, who had competed for first place in everything she'd done all her life. Where was that competitive spirit when it came to her career now?

'Good. Just checking.' He shifted his weight, shoulders relaxing, and somehow the tension that had bound them for the last several minutes just...disappeared. She saw it in the way his mouth softened, in the way he tucked his hands into his pockets and angled his body towards hers, not away.

They stood that way for a long moment, neither of them willing to break the fragile truce, until finally Theo said, 'So are we good?'

Catalina took a breath, then another, and found that the answer was yes—even if she still didn't fully understand what 'good' meant for them. 'We're good.' She even managed a small smile and hoped it was convincing. 'If you tell me where you've been staying. Your refusal to answer the question is concerning.'

Theo sighed and shook his head. 'You're really going to drag it out of me, aren't you?' His words carried an undertone of admonishment, but then he continued, 'I'm not avoiding the question for any nefarious reasons. I just... Amelie clearly didn't think this swap through in its entirety, and I didn't want to be a presence in your personal space when I know you don't want me there.'

Catalina's first instinct was to insist that she didn't mind having him in her space. That he'd been wrong to assume she wanted him as far away as possible from her. But she couldn't say it because it would put her across the boundary they'd just re-established. The more distance there was between them, the better.

'I appreciate it,' she said instead, giving him a small smile. 'But this still doesn't answer my question. Like, have you been sleeping on the loungers on the pool deck all this time?'

Catalina laughed as she said it, going for the most absurd scenario she could come up with. Sure, he'd wanted to make her feel safe, but even Theo wouldn't go to such lengths.

He didn't laugh. Didn't say anything, either. His mouth twitched as if caught between a smile and a frown, and as the silence stretched between them, Catalina gasped. 'You did not!'

'Not that often on the pool deck,' Theo said, raising his hands in defence.

'Oh, but in other parts of the ship? Have you been sneaking into the cinema at night, living there like a stowaway?' There was no way Theo had done that, right? He would have arranged his own cabin.

'No, not the cinema. I don't think that would have been particularly comfortable.' He gave another shake of his head, and she could see the different thoughts rippling over his face. Theo was debating whether he should tell her. But why would he...?

'Until yesterday, I was mainly staying in the little hospital-like room we're now using to isolate worse cases of the virus,' he said, voice low as if he had to force himself to speak.

'Theodore!'

'It's *fine*. They didn't have any empty cabins, so I made do with it. I didn't tell you because you don't need to worry about it. Okay? I got it covered.'

Her brain short-circuited, skipping every reasonable follow-up and landing on the most indelicate one. 'Wait—how have you been showering?' The words came out before she'd realised she was thinking them, and the flush of embarrassment hit her half a second too late to reconsider her words.

A slow smile crept across his mouth. 'The gym's open twenty-four hours. I use the crew showers there.' He shrugged, as if the image of Theo, alone at three a.m. towelling off under the fluorescent lights, was entirely mundane.

It was not. It was really, really not.

'Oh my God. You really are a stowaway,' Catalina said, but it came out more fond than frustrated. 'You can't keep living like that for almost two more weeks, Theo. You're coming back to the cabin.'

The invitation came out with far less resistance than she'd expected. Because at the very front of her mind she knew with absolute certainty she couldn't have Theo Morgan next to her in bed. The split second she took right now to consider her proposal was enough to fill her head with all sorts of ideas and pictures she knew she needed to stay away from.

Yet she didn't take the offer back. Everything about Theo might spell danger to her, but she couldn't leave him to sleep on a lounger on the pool deck all night. Or worse, have him sneak into the quarantine ward and risk getting sick himself.

'Cat—'

She knew that stern expression far too well and shook her head.

'Nope. Don't argue with me, Theo. I know you are trying to be considerate, and I appreciate it. But this is not an adult solution. We can *share* a room without issues. Right?'

He hesitated. She could see the calculation of reluctance on his face before the words arrived. 'If you're sure.'

'I'm sure,' she said, more firmly than she felt. 'No drama, no tension. We're both adults. And besides, Amelie would murder me if she knew I'd let you sleep in the quarantine room instead of a real bed.'

Catalina owed him this measure of consideration even if it made her squirm. He had dutifully gone out with her a couple of times and played her wingman, even if he'd done a poor job of it. Catalina might be hyper-competitive and always looking for the challenge in anything she did, but that didn't mean she wouldn't look out for others. Maybe it was her ultimate flaw, having always put herself second whenever her siblings had needed something. She had somehow set the precedent of being a third parent to both her older and younger siblings, taking care of all the things they needed.

Never being asked what she needed. To the point where she now didn't know how to continue her life when it was time to put her needs first.

Or maybe the challenge here would be how to resist

Theo while still chasing the fun she'd come here for. Ugh, when had this become so complicated?

'But no shenanigans,' she said, glaring at him even though the words were meant for herself.

Theo's mouth quirked. 'No shenanigans,' he agreed solemnly, as if swearing the Hippocratic Oath again.

'Great. Settled.' Catalina exhaled all the pent-up nerves like a diver coming up for air. 'Now that you're officially not homeless, let's get moving. Ship's leaving in, what, two hours?' She checked her phone and did a double-take. 'Forty-five minutes. Crap.'

They both glanced at the port, then at the warren of alleys winding down towards the water, and realised they had quite a way to go to reach the ship. With no further ceremony, Catalina whirled around and strode towards where Theo stood, when her foot caught on an uneven cobblestone.

The world tilted beneath her as she lost her balance, falling face first towards the ground.

She didn't have time to brace or even panic. Two strong hands closed around her waist, righting her with a jolt that slammed her back against the wall of Theo's chest. For a breathless second she felt his pulse thundering against her spine, the heat of him steadying her as if they were the only two people in the city. His arms didn't let go immediately; instead, one palm hovered at her ribs, the other settling just above her hip, anchoring her with a gentleness she'd only recently learned was so *him*.

'You okay?' His voice was low, soothing her panic even as embarrassment spiked through her.

'Yeah, I just—' She tried to laugh off the humiliation, but it came out shaky. 'I guess I got too excited about going back to our shoebox cabin.'

Theo's hand lingered. If she'd wanted to escape, she could have. Instead, she stood there, half-turned in his arms, her own hands braced on the flat planes of his chest. So close, their breaths mingled. She'd never realised how much softer his mouth looked without the beard, or how the new smoothness sharpened the lines of his jaw, made all that intensity feel exposed and dangerous.

His eyes flickered down to her lips, then up again, searching for permission.

Catalina should not give it. They'd just agreed to no shenanigans, and standing this close to him had to fall in that category, right? Plausible deniability had stopped the moment neither of them hadn't immediately moved away after righting her.

But instead of doing that, she pushed her chin out, enough to close the distance between their mouths and give Theo the consent he'd been asking for.

Her eyes fluttered closed when his warm breath grazed her cheeks, and her heart lurched, bracing for his touch with a giddiness inappropriate for what they were about to do.

Except this time, Theo didn't close the distance. The expectation built, balancing on a knife edge, and then—he ducked his head, brushing his lips against her forehead instead. It was brief, featherlight, barely contact at all. When he drew back, his hands fell away, a careful step creating enough space that the cold air rushed in between their bodies.

'We should go,' he said softly, voice so low she almost didn't catch it. There wasn't a trace of mockery or indifference, just a complicated knot of longing and regret, the kind of gravity that threatened to pull her straight under if she let herself look too hard.

She wanted to say something—anything—that would make sense of the whiplash between her pulse and what he'd just done. Catalina couldn't decide if she was relieved or devastated.

But she just nodded, following a step behind Theo as they walked the winding alleys of Dubrovnik back to the shuttle that would get them to port.

CHAPTER EIGHT

Day Ten, at sea

THE DRONING OF the bass was particularly obnoxious tonight. Or maybe it was Theo's mood. Or perhaps his general dislike of literally everything might have to do with Catalina standing at the bar and talking to some guy who clearly saw her more as an object than a person.

Not that it was any of his business. Theo was supposed to be her wingman. Talk her up to potential matches and then make himself scarce. Right now, the scarce bit was the only one he was following. In fact, he wasn't entirely sure if Catalina even knew he was here—watching like some kind of love-sick creep. How could he even tell her who would be a good match if he himself was resorting to such behaviour?

Hanging his head, he looked down at the half-empty beer bottle. His finger rubbed along the label until a corner of it peeled off, leaving a sticky residue behind.

He needed to get a grip on himself. After Dubrovnik, they'd come to a tentative truce and the agreement not to let any of their hormone-driven feelings get ahead of them. Unlike strangers on a cruise, they would still be in each other's life in some capacity. Though after what had happened at Morgan Greywater, he didn't know what that would look like. Would he ever again be welcome at his parents' home? Amelie had been able to form a relationship with them despite her refusal to have anything to do with the family legacy. But she'd made that choice early on, rejecting the name and all it entailed to pursue her own happiness.

His parents had been sceptical back then, but had quickly shifted their attention back to their son. His failure to live up to expectations wouldn't go down as easily. They hadn't even reached out to him since he'd walked out of his office, never to return.

'This is what you do for fun? Brooding?' Theo looked up as Dr Chen slid into the chair opposite his, holding her own drink in her hand.

'Dr Chen, good to see you,' he said, but the woman shook her head.

'Please call me Sarah. I'm all for reporting structure, but neither of us is working right now,' she said with a smile infectious enough that Theo felt his own lips twitch.

'Very well, Sarah. How are things?' He gave her a cursory glance, surprised by how different she looked outside the clinic. They hadn't ever interacted when it wasn't about work, and he hadn't even considered socialising with her until the moment she'd sat down. Truth be told, he still wasn't in the mood to talk to anyone as his eyes kept flitting back to where Catalina stood, leaning against the bar, talking to…whoever that was.

'Good. Enjoying some time off for once. The situation with the virus is somewhat contained now, thank God. We had to disembark so many people and transfer them to the hospitals in Dubrovnik to reduce the risk for the passengers but, as you can see, things have been much calmer today,' she said, settling back in the chair and letting out a sigh. 'I thought it was about high time I came out for a bit, and imagine my surprise when I found you brooding here.'

Theo bristled at her words, though he wasn't sure why. Objectively speaking, he *was* brooding. Even he could acknowledge his mood. He just wasn't keen on talking about the why of it, and he got the feeling that was what Sarah was here to do.

She surprised him again when she said, 'So, Morgan Greywater? Not often we get such a big name to join us on a cruise.'

His stomach flipped over, muscles tensing at the mention of the hospital that had cost him so much.

'Not what I was planning on doing after leaving my position. You know my sister was supposed to be here.'

Sarah chuckled. 'Yes, and the only reason I even agreed to such a controversial swap was because of the guarantee your name carries. It doesn't mean much to the cruise as a whole, but I've read the articles you've published.' She paused, giving him a well-meaning smile. 'Doctors usually don't get to send someone else just because they can't make it.'

Of course, his being here was somehow another twist of the privilege his name brought. It was the thing people saw when they learned his last name—the fame and the doors it might open. No one took even a moment to look beyond and acknowledge the pressure that came with it. How much the name *Morgan* demanded on a personal level.

All the smoke and mirrors had ultimately led to his cracking.

'I appreciate your flexibility,' Theo replied, voice clipped despite himself.

Sarah tilted her head, studying him. 'May I ask you a personal question?'

He furrowed his brow, but gave a nod for her to continue.

'Why did you accept the swap? I understand helping your sister, but it's not like your family couldn't afford the contract penalty associated with a last-minute cancellation. Don't get me wrong; your work is excellent. I just don't get the feeling you want to be here.'

He let out a soft breath, gaze slipping past her to the dance floor, where Catalina's laugh rang out above the club noise. 'I didn't come here to enjoy myself, no.'

'So why come at all?'

Her direct question drew his gaze back to her, his mind stalling when he couldn't come up with an immediate answer. It should be clear to anyone *why* he'd come—including himself.

'My sister needed my help.'

His mouth snapped shut when Sarah shook her head.

'No, we've been over this. With who you two are, no one *needed* anything. So, try again. Why did you even bother to come here?'

Theo bristled, his pride making him want to push against Sarah and turn the question around on her. Who was she to him to even ask these questions? They weren't friends just because they worked together—and even that was a stretch. Most of the time Theo spent on his own in one of the exam rooms.

His jaw muscles tensed, molars grinding against each other as he shut those thoughts down one by one. Why was he reacting like this to what was only an innocent question? Sure, one that was designed to uncover more of him, but he reminded himself that colleagues *liked* to get to know each other better. Just because he'd been raised from early on to see everyone as competition didn't mean others functioned the same way.

Hadn't he spent the time after quitting trying to de-program himself from all those things his parents had forced on him?

'This offer arrived when I was craving a change. It seemed wrong to refuse just because cruise ships aren't all that appealing to me when I didn't specify *what* change I wanted to see.' The words got as close to the truth as he felt comfortable with.

Catalina's laugh reached his ears again, the sound loud in his ears despite the murmuring of the crowd and the buzz of music filtering through the speakers. His gaze darted up again, examining her from head to toe, looking for a sign—or maybe an excuse—for him to show up and disrupt whatever she was doing. Except that would fly in the face of being a *good* wingman, which he had agreed to be for her against his better judgement.

'I see, and I guess this is you trying to make the best of it? Or is your reluctance more tied to the fact that there *is* something on this cruise ship that you *do* want, but you would prefer not to want it?' Sarah smiled when he raised his eyebrows, failing to hide the shock her words kicked loose in him.

'How did you…?'

She shrugged. 'This isn't a holiday for me; it's my life. I spend most of my year bouncing between ships on different assignments. Which means I get to know a lot of people. Enough for me to categorise them. Doctors and other medical professionals sign up for different reasons, but if you boil them all down to their core, there are really only a handful of reasons someone works on a cruise rather than a hospital or a clinic.'

Theo opened his mouth to protest, but again shut it without giving in to the impulse to say the first words coming to him to defend himself. He'd not let himself dwell on *his* reason for being here, instead feeling far more comfortable hiding behind the excuse his sister had provided with her broken ankle. Sarah was right, though. If he really hadn't wanted to do this, he could have refused. Offered to pay the penalty in the contract himself.

Deep down, he knew his decision had been swayed by more than what he was willing to admit. Yes, doing a job with far lower stakes than what he'd been doing all his career was helping him appreciate why he'd gone into medicine in the first place. But then there was Catalina. Amelie had mentioned how her best friend was still going, and that had been when the *no* building in his throat had died.

But Theo couldn't admit that out loud. Quietly pining for a woman who'd always seen him more as a rival than a potential love interest was one thing. But deciding to come on a cruise because the aforementioned woman would be there too? That fell squarely into the territory of stalker vibes.

Sarah gave him a knowing smile. 'You don't have to tell me anything. I'm just an old medical officer who has seen this exact scenario play out in front of her more times than she can count.' She turned around, following his gaze as it landed on Catalina. 'And I think from all I've seen over the last few days, she might appreciate you rescuing her right now.'

He tensed at her words, focusing on Catalina's body language while trying not to get distracted by what simply *looking* at her did to him.

'I can't force myself into a situation simply because I don't like seeing it,' he said, the words an assurance to himself as much as to Sarah.

But the woman shrugged as if he hadn't laid out some

solid reasoning. 'The face she's making—that's not someone who is enjoying themselves right now. And I know what her expression looks like when she *is* with someone she likes,' Sarah said with another shrug. 'But don't listen to me if you disagree. I hardly know you two, after all.'

What was he doing, standing by while Catalina tried to find someone else when *he* was right here? When he wanted this? *Her.* Sure, the hundreds of reasons why they didn't make any sense together stood right in front of him like a mountain. For one, his life was in complete disarray, and coming here on the cruise had been like hitting the pause button on that. The moment he got back to the States, it would all come back like a tidal wave. Sorting through the fallout with his parents—figuring out what *he* wanted rather than what they expected from him—would require time and space. Neither of those things would be fair in a new relationship.

Plus, she had her residency ahead of her. Theo wasn't sure if she'd applied anywhere, but with how he'd left things with his parents, he wouldn't be surprised if they'd blacklisted him across all prestigious institutions. Association with him would only hurt her chances of getting a good placement. He couldn't let that happen to her.

But what if it wasn't a relationship? From what Catalina had told him, she was looking to reclaim her life by pursuing things that brought her pleasure rather than trying to be the most impressive person in the room. Could that be what he had to offer her? A safe space to explore, confined to the duration of their trip?

'I have to go,' Theo said, pushing himself upright before he could talk himself out of it. 'Thanks for the chat,' he added as he passed by Sarah, giving her a small smile before weaving through the crowd to get to the bar.

* * *

Was she just not into men? It was the only thing Catalina could think of to explain the complete lack of chemistry she'd experienced with every single person since embarking on this cruise adventure. Surely they couldn't all be trash like Dave?

To be fair to the men who'd approached her, none of them had sunk to Dave levels of creepiness, but neither were they conjuring butterflies in her stomach, to the point where she was seriously questioning her sexuality. Had she *really* never been attracted to a man before? No, that couldn't be right.

She knew what she wanted and also what she expected. It was the swooping stomach, the bursts of electricity shooting through her entire body as Theo's lips pressed down on her—

Oops.

A flush crept up her neck, temporarily rendering her incapable of hearing anything. Not that it mattered because Brian over here wasn't getting an invitation back to her cabin. Especially not now that she'd asked Theo to move back in. He'd gone to fetch his things as soon as they'd got back from Dubrovnik, and to avoid seeing him after that almost-*whatever* at the lookout point, she'd gone straight for one of the ship's bars, intent on turning her virginity mission into reality.

Okay, so there was *one* man to whom she was attracted. Progress, right? At the very least, she could now confirm she was *capable* of attraction to the opposite sex. Just not the Brians and Daves of this ship. No, she needed to find a Theo-type person who wasn't Theo himself.

A part of her had briefly considered the possibility of going down that path with him. She'd told him everything, including her reasons. A man of his age and calibre would have more than enough experience to guide her through this.

And perhaps most importantly, one look from him was enough to turn her into a puddle. Had been for years now. Maybe that was what was happening between them. With the impromptu kiss and their renewed closeness from earlier, there was clearly something between them. For the longest time she'd thought her crush was unrequited, and she'd lived quite peacefully with that fact.

'You said you are part of the crew?' Brian asked, voice hoarse enough to scratch her ear canal. Yeah, there was no way this was going to happen tonight. Catalina had struck out once again—was that the right use of the sports metaphor?—and she would be going back alone.

Mostly alone. Were it not for her old/new roommate, who would no doubt be waiting for her.

'Yeah, I'm a doctor,' she said, her eyes roaming around the room to plot her escape route. After the encounter with Dave, at least she was getting better at that. 'And I actually have an early shift tomorrow. You know, saving lives and whatever. One alcohol poisoning at a time. It was nice to meet you.'

She plastered on a smile and, before Brian could react, she moved away and into the crowd, ready to slink back to her cabin and lick her wounds. With every day that passed, her hopes of accomplishing her goal sank lower. Who would have thought that a virgin wouldn't just be shy about sex but also about all the preamble that led to it? The thought of suffering these conversations long enough to get to a point where she would let any of these guys near her exhausted her.

Or maybe *one* specific man had ruined her, since all this

didn't apply to him. No, conversations with Theo were easy. So were the silences. And the moments in between, when they weren't really doing anything but still hanging out. Hell, even in Dubrovnik, after the world's most awkward encounter the night before, the moment they'd found each other again, it just worked. The tension had ebbed away within seconds as they'd found their rhythm again, and then it had been as if they'd never accidentally made out.

Why were things so *natural* with him, but other men were downright excruciating?

As she reached the edge of the room, a hand closed around her arm—stopping her in her tracks. Catalina whirled around, ready to tell Brian what she *really* thought of him. But the words died in her throat when she stared into the grey eyes of Theo, the sight instantly familiar and putting her at ease.

Though that lasted for a mere second before she saw the fire ablaze in his stare. Somehow the flame jumped the space between them, building up beneath her skin until her own body temperature spiked to an infernal level. She swallowed, her throat dry from the alcohol and the shouted conversation of the evening.

Theo towered over her, and when he took another step towards her she had to tip her head backwards so she could still see him. Her back pressed against the floor-to-ceiling windowpane behind her, the glass doing precious little to cool her down.

'I don't think I can be your wingman any more,' he said as he bent down next to her ear so she could hear him without shouting. His voice was low and filled with gravel, sending a shiver down her spine.

'If you were doing your wingman job today, then I have to agree. Not your best performance, seeing I'm once again solo,' she replied, though why they were taking the conversation in that direction, she wasn't sure. Nothing about his body language—or how close he stood—gave her any specific indication.

'You said I should stay away. That I frighten the men you're trying to court. So I stayed away, even though I hated sitting over there being forced to watch you pursue *other* men.' There was an edge to his voice that shot right through Catalina, settling in a swirling vortex in the pit of her stomach. What he was saying wasn't hot. It wasn't even cute. Why was she reacting as if it was?

'I'm not forcing you to watch anything,' she hissed, though the thought of him standing somewhere in the crowd and watching her did something funny to her insides. Twisted and shook them until they were completely rearranged. 'Maybe you should work on yourself before you come here on your high horse, lecturing me.'

'I promised you I would help. That doesn't just go away because I can't keep a lid on my jealousy.' His words turned into a growl—or at least that was the only word Catalina could come up with that fitted.

But her mind latched onto something else. 'Jealousy?'

His huffed laugh was warm against her cheek. 'What? You think I'm unaffected by all this? That I just kiss you one day and forget about everything the next? You are vastly overestimating my compartmentalisation skills.'

He paused, and when he breathed in his chest expanded enough for their upper bodies to touch. Her knees grew weak, and her hands—developing a will of their own—came down on either side of his collar, hanging onto him. A tremble went through Theo at the light touch. Or maybe she was the one trembling; she wasn't sure.

'Cat—' her name somehow echoed through the tiny

space between them '—don't make me watch from the sidelines again. I don't think I can.' His head dipped lower, his nose pressing against the side of her throat so she could feel every exhale dance over her skin. Her grip on him tightened, fingers fisting into the fabric of his shirt.

'I'm not making you do anything,' she repeated, though keeping track of the conversation was becoming harder by the second, her brain filled with this lusty haze only *his* touch could conjure within her. Was that even possible? Could someone simply be attracted to one person and only them?

'You're not. But you're still the one who holds the solution to my dilemma.' His mouth trailed down her neck, each kiss sending renewed shivers through her until she was nothing more than a trembling mess.

'What dilemma?' Deep down, Catalina knew his struggle because she was experiencing the same one whenever she went out to find someone who would never live up to the comparison to Theo. Would never hit the same nerve or hold her attention the same way. It had been going on for years, her nurturing a one-sided crush, which had now turned out to be far less unrequited.

Only she didn't know what it meant for her—for them.

'Every person I watch you with, every time I see you laugh or smile or even touch someone's arm in a friendly way, something jolts through me and I think: this should be me.' His breath was hot against her neck, raising the hairs all the way down her arms. 'Let it be me.'

His voice was low and pleading in a way she'd never heard from Theo. It sent a thrill through her, knowing how he'd considered her. In a way that wasn't derision or cold calculation. No, he *wanted* her, the way she wanted him. Had that always been the case?

'What about…your family? Your life outside of this ship?'

Her conversation with Amelie flashed through her mind. Even though her best friend had told Theo to stay away, Catalina knew that had been a pretext. Though what exactly the younger Morgan sibling was planning was beyond her. Only that it could be nothing good.

Theo hummed, the vibration ghosting over her skin and making her arch her back to get closer to him. His lips brushed over her collarbone, and she gasped when his tongue found the hollow of her throat.

Then he straightened, touching their foreheads against each other. There was nothing but fire in his eyes. 'You're looking to break out of this pattern you're in. Choose yourself, you said? I can do that right here, within the confines of this cruise. And after it's over, we go back to our separate lives.'

A pinprick of worry broke through the tidal wave of lust crashing through her at his words. Catalina hadn't put much thought into the after. Or into the future in general. There was the matter of continuing her education as a doctor, but when she and Amelie had made the plan for the cruise they'd both promised not to think about anything else.

So Theo didn't want a relationship. That made sense. Catalina didn't want a relationship either, right? That hadn't been the goal of this entire endeavour. No, coming here had been a radical act of self-love, letting herself experience new things and leave the humdrum of her daily life behind for a bit. Gain some distance to understand who she wanted to be in the future—in her personal and professional life.

And yes, there was also the bit about her sexuality and figuring out what she liked there—in a no-strings-attached and emotionally safe way. No room to overthink things or get stuck in the same pattern of people-pleasing she had barely broken out of with her parents.

'Okay.' She breathed the word out. Through the noise of the bar, she thought he hadn't heard her when he kept staring at her, blinking almost in time with the bass vibrating through the dance floor.

But then his mouth crashed down on hers, tongue swiping over her lips and into her mouth in a greedy kiss that stole all the air from her lungs.

CHAPTER NINE

Day Ten, at sea

THEY'D BARELY MADE it through the door when Theo pounced on her. Caging her body with his, the way he had back at the bar, he pushed her against the closed door of her cabin and drew her into a lingering kiss. His hands found her hips, thumb tracing a lazy upward spiral across the fabric of her dress, kneading the spot he'd already learned was hypersensitive. Catalina caught herself half-laughing, half-moaning as the world began to contract—there was only this cubic metre of space, the twin heartbeats thudding in her ears. There was no more space for overthinking or wondering about the consequences. Theo's words had been clear. They would treat this like people treated Las Vegas: what happened on the ship, stayed on the ship.

Theo's grip tightened around her as she moaned, and the contrast between their first kiss and now was so stark it sent sparks shooting across her body. There was nothing gentle in how he held her, the hunger coiled in his fingertips, the press of his chest pinning her so tightly that every shallow breath was inhaled from him. He kissed her as if he'd been planning this for years—and for a broken fragment of a second, Catalina let herself believe he had. That this wasn't a result of circumstances but that he'd been quietly pining for her the way she had for him—hiding his true feelings behind derision.

She knew this was a dangerous path to walk down but, caught up in the moment, she couldn't stop herself.

Her hands slid under his shirt, desperate for skin and certainty. He growled, a sound that vibrated against her lips and down her spine, and then he broke the kiss just long enough to look her in the eyes. 'Stop me if you want to,' he said, voice unsteady but true.

She shook her head, incapable of words. If anything, the pressure of his restraint—the tension in his jaw, how much he was obviously holding back—made her want him more. She wanted him unspooled and raw, not the carefully presented version of Theo Morgan the world saw.

He dropped his head to her throat, mouthing kisses across her collarbone while his hands mapped her body as if he were learning it in Braille. She gasped, legs turning to water as her back arched, every gentle scrape of his stubble drawing a soft moan from her.

'I never want you to stop,' Catalina replied, unable to keep the truth of her feelings hidden. Not when they were so close, his breath mingling with hers and his hands touching her skin reverently. Delicately. As if he wanted her for more than just this moment.

Theo responded with nothing more than a growl, and his hands slipped to the hem of her dress, fingers toying with it while he pressed his face into her neck. She tipped her chin, hungry for more, but he bunched the fabric of her dress and palmed her hips, steering her from the door to the bed with stumbling steps. They crashed onto the narrow mattress and she caught herself with a laugh, the sound melting into another gasp as he pressed her down, hands bracketing her ribs, kissing her as if he could swallow the sound of her moans to keep them forever.

'You really thought we could sleep on this bed together for the rest of this cruise without anything happening?' he asked as he pushed himself up on his elbows to look down at her. He settled in the cradle of her parted thighs, and when she felt his arousal press against her this time Catalina braced herself for the same panic to sweep through her.

It didn't come. No, she stayed wrapped in the luscious fog of passion, her mind not drifting to the thought of her virginity, of the consequences that might await them if they did this. Tomorrow seemed too far away to consider when she was burning up inside.

Theo *wanted* her. It was as clear as it could get. Undeniable, yet her mind still grappled with the idea. How long had this been going on right in front of her eyes? Had Theo always been interested, and somehow she'd not connected the dots? Was this the reason for their antagonistic relationship? She tried to remember who had started the sniping between them all those years ago, but she couldn't. Not when Theo's hands found their way under her dress again, callused palms scraping up her bare thighs until he got to her stomach.

His breathing hitched. She felt it; the tremor travelling down the line of his forearm as he raked his knuckles up her side. 'I'm going to lose my mind,' he muttered, half to himself and half to her, before ducking down to mouth along her jaw. There was reverence in the hunger, every kiss and squeeze a question—*Are you sure? Do you want this?*—that kept repeating until she wanted to sob *Yes, yes, yes* into the hot space between their bodies.

She found herself greedy for every new sensation: the velvet heat of his tongue at her ear, the pressure of him nudging her thighs further apart, the way he seemed desperate to touch all of her at once.

'Cat,' he said, voice raw.

She opened her eyes—when had she shut them?—and the pure need in his gaze sent her head spinning. But beneath it was something more. A glimmer of concern? When she realised it, Catalina almost burst out laughing. Of course he would worry about her—about taking advantage of her?—even when it was clear as day she wanted him. Had wanted him for far longer than she was willing to admit. Even though she'd tried her best to fulfil her mission and reclaim control of her life, none of the men she'd met had been even remotely interesting to her. Only Theo had caught her attention in every way she needed.

Theo's lips hovered just above hers, his weight braced on trembling arms. For a moment, he seemed on the verge of pulling back, the old reticence fighting with the heat in his gaze. Catalina reached, curling her fingers into his hair. She pulled him close enough that his breath fanned her lips, close enough she could taste the doubt, the want, the worry.

'I want this,' she whispered. 'I want you.' The words bubbled out, unpractised and rough, a confession more than a command.

But it worked as the latter. Theo's mouth crashed onto hers, bruising and needy. Catalina arched up against him, fingers tunnelling beneath the collar of his shirt, frantic to feel the heat of his skin. She clawed at the buttons, popping the first two before he even registered her intent. A helpless, strangled sound broke in his throat as she yanked his shirt from his waistband, hands spreading over the hard terrain of his chest. He tensed beneath her touch, every muscle drawn taut, then seemed to melt at the sweep of her palm up and over his heart.

Catalina let out a moan when Theo pressed closer, her hands skimming across his skin. Was this what it felt like to touch someone else? As if there was a low current running beneath their skin, making electricity jump back and forth between them.

'Do you like touching me?' he asked.

She blinked, startled by the vulnerability in it. As if he worried the answer could be anything else but the one she gave.

'Yes,' she said, and her palms pressed harder, as if to demonstrate.

His smile was slow but radiant, forcing the breath out of her lungs. 'Good. I want you to enjoy every touch. Make sure you're ready. And if things are going too fast, let me know.'

Theo didn't wait for her reply. His hands tightened around her hips and then he flipped her around, face first into the cushions. Fabric rustled above her—no doubt the shirt she'd only bothered to half remove—and then his fingers brushed over the nape of her neck. It was enough to send another wave of heat through her, tiny fires following as Theo opened her zip all the way down to her spine.

He splayed his hand over her skin, fingers fanning out and touching both of her shoulder blades. In her peripheral vision, she could see him move his other hand to peel the dress away from her body. Then he bent over, his hand vanishing—replaced by his face. His mouth, more specifically, lavishing her heated skin with more feather-light kisses. She gasped when his tongue darted out, licking her in a place she'd never thought to be particularly sensitive.

But then again, what did she know about sex? A half-drunk make-out session with some guy she couldn't remember was as far as her physical experience went. Not really something she could call *adventurous* by any means. No, as far as exploration was concerned, falling onto a far too soft mattress in a tiny cabin on a floating hunk of steel with her best friend's brother was the most adventurous Catalina had got in, well, ever.

And yes, having it all laid out like that, she might be in *a bit* of trouble. Was this actually the worst idea she'd ever had?

But before her thoughts could stray too far from the present moment, Theo reached the base of her spine and placed an open-mouthed kiss there. Even though her skin was heated all over, his breath still scorched her when he let out a stuttering breath that gave her an idea of how much this affected him, too.

This was the thought she kept coming back to. The idea that almost turned incomprehensible if she thought about it too long. No one had ever *wanted* her, at least not in the form she came. Hadn't she spent years struggling to be recognised by her family, until she'd simply given up on trying?

'Will you get on your knees for me, Cat?' Theo's words were a hushed whisper, his hands skating up her thighs and pushing up the fabric of her dress until it was bunched around her waist.

He lifted her up when she moved her already rubbery limbs, helping her get off the mattress enough so he could peel the dress away from her entirely. But instead of putting her back down on the bed, Theo pulled her towards him until her back was flush against his front. His arms snaked around her, caressing her stomach before tracing lazy circles upwards until he reached the underside of her breasts.

'You're not wearing a bra,' he whispered next to her ear

before placing a kiss below it. Catalina wanted to respond, but her words turned into a moan when he palmed both of her breasts.

'The advantage of having small boobs,' she breathed out between pants, losing most of her faculty to speak when his thumbs brushed along her nipples.

'Am I completely vain for wanting to believe you did this for me? You knew how I would react to seeing you walk around in this dress, looking at everyone but me?' He growled the words, punctuating every pause with another kiss or lick to her neck while his hands lavished her with the attention she'd known she'd wanted but hadn't realised just *how good* it would feel.

She had thought about Theo when deciding what to wear, though even now, in the position they were in, there was no way she could admit that. They might be naked in front of each other, but there were still some boundaries, right? And admitting how hot this jealous act of his was getting her—and how unnecessary it was for him to compare himself to anyone in her eyes—crossed a line. Their dynamic was already shaky, and she was under no illusions that this wouldn't change it further.

But right now, Catalina didn't care. She'd come here with a goal, and the only person capable of getting her to this point seemed to be Theo.

'If I say yes, will you touch me?' she said instead, head lolling back onto his shoulder when he squeezed her nipple hard enough to bring her to the edge of pleasure and pain.

He didn't answer. Instead, he moved his hand downward, playing with the seam of her underwear for a few excruciating seconds before dipping below the fabric. 'You tell me what feels good, okay?'

She meant to tease him, to say something snarky, but

the moment his fingers slid over and inside her—one, then two, with a slow and deliberate push—words simply vanished from her mind. He curled them as he pumped in and out, drawing a sound from her chest she'd never made before, a whimper that seemed to please him as much as it shocked herself. Theo's chin pressed to her shoulder, his mouth collecting every gasp and *'yes'* as he worked her with slow strokes and caresses, learning every twitch and spasm and shiver like a language only they spoke.

Her limbs and muscles stopped working altogether as the pressure at her core built, but his other hand wrapped around her waist, bracing her. Holding her up, holding her together. The world shrank to the slick, rhythmic pressure of his touch, and the only thing she could manage was to press her hips back, greedy for more friction, more of him. When he added his thumb, circling tight and insistent, the pleasure became a throttle, making her collapse back into his chest with a hoarse, shuddering exhale.

Theo's mouth worked up her neck, nipping and sucking at the tender skin below her ear as his fingers coaxed her higher. 'That's it, Cat,' he murmured, voice dark and raw. 'Let yourself go. Don't hold back.'

She didn't. She couldn't. Not when her knees were buckling and her hands scrabbled for purchase against the wall, not when every expert curl and stroke set her aflame.

Her climax took her by surprise, erupting from the depths of her core and radiating outwards like a shot of liquid sun. She locked up for a moment, then splintered, gasping out his name so loud she thought it might echo through the bulkhead. Theo steadied her, hands unyielding and gentle all at once.

For a suspended moment, neither of them moved, the air thick with something elemental that had never existed between them before. Eventually, he eased her back onto the bed, settling her gently and smoothing a damp strand of hair from her brow.

'You good?' he asked.

Catalina rolled over onto her back, blinking up at the ceiling, vision blurring at the white swirl of cheap cabin paint. She felt emptied out and refilled in equal measure.

'I'm—' Her voice faltered, threaded through with laughter. 'Yeah. I think I'm better than good.'

Theo came up to drag her into another kiss, layered with the want she could feel radiating from herself. There was a subdued franticness to it, and it was enough to stoke the cooling embers back into frenzy.

'I'm glad,' he said between kisses, his weight settling against her—somehow already familiar. 'Do you still want to continue?'

Would any other person have been this careful with her? This reassuring and checking in at every turn? Catalina couldn't imagine it. Then again, her entire mission had been about simply getting it done. Striking it off the list so she could move on with her life. Shed the final vestiges that were holding her back and mould a version of her life she wanted to live in. Not the version she'd chosen for her parents' sake. Not the one she thought her ambition dictated.

Was it odd that, looking up into Theo's passion-glazed eyes, she could see that future, despite not really having thought about it?

She nodded, and when he still hesitated, Catalina wrapped her legs around his waist and pulled him closer until his length pressed against her through the fabric of his trousers.

'Are *you* sure?' she asked, letting her body guide her into what felt good as she ground against him. His low hiss at the continued touch sent a thrill through her.

'I've never been unsure about wanting you, Cat. Ever.'

Catalina writhed against him, the intimate form of her name doing something to shut down her brain. There were only two ways she'd ever heard him call her 'Cat'. As a warning had been the top contender. But now—pure want. It was the better version.

'Then do this with me. Let's just...do what we want for the first time in our lives instead of what is expected of us.' She reached out to cup his cheek as she spoke, her fingers trailing along his jawbone. Theo turned his head to the side, and Catalina shivered when he pressed a gentle kiss at the centre of her palm.

'Okay,' was all he said. Then he shifted onto his knees before getting off the bed entirely. His sudden absence was disorienting, and for a panicked second she thought she'd said the wrong thing. But then Theo reached for his belt, unbuckling it with a clink of metal before it joined the heap of clothes on the floor. Catalina's gaze dropped to his hands, watching him as he undid the button on his trousers and then pushed them down. Stepping out of them brought him closer to the bed again, and even in the dim light filtering through the window she could see the impression of his manhood through the fabric of his underwear.

'Cat.' He repeated her name, and her head whipped up. 'Since you've been planning this, do you have protection?'

Why did the words make her blush? She was a doctor, for goodness' sake. Of course she had prepared. In fact, she had prepared maybe a bit too well by buying different sizes and types. If any customs agent had looked at the luggage from her flight they probably had a very different idea of who she was as a person.

And now she was about to show Theo the pile of condoms she'd brought with her. Oh God. In all of her weirdly analytical fantasies of losing her virginity, that hadn't been a problem because, well, Theo was nowhere near them.

Whether her temporary dismay was obvious or Theo was simply that good at reading her, she wasn't sure. His mouth softened into a smile as he asked, 'Did you overprepare for this occasion and now you don't know what to offer me?'

Catalina couldn't help but laugh. He knew her that well, didn't he?

'I may have,' she hedged, even though there was no reason to, but their ingrained dynamic was hard to shake. Also, something about the familiarity put her at ease.

Taking a breath, she nodded towards a tote bag hanging from a hook. Theo turned around, and she couldn't stop her eyes from taking him in from head to toe as he reached over and took the bag. The cardboard boxes knocked against each other as he rifled through them, and when his hand disappeared again, he held up a box.

'You really had big plans for this cruise,' he said as he came back, opening the box and fishing out one of the foil-wrapped condoms. Then—faster than Catalina could process—Theo hooked his thumbs along his waistband and pulled his underwear down. The condom came next, rolling on in one smooth motion.

The heat in her cheeks renewed. 'Shut up. There were twenty types, all promising different things. How was I supposed to know which one to bring? I didn't know there were so many types of penises.'

Theo cocked his head to the side, his lips widening in a grin. 'You're a doctor, Cat.'

'Yeah, a general medicine doctor.'

'The male anatomy is covered in there.'

Catalina pouted. 'Just…shut up and come over here before you ruin the mood.'

She knew as she said it that this wasn't the sort of challenge she should throw at Theo. The grin turned into a smirk.

'My mood has never been better.'

'Ugh, where is the Theo that was all worried about this?'

She should have expected the teasing. The heat of the moment had distracted them both, though it wasn't like their need for each other was diminishing. No, the tension remained thick between them.

Theo's eyes slipped down her body when she pressed her thighs together in search of some friction, and the smirk slipped for a second—giving her just the idea she needed. If he was going to drag this out just for his own amusement, she would see how tough his restraint really was.

She brought one of her hands up to her chest, palming her breast and flicking her thumb over her nipple. Her gasp turned into a laugh when his eyes darted up, smirk wiped off his face.

'What are you—?'

His words trailed off when Catalina moved her other hand down over her stomach and between her legs, where she stroked herself just the way he had a few moments ago. She watched him with delicious intent, waiting for him to make his move as she pleasured herself. Theo's eyes flared, pupils blown wide. He stood frozen for a few moments, then he was on her, replacing her hand with his. His mouth crashed down on hers and swallowed the building moans and just as Catalina thought she was ready to flow away into the clouds again, she felt him between her legs.

Pressure built in a way both strange and deeply familiar, and she let out a gasp when he pressed into her, slow and careful. The burn was exquisite and foreign, a tight, bright flash of sensation that made her hips buck and her hands fist in the sheets.

Theo stilled, holding absolutely silent. 'This okay?' he asked, his mouth brushing the damp wisps of hair at her temple.

It took her longer than expected to find her voice. 'Yeah—just…keep going.'

He nodded once, the movement sharp with restraint. He thrust again, a little deeper this time, his gaze never leaving her face. It was almost too much—the intensity behind those eyes, the feeling of being opened and taken, but also the way he seemed to want to memorise every millisecond. Catalina squeezed her legs tighter around him, needing the extra pressure, and he hissed out a soft expletive that made her laugh. How often had she seen him lose his composure like that? Never.

She wanted to tease him for how serious he looked, but then Theo started to move in earnest, and it was like nothing else had ever mattered. The rhythm built between them, slow and relentless, and he was so precisely attuned to her she lost track of her own body, just feeling and being felt. His hands covered hers, fingers interlocked. Every movement tugged a new sound from her until she was making noises she'd never heard before.

'God, Cat,' he breathed into her neck. 'You're incredible.'

She wanted to laugh, to dismiss or deflect, but there was nothing left in her to argue. Just the heat of him, the way every thrust felt like it fused them closer together—sealing a bond that had been in existence since the day they'd met.

She didn't know exactly when the second climax started, only that it was an avalanche from her core—an aftershock that rippled through her legs and pulled an answering groan from Theo. He slammed in harder, dragged out, and her world snapped to a pinhole of white, her body clenching hard and then shattering in a way that was so raw and so good she thought she might dissolve right there between the sheets.

Reduced to nothing but the sensations running through her body, she cried out his name and felt him stiffen around her.

Theo lost all composure then, the carefulness replaced by something wild. He pushed in once, twice, and then let out a hoarse cry. Their bodies kept pressing against each other, sweat-slicked and trembling—boneless. For a long, suspended second, nothing existed but the hiss of their mingled breath and the thump of blood in her own ears.

Finally, Theo slumped gently to one side, rolling to face her so their bodies stayed entwined. He cradled her cheek, tracing her jaw with a thumb, blinking as if sight itself was a new sensation. Neither of them spoke for a while. They were both too spent, too stunned, too raw for words. But the silence wasn't awkward.

It felt as if something long lurking between them had been fused together and made whole by the fire of their passion.

CHAPTER TEN

Day Fourteen, Florence

SOMEHOW, THE CRUISE had turned out so much different from what Theo had anticipated. Sure, his expectations had been low to begin with since he wasn't really a person known to 'have fun' easily. And a part of him still suspected his sister had somehow orchestrated this. Though breaking her own ankle to push him in this direction seemed extreme even for Amelie.

Then again, they were Morgans. She might have rejected the family dynasty, but that didn't make her less tenacious than the rest of the family. She simply channelled those feelings to her advantage. Unlike Theo, who had spent far too much time doing exactly as he was told.

At least that had changed on the cruise, for better or for worse. The old Theo—the Theo from before, who hadn't failed miserably at the one thing he was supposed to be good at—wouldn't have given in to a jealous impulse and gone back to Catalina's cabin. The old Theo would have missed out.

'Have you been to Italy before?' Catalina asked next to him, arm slung through his and pulling him closer into her with every other step.

He chuckled, looking down at where her hand rested

on his bicep. It was an oddly comforting gesture. Not just her holding him but all the other brief moments they'd shared in the last few days—ever since they'd slept together. 'You seem to be under the impression I've led an incredibly adventurous life, when nothing could be further from the truth. When do you think I had the time to travel the world?'

Catalina shrugged, a smile dancing on her lips. 'I don't know. After you finished up med school, you must have gone somewhere. Don't important people travel around for conferences and consultation and all that stuff?'

Not in the field of emergency medicine, he wanted to say. But instead, what came out was, 'You think I'm important people?'

Her hand tightened around his upper arm in an affectionate squeeze. 'You are to me.'

She had said things like that before, off-handedly. Always at the end of a conversation and never with enough intention for Theo to dig further.

But the words stuck with him, slow-release, winding through the soft, unremarkable Sunday morning in Florence. They strolled along the bank of the Arno River, the air sharp with salt and rosemary from the row of restaurants across the water. Couples and families drifted by, unconcerned by the heaviness slowly building in Theo's chest.

He waited for the anxiety to fade, but it stitched itself tighter with each step. He searched for the right moment to bring it up, to ask Catalina what she thought would happen after this. After the cruise, the ship, the bubble. In a week they'd return to port, and she'd be off to find her residency, and he—what was he now? A man who'd burned all his bridges except the one they both stood on together for as long as the steel hull surrounded them.

He tried to picture her in Chicago, doing rounds, laughing with the other residents over takeout. He tried to picture himself still in New York City, calling her after a shift, making plans, fighting for a corner of her life she'd already spent so long defending from the world. Would she want that? Could he even do it, after years of keeping everyone—especially *her*—at arm's length? Did he even know how to let her in?

Catalina stopped short, shifting her weight so abruptly he nearly walked into her. She'd spotted something on the other side of the street—some architectural curiosity, a lintel carved with cherubs, nothing that would have caught his eye. She snapped a photo with her phone, then glanced at him with a bright smile that showed him far more of the future than he wanted to admit.

If he were a different man, maybe he could find a way to keep her. But it would be too selfish, dragging her into the world he'd burned to the ground around himself.

'I love this place. Similar to Sicily but somehow completely different. Do you know what I mean?' Catalina looked around, her skirt billowing as she whirled, and her eyes sparkled when they landed back on him. 'No wonder this is one of the top honeymoon destinations. It's so romantic.'

The smile on her lips froze. Or maybe it was his lips feeling less flexible than usual. Her words sank into the silence between them. Catalina's eyes widened a fraction before she said, 'Platonic, I mean! It's all super *platonic* here.' Then she spun around and stalked on ahead, taking pictures now and then without actually looking at her phone.

Her awkward giggle was almost enough to make him laugh if a version of this moment hadn't happened every day since their night together. They hadn't slowed down that night—or any night since—though the next morning they hadn't spoken about what it meant. They couldn't get entangled with each other beyond this trip, and Theo needed them both to remember that.

No, that wasn't true or fair. He needed to remind *himself* of that far more than Catalina. Because the moment he'd felt her around him, under him, something formless inside him had solidified. The way he'd felt about her since they'd first met finally blossoming into something he'd known had been there all along: affection.

Love.

Theo was so gone for Catalina—had been for a pathetically long span of his adulthood—that the kiss they'd shared had been enough to tip him over the edge.

He could no longer deny his feelings and how they had been brewing inside him. Or how kissing her—sleeping with her—had changed everything for him.

He was in love with her, and he could do nothing about it. Couldn't change what was inside him, but neither could he accept it. It wouldn't be fair to her. Catalina was starting her medical career, choosing a specialty that would determine the rest of her life. There were few more important decisions in the life of a career physician, and Theo would not stand in the way of that. Would not let her attach her name to his, even romantically, when he had tarnished his career and his name beyond repair.

He just needed to figure out how to walk away from her without breaking.

Romantic. The word echoed through Catalina's head for the duration of their visit in Florence. Theo hadn't responded— even when she'd gone on to make it worse by saying she thought Italy was super *platonic.*

At the time it had felt like a good save, but she had to admit now, her brain had gone into a weird survival mode she hadn't intended.

Things had been quietly tense between them since then. Or maybe it was all in her head; Catalina wasn't entirely sure. Because he hadn't sought to distance himself after that. She'd made sure he had plenty of opportunity at every stop they'd made in Florence. Now she stood at the sink of the cabin—*their* cabin—brushing her teeth while Theo sat on the bed with a book in his hand.

She looked at him through the mirror, her chest squeezing tight. Despite knowing this should be casual and that reacting any other way would be misguided, Catalina couldn't stop her brain from latching on to the mundanity of what she was seeing—and how much she craved it. How much she *wanted* to stand at a sink every night and see Theo sitting on a bed. Her bed. Their bed?

There was nothing sexual about this moment, and that was the worrying part. The thing between them was supposed to be *only* that. Heat and sweat and slick skin against each other. Not…this. Not quiet moments in the evening, not living side by side as if it was the most natural thing in the world.

'So, what's your plan after this?' she asked as her thoughts veered into a direction she didn't want them to take.

Theo looked up from the book, and something flickered over his features—shock? It had gone too soon for her to catch, but her heart lurched anyway. Were they not supposed to speak about *afterwards*? Was that somehow also indicative of her growing feelings for him, like using the word *romantic*?

Or telling him he was important to her?

Theo looked back down at the book. Stared at it long

enough that Catalina thought he might have decided not to answer her question.

Fair enough. Why should he answer? Asking questions like that about each other was more than they had agreed on, after all. It wasn't as if she'd spoken about these things before with him. Why should she ask now? Nothing had changed between them, other than she'd finally lost her virginity, putting her own happiness first after years of denying it.

Putting her heart on the line for a man who'd told her—shown her—over and over again that he wasn't interested in her like that.

'I don't know. To be honest, I've so far avoided thinking about the *after* because I have no idea what to do.' The words were so quiet that for a moment she thought she'd imagined them. But when she looked up at the mirror and at his reflection again, his eyes were on her.

Putting down the toothbrush, she turned towards him. And then she asked the question that had been on her mind since even before they had come on this cruise together.

'What happened to you?'

Theo had hinted at things here and there, granting her tiny glimpses into a still deeply hurtful episode in his life. But he had yet to share any details. A part of Catalina didn't want to pry. Mainly because it wasn't her place to know him like that, right? As they had discussed, this was a casual arrangement and he was helping her out. None of this was supposed to mean anything, and she would be damned if she was the one to suddenly change their arrangement.

Wouldn't that be what he would expect from her? The virgin falling in love with her first lover?

Except maybe it was already too late for that.

'I crashed out.' Three words and nothing else. Yet Catalina's heart stopped when she heard them. Turning around, she stepped out of the tiny bathroom and leant against the doorframe while looking at him.

'I don't even know how it happened. The work had always been stressful, but something on that day just snapped in me. I realised I could spend my entire life chasing this idea—this legacy—and still never succeed.'

Catalina's grip on the doorframe tightened as his words echoed within her, finding a vulnerable place within her. She knew the meaning behind them, even though she didn't know what it felt like to be him. But she too had chased something she would never reach. Was standing right here because she'd had enough. Didn't want to centre her self-worth on the approval of others.

Theo shook his head, letting out a mirthless laugh. 'One day I woke up and I realised I didn't want any of this. Have never wanted to be a Morgan but was pushed into it my entire life. I realised that the reason my chest feels tight when I see my sister calling is because she reminds me of what I could have been. If only I were braver. But instead of being an adult about it, I burned it all to the ground. Left the hospital and my family with no notice. Just turned my back and walked out.'

His voice grew more monotone as he went on until he sounded as if he were far away. It broke something inside Catalina seeing him like this. Before she could decide if her action was appropriate in their not quite friends with benefits arrangement, she stepped forward and pulled the book out of his hands. Then she took them and put them around her waist while pulling him closer towards her.

Her fingers tunnelled through his hair, pressing his head against her stomach in an embrace that was somehow more intimate than what they'd been doing.

'Don't be so hard on yourself. You were thrust into a position you didn't want because of family obligations. I don't know what you went through, but I know the stories about your parents. Know what Amelie went through herself.'

The Morgan parents had earned a reputation for being ruthless; Catalina knew that much. They'd been less than enthusiastic to learn their daughter would rather do her internship at the same hospital as her best friend than a Morgan-approved hospital. They'd never been overtly negative towards Catalina, but she'd wondered at times if they blamed her for Amelie's decision to carve her own path.

'I was raised to be exactly like this. From early on, I knew what was expected of me and what my future would look like. I knew it would be a long and hard road, but also that I'm lucky to be in this position. Many struggle to get to where I was, and that is due in large part to my privilege.'

Catalina wanted to object, but the words caught in her throat. Hadn't she thought the same thing? Not about Theo specifically, but about how hard she'd had to work to get accepted into Attano Memorial for her internship when Amelie had simply walked in and received a space due to her name.

She finally found her voice. 'You're not your parents' expectations, Theo. You're not even the version of yourself they imagined. You're just you. That's always been enough for everyone except maybe them.' She slid her hands to either side of his face, forcing him to look at her, and the desperation in his eyes made her chest hurt. 'You don't have to be the best. You don't have to fix everyone. You can just… be. No one who matters would be disappointed by that.'

Theo's eyes flinched from hers, a muscle jerking in his jaw as he looked away, but she felt the shift in him. She could see it, the way her words had unsettled his foundation. For a moment, he looked almost offended at the suggestion. As if she couldn't possibly know what she was talking about, when she might in fact be the only person who understood what he was saying right now.

'You don't know that,' he said, so quietly she almost missed it. 'You don't know what it's like to have this expectation hanging over your head. To have all choice removed from you before you even knew they were there. My parents—they didn't get to build a dynasty upon failure. What I did to them, the way I left, will have harmed their relationships. Their reputation. I won't be able to—'

'Who cares about their reputation, Theo? They will be all right, even without you.' The look in his eyes, the genuine hurt she saw there, was almost too much to bear. Was this what he'd carried around with him since leaving the hospital? 'My parents might not have built a dynasty, but they still act like I was never enough, no matter what I do or did or am. All they care about is... See, I don't even know. I just know that I spent far too much time trying to please them when I should have been living my life.'

Theo breathed out, his head drooping back down. The stubble on his cheeks scraped against her exposed stomach as he pushed his face against her. They stayed still like that, and Catalina thought the conversation was over when he said, 'How did you free yourself from that? Because I don't know who I am outside of what they expected me to be.'

Catalina's arms tightened around him, her heart breaking at the fragility in his tone. In all the years of knowing him, she'd never seen him like that. Never imagined him as someone who could get to this point. But of course he could. He was made out of flesh and blood and bones and feelings, like herself. Something that had been so easy to forget when she'd put him on a pedestal for the entire time they'd known each other.

She had thought seeing Theo come was the pinnacle of

beauty. But watching him unravel like he was right now was something completely different. More profound and intimate than sex could ever be.

And it pushed her right over a cliff she knew she couldn't go over.

'You are Theodore Morgan. You are a caring older brother. A competent doctor. And the most thoughtful lover I could have asked for.' Her cheeks burned as she said that, and her heart accelerated to the point where she thought it was going to leap out of her body. But she continued on, letting the words she'd kept bottled inside her for the last few days out—even though she knew she shouldn't. Knew it went against what they'd discussed. But they needed to come out because she knew that even if he might not feel the same way, the hurt part of Theo she saw right now deserved to know that he was loved. Even if it was one-sided.

'You are worthy of whatever you put your mind to, and you are not beholden to other people's expectations. I know this even though it took me so long to see it for myself.' She paused, her voice quivering. But she couldn't let herself hesitate for too long or she wouldn't be able to say it. 'If you were standing right here where I am, looking at you through my eyes, you would see a caring, resilient man. One who was pushed to the brink by expectations far too big for anyone's shoulders. You would see a man that's loved.'

Were her words too obscure? Because if she flipped them around, they could mean something else. Of course Theo was loved—he probably knew that. Oh God, she'd never had a conversation like this with anyone ever. And here she'd thought losing her virginity would solve all of her problems, only to find herself plunged into an even deeper mess. Because she'd slept with the one man she had feelings for, and even though she'd convinced herself she wouldn't slip deeper into it, she couldn't deny the feelings fluttering alive inside her every time she looked at Theo.

The feelings that had been building since that night. No, even before that. Their first night together hadn't been the start of this but the catalyst bringing it all out of hiding.

Theo's gaze shot up to hers. Her chest squeezed so tight, the air fled her lungs. Catalina wasn't sure what she was waiting for. What she was *hoping* for. In truth, there were no plans or expectations or anything. Yet something inside her gave in when she saw his eyes shutter.

Slowly, as if he had to think through it, Theo shook his head. Kept shaking it until she wasn't sure if he was stuck with something in his ear. The silence spread, unlike any other between them. Thick and ready to cut with a knife. Tight enough to snap. Hard enough she knew it would hurt.

'Theo, I...'

'No.' The one word echoed through the tiny cabin in an unexpected acoustic phenomenon. Catalina flinched despite herself.

'Theo, I'm trying to tell—'

He didn't let her finish her sentence. 'No, you can't do that, Cat. We had—an agreement from the beginning. About what this could and couldn't be.'

'I know that.' Her voice failed her, turning frail when she needed to be loud. Confident. Because that was the kind of man Theo was. Even if he thought he was at his lowest, he was still so much more confident and poised than she could ever imagine being. She'd struggled to make her parents proud even after years of trying. Then she had given up rather than have her spirit crushed one more time.

'I think I should take a walk,' Catalina said, her voice barely a whisper. She needed to get out of this room.

Theo jumped to his feet at her words. 'No, please... I—'

He sighed, hand half outstretched towards her and hanging in midair.

'I'm sorry,' he said, his voice so hollow it barely filled the gap between them. 'I'm sorry for being like this. You deserve someone who isn't—' He cut himself off, the look in his eyes so raw she almost reached for him again, despite everything.

'I don't want someone else,' Catalina said. She wasn't sure what had possessed her to tell the truth—stubbornness, or simple exhaustion from holding back. 'I want you, Theo. Like, I thought I could keep it contained to just now. This ship. But you and I both know this has been going on far longer, and taking that step with you didn't make my feelings for you any less.'

He stared at her, and for a moment she thought he might say it, whatever was building at the back of his throat. Instead, his hands clenched, then released. 'Catalina, you have a whole future ahead of you. You're going to pick your residency, excel in your specialty, build your own name. You shouldn't be…tied to someone like me, especially after what I've done. It's not fair to you.'

She swallowed, feeling the heat in her throat, hating how every word made her want him more, not less. 'I'm not afraid of that, and I do not think you should be either. No one is going to judge me by the company I keep, Theo. I know your family is famous, but even the Morgans have limits.'

Theo shook his head, unwilling—or maybe unable—to see her point. To trust her when she said she wanted him, even if it came with its issues. Her entire life had been nothing but difficult. There was no way she couldn't handle whatever he brought with him.

'You don't— There will be consequences waiting for me back home. You don't just up and leave in my world. Not with a name like mine and the weight that comes with it. My parents will have done some damage control for their brand, and there's no doubt in my mind they did it at my expense. I wouldn't be surprised if I'm blacklisted at every major institute in the States.' Theo dropped his hand, his gaze turning sharp. 'I don't want you to wake up months from now and realise I'm holding you back. That being with me ruined your chances at important things—your career.'

Catalina could almost laugh at the irony—after all these years, after all those late-night panic sessions with Amelie about how she was always second-best, it had turned out she'd fallen for a man who'd put himself at dead last. She wanted to kick something. She wanted, even more, to shake Theo until he admitted he was worth as much as anyone, that what he'd done was survive, not destroy.

Hell, he was so worried about her career when she didn't even know where she wanted to go. What to do.

She shook her head, arms crossed to keep herself from reaching for him. 'You won't ruin anything for me,' she said, the words hot and desperate and, honestly, a little humiliating. But Catalina didn't care. Not after all this—she'd flung herself off the edge, and she refused to hide her feelings just because he wouldn't catch her on the way down. 'I don't want to wake up in five years and wish I had been braver. I can fight my own battles, Theo. I want to choose you.'

He stared at her, his silence hammering out a new pulse in the room, until Catalina had to close her eyes. The cabin's fluorescent light suddenly felt raw, the sheets a mess on their bed. *Their bed.* If she started crying, she'd never stop. Not until they reached port, or maybe never.

She forced a laugh, brittle as dry leaves. 'God, I sound like an idiot. I know you said you didn't want anything serious, and now I'm—'

Theo cut her off, voice rough. 'You're not an idiot, Cat. You're the only person on this planet who's ever made me want more.'

Any second now he'd start making sense, right? Because right now he wasn't, with his words contradicting each other from one breath to the next. He wanted more—wanted her? But he said no more, not giving her any indication of where they could go or what was left to do.

She made him want more. Surely that had to mean something?

'So, what? You want this. I want this. Yet we can't have it because of some arbitrary thing you invented?'

That was what it boiled down to and that was what she couldn't understand. There was nothing standing in their way. No reason why this couldn't be real. Not unless…

'Is it because of my lack of experience? You don't see yourself with someone who you have to teach stuff. It's fun for a temporary arrangement, but not something you want in your actual life.'

This had to be it. Even though it had been revelatory for Catalina, she was under no illusions that it might have been more skewed towards her pleasure than his. With someone more experienced, he probably wouldn't have to go as slow, or explain things or—only one time though—stop in the middle of it because of some discomfort.

Confined to a ship in the middle of the ocean, maybe she was simply the easiest option. But there were others out there. Better options.

A line appeared between Theo's brows, confusion mixing with something else in his gaze. But there was no denial. Not immediately. No, he was thinking—about how to let her down easy? Or how to lie to her because he didn't want to hurt her feelings?

'Oh my God, *this* is the reason? Are you serious?' All that talk about careers and his life being in shambles, but in truth he just didn't want someone like her.

Catalina was the problem here.

'No, Cat. Now you're putting words in my mouth. I hesitate because…'

Catalina gave him two shaky breaths to get his thoughts together, but when he still looked at her without saying anything, she shook her head. 'I need to leave,' she said, though she had no idea where she'd go. They were about to leave Florence, and even if she could get off the ship, she still had responsibilities. Even though another week trapped in close proximity with Theo sounded like the worst experience on the planet.

Maybe it was her turn to sleep on the lido deck. The temperature would be warm enough. Before she could think about it for too long, Catalina began to scrabble around in the drawers, putting on whatever clothes she could find. When she was ready to leave, she found Theo standing in front of the door, pleading in his eyes.

'Catalina, you don't understand. This has nothing to do with you and everything to do with me. I'm the one who has problems—who isn't in the right space to give you what you deserve. Don't even think for a second this is about you.'

Catalina felt the air compress in the tiny cabin as she reached for the door, her hand trembling—anger or heartbreak, she couldn't tell. 'You don't get to make that decision for me,' she said, each word scraping raw against her teeth. 'If you want to finish things, fine. But don't spin it as some noble sacrifice on my behalf.'

Theo's posture stiffened. For a split second, she saw the old version of him, the one who could freeze a room with his presence alone. But it crumpled just as fast, dissolving into a slouch she'd never seen before.

'I should be the one to go. You shouldn't have to leave your own space.' The words were stiff, but there was nothing performative about the way he balled his hands into fists at his sides, as if the only thing keeping him there was sheer will.

Catalina hovered between the bed and the door with Theo blocking her way—frozen mid-step. She didn't know what she'd expected. A fight? Pleading? An explanation that didn't feel like it fell apart under the slightest scrutiny?

'Don't worry, I'll stay out of your way,' he said. Theo shot her one look filled with the agony unfurling in her own chest, and then he pushed the door open and left. In the same way he had on that first day, only now everything was different between them. It was what Catalina had wanted, right? To be a new person at the end of this trip. Someone in charge of her mind and body, doing what she felt was right for her for the first time in her life.

She just hadn't considered that it would feel so miserable, and all because of Theodore Morgan.

Catalina took a deep breath, but when she released it, it came out in a rattle. They still had a week left on the cruise and whatever had been between them had blown up in their faces. He'd said he'd stay out of her way, but how was he going to do that? Avoiding him at work would be simple enough, but what about the cabin? The rest of the trips?

They'd have to be adults and find a solution. *But not now*, Catalina thought as she let herself fall on the messy bed.

She could think about all of the consequences later. For now, all she wanted to do was curl up into a ball and listen to the low rumbling of the ship passing through quiet waters.

CHAPTER ELEVEN

Day Thirty, New York City

ODD HOW THINGS were exactly the same as he'd left them. Well, not *quite* the same. Theo was still very much unemployed and no closer to establishing contact with his parents. They knew he was back in the city since he'd gone by Morgan Greywater to drop off some files he had found in his home office. Of course, they hadn't come to see him, nor had he asked to see them. But there was no way the receptionist hadn't alerted them to his presence in the hospital for the brief thirty seconds this exchange had taken.

What had shocked him, however, had been his colleagues reaching out when they heard about his being back. One of the senior doctors he'd worked with had come jogging out of the building to talk to him at his car. She'd assured him how they understood the pressure he'd been under and that it would have got to a lesser person far sooner. That none of them resented him for leaving, regardless of what he might have heard from the rumour mill.

Something inside Theo had lifted at her words, setting him free of a burden he hadn't been aware he'd been carrying around all this time. The people he'd feared he'd disappointed most had understood why he'd left. Or rather that he hadn't meant to leave in the way he had, but he'd cracked under the pressure of the neverending work and the constantly moving goalposts.

Until that moment, he'd avoided thinking about the future or his place in the world. But the longer he sat idle, the more he realised he needed to do something. Wanted to be a part of something bigger than himself—just not the way his parents had imagined it. The cruise, as much as it hurt to think about it, had shown him how he could make a contribution and use his skills without feeling as if the world was caving in on him.

Theo had got lost, but the last month had shown him there was a way forward. He just needed to figure himself out.

'I'm glad you seem more relaxed,' Angela had said as a goodbye, and her words were still rolling around in his head days later as he sat in this café with a coffee, waiting for a familiar mop of brown hair to appear.

Only apparently Amelie had something else in mind, because when she plonked down on the seat opposite him with her own coffee, her hair sparkled with a deep red colour.

'Can't believe you made me come all the way to New York,' were the first words out of her mouth in weeks, and Theo couldn't help but laugh. It was very much like his sister to start a conversation like that. No preamble. It calmed some of his nerves because he wasn't quite sure *why* she wanted to speak to him.

There were many possible reasons. They were siblings and had grown much closer over their adult years, with the somewhat shared burden of their parents' expectations. They still hadn't really spoken about the cruise and what it had been like to fill in for her. Though if Theo had to guess, there was only one topic that would interest Amelie enough to make her come all the way to New York.

It was also the one thing—one person—he *didn't* want to talk about. In fact, he would much rather go to his parents' place right now and face the music there than sit here and have this conversation. But he knew he needed to have it.

As he'd promised Catalina, he'd managed to stay out of her way—finally snagging a cabin for himself after confiding in Dr Chen. He'd caught glimpses of her at the clinic now and then, though she'd moved around so fast, the message was clear as day: she preferred for him to stay out of her life.

And part of him also wanted to know how Catalina had been. If she was okay. If her life was progressing exactly how she'd hoped it would. Maybe a bit ambitious to expect changes in the span of two weeks, but Theo couldn't help it. Not when the reason he'd walked away from her rather than bury himself inside her for the rest of his life was to ensure she could have the future she wanted. Because being with him would have just traded one cage for another—replacing the awareness of her parents' disinterest in her with the undue scrutiny he knew his significant other would face.

One couldn't avoid it. Except if you were Amelie. Somehow, his sister had untangled herself from everything, and he wasn't sure how she'd done it.

'I didn't make you do anything. You're the one who texted me a time and a place with no other context. A part of me thought this might be an assassination plot.'

Not entirely true. He *wished* it was that rather than what he knew was about to happen. Theo had no idea how much Amelie knew about what had happened between him and Catalina. They were best friends, so he assumed she'd told her a lot. But Amelie was also his sister and maybe didn't *want* to know all the intimate details about her brother helping her best friend lose her virginity—and catching feelings in the process.

'Right, because you were absolutely going to come to Chicago to have a chat with me if I asked you? Even though it's not like you're doing much these days.' Amelie levelled a glare at him.

Theo shrugged. 'There is an invention called the telephone. People use it to communicate with each other over a long distance without having to travel. Did you consider making use of that?'

'Ha-ha, I'm glad you found your sense of humour again. Of course I would have called you if I thought you'd actually pick up the phone.' She paused to look him up and down. 'Ah, you would have picked up. But then I would have had to figure out your prolonged silences over the phone without seeing you. Which was more of a challenge than coming here.'

'How is the hunt for a residency going? Decide on a specialty yet?' he asked, hoping he'd hit the right tone of concerned brother showing an interest in his sister's career rather than the blatant deflection tactic it was.

Amelie's eyes narrowed with a dangerous spark, and he knew she wasn't going to bite. 'That's none of your business, brother. Unless you want me asking a similar question.' She paused, leaning back in her chair and crossing her arms in front of her chest. 'Actually, that's not a bad idea. I'll let you decide what we want to talk about: Catalina or *your* work.'

Theo's stomach tumbled at the mention of the two things in his life that were in complete disarray. Ironic how they also seemed to be the only two things in his life that had ever mattered to him. He'd been adrift before the cruise, thinking of nothing except the next day. Working on the ship—as mundane as the work had been most of the time—had anchored him with a new purpose. Something to hang on to.

And then Catalina had upended it all by making him want more. Teaching him he wasn't just defined by his last name or his achievements. They'd learned the lesson together, choosing to do things because they wanted to rather than living up to ideals or expectations.

Now it was all gone. Theo was drifting again, but this time it was of his own making. He was choosing to be directionless because it was easier than dealing with the storm inside him. Picking up the pieces Catalina had knocked loose simply by being her. Not dealing with how much he *wanted* her to bring such chaos into his life.

'Amelie, I know you mean well...but there's nothing to discuss. I went by the hospital the other day, and I was fine. No discomfort, no triggers. Nothing.' He crossed his arms, then quickly uncrossed them when Amelie's eyes dropped downward. His body language wasn't exactly saying, *I'm totally fine with all this.*

'Fair, but you didn't go inside the hospital. You just went to the lobby, dropped off some stuff, and maybe someone saw you. Definitely not someone with the power to crush your career the way our parents could.'

She wrinkled her nose at the mention of their parents, though something else gave Theo pause.

'How do you know all of this? Did you talk to someone?'

She'd only arrived in New York City a few hours ago. How had she been able to recap something he hadn't told her this accurately?

Amelie scoffed. 'Please, brother. If you are anything,

it's predictable. That's why our dear parents put everything on you and were happy enough to let me slide into obscurity. It also means I know exactly what you'll do at any given moment.'

Something about her words grated, and he knew it had to be a childish sibling rivalry making him bristle at his sister's claims. He couldn't help but rise to the challenge—prove her wrong—so he said, 'I bet you didn't see the thing between Catalina and me happening.'

It sounded *way* too braggy, and the moment he said it pain unfurled in his chest, pushing him into instant regret.

'Why did—I shouldn't have said that,' he blurted out almost immediately.

But Amelie was already grinning, eyes sparkling with far too familiar mischief. 'Actually, I did. Like, it was ridiculous how easily you two fell over each other. And I didn't even do much, other than say, "Stay away from her". Which, by the way, was such an obvious piece of bait, but you gobbled it whole.'

She sounded far too pleased with herself, and Theo would be annoyed if his entire brain power wasn't occupied with interpreting her words.

'You did this on purpose?'

His sister gave him a sheepish shrug. 'I wasn't as discouraging as you might have interpreted from my words.'

No, that couldn't be right. How had she—?

'Even your ankle? The accident?'

Amelie's eyes widened, and she let out a laugh loud enough to draw attention towards their table. 'What? No! My God, you think I would— Theo, I'm whimsical, but even I wouldn't risk a permanent injury just to get my best friend laid. No, when I realised I couldn't go, and you were conveniently out of work, that's when the plan came together.'

'And the plan was what? To "get your best friend laid"?' The words tasted like ash in his mouth. He knew it was a ridiculous oversimplification of what they'd shared on the cruise, though now he wasn't certain how much Amelie knew. Had Catalina told her everything?

His sister's expression softened, sending a stab through his chest. She definitely knew enough.

'I wanted you out of New York for a bit. Away from our parents. Give you some perspective on what's out there. You both needed that.'

Real feelings. The words bounced against Theo, looking for a way under his skin. And he felt a pull from within him, wanting to answer the call. Give in to those real feelings even as he said, 'There was nothing. We took things too far, but the agreement was always that things had to end after the cruise.'

The remaining days on the ship had been agony. But throughout it all, Theo had kept telling himself that it was always meant to play out like that. Catalina had just had her first experience with anyone, and anyway, he was wrapped up in so much drama. Dragging her into this—confessing his enduring feelings—wouldn't be fair to her.

'Why, though?' Amelie leant forward, elbows coming down on the table between them.

He shook his head, confused. 'What do you mean?'

'Why contain it to the cruise alone?' She huffed out a laugh. 'I have watched you slyly moon over my best friend for, what, five years now? And yeah, at the beginning I was annoyed. Like, get your own friends to moon over. But then I realised Catalina is one of the most amazing people on the planet, and if I were so inclined I would have mooned over her, too. Sadly, I'm straight.' She let out a sigh dramatic enough to cut some of the tension between them. 'You finally *got* her, Theo. And it became blatantly apparent to me over the course of this cruise that this is more to both of you than some silly forbidden-fruit crush. Why are you letting go of it all?'

'I don't have her and never had. This was designed to be casual. A...favour wrapped in companionship.' He felt dirty even as he said it—reducing what they'd shared to nothing more than a deal. But how else was he supposed to protect her?

'I know it was more for her, and I'm pretty certain that you aren't being completely honest about your feelings, either.'

Amelie examined him, and he forced himself not to squirm under her probing gaze.

It was more for her? So she did talk to Amelie about everything?

'I can't let her—she doesn't know what she'd be agreeing to, being with me right now. You know our parents have probably already blacklisted me from every single noteworthy medical institute in the States.'

To his surprise, Amelie simply shrugged. As if all he'd laid out for her didn't matter.

'Our parents are maniacs, and I'm sure they did some damage control in the background. But what does it matter if you are blacklisted at every noteworthy institute? Didn't stop you from working as a doctor on the cruise, did it?'

'But that was a cruise. I can't spend the rest of my life doing that.'

'I mean, you could if you've fallen in love with the lifestyle. But that's not what I mean.' She shook her head, and her expression relaxed into an uncharacteristic softness.

'There are plenty of hospitals out there that will hire you on the spot, no questions asked. Plenty of places where the influence of our parents is non-existent. Hell, there are even institutes like Attano Memorial, which have an active rivalry with anything Morgan related.'

Theo's eyes widened at that. 'Is that why you went there? Some kind of corporate espionage?'

'No, nothing of the sort. You think I know anything about our parents' business? But...' She paused, mulling his comments over. 'I guess *you* know enough that people might just hire you to get some insider info on the Morgan empire. Something to consider.'

Was it really so simple? Theo couldn't believe it. His entire life—his career—had been laid out the moment he'd finished high school. College, med school, internship, residency—they'd all been selected ahead of time for him. Given to him like a blessing, with the promise of how many great things he would do. How he was now responsible for the continued success of Morgan Greywater.

He had never considered anything else. Not until he'd walked out of the emergency room, never to go back. Not until...Catalina. Working side by side with her on the most mundane cases imaginable had unlocked a deep yearning within him. One he'd tried to smother over those two weeks, too scared of what might happen if he let it go on.

The fantasy of *what-if* was so close, he could almost grasp it.

When he remained silent, Amelie reached out and put a hand on his arm. 'I think you've been so wrapped up in talk of legacy and carrying on the name and whatnot that you've never stopped to consider what you want. Are noteworthy institutes even something you want? Or would you be happy just to open up a clinic somewhere? Live your best life?'

He had thought about it, but only in the quiet moments. How refreshing it had been to go to the ship's clinic every morning and see what the day brought in. Even the more stressful days had still been such an improvement on the pressures of the ER at Morgan Greywater.

He had considered it, yes. But… 'Only more reason why Catalina shouldn't associate with me. I might not want the big career, but she's choosing her residency spot, and she should do that without any other consideration than herself.'

Amelie let go of his arm and leant back. 'I'm pretty sure she's done with the ambitious life. It's brought her more trouble than pleasure. But I think you know that.'

Theo was surprised that he did. So much of her ambition and self-worth had been driven by the need to gain her family's approval and love, only for them to hold her at arm's length. The trip had been the ultimate tribute to rejecting a life of chasing those things which wouldn't bring her happiness.

Theo stared at the dregs of his coffee. The silence between them was no longer heavy but clarifying. Maybe for the first time in his life, he understood what it meant to want something without being told he should. Not because it was expected or strategic, but because *he* wanted it. Not the name. Not the empire. Just Catalina—her laugh, her chaos, her ridiculous way of turning everything into something fun.

And maybe that was the problem. He hadn't just walked away from a relationship—he'd walked away from *wanting*. From the one person who had asked nothing of him except honesty. He'd called it sacrifice, claimed it was for her sake, but the truth was simpler and far more cowardly:

he'd been terrified he might no longer be a person worthy of her love.

He stared at his hands. How many times had he held her with them? How often had he longed to? When he recalled the way she'd looked at him that last night, the impossible tenderness, he realised he'd been helpless from the beginning. Even if he'd planned the exit perfectly, it wouldn't have made the absence easier.

'What if she's moved on?' he blurted, the words slipping out before he could crush them under his tongue.

Amelie's mouth curled, but not in the way he was prepared for—there was no smugness in it, just a painful kind of fondness.

'I'm honestly not sure she can. She's an all-or-nothing person. Like someone else at this table.' She sipped her coffee, eyeing him over the rim. 'You know, when she got back from the cruise, she called me at two in the morning. Didn't say a word for the first couple of minutes, just sobbed. You've kind of pissed me off with this whole thing, actually. You're not using your head.' She set the cup down. 'I think she's hoping you'll get over yourself and call her.'

He stood so abruptly that Amelie startled, nearly knocking over her half-empty cup. She raised an eyebrow, lips already twitching into a smirk. 'You're going to do it, aren't you?'

Theo blinked, still feeling the aftershock of his decision. 'Do what?'

'A grand gesture!' She slapped the table, looking so gleeful he almost reconsidered. 'You're going to run after her right now, like in the movies. Only please, for the love of God, do not try to get through TSA with a bouquet. It's embarrassing for everyone involved, and Catalina doesn't even like flowers.'

He pressed his lips together. The idea of running—towards, not away—had never occurred to him in such a literal sense.

'I don't have a plan. I just need to see her.' Even as he said it, something in him clicked into alignment. He needed to see Catalina. Not for closure, not to beg forgiveness, but because he was afraid if he waited much longer, the space she'd carved out of him would calcify. Become permanent.

He couldn't let that happen.

CHAPTER TWELVE

Day Thirty, Chicago

'AND WITH THIS, you're all set to go.' Catalina pressed a small box into the woman's hands, giving her a smile as she thanked Catalina and hurried out of the exam room.

Catalina slumped back when the door behind her closed. It had been a week and a bit since she had returned to Chicago. Most of the time she'd spent hiding away in her room so that she could avoid Amelie and her inevitable probing questions about Theo. Though part of her was certain her best friend already knew everything. She just didn't know how.

Theo wouldn't tell her anything, would he?

Just thinking his name sent a painful flutter through her, and she pushed all of those thoughts away. Needing a distraction was also the reason why she was at the free clinic run by her former hospital, Alexander Attano Memorial. Dr Santos-Henderson, the lead of the clinic, hadn't asked any questions when Catalina had shown up, volunteering her time. Anything to get out of the apartment and, more importantly, out of her head.

If she didn't, she would no doubt do something foolish like break down and call Theo. Or worse, book a flight to New York and track him down like some lovesick maniac.

Because that was where she was now—pining. *Still*. He'd broken her heart into pieces, confirming her worst fears in the process, and she couldn't get him out of her head. Couldn't scrub the ghost of his touch from her skin, no matter how hard she tried.

As if he lived just below the surface, where it would be the most painful to extract him.

A knock sounded on the door, making her sit up straight. 'Yes?'

Emma Santos-Henderson stuck her head in. 'That's the last one on the list,' she said with a warm smile that set Catalina at ease.

During her internship at the hospital, she'd spent more time with her husband, the head of oncology, than with Dr Santos-Henderson, though her time in the free clinic had been one of her favourite times here. Something about knowing her skills were helping the people who needed them most sat right with her.

Was that maybe what she should do? On top of the broken heart, she could add a professional crisis, given she was nowhere closer to figuring it out. Another thing the cruise should have helped with. Now that she was back, Catalina could safely say the entire thing had been a complete bust.

Instead of hooking up with some random but cute guy, she was stuck with her head and her heart wrapped around the ultimate cute guy who didn't want to have her. Somehow it had turned out the opposite of empowering.

'Okay, thanks for letting me know.' Shaking her head, Catalina got off her chair and shut down the computer before leaving the exam room.

With the clinic being as small as it was, it didn't have a dedicated staffroom. Instead, they used a small cupboard behind the front desk to stash their personal belongings during the day. When Catalina opened it, only one other bag hung there along with her own. Turning around with her tote slung over her shoulder, she looked towards Emma. 'Same time tomorrow?'

The other woman gave her a small smile. 'Sure. We're not in a position to turn down any help here.'

Catalina was about to leave when Emma chuckled, and the sound was such an odd surprise that she stopped in her tracks and turned back.

'What's got you in such a good mood?' she asked, feeling as if she'd missed out on the joke. Emma wasn't a particularly stone-faced person, but during their collaboration she'd never approached Catalina with anything more than friendly professionalism. Had she ever heard the woman laugh like that?

'Ah, I said the same thing to my husband years ago when I first wandered in here. Funny how it's come full circle.' She laughed again and then her lips closed in a wistful smile. 'This clinic used to be his side project, but when we came back to Chicago, I spent more time here until I became the natural choice to lead it. Not where I saw my career going, but exactly what I needed, and still do.'

A million questions popped into Catalina's mind. Mark Henderson used to take care of this clinic? Knowing how much research he did, how many papers he wrote and the groundbreaking work he did as a surgeon, she couldn't even imagine where he found time for anything else. How did he stay married—happily at that, going by Emma's soft expression as she spoke of her spouse?

Theo was a Mark Henderson-type person. Or at least he had been before he'd walked out of his job. Now he was lost in what to do next, so unsure of where life would take him he couldn't imagine sharing even a part of it with Catalina.

Not that she could do much talking on that front. She was spending her days at the free clinic because she equally did not know what to do with her life. What gave her the confidence to know she could figure it out while still being with Theo and taking him into consideration?

The fury at his actions had lessened to a low simmer of indignation—one which had been tested every single day since. On the first day back home, she'd woken up with a small voice in her head, asking her if Theo had been right. Was she able to pick her path forward just based on what she wanted, or would she automatically compromise because of him? Seek his approval in her next step, the way she'd always had with her parents?

Catalina had operated like that for so long, a part of her believed she didn't know how to do things that weren't focused on chasing approval.

'If you don't have anywhere urgent to be, would you like to sit with me for a moment?' Emma asked, snapping Catalina out of her thoughts.

She followed Emma's gaze, trained on the chair Catalina had been clinging to with her hands as she'd gone down the mental spiral.

'Oh...' The metal legs scraped against the linoleum flooring as she pulled it out and plopped down with a sound rather lacking in any grace.

Emma continued to smile at her, though something now lurked beneath it. She didn't let Catalina guess for long before she said, 'As much as I love having you here, why aren't you out there looking for a residency spot? Most of your peers from earlier in the year are already in their residency programs.'

Oh, good. Another person to disappoint with her indecision. She hadn't even thought that Emma Santos-Henderson would have noticed, yet here she was, struggling to come up with the words to explain why she was volunteering at a free clinic instead of building her career just like everyone else in her peer group.

Except there was no judgement in Emma's gaze, as Catalina had expected. And it was the gentleness that broke through Catalina's reserves, breaking the dam and letting the truth come spilling out of her.

'When we finished up here, Amelie—Dr Morgan—suggested doing something fun for the summer before we go into our specialisations. So we signed up as medical staff for a cruise through the Mediterranean. Only, a few days before we were shipping out, Amelie broke her ankle and so she asked her brother to sub in for her. A brother who, I'm annoyed to say, I've been crushing on since we met in med school. Part of me thinks Amelie did this on purpose, because that would be just like her. But she clearly hadn't thought any of this through because now I'm here, an absolute mess because of Theo.'

The words wouldn't stop coming, and as Catalina went on, Emma's eyebrow wandered further up. When she stopped, it was almost at the other woman's hairline. Silence stretched between them—long enough for Catalina to regret her emotional outburst—but then Emma said, 'Dr Theodore Morgan went on a cruise as medical staff? Of all the things he was rumoured to be doing, this one wasn't on anyone's list.'

Now it was Catalina's turn to be surprised. 'You know Theo?'

Emma's smile was gentle. 'Everyone knows the Morgan Greywater Institute, including who is currently attached to the highly prestigious emergency room. Theodore Morgan isn't on nearly as many front covers as Mark, but I think that says more about how much my husband likes to see his face out there.' She chuckled before she continued. 'It set tongues wagging when Theodore left the way he did. Not that I'm entirely surprised he did. The job is far more pressure than one person alone can handle, and being under the watchful eye of the Morgan Greywater Foundation can't help. There's been talk going around in the medical community that its biggest priority is preserving its good name rather than caring for the mental health of its doctors.'

Catalina stared at Emma, absorbing the new pieces of information. Some of it sounded familiar. The pressure of the job and how the Morgans were more concerned about their image matched the things Amelie had always said about her parents. It was the reason she wanted nothing to do with the dynasty and had chosen a different path.

'I wonder if Theo still has the option of a different path,' she said quietly, more to herself.

But Emma picked up on it anyway. 'What do you mean?'

'Amelie—she came here to be with me. Her parents had her entire internship path sorted out. But she said while she loves medicine, she doesn't like what her parents are asking of her or her brother. But she's free-spirited like that, unlike Theo. I think he grew up with all this expectation on his shoulders and now that he's walked away from it all, he doesn't know what to do.' Amelie rarely spoke about her parents, but when she did, their controlling nature came across without a doubt. Something Catalina could understand. Her parents had been controlling, too. Not by demanding she did certain things, but rather by withholding things from her—affection and love—when she didn't meet their arbitrary threshold. And of course she'd never been able to find the right things to do or to say when the goalposts moved at random.

'I'm not going to pretend to know what Theodore Morgan's journey of self-discovery has been like, but we all carry some things with us, for better or for worse. For years, I let some unprocessed things from my family's side stop me from making choices I needed to make for myself. The same can be true for our loved ones. Sometimes we think we know what's best for them, and that's how we act.' She paused when Catalina looked at her with wide eyes. 'Something I said resonating with you?'

A lump appeared in Catalina's throat, and she tried to swallow it down. Her voice still sounded rough when she replied. 'Most of my choices came from a place of wanting to impress my parents. As the middle child out of eight, I got the bare minimum of attention from them, and only ever when they thought I was excelling. And so of course I made that my entire personality until very recently.'

Why was she telling Emma Santos-Henderson any of this? Of all the people to spill her guts to, the doctor leading up the free clinic where she spent some of her time seemed like a strange choice. But her eyes remained kind—so did her smile—and Catalina felt encouraged to continue.

'I understand now that I was never going to get what I wanted that way. Like, I'm a doctor. I've done the few hours of mandatory psychology training sufficient to recognise this dynamic as toxic.'

'But it's one thing to recognise it and an entirely different thing to break it,' Emma said, getting an emphatic nod from Catalina in return.

'Right. And while I loved doing my internship here, and I'm grateful to have made the cut, I've realised this was just another move to please people who don't see me for who I am. I thought an internship at a big-name hospital after graduating top of my class from a respected med school would net me what I want. But it hasn't. And the cruise... It was my way to break free from expectations. Reclaim some space inside myself. And it worked, because I enjoyed myself for the first time in so long. Sure, the work was often easy and sometimes monotonous, but there's nothing wrong with that, right? If I enjoy it...'

Throughout the cruise, this had been eating at the back of her mind—whenever her entire thought process wasn't occupied with Theo and the riot of feelings he inspired in her.

'Nothing wrong with that. I thought once I wanted the same career Mark has, but then I found my calling here in the free clinic. If you found something that makes you happy, go for it.'

Catalina's brain grappled with Emma's words, so casually given, yet their impact undeniable.

But before she could say anything, the other woman continued. 'It sounds like you've made peace with never getting the recognition you want from your parents. Meanwhile, Theodore has been raised to do this one thing, and has both the recognition and the responsibility that comes with it. Or had it until he walked out. It's like you are different sides of the same coin.'

'How do you know so much about him?' Emma's words were way too accurate for someone who had never interacted with Theo. Had she formed this opinion from Catalina's emotional ramble alone?

'The medical community is an odd one. Because of Mark's position, he often rubs shoulders with the chiefs of these places, trading pleasantries and whatnot.' She waved a hand in front of her. 'Through him, I've met Sinclair Morgan a few times, and the only thing he drones on about is his family's reputation and the legacy they're creating. I'm not going to judge anyone trying to escape such an environment, but I do understand caution. It's a sticky web to untangle, with so many eyes on him. Even I heard about his exit, so it's more than likely he's spending his days now dodging scrutiny.'

Catalina had to admit that even though she understood difficult family dynamics, the political side of medicine was foreign to her, and would remain so. With the clarity she'd gained on the cruise—and through this conversation, surprisingly—the picture of her future became clearer. The high-octane environment of a top-performing institute wasn't where she could see herself. No, the pace of the cruise had been exactly what she wanted professionally—and she had more than enough training to do that.

Maybe this is genuinely why Theo walked away.

The thought fluttered in on silent wings, yet somehow performed a crash landing—making it impossible to think about anything else. Could it really be…?

The man she'd got to know on the cruise wasn't uncaring. Quite the opposite. What if he really had walked away because he cared? So much so that he couldn't bear the idea of her giving things up for him. If Emma knew all these things about him, so must many other people. Enough for him to genuinely worry about what kind of impact her association with him would have on her further training.

Catalina hadn't believed it, but now it looked more like she was the one who hadn't known enough about the situation to judge his actions. He'd been trying to protect her in the only way he knew how.

The ache in her chest shifted—no less painful but different.

All this time, she'd thought she wanted to be chosen. That if someone looked her in the eye and said she was enough, all those years of silence from her parents would dissolve. But Theo *had* looked at her like that. Held her like she mattered, and still she waited for more.

He had chosen her, but she had been too wrapped up in her own version of wanting to be chosen to see him.

Her breath rattled out of her, and she scrubbed her palms down her thighs as she met Emma's gaze. Something new stirred just behind her ribs. Not certainty or hope. But the pull of something worth chasing.

If she could muster the courage.

CHAPTER THIRTEEN

Day Thirty-three, Chicago

COURAGE ONLY CAME to Catalina three days later, and it came in the form of a shirtless paramedic on a TV commercial. Well, not really, but that was how she would later go on to recall the story. What actually happened was her phone pinging and jolting her out of her half-sleep to the picture of the muscled-up paramedic on her television.

Groping for her phone, she squinted as the too-high brightness burned into her retinas for a second too long before the phone adjusted to its dim surroundings. On the top of her list of notifications was a message from Amelie. No, an email. Since when did her best friend send her emails?

When she tapped on it, it contained nothing but a blue link to a news site. The words *Morgan*, *Greywater* and *Emergency Room* jumped out at her from the URL. With her thumb hovering over the link, Catalina blinked several times.

She pressed, and the screen loaded, sluggish on her building's mediocre Wi-Fi. The article banner was a high-contrast photo of the Morgan Greywater Institute—a slab of glass and steel, severe as a confession. The headline read: *Morgan Greywater Appoints New Head of Emer-*

gency Medicine. Underneath, another line: *With the sudden vacancy, Sinclair Morgan lauds the appointment of Dr Priya Deshpande as the future of patient-centred trauma care.*

Catalina's eyes searched the first paragraphs—her brain assembling and reassembling the context, looking for Theo's name. She expected a mention of the predecessor, maybe a sentence or two about his 'sabbatical' or 'pioneering work'. Instead, there was only a brisk summary of Dr Deshpande's accolades, her years of service at a different Greywater hospital, and a cloying quote from the patriarch himself about 'family legacy and renewal'.

Theo's name did not once appear.

It was as if he'd never occupied the role, never helmed the ER. As if he had been scrubbed from its institutional memory in the span of one cruise. Yet his father still had the gall to talk about legacy with a bright smile when the pressure of that had broken his son—the man who had given everything to preserve the reputation of the Institute. Who had *lost* everything because of it, too.

Including her. She hadn't believed him when he'd told her about his reservations. She'd assumed it to be an excuse because it had been what she'd heard so often in her life from her parents. And then from herself whenever she failed to get the acknowledgement she wanted.

But what she and Theo had wasn't about acknowledgement or attention or anything this tenuous. It had *never* been about that. How had she ever reduced it to just this? Okay, yes, the entire cruise had been designed to get her laid, as a first step to reclaiming her life and her confidence and finally getting to choose the things she wanted to do.

But what if those things were Theo? She hadn't even stopped to consider that.

'Damn you, Amelie,' Catalina muttered as she climbed off the couch with her phone in her hand.

She shouldn't have walked out on Theo, and it had only taken her two weeks and a bit to figure that one out. Great. That wasn't a long time, was it? Was there a chance if she booked a flight to New York right now that he'd be horrified to see her, having somehow already moved on to the next iteration of his picture-perfect life?

Because Catalina needed to tell him she'd made up her mind. That she would be happier with him and working in a free clinic for the rest of her life than living without him and pursuing a high-powered career that would only lead her down a path where unscrupulous people could erase her existence in flashy news articles the moment she did something they didn't like. Where she would end up replacing the approval of one person with another without ever considering what she wanted.

Life was too short to chase unattainable glory when the possibility of a lifetime with Theo was right in front of her. If he would meet her there. There was the chance he was dead set on his impression that associating with him would ruin her, when actually the opposite was true.

But she needed to tell him. Over and over again, if that was what it took.

She dialled Amelie before she'd formed a plan, the phone ringing three, four, five times before her best friend's voicemail kicked in. Catalina paced the length of the apartment, one hand pressed to her temple, the other cradling the device as she waited for the beep.

'Amelie. I know what you did. I know—' Her voice

cracked, and she stopped, staring at the peeling laminate of the kitchenette as if it could explain to her the depth of her own idiocy. 'You sent me that link because you're an evil mastermind, and also possibly a romantic villain, and I swear to God I'm going to pay you back for this.'

She slumped against the counter, the late-afternoon sun throwing a wobbly rectangle across the debris field of her living room. The tote bag from yesterday's shift lay crumpled where she'd dropped it.

'I'm not mad,' she said, more to herself than Amelie, 'but just so you know, I'm about to make the single most impulsive decision of my adult life, and if this blows up in my face, I'm blaming you for the next five years.' Why five years? She wasn't sure, but it seemed like an appropriate timeframe to hold a grudge.

She inhaled, steadying. 'I'm in love with Theo. And I need to get that through to him so he can stop being all perfect and self-sacrificing and whatever other heroic things go on in his mind.' Catalina paused, staring at the clock hanging on the wall. Could she get out of here tonight and see him? She had to try. 'I'm going to fix this. I'm going to New York. If you have any last-minute advice, text me, but only if it's not "Go get a grip, Catalina, you're being ridiculous".' Because if she was being honest, this was the most Amelie thing to do.

She hung up, finished packing her bag in a tornado of limbs, and yanked open her apartment door with an impatient flourish—only to nearly collide with the man she'd planned to hunt down across the country.

Theo stood in the doorway, hand raised, inches from rapping on her door. He wore no coat, only a cable-knit navy sweater stretched over his shoulders, as if he'd left in a rush. His hair was mussed, his shoes scuffed and everything about him was imperfect—unlike Theo and yet somehow exactly how she remembered him.

For a second, neither of them spoke. The silence grew—awkward, electric, full of unsaid things.

Theo dropped his arm and stared at her, as if he couldn't believe what he was seeing. 'Hi,' he said, his voice cracking on the word.

She stared at him, heart hammering so loud she was sure it would rattle the windows. 'What are you doing here?' In her shock, the words came out sharper than she meant.

He looked down at his shoes. 'I didn't want to call. I thought you'd just—' He broke off, mouth twisting. 'Honestly, I wasn't sure if you'd want to see me.'

'I didn't want to see you—' she started, and his face crumpled—actually crumpled, as if her words were a fist. 'No, that's not right. I meant I didn't think you would want to see me. I was about to walk out my own door and hunt you down like a crazed stalker, Theo, so maybe let's call it even.' She winced, breathless. 'I mean, I was going to New York, and now you're here, and I—' She broke off, closing her eyes. The world felt as if it was buzzing, her hands trembling so hard she gripped the doorframe for support.

Theo blinked, then his mouth did a twitchy half-smile, the kind that used to surface only when she'd said something that genuinely surprised him. It was so familiar it made her knees tremble. 'Really?'

She nodded, swallowing around the lump in her throat. He was *here*. Theo had beaten her to it and appeared in front of her like an apparition. She wanted to reach out, throw herself at him and bury her face in his neck. But she couldn't—not yet. There were still things to discuss, even if her heart was telling her these were no more than details. He was here, and that was all that counted.

'Really,' she forced out, echoing him. 'I was about to leave and tell you that I was wrong not to listen and—'

Theo stepped forward. The scent of sandalwood hit her first, and then his arms came around her, pulling her against him in an embrace she hadn't realised she'd been longing for all this time. A shiver ran down her spine when his hands found their way up her back, almost lifting her off the floor.

'I won't have you apologising for even a second. This is all my fault, so I'll have none of that from you.' He straightened himself enough to look at her, and what she saw glittering in those eyes stole the breath from her lungs. 'I'm sorry I pushed you away. I thought I was protecting you from my influence—letting you have the career you always wanted without having to explain who I am. I'd never forgive myself if I was the reason you couldn't follow your dreams.'

Her chest tightened when his voice wobbled, and she shook her head before he could continue. 'No, I understand now. I didn't on the cruise, but now... I get it. What your family can do if they disagree with you. How they all but erased you from their history. For what? Wanting to live your life on your own terms?' Catalina still reeled from the realisation. 'I get you wanted to protect me from this. But I just—the life you think I wanted, it's not real. I don't want something where I can't be with you, Theo. I love you.'

The confession seemed to detonate in the narrow hallway, expanding to fill the space between them. For a heartbeat, Theo simply stared at her. Then something radiant and reckless lit behind his eyes, and he closed the small distance between them, his mouth finding hers in a kiss that expressed his feelings the way his words couldn't.

She gasped, but not from surprise. It was oxygen after having drowned for weeks. She pressed herself up on her toes, tangled her hands in the hair at his nape, and let herself be gathered. His mouth was greedy and his arms a cage, but she had never felt more free. The air between them crackled with the aftershock of her words, and Theo's trembling hand cupped her jaw as if to keep the moment from running away.

When he finally broke for air, his forehead dropped to hers, and she felt the shudder of his exhale against her lips.

'Say it again,' he whispered, voice frayed at the edges. 'Please.'

She laughed, heart beating in her throat, but she didn't hesitate. 'I love you, Theo.' Each word a stone thrown through the window of her old life.

His hands were everywhere—her cheeks, her hair, her waist—and his own confession barrelled out of him, helpless and raw: 'I love you, too. I have for longer than you know. God, Cat…'

She smiled against his cheek. 'I know now.'

They stood there, suspended in each other's gravity, until he caught her chin and pulled her back to eye level. 'You need to understand, though. I meant what I said about the fallout. I may never work at a big hospital again. I have no idea what's coming next. And I don't want you to regret this, Catalina. Not a year from now, not ever.'

His voice was raw, so unguarded it nearly broke her. But for the first time, she didn't feel the sharp reflex of competitiveness. Rather, a warm feeling spread through her. She reached for his face, thumbing the faint stubble along his jaw, and felt the ache in her chest expand into something fierce and shining.

'I don't want any of the things I used to want, Theo—if I

ever truly wanted them for myself anyway. If I had wanted them, I would have stayed on the path. But I'm off it—and I like the view from here. I don't care where we end up, as long as we're together. I don't need anything fancy. What we did on the cruise, working one-on-one with people—it was the best experience I've ever had. So if you tell me we'll be cruise doctors for now, sign me up. As long as it's with you.'

He let out a shaky laugh and buried his head in her shoulder, breathing her in.

'You know, I had this whole speech planned out on the plane. How I was going to stand here and tell you I love you but that I couldn't be selfish enough to ask you to choose me. But now you've upstaged me.'

Catalina laughed—full and unguarded. Happy. 'Upstaged you? I *was* about to cross state lines in your honour. You're lucky I didn't show up at your door holding a boom box.'

Theo pulled back just enough to look at her, brows lifted. 'I don't think you'll ever stop surprising me, Cat.'

'I contain multitudes…' She shrugged, each word they exchanged lifting her spirit. This was happening. This was really happening.

'You do,' he murmured, brushing a strand of hair from her cheek with a touch that made her breath catch. 'And I want a front-row seat to all of them.'

Theo took her hands and held them between his, the weight of everything they weren't saying behind the simple touch. 'Let's figure it out. The future. I don't care where or how. Clinic, cruise ship, cabin in the woods—I'll start googling job boards tonight if you want. As long as I get to build it with you.'

A lump caught in her throat again, but this time it didn't hurt. 'No more running?'

He shook his head. 'Only toward you.'

And then he kissed her again, slow and certain this time, sealing the beginning of everything.

* * * * *

If you enjoyed this story, check out these other great reads from Luana DaRosa

Falling for the GP Next Door
Faking It with the Doctor Prince
Falling for Her Miami Rival
Hot Nights with the Arctic Doc

All available now!

MILLS & BOON®

Coming next month

SURGEON'S SECOND TIME LUCKY
Karin Baine

'Now, where do you need me?'

It was the voice behind her which sent chills along the back of her neck, before she turned around to face him.

Time had chiseled his features into that of a handsome, mature man, from the teen she had known, but the swoop of dark hair, deep brown eyes and full smile hadn't changed that much. Harrison. Her ex-husband. Father to the baby she'd lost. The love of her life who hadn't loved her enough to stay. And now he was here, in front of her.

It took a moment for Ruby to compose herself, not wanting to give away the nature of the relationship they'd once had to any of her colleagues. No one here knew of her life before she'd qualified as a nurse, and that was the way she wanted to keep it. Especially if she and Harrison were apparently going to be working in the same hospital from now on.

She saw the moment too when he recognized her, the almost imperceptible sharp intake of breath, and flare of recognition in his eyes.

Continue reading

SURGEON'S SECOND TIME LUCKY
Karin Baine

Available next month
millsandboon.co.uk

Copyright © 2026 Karin Baine

COMING SOON!

We really hope you enjoyed reading this book. If you're looking for more romance be sure to head to the shops when new books are available on

Thursday 23rd April

To see which titles are coming soon, please visit
millsandboon.co.uk/nextmonth

MILLS & BOON

TWO BRAND NEW BOOKS FROM
Love Always

Be prepared to be swept away to incredible worldwide destinations along with our strong, relatable heroines and intensely desirable heroes.

OUT NOW

Four Love Always stories published every month, find them all at:

millsandboon.co.uk

FOUR BRAND NEW BOOKS FROM
MILLS & BOON MODERN

Indulge in desire, drama, and breathtaking romance – where passion knows no bounds!

OUT NOW

Eight Modern stories published every month, find them all at:
millsandboon.co.uk

LET'S TALK
Romance

For exclusive extracts, competitions and special offers, find us online:

- **f** MillsandBoon
- **X** @MillsandBoon
- **◉** @MillsandBoonUK
- **♪** @MillsandBoonUK

Get in touch on 01413 063 232

For all the latest titles coming soon, visit
millsandboon.co.uk/nextmonth

OUT NOW!

Available at
millsandboon.co.uk

MILLS & BOON